Echoes of the HEART

OTHER TITLES BY L.A. CASEY

Slater Brothers Series

Dominic

Bronagh

Alec

Keela

Kane

Aideen

Ryder

Branna

Damien

Alannah

Brothers

The Man Bible: A Survival Guide

Collins Brothers Series

Dateless

Maji Series:

Out of the Ashes

Ripples in Time

Standalone Novels

Frozen

Until Harry

Her Lifeline

My Little Secret

Forgetting You

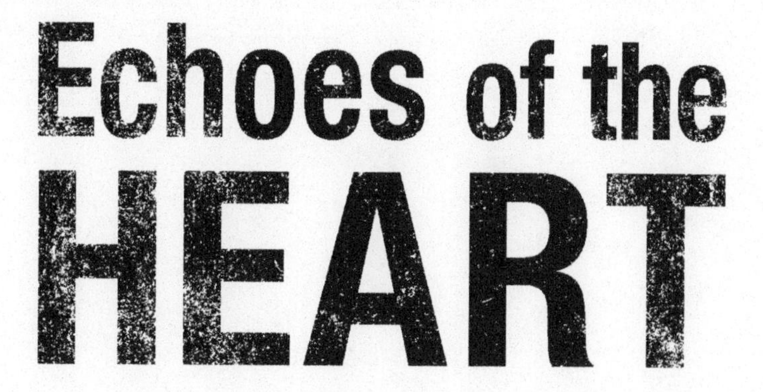

L.A. Casey

This is a work of fiction. Names, characters, organizations, places, events, and incidents are either products of the author's imagination or are used fictitiously. Any resemblance to actual persons, living or dead, or actual events is purely coincidental.

Published by Montlake, Seattle

www.apub.com

ISBN-13: 9781542023320
ISBN-10: 1542023327

Cover design by Plum5 Limited

Printed in the United States of America

For my mother.

PROLOGUE
FRANKIE

Nine years ago . . .

I awoke to the heart-stopping sound of thunderous banging.

I shot upright and stared around my darkened bedroom. I reached over to my left, expecting to find the warm body of my boyfriend, but his side of the bed was empty and cold. I didn't have a spare moment to think of where he was because the banging quickly resumed. I kicked my duvet off my body and hopped down from my bed. The harshness of the hallway light almost blinded me the second I opened the door. I rubbed my eyes with my fingers as I scurried down the narrow passageway and came to a stop at my front door.

"W-Who is it?"

"It's Michael, Frankie. Open up."

I felt relieved when I recognised the voice. I undid the lock, pulled the door open and stared up at the tall, stocky, brown-haired man who I was not expecting to be banging down my door in the middle of the night.

"Dr O'Rourke?" I blinked tiredly. "What's wrong?"

"Frankie." His hands were on his hips, his bushy eyebrows drawn in tight. "I've been callin' ye for the last hour."

Dr Michael O'Rourke was a Dubliner, from Ireland, but had lived in Southwold for a long time. He was my GP and had been for as long as I could remember. A mentionable fact was that he was also my mother's boyfriend. My mum having a boyfriend wasn't a problem for me, it was actually welcomed. I had just turned eighteen and she was a forty-six-year-old widower who deserved to find a good man who loved her. It was just a little bizarre that that man was my GP. They had been dating for a little over three months and I still didn't know how to act around Dr O'Rourke so I always remained polite, but a little standoffish.

"It's on silent." I shivered as the crippling cold of the winter's night slithered around me. "I was out until late with Risk."

Upon saying my boyfriend's name, I remembered where he was. He was a musician who lived and breathed music. When he and his band, Blood Oath, weren't travelling around the UK playing as many gigs as they could get, anywhere they could get them, they were in a tiny studio writing and recording. Risk Keller spent as much time in that studio as he did with me; if he wasn't by my side, he was there.

Dr O'Rourke coughed into his elbow. "Can I come inside?"

"Of course."

I backed into my home as Dr O'Rourke stepped inside and closed the door behind him. For a few moments, neither of us spoke and all that could be heard was the low whistle of the wind outside. It was awkward.

"Uh, would you like a cuppa tea?"

"Please."

On autopilot, I turned and entered my small kitchen, flipping on the light as I went. I grabbed my kettle, filled it up with water, set it on its stand, plugged it in and switched it on. I grabbed two cups, popped a tea-bag into each one then turned and leaned my lower back against the counter-top. Dr O'Rourke was seated at my two-person table. His eyes were on his hands, which were resting on the table's surface. They were clasped tightly together.

"Dr O'Rourke—"

"Michael." He looked up with a tired smile that didn't reach his brown, hooded eyes. "I've been datin' your ma for a few months now, Frankie. I think ye can call me by me name. Don't you?"

"I'm sorry," I said, flushing. "It's a force of habit, I've only ever called you Dr O'Rourke."

He nodded and we fell back into an awkward silence.

I looked from him to the clock on the wall and stared at the two hands. Twenty-five past five in the morning. Dr O'Rourke was in my home at twenty-five past five in the morning. He had never been inside my cottage before, let alone this early and unannounced. I felt my body began to shake as an overwhelming sensation of dread filled the pit of my stomach. It was an odd experience, to feel my body fall into a hole of panic so rapidly. I could already hear the familiar tell-tale musical sound from my lungs that told me an asthma attack was fast approaching.

"Something's happened to my mum," I rasped. "Hasn't it?"

When Dr O'Rourke looked my way, his clouded eyes were filled with untamed despair and I suddenly felt like I couldn't breathe. My chest tightened and drawing in air became increasingly difficult, like someone had poured concrete down my throat. I felt the blood rush inside of my head. My feet tingled, my hands shook and my vision distorted, like I was looking through a shattered piece of glass.

I was on my knees without realising I had fallen to them.

I felt calloused hands on either side of my face and a voice that sounded like it was a long distance away. I couldn't understand what was being said, but when I felt an object being pushed inside of my mouth, my instant reaction was to inhale. The instant I breathed in, a familiar puff of air that tasted like chemicals assaulted my taste-buds on its way down to my lungs. Robotically, I held onto the puff of air for a few seconds before I exhaled it. This process was repeated a few more times and just as quickly as the pain began, it faded.

I opened my eyes, not realising they had closed, and stared into Dr O'Rourke's worried ones.

"You're okay," he said, his hands on my shoulders. "Don't talk, just breathe in and out."

I followed his instructions and remained on the cold, tiled floor of my kitchen until the threat of my attack passed. When I felt better, I made a move to get back to my feet and Dr O'Rourke helped me. I was a tiny bit unsteady, but my senses had returned to normal. Dr O'Rourke didn't take any chances as he aided me in walking over to my table. I eased down onto the chair, leaned my elbows on hard wood, turned my head and watched in silence as Dr O'Rourke re-boiled the kettle and after a couple of minutes, brought over two steaming cups of tea and placed one on a coaster in front of me and the other in front of him. He got milk from the fridge as well as the sugar-pot and two spoons and placed them on the table too.

I said nothing, I only watched him.

"Much milk?"

I bobbed my head to his question. He poured milk into my cup and followed it up with two spoonfuls of sugar. He mimicked his actions with his own cup of tea then sat across from me. We both stared at one another until I broke the contact and picked up my cup. I blew across the top of the steaming hot liquid for a dozen or so seconds, then took a sip, then another. I felt my body loosen as the sweet, familiar taste slid down my throat and did its job of calming me.

"A cuppa Rosie Lee always hits the spot."

I couldn't smile, laugh or do anything other than look up and stare at this man who had come to tell me something had happened to my mother. I knew he had and I knew that he knew that.

"Is she . . . is she d-dead?"

My voice broke with the last word as flashbacks of my mother sitting me down when I was thirteen and telling me that my father had gone to heaven and wouldn't be coming home to us, entered my mind. I could remember screaming as overwhelming pain filled my body. I still carried that pain around to this day.

"No, no, no," Dr O'Rourke shook his head. "She's alive, she's just not well."

The relief I felt was almost enough to make me sick.

"What's wrong," I said, gripping my cup. "Just tell me."

"She drove to the twenty-four-hour garage a couple of hours ago for some cigarettes and was hit by a drunk driver but she's doin' okay," Dr O'Rourke said in a rushed breath. "Her leg is fractured quite badly, but that is the only physical injury she has sustained apart from a dustin' of minor cuts. The driver of the other vehicle wasn't so lucky: he was pronounced dead at the scene. He wasn't wearin' a seatbelt."

I felt like I was having an out-of-body experience. I was looking right at Dr O'Rourke when he spoke, I could hear each word he said clearly, but none of it felt like it was really happening. I don't know how to explain it other than that I was imposing on an important moment in someone else's life.

"I . . . I can't believe this."

"It's hard to believe, I know, but your ma wanted me to come and tell you instead of the police showin' up to inform ye since they took a statement from her about what happened. Luckily, she has her dash cam that you gifted her at Christmas last month as evidence since it was recordin' at the time of the accident."

I felt my head bob up and down.

"I can't process this," I said, lifting a hand to my temple and rubbing. "This feels like it's not happenin'."

"That sounds a lot like shock to me," Dr O'Rourke said. "Drink some more of your tea."

I did as suggested and drank some more, but I couldn't shake the feeling that there was something I was missing. Dr O'Rourke was speaking and acting normally, but his eyes . . . I could see a haunting wave of turmoil within them. I knew there was something that he wasn't telling me.

"There's more," I said, setting my cup down. "Somethin' else is wrong."

Dr O'Rourke lifted his hands to his face and scrubbed up and down until his skin was flushed. When he lowered his arms, he took in a deep breath and exhaled it before he glanced around, looking for something.

"Where did I put your inhaler?"

Automatically, I looked to the white plastic box on the wall of my kitchen that Risk had drilled into place. We had one in each room of our cottage; we jokingly called them my air boxes because inside of each container was an inhaler. I had severe asthma and was also prone to panic attacks. I always carried my two inhalers, a blue emergency inhaler for when I had attacks and a brown inhaler to combat symptoms throughout my day-to-day life. I always had a blue reliever inhaler in each air box inside my home just in case.

The air box I was staring at was open and empty.

"There it is."

Dr O'Rourke got up, moved across the small room, and picked my inhaler and its cap up from the floor. He shook the inhaler, then pressed on it and sent a puff of life-saving medicine into the air.

"Still works," he relaxed. "I was worried I'd broken it."

He capped my inhaler then placed it in front of me. I looked from it to him and blinked. "D'you think whatever you're goin' to tell me will trigger another attack?"

He shrugged his broad shoulders. "I dunno, maybe."

My gut clenched. "Just tell me, sir. Please."

He exhaled another big breath and for a few seconds he said nothing. It frustrated me; I wanted to reach over and shake him until he said whatever it was that needed to be said. The suspense was killing me.

"A couple of months ago," he began. "I noticed a pattern with your mother."

"Okay."

"Nothin' major, just little things. Forgetful moments."

I raised a brow. "You noticed she's been forgetful? She had a stroke three years ago, of course she's goin' to be a little forgetful now and then."

Since her unexpected stroke, she had some problems with her memory as well as having a little difficulty swallowing, but other than that, she had recovered.

"Now and then isn't a pattern, Frankie. She is forgetful frequently; forgettin' newly learned information is worryin'."

I shifted. "How worrying?"

"Worryin' enough for me to be concerned. A few weeks ago, I made some at-home tests for her, simple memory tests that a child could complete. She got four out of ten questions correct. She couldn't remember the things I'd asked her to remember over the period of a week and it was a red flag for me. I talked her into havin' some scans done a week ago."

"Scans?" I repeated. "What d'you mean?"

"CT, MRI."

"Right," I leaned back in my chair. "Brain scans."

"Yes," he shifted. "Last week, we got the results."

"And?"

"And," he looked down to his hands. "Accordin' to the scans that were taken, she has a build-up of beta-amyloid plaques and neurofibrillary tangles in her brain."

I scowled. "I don't know what any of that means, Dr O'Rourke."

"It's a diagnosis."

"A diagnosis of *what*?"

"Early-onset Alzheimer's."

I didn't know what I was expecting the man to say, but those words were absolutely *not* it. For a moment, I said nothing and didn't move, then I huffed a puff of air through my nose as I silently chuckled at the ridiculousness of what I was hearing. It was entirely too insane to even comprehend.

"She's forty-six." I shook my head. "She doesn't have Alzheimer's. You're crazy."

Dr O'Rourke closed his eyes and rubbed a hand over his stubbled face. When he lifted his eyelids and looked back at me, I wanted to cry, but I couldn't. The man's eyes were a bottomless pool of misery. He was hurting.

"No," I practically snapped, all traces of humour vanishing. "D'you *hear* yourself? Alzheimer's? That is an *elderly* disease. She doesn't have that."

"It's more common in people older than sixty-five, but a lot people below that age have the disease too. It's just not as prevalent so ye rarely hear of it, especially in a town as small as ours. People who have suffered from a stroke are at risk of developin' it."

I lifted my trembling hands to my face and tried to think. Processing the doctor's words was like swallowing ground chalk, I couldn't do it. Risk popped into my head. I needed him. I needed him next to me so I could try and make sense of what Dr O'Rourke was telling me.

"I can't believe this." I dropped my hands, not being able to accept what I was hearing as the truth. "There has to be some sort of mistake. A misdiagnosis. That's what this is. The doctor was wrong."

"Your ma's scans have been reviewed by a team of doctors at the hospital, Frankie, as well as specialists in London. They all came to the same conclusion with their diagnosis. It's Alzheimer's."

My body began to shake uncontrollably.

"She'll have treatment," I sputtered. "We'll find the best doctor who specialises in Alzheimer's and we'll go from there. She's young, she's mostly healthy if you don't count what happened when she had her stroke. She'll be fine, she'll beat this easily."

"Honey," Dr O'Rourke frowned deeply. "There is no cure for Alzheimer's. It is a progressive disease."

"Shut up!" I jumped to my feet. "Shut the fuck *up*! You don't know what you're talkin' about! She'll be fine. D'you hear me? Fine!"

I heard the familiar wheeze as I breathed and felt tightness across my chest, so I grabbed my inhaler and took a puff before breathing became too hard and another attack had me in its clutches. I repeated the step with my inhaler two more times until I had somewhat of a handle on my situation and could breathe easily. I felt sick to my stomach. It'd been a couple of weeks since I'd had such a bad attack, with another looming not long after the first one had ended.

"Honey," Dr O'Rourke said gently. "I know tellin' ye to relax is stupid, but what ye need to do is calm yourself all the way down."

I found myself nodding as I focused on my breathing. I went to my quiet place where I blocked everyone and everything out, and focused on nothing other than breathing in and out. It had taken years of practice to be able to acquire this focus but it helped me massively and had done since I was a young child.

"I know you wouldn't lie." I opened my eyes. "But I just can't believe what you're tellin' me."

Dr O'Rourke grunted. "I've been in shock since I found out, but I've had a few days to process the news. So has your ma."

I jerked in response to his words.

"*She knows*?"

"Of course," he answered. "I was with her when she got her diagnosis."

"And she remembers the conversation?"

"Yes. We've spoken about it a lot, about how to go forward. Like I said, it is a progressive disease. She isn't goin' to just forget every single thing right away. It's small things right now. Like where she put her keys, forgettin' recently made appointments, buyin' extra milk because she forgot she already bought some, or cookin' food and forgettin' about it."

I felt a gigantic wave of shame crash into me.

"I had no i-idea," I stammered. "I had no clue she has been goin' through this."

"Frankie, neither did she. This is all as new to *her* as it is to *you*."

I understood that but I still felt like I should have noticed the things that Dr O'Rourke did. I was incredibly close to my mother, she was, in many ways, my best friend. We spoke every single day and saw each other frequently too. I had only moved out of her house in the past few days and moved in with Risk, into a cottage near the pier. The only reason we even got the cottage was because Dr O'Rourke was our landlord.

He offered to rent to us during dinner a couple of weeks ago when I brought up that Risk and I wanted to move in together as soon as he turned eighteen. I was hesitant at first because my relationship with Dr O'Rourke had shifted from strictly being a doctor and a patient to a new sort of family unit. It wasn't a problem though, he used a letting agency so we never had to deal with him directly, which made it feel less personal.

This man noticed the signs in my mother that I should have spotted first; the guilt I felt was incredibly hard to stomach.

"She asked me to tell ye about her diagnosis while I was here," Dr O'Rourke continued. "She was alert when she was brought into the hospital earlier and asked the on-call doctor to notify me. She didn't want ye to learn about her accident over the phone, she was terrified ye'd have an attack."

"Which I did," I swallowed. "She knows me like the back of her hand."

I thought I knew her like the back of mine too, but all of the signs that she was ill were right in front of me and I missed every single one of them. I couldn't describe the emptiness that brought. She was my mother, my best friend, and I didn't see that she was sick. I didn't see it.

"That she does," he said with a sad smile. "She thinks of everyone before herself. You're the light of her life, ye know?"

A lump formed in my throat and I sucked in a breath when a lone tear fell from Dr O'Rourke's eye and meandered down his cheek. I had never seen him cry in my entire life. I had never seen him in a situation that was personal to him where he was vulnerable. It was entirely new ground for me to walk on, but my heart went out to him.

"I love your ma, Frankie." He wiped his cheek. "She has made me happier than I ever thought possible. I promise ye, I'm goin' to be standin' right by her side with you. She won't go through this alone. Neither of ye will, I swear."

My chin quivered. "Is it goin' to kill her?"

Those words were thick enough for me to choke on.

"You're thinkin' of the worst possible scenario right now because you're scared. You're lookin' too far ahead; with this disease we need to only look as far ahead as the minute we're in. Okay?"

The fact that he didn't answer my question with a solid no was not comforting in the least.

"I want to see her." I pushed loose strands of hair from my face. "Right now."

"I'll drive ye," Dr O'Rourke nodded. "Ring Risk, he should be with ye right now."

Before I hurried out of the room, I put my inhaler back inside its air box and closed it. It had been ingrained in me to always put them back when I took them out for use. A good habit to have when my asthma was as bad as it was.

When I left the kitchen and entered my bedroom, I flipped on the light, closed the door and crossed the room to my wardrobe. I flung it open and grabbed the first items of clothing I could get my hands on. That ended up being a pair of black leggings and a white hoodie with the name of Risk's band, Blood Oath, designed to look like it was spray-painted across the front in black.

I didn't even stop to search for a T-shirt or bra to wear under my hoodie, I simply grabbed a fresh pair of underwear and stripped out of my pyjamas then put on the clean clothes. I grabbed an old pair of blue Vans and slid my bare feet into them then tied the laces up tight. I grabbed a hair tie from my vanity table and gathered my mess of thick, unruly, curly, waist-length auburn hair and piled it to the top of my head and tied it into an ugly bun. I didn't pause to perfect the look; I didn't care about my appearance.

I grabbed my phone as I went into my bathroom and called Risk, putting it on speaker as I washed my face and brushed my teeth. The phone rang and rang, but he didn't pick up. I rinsed my mouth out with water followed by mouthwash as my call went to voicemail instead.

"Hey," the husky, deep voice of the boy I loved filled the quiet room. "Sorry I missed your call. I'll hit you back when I have a sec."

When the tone beeped I said, "Risk, answer your phone. My mum was in a car accident, I'm going to the hospital with Dr O'Rourke. Please. I need you."

I ended the voicemail and instantly tapped on his name again. I took the phone off speaker and put it to my ear as I left the bathroom, then made my way into the kitchen where Dr O'Rourke was still sitting at my table, drinking what was by now likely to be a cold cup of tea. Risk's voicemail played again in my ear. Annoyed, I ended the call before I could leave another message and sent him six back-to-back texts asking him to call me as soon as he could.

"I'm ready." I grabbed my bag from its hook. I checked it had an inhaler inside and once I saw it did, I closed it and grabbed my keys. "Let's go."

Dr O'Rourke rose to his feet and, wordlessly, we left my home and headed to his car that was parked out front. We both hurried to get inside as the ice-cold breeze of the January winter night curled around us. It didn't help that it was drizzling either. As soon as I buckled my seat belt, I said, "We need to stop off at Mum's house to get her clothes and—"

"I went there before I came here." Dr O'Rourke interrupted as he buckled his belt and started the car. "I grabbed some underwear, pyjamas and some toiletries. I figured if she needed anythin' more specific, we could grab it in a few hours when shops open up."

I nodded and looked down to my phone as he pulled the car onto the main road. Risk still hadn't replied to me and there was no way in hell I was asking Dr O'Rourke to make a detour to the studio so I could see him. The studio was built right next to May Acton's parents' home. He was a member of the band and Risk's best friend. I rang Risk a few more times. I phoned his friends too, to no avail. I sent him more back-to-back texts and received no response. I began to grow angry with him for not being there when I needed him, but I told myself that he was asleep.

He'd answer my calls and texts otherwise.

"How is Risk's band gettin' along?" Dr O'Rourke quizzed as we drove. "What's the name of it again?"

"Blood Oath," I answered, appreciating the small talk. "They're doing really well. They released their first EP last month and they've received lots of notice from it. One of the songs off it became really popular on Blink so their fanbase has grown hugely thanks to that. You know the way fanbases have their own names? Well, now so do Blood Oath's fans. They're called Sinners."

"What's Blink?"

"Just an app used for skits and dances and stuff."

"Oh, right."

The conversation died down and we spent the roughly thirty-five minute drive in silence. I was tense the entire journey and I sensed that Dr O'Rourke was too. I had so many questions that needed answering, but I couldn't bring myself to ask a single one of them because I was too scared of what the answers would be. It had just gone half past six by the time we reached the hospital and parked. It was still pitch black outside, but there were more cars on the road as people began to wake up to start their day by heading to work. Quickly, I sent Risk another text telling him which hospital I was at so he'd know.

"We'll be allowed in, right?" I unbuckled my seatbelt. "Even though visitin' hours haven't started yet?"

"I was told she would still be in casualty for a few hours until a bed opened up on one of the upper wards. She'll probably have her surgery before then, though."

My heart stopped.

"Surgery?" My voice cracked. "She needs *surgery*? You never said anything about her having a bloody operation!"

"Her leg is badly fractured, Frankie." Dr O'Rourke switched the engine off and pulled the handbrake up. "It won't heal correctly on its own so she needs surgery."

"What will they do to her?"

"They'll likely insert pins, screws and a metal plate. That is standard for fractures that need surgical repair. I haven't seen her X-rays, but the surgery is pretty straight forward."

I tried to remain calm, I told myself my mum getting surgery was a good thing. It would fix her leg and give her a better chance at her bones healing correctly. I repeated this over and over in my head, but I felt panicky. I needed Risk; we had known each other since we were in reception class, but we only started dating three years ago. He had rapidly not only become the love of my life, but a rock for me too. He never made me feel like a burden with my asthma or anxiety, he helped me through every attack I had and held me afterwards.

He was my person and I needed him right now, to cope.

"Right," I said to Dr O'Rourke. "I understand, but does she *know* she needs surgery?"

"Yes, she is aware."

We got out of the car and hurried into the hospital's entrance to get out of the rain and bitter cold. I followed Dr O'Rourke through casualty and I was so glad that no one stopped us or asked what we were doing. I needed to see my mum more than I wanted my next breath.

"Just through here," Dr O'Rourke whispered.

We entered a room full of cubicles that had their curtains drawn. There wasn't much activity, but I could see a couple of nurses chatting as they sat behind the nurse's station on the far side of the room. Dr O'Rourke approached cubicle six and I was right on his heels. He dipped inside and I heard Mum say, "You're back, hon."

When I hustled inside and saw my mum for the first time, tears came fast and furious. She looked so small and weak in the bed before me. Her leg was in some sort of bandaged contraption. Her beautiful face was bruised and swollen all over and I saw she had gauzes on the back of her right hand along with one on her neck. I felt like someone was choking me.

"Mum."

Her hazel, doe-eyes moved to me and instantly she lifted her arms and said, "I'm okay, honey. Come here."

I moved around the empty side of her bed and leaned down into her embrace as I burst into a sob. She put her arms around me, kissed my face and held me, swaying me slightly. She moved her hand to my lower back and began to pat the spot. She was calming me to prevent me from having an attack.

This was a method we found that comforted me immensely when I was a child, and to this day it still relaxed me. Risk frequently did this whenever I was getting antsy or coming down from an attack. Sometimes I hated that I needed this kind of comfort because I wasn't a child anymore, but I couldn't help the fact that it was a source of solace for me.

No one seemed to mind it except me, though.

"Don't be scared," Mum said into my ear. "I'm okay."

But she wasn't okay.

Her leg being injured was just a minor black brush-stroke in a big picture of colour. My mind was revolving around the fact that my forty-six-year-old mother had Alzheimer's disease. It was something I never even considered in a million years. I didn't even know it was possible for someone so young to suffer from the disease. It was so far-fetched that it just didn't feel real to me yet. That really bothered me. I was already terrified and the full weight of my mother's health hadn't even had time to settle and marinate in my mind.

I didn't know what I would do when I had the time to process it.

"Are you really okay?" I whimpered. "Be h-honest with me."

I leaned back and Mum used her thumbs to wipe away my tears.

"I was pretty sore," she told me. "The doctors gave me some morphine so right now I feel a little loopy."

I managed a little laugh as I tried to force myself to stop crying. Mum was going through enough, she didn't need to see me so upset. I already knew she worried about me constantly, her biggest fear was me being alone when I had an attack.

"Where is your inhaler?"

"Right here, Mum." I patted my bag. "I checked before I left my house."

"Good girl. Did . . . Did Michael speak to you?"

I nodded, blinking back another wave of tears.

"Mum, I'm so sorry. I should have noticed the signs that Dr O'Rourke could see. I'm *so* sorry. I wish I could make this go away for you. I'd give anythin', I swear I would."

"Little, I know you would, but what's happenin' to me is *not* your fault. It's nobody's fault, it's just the cards I have been dealt. We have to roll with the punches, okay?"

I bobbed my head as I sniffled.

Hearing her call me the nickname she had called me since I was a child made me want to curl up next to her and cry myself to sleep. This was my mum and she was really sick. I couldn't even allow myself to think of what was going to happen to her because it made me feel trapped in a room with no air. That was how I had felt when my dad died, it was how I still felt every day when I thought about him.

"What are you of thinkin', Frankie girl?" she asked, moving her hands to mine. "Tell me?"

"Dad," I choked. "I can't lose you too, Mum. I can't."

It had only been five years since my father passed away during an accident at his job and most days it didn't feel like that much time had passed by at all. He was an electrical lineman. He was working on the line of a blown transformer the evening he died. He was electrocuted by a line that was exposed and had power when it shouldn't have. He died instantly and just like the snap of my fingers, he left me and my mum all alone with nothing but his clothes and our memories of him.

"Oh, honey." Mum hugged me to her once more. "Please, don't think like that. Okay?"

It was impossible not to, but for her sake I nodded and tried my hardest.

"Listen to me," she took my face in her small, soft hands. "We're going to get educated in this disease and we're goin' to do everythin' we can to help me stay strong for longer, okay?"

I hiccupped. "Okay."

She kissed my cheek then said, "D'you have your inhaler?"

I frowned because she had already asked me that. I glanced at Dr O'Rourke, he gave me a discreet nod that he had caught it too. Mum had forgotten she had already asked me that question. This was my first experience with her disease now that I was aware that she had it. A feeling of helplessness that I had never felt before overcame me.

"Yeah, Mum," I answered. "I have it right here in my bag."

"Good girl," she sighed. "You're due a refill soon."

"Two weeks' time," I nodded. "I have it on a reminder in my phone so I don't forget to go to the pharmacy."

Mum relaxed like she always did when she heard I was on top of taking care of my asthma. Ever since I moved out, she had been constantly worried about me since she wasn't there to check that I had inhalers always stocked and on hand should I ever need them. I took her hand in mine and stroked my thumb back and forth, and before either of us could say another word, the curtain to her cubicle was pushed aside.

"Good morning." A brown-skinned, middle-aged, balding man inclined his head. "I'm Mr Coleman."

"Nice to meet ye, sir. I'm Dr O'Rourke, Mrs Fulton's GP and partner."

The doctor looked to me after he shook Dr O'Rourke's hand.

"I'm Frankie." I gripped his extended hand. "Mrs Fulton's daughter."

"Lovely to meet you," he retracted his hand and looked to my mum. "Sorry we have to meet under these circumstances, Mrs Fulton."

Mum smiled. "Me too."

"I know you've been told you need surgery on your leg, I will be the surgeon leading it. I just want to examine your leg, if you don't mind?"

"Go ahead."

The surgeon carried out his examination and I had no idea what he did because I was staring down at my mother's face, trying to gauge if she was in any more pain than necessary the entire time. A couple of times, she made a face and I squeezed her hand to offer her as much support and comfort as I possibly could. I hoped I was helping her by being here because I felt as useless as a miniskirt on a windy day.

"I'm happy to take her down now." The doctor gained my attention. "I was concerned the swelling would be too much for surgery today, but it's fine."

I gripped my mother's hand tighter.

"How long will the surgery take, sir?" I enquired. "And what will you be doing?"

"The fracture your mum has is placed in such a way that would make it difficult to heal well on its own. I'm going to insert a small metal plate and have half a dozen screws seal it to the bone. This will ensure the fracture heals correctly, and the plate and screws will give the bone added strength and protection. A surgery like this can run from two to three hours, maybe more, maybe less. Each operation is different."

I looked to Dr O'Rourke, making sure he was okay with what this other doctor was saying. I knew he was a general practitioner and didn't operate on people but he was a doctor, he knew a hell of a lot more about this kind of thing than I did. I was silent as Dr O'Rourke asked a few questions that I didn't know the meaning of so I looked back at my mum. Her eyes were on mine.

"You're so pretty." She hummed. "My little."

I huffed a laugh. "You're definitely high, I look like a girly version of Dad."

"Exactly," Mum chirped. "You're beautiful. My green-eyed angel."

I leaned down and kissed her cheek. "I love you, y'know?"

"I love you too," she winked. "More than all the water in the sea."

We both turned our to attention to the surgeon when he addressed my mother.

"I'll see you down in theatre in about thirty or so minutes, Mrs Fulton."

"Thank you, sir."

He inclined his head to us both, shook Dr O'Rourke's hand once more then he left the cubicle. I exhaled a big breath and looked at Dr O'Rourke.

"Is everything okay?"

"Yes," he nodded. "We were discussin' the surgery and his plan."

"Are you happy with it?"

"Yes."

I relaxed. "Okay then."

The next thirty minutes sped by and before I knew it, Mum was changed into a hospital gown, had a shower cap on her head and was being wheeled by a porter down a long hallway towards the surgery rooms. A nurse accompanied us with Mum's chart, Dr O'Rourke and I trailed behind them but as we neared the door, I suddenly broke into a run to reach Mum's side. I leaned in and kissed her.

"I love you."

"Love you more, little."

The porter stopped moving and allowed Dr O'Rourke to kiss and cuddle my mum too. Then with a smile and a blink, she disappeared behind double doors leaving us to stare after her. A glance around showed the hallway that led to the operating theatre was devoid of chairs. It was an empty, white-walled passageway, but I didn't care that I had nowhere to sit, I wasn't leaving until my mother came back through those doors. Dr O'Rourke seemed to sense this too.

"She won't want ye out here worryin' like this, kid."

"I'd rather be out here worrying than inside a waiting room feeling trapped and panicked. I need to be close to her and this is as close as I can get right now so I'm staying right here."

Dr O'Rourke didn't argue with me, he simply nodded and leaned against the wall next to me.

"Aren't *you* going to wait in the waiting room?"

"No," he answered, glancing down at me. "I need to be close to her too."

Something changed between us in that moment. He was still Dr O'Rourke, but he was also my mother's partner. I wasn't the only person in the world who loved my mum, Dr O'Rourke did too. He looked at her like she hung the galaxy, never mind just the moon. He was a good man and I was happy Mum had found him, but right then and there, I was really happy that he was the man she picked.

"You're a good man, Dr O'Rourke," I said, offering him a tired smile. "My mum really does love you."

"I love her too," he replied, his eyes crinkling at the corners as he returned my smile. "I think we're goin' to get along just fine movin' forward, what d'ye think?"

"I think you're right, we need to be a team to help Mum."

"Sounds like a plan to me, little."

I looked up at him, surprised he said the nickname only my mum has ever used, but touched that he wanted to forge a bond with me. Without warning, I stepped towards Dr O'Rourke and wrapped my arms around his stocky build. He returned my hug wholeheartedly.

"Everything will be okay," I said. "Won't it?"

"I bloody well hope so, kid."

I stepped away from Dr O'Rourke and leaned back against the wall next to him. I checked my phone for the hundredth time and sent Risk another text. I needed him. I felt constricted with the weight of the situation I had found myself in. My mother was sick . . . really sick. I didn't know how to cope but I knew that Risk would help me. He always did. I needed him to breathe. I needed him more than ever before.

"He'll be here."

I looked up at Dr O'Rourke and blinked.

"Risk." He clarified. "He'll come runnin' once he knows ye need him, Frankie. He always does."

"Frankie!"

I spun around the second I heard his voice and when my eyes landed on him, I began to move in his direction without thought. Risk ran down the entire length of the corridor, only slowing down when he neared me. When he was a couple of metres away, I could see his round, ice-blue eyes clearly. His white-blond hair that was normally perfectly styled was messy and unkempt. His handsome, freckled face was flushed from running and his clothes were an iron's nightmare. I didn't think we would ever get the creases out.

I wrapped my arms around his body the second I got my hands on him. I moved my arms up to his neck when Risk bent at the knee, picked me up and hugged my body to his. He squeezed me so tight that it was almost hard to draw in a breath. After a few seconds, he sat my feet back on the ground. I leaned back and his hands went to either side of my head. His eyes locked on mine.

"I'm here." He panted. "I'm here, love."

I could feel Risk's worry and confusion, just like he could feel my pain and fear. Dr O'Rourke was right. He always ran to me when I needed him with no questions asked. In that moment, I didn't know that this time would be the last time he would do so. That very day turned out to be that start of the worst week of my entire life. I had not only learned that my mother had a progressive, terminal disease that would rob me of the woman I loved so deeply, slowly over time, but I would also push the love of my life away for reasons he couldn't understand.

I pushed him away until all that was left of him were echoes in the melody.

CHAPTER ONE
FRANKIE

Present day . . .

Today will be a good day.

I read somewhere that if a person believed in something so deeply they could positively manifest it into reality. I didn't know whether *I* believed that or not, but I didn't have much in the way of luck, so trying to manifest my wants into reality might not have been the dumbest thing in the world. I mean, what was the worst that could happen, right?

I tapped my hand against my thigh as 'Kryptonite' by 3 Doors Down played through my earphones while I waited for the lift to arrive on the lobby floor of St Elizabeth Hospice. It was Monday, my only day of the week that I had off work. While most people hated Mondays, I loved them because it meant I got to spend all day with my beautiful mum. Nine years ago to the day, when I was eighteen and she was forty-six, we found out the she had early-onset Alzheimer's disease. Hearing those words had shattered a piece of my soul. It was hard to believe at first, even harder to accept, but nine years later and Mum's Alzheimer's was now as much a part of my life as it was hers.

It was odd, but I now couldn't imagine my life without Mum having this illness. My life revolved around her *because* of this illness; remembering a time before it was too bizarre to comprehend. As much as I hated the disease, and I hated it with every fibre of my being, it shaped me into the woman I had grown into over the past nine years. It taught me patience, understanding and compassion on a much deeper level. It also made me adore my mother that much more. She was my hero. I had never known a woman as strong as her and I doubted I ever would.

"*Oft*!"

I stumbled forward when a small body knocked into mine. I fell to one knee, but before I could faceplant on the ground, a hand wrapped around my upper arm and halted my movements. I was pulled to my feet a moment later. I turned to the dark-skinned teenage boy who was staring at me with big brown eyes. He couldn't have been older than sixteen.

"I'm sorry, missus," the boy spluttered. "I wasn't watching where I was going."

I smiled and waved my hand in the air, catching my earphones because they had fallen out of my ears. "No harm done. Don't worry about it, hon."

The kid visibly relaxed when he realised that he wasn't about to get into trouble. Both of our attention turned to the right when a ding sounded and the doors to the elevator I was waiting on opened wide. No one was inside, so I glanced at the boy who gestured for me to walk into the lift first so I did with a grateful smile. When I turned, I took in the rest of the boy's appearance for the first time. It was a school day, but I assumed the boy was visiting a patient of the hospice and got the day off. The second I locked eyes on the black T-shirt that he was wearing, my heart sank.

Staring back at me was the logo for Blood Oath in bold white.

My eyes moved to the left hand of the boy and I realised he was holding a smartphone, I squinted and saw he was on YouTube watching a video of some kind. He noticed me watching it so he pulled his earphones from the jack port and said, "It's a Blood Oath music video, in case you're wondering. They're a mint rock band. D'you want to watch it too?"

I recoiled from the boy like he'd hissed at me.

"Oh, no, that's okay, honey." I fumbled with the wire of my earphones, trying to untangle them. "Thank you, though."

I was relieved when I pushed the pods back into my ears and another song from my playlist blocked out everything else. I must have seemed like a crazy woman to the kid because he inched his way closer to the elevator's doors. He repeatedly tapped on the button of the floor he wanted to get off at and when the doors opened, he bolted through them quicker than a hiccup.

I leaned my head back against the steel wall and exhaled a deep breath. That was a close encounter. I had had more than a few of them over the years, but I had been so close to hearing *his* voice this time that I could feel my heart pound away inside of my chest. I wore my earphones everywhere for a reason, so I would never have to hear his voice. Nine years ago my mum got sick, but that wasn't all that happened that turned my world on its head. My ex-boyfriend and the love of my life, Risk Keller, walked out of my life at my request.

He had been a musician who, along with his band, got the big break they had been waiting for. The opportunity to sign a record deal with a small-time record label. I knew from the moment that my mum got sick that my life would forever be in Southwold because I was never going to leave her. Never. Risk's life was never meant to be lived out in one place. He was too great for this small, coastal town. I knew that even if he didn't.

Breaking up with him was the only way he could pursue his dream because I knew if I stayed in Southwold while still dating him, that he would eventually give up his career to be with me. That was how much he loved me, that was the kind of person he was. I didn't want that for him, but that didn't mean I wanted to break up with him. I wanted to hold on to him forever and never let him go, but that was selfish because his happiness mattered, not only mine.

Staying in Southwold would have ruined Risk. Leaving Southwold would have killed me.

The only solution was to break up, so that was what happened between us. The boy I had known my entire life, and dated and loved hard for three years, was suddenly no longer a part of my life. He did achieve his dream of being a successful musician just like I knew he would. A year and half after Risk, Hayes and May, his friends and bandmates, moved to Los Angeles, their debut album reached number one on the Billboard 200 chart. They broke records for the quickest debut album of a rock band to go straight to number one in over fifty countries, as well as having the highest first-week album sales of any rock band in their rookie year with their debut album in the US and UK.

That was only the beginning for Blood Oath.

Just like I knew they would, they exploded onto a global stage and took the world by storm. Everyone knew who they were, not only for the handsome faces of the band members, but because of their raw talent. They didn't play anything safe. They didn't censor themselves, they were the embodiment of rock and roll. They had won multiple Grammys, Brits and even bagged an Oscar for an original song that was featured in a major motion picture.

Everything that the lads had ever wanted, they achieved it and beyond. I couldn't have been happier for them. No one but the guys knew it, but I was the original Sinner.

The first ever fan of Blood Oath, but even back then I knew I wouldn't be the last.

Their achievements were as far as my knowledge about them went and that was only because it was safe information that I could research. I knew Blood Oath were famous and that they were known by many around the world, but I hadn't heard a single one of their songs in nine years, apart from the instrumental versions. Not that I didn't want to, but just because I couldn't cope with it. Risk was the lead vocalist of the band and his voice, his stunning voice, was one of the few things in this world that could shatter me instantly.

It was coming up on nine years since we broke up, since I last saw him in person, since I last heard his voice, since I last got to experience what it was like to kiss him, and if I heard him sing, even just for one second, I would be thrust back into the pain of losing someone who I had loved so desperately. Risk was once my rock, my coping partner, my favourite sound but now . . . now he was a trigger for pain. A trigger to remind me just how perfect my life once was and what I had with him. A trigger to remind me how I was just barely holding things together now.

I wore my earphones to protect me from him.

When I opened my eyes, the doors to the lift were closed so I had to hit the button for the floor I wanted to go to and wait. When I left the elevator and walked the familiar hallway towards my mother's room, I realised that it had been one full week since my mother had arrived at the hospice. She had previously been in the hospital for weeks with pneumonia that had gotten worse and worse. She had reached a point in her illness where nothing more could medically be done for her. We were recommenced to have her transfer to a local hospice where she could live out the remainder of her life in comfort.

Nine years ago she was in the early stages of Alzheimer's, and now she had entered the late stages. Her disease had progressed quickly over the years and now she was speeding towards the end of her life and I couldn't slow her down.

The mother who I visited now was only a shell of the lady I once knew, her moments of clarity were now few and far between. She couldn't do much for herself in terms of mobility and her speech was starting to get worse and worse. It hurt my heart each time she asked me who I was and looked at me like I was a stranger off the street, but I always made sure to keep a smile on my face because while it was difficult for me, I knew that it was absolutely terrifying for her. She was in a constant state of confusion, she was often ill and she never knew what was going on.

The only other person who experienced what I felt was my stepfather, Michael O'Rourke. He and my mum married three months after her diagnosis and while I called him by his first name now, he was, in many ways, my dad. I bonded with him during a very dark and lonely time in my life and I knew with great certainty that I wouldn't have been able to get through the past nine years without him by my side.

"Frankie?"

I looked up and smiled, the very man I was thinking of called out my name but as I neared him, I saw the look of concern on his face and felt my stomach flip. I removed my earphones, and tucked them and my iPhone into my bag as I approached Michael.

"What's wrong?"

He placed his hand on my shoulder when I came to a stop before him.

"Bad day," was his response.

My shoulders slumped. So much for manifesting my good day into reality.

"Crap," I pushed hair out of my face. "What happened?"

"She got violent with a nurse earlier. Luckily she didn't injure the woman."

I felt my heart drop to the pit of my stomach.

"Violent?" I was astounded. "Mum was violent?"

"I know, honey. She's the sweetest lady we know, but ye know how this disease progresses. Things about the person change with time, she's reactin' differently the past two days. She's angrier, more prone to snappin' and cursin' at the nurses."

I lifted my hand to my neck and rubbed.

"How is she now?"

"Sleepin'," Michael answered. "She was very agitated when I got here at nine, but she's just fallen asleep not too long ago. She was given a sedative to help her relax."

I nodded. "How is her chest?"

"Still the same, I was hopin' it would have cleared a little, but nothin' has changed."

We went inside Mum's room and sat on either side of her bed. She was a heavy sleeper, even more so when she was sedated, so we didn't have to worry about every little sound waking her up. While Michael went to fill her pitcher up with fresh water, I adjusted her blanket around her body and tucked it back into place. My eyes moved to her face and my heart hurt. She was fifty-five years of age, but she looked like she could have been in her late sixties. Her disease had taken its toll on not only her mind, but her body too.

I sat down just as Michael re-entered the room.

We celebrated his sixtieth birthday last week and the week before that we celebrated his partial retirement. He didn't have his usual lengthy client list at the doctor's surgery he owned, he filtered those patients to two new doctors he had recently hired. He only went into work on days when things were very busy and, luckily for him, those days were few. This meant he got to spend a great deal of time taking care of my mum, which put my mind at ease for the times when I could not be there.

"Was she bathed today?" I asked Michael. "It doesn't look like her hair has been washed."

"She was going to be but that's when the episode happened with the nurses," he explained. "They'll try again later, she's much more mellow in the evenings and lets them take care of her without much of a fuss."

I was about to speak when my phone rang from inside of my bag. I hurriedly took it out, saw the call was from my boss, Joe, and sighed before I answered it.

"Hi, Joe."

"Kid, I'm sorry to call you on your day off, but is there any way you could come in and help us? Tiffany finishes at lunch to go and take her kid to the dentist, Deena is here but I don't know what's going on, we have more people in for lunch than she can handle."

I lifted my hand to the bridge of my nose.

"The twins aren't around?"

"Their phones are off."

Typical.

"Okay," I relented. "I'll be there in thirty, forty minutes at most. I'm visiting Mum."

"I'm sorry, kid. I wouldn't call if I had someone else to cover the shift."

"Don't worry about it, Joe. See you soon."

I hung up and looked at Michael.

"Joe's run off his feet at the diner, he needs another waitress."

"Go," Michael said. "She'll be sleepin' for a couple of hours yet."

I nodded, leaned over and kissed Mum's cheek, then rounded the bed and did the same to Michael. "I'll call you later. Love you."

"Love you to, little."

I smiled as I left the room.

I spent the next thirty-five minutes rushing home so I could change into my uniform and get into work as soon as I could. When I showed up at the diner, Joe wasn't lying. The place was packed with people. I didn't have a chance to properly greet Deena, or Joe, as I jumped straight into taking orders, serving orders, then making milkshakes and desserts for those who requested them. Hours ticked by until the storm of customers had died down enough so Deena could clock off early to pick up her kids from her parents and visit her husband who'd had foot surgery the day before. It was near closing time by the time I felt like I could think straight.

"Frankie, order's up!"

I sat back on my heels, placed my hands on my hips and, with a tired puff of air, I blew strands of auburn hair that had escaped my hair tie out of my face. I wasn't sure what ached worse, my feet or my back. I grabbed the bucket beside me and tossed the rags I'd been using to clean the base of one of the corner booths into it. Not too long ago, some kid had been running with a chocolate milkshake in his hands and when he tripped the shake went *everywhere*.

I had been the sorry sucker charged with cleaning it up.

I stood up and softly groaned when my back clicked in protest. I rubbed the base of my spine before I grabbed the bucket and walked through the door that led into the kitchen. I placed the bucket in its designated spot, then headed back out front. When I was in front of the hatch that gave all the customers a partial view of the kitchen, I picked up the two plates of freshly made-to-order food. I checked the table they were for and headed in that direction.

"Here we go," I smiled at the teenage boy and girl who looked up upon my arrival. "A double cheeseburger with everything on it and extra chips?"

"That's mine," the boy chirped.

He eagerly rubbed his hands together and eyed the plate like it was his very life force. I placed his food in front of him then with the other dish, I placed it in front of the girl.

"Can I get you both anything else? More drinks?"

"No, thank you," the pair said in unison.

"If you need anything, just give me a shout."

I glanced around the diner and when I saw I had no other customers I walked back towards the kitchen. Once inside I leaned against one of the counters, applying weight onto my hands, just to take some pressure off my throbbing feet. I had been working for nine hours straight, since I came in at one, and couldn't recall sitting down once during the day. Things were so hectic that I had no other choice except to work through my breaks. I had one hour left on my surprise shift and I had never willed time to go faster in my entire life.

"This has been the longest shift in existence," I proclaimed. "And the most uncomfortable, my bloody feet are throbbing. My back is hurting too and my back *never* hurts."

Joseph Reeves, the owner and chef of Mary Well's diner, grunted in agreement.

"Lunch hour was a nightmare," he said as he cleaned down one of his worktops with a cloth. "I haven't seen things that busy since the circus was in town a couple of months ago. It's winter, I wonder what has so many tourists in town."

I folded my arms across my chest and fought off a yawn.

"I've been wondering that too." I rolled my shoulders to stretch them out. "I had half a mind to ask people if something was going on, but I was too busy seating everyone and taking orders to get around to it. It was like a madhouse."

"I saw." Joe's lips twitched, and that was as much as a smile as anyone could ever get out of him. "You were like a headless chicken running back and forth, Deena too. Best entertainment I've had in a while so thank you."

"You're welcome." I snorted. "I'm just glad we made it through it."

"I know," he agreed. "The one day we're overwhelmed with customers and only three of us are working."

"I'm *still* pissed about that," I scowled. "And not for a second do I believe it wasn't done on purpose by the twins."

The two other waitresses at Mary Well's were Anna and Hannah Porter. They were twin sisters and where there was one, there was the other. When they weren't working, and sometimes when they *were* working, they had their phones glued to their hands so for the pair of them to have their phones switched off was suspicious. I had known both girls for years, I was a year ahead of them in school. Since phones and social media became a massive thing, I had never known either sister to have a blackout from both.

They disconnected their phones on purpose, I was sure of it.

"The upside is," Joe winked, "you get to keep the rest of the tips since Deena already got her cut before she left for the day."

The tip jar had had to be emptied into the collection bag two times after Deena left, and one of those times was because I couldn't stuff any more notes into the jar. As crazy as the day had been for service, it had been incredible for tips. There was no doubt about that. I never expected tips, but when I got them, it put a smile on my face. Today's tip load would have me grinning from ear to ear for the next week.

"Me?" I questioned. "You're here, too."

"Tips are for the waiting staff, you know that."

"Yeah," I began, "but you've been cooking up a storm in here all day. You deserve half."

"You're a sweetie, Frankie, but those tips are yours. You've worked hard today, I don't know what I would have done without you."

I felt heat stain my cheeks.

"Thanks, Joe, I appreciate it."

"And I appreciate *you*, kid."

I smiled as he turned and got back to work cleaning his workspace. Joe could hold a steady conversation, but he preferred to be alone in the kitchen with his thoughts for company as he cooked. I never felt brushed off by him. In fact, whenever I managed to get his attention and talk to him, he had a way of making me feel like a well-loved and appreciated little kid. I loved that about him.

I looked from Joe and focused my gaze through the hatch. I was glad to see no new customers had come into the diner. I leaned forward, relaxing when I saw my only table were smiling and chatting away as they ate their meal.

I studied the pair, wondering if they were friends, relatives or a couple on a date. From the way the girl kept stealing glances at the lad, and the way he kept licking his lips when he looked at her, I was edging more towards them being a couple on a date. Maybe even their very first date. Thinking of that made me think of *my* very first date, and funnily enough, it took place in Mary Well's diner, too, in that exact booth.

I was a few days away from turning fifteen and I had been asked out by my long-time crush . . . Risk Keller.

"Aren't we supposed to share a milkshake?" I quizzed, trying to downplay the fact that I was so nervous that my palms were sweating. "All the romance movies I've seen will have been for nothing if we don't drink a large strawberry milkshake with two straws while we stare deeply into each other's eyes."

Risk stared at me, unblinking. His bruised right eye making him look rugged, dangerous, and a hell of a lot more handsome than he already was. I didn't ask how he'd gotten it because I knew it was his foster father's fault. I didn't want to bring it up and upset him so I kept my mouth shut.

"For that sentence alone," he began, "I'm considering walking out of this diner and never contacting you ever again."

"Considering the way you've stalked me lately, I find that hard to believe."

"I can dodge you easily."

"How easily?" I leaned forward. "How easy would it be to stay away from me?"

"As easy as taking sweets from a baby."

"You're a pig," I said, fighting off a grin as I sat back. "I should have made you buy me chocolates to make this date bearable."

"How about I give you a kiss instead?" Risk waggled his thick, white-blond eyebrows. "Right here and now. I'll make it quick in order to put a smile on that semi-decent face of yours. I still remember how much you liked my little peck when I asked you out yesterday."

I yawned, feigning boredom but Christ, my heart was pounding.

"I agreed to this date because I felt *sorry* for you. If my answer was based on that embarrassing thing you called a kiss then I wouldn't be here. For future reference, I need a little more time and appreciation put into my kisses. So unless you can kiss me until I'm weak, thanks but no thanks, rock star."

Risk, who was looking at his nails, looked up at me and blinked, "I'm sorry, did you say something? I tuned you out; your voice is so bloody annoying."

"That's funny," I blinked. "I was going to say exactly that when you sang earlier."

Risk sucked in a sharp, dramatic breath. He even placed his hand on his chest in shock. "That was too far," he scowled. "There is a limit to sarcastic insults and you just exceeded that limit with the biggest lie *ever*."

"Who said I was being sarcastic?"

"I am, because you're obsessed with my voice and you know it."

"And *how* do you know that?" I questioned, trying not to let on how close to home he was with that comment. "I could only be on this date because I know you're gonna be a rich and famous rock star one day and I want you to buy me some pretty things."

"I know you're obsessed with me," Risk smirked. "Because you talk in your sleep."

I froze. "You lie."

"I would never."

"You would too and you know it."

"I'm a midnight slasher, and when we were camping on our last school trip, I walked right by your sleeping bag. You talk in your sleep, Cherry."

I felt my cheeks burn. He had recently started calling me Cherry because of my hair colour and each time he called me it, my heart pounded because of how much I loved it, but of course, I couldn't let him know that.

"You shut your stupid mouth, Risk Keller."

"You spoke clearly," he continued as if I hadn't bellowed. "I stopped walking when I heard my name. My name being moaned from your sweet lips in a deep sleep."

I choked on air. "Liar."

"Truther," Risk grinned. "Why do you think I asked you out yesterday?"

"Because you're in love with me and always have been!"

"Maybe," his lips curved up at the corners. "But also because I want to hear you moan my name again, but this time, while I'm looking into those pretty green eyes of yours."

My cheeks were absolutely scalded.

"You're a dumb arse."

"And you have a nice arse."

"You're not allowed talk about my arse, Risk Keller. I'll thump you something fierce otherwise."

He pointed to his blackened eye. "Get in line, Cherry."

I scowled at him and he cheekily smiled, making my pulse spike. He sat up and leaned right over our empty table and brought his face so close to mine that I could feel his breath on my skin and count each of his freckles if I wanted to. I could feel my body tremble.

"You want me to admit how much I like you, Frankie?"

Wordlessly, I bobbed my head.

"You're not just my muse, you're my music," he said. "And I want you to be my girlfriend . . . will you?"

He had barely finished asking me when I blurted, "Yes."

Risk's face lit up. "Told you that you were obsessed with me."

"Shut *up*."

"Time and appreciation," he said, his ice-blue eyes locked on mine. "That's what you want put into your kisses, isn't that what you said?"

I couldn't speak, the ability was suddenly lost on me, so I only barely managed to nod.

"Good, because Cherry," he slid his tongue over my lower lip. "I wouldn't have it any other way."

His lips pressed against mine then and if I thought the little peck we had shared previously was something to gush over, Risk was about to show me that I had seen, and felt, nothing yet.

◆ ◆ ◆

I was jolted back to the present when loud laughter snagged my attention. I blinked, focusing on the young couple who were beaming at one another and playfully throwing chips, before having the good sense to tidy up after themselves. I swallowed the lump that suddenly formed in my throat and forced myself to relax. I closed my eyes, hoping to regain some sense of calmness, but I knew it was futile so lifted my lids.

Risk Keller.

My first and only boyfriend. I had never been interested in another relationship after we broke up. What started out as lighthearted and fun coupling turned into an intense burning passion very early on, and it didn't take long for me to fall in love with Risk. It was the reason why letting him go hurt so much. My heart needed an abundance of time to heal from the break that letting Risk go caused. Nine years later and I was still no closer to putting myself out there again.

I lifted my hands to my face and scrubbed my skin, trying to put all thoughts of Risk and our previous relationship to the back of my mind where it belonged. Another glance at the smitten kids in the booth Risk and I always shared was like a smack in the face and I willed my shift to end faster than ever before. I wanted to go home, take a shower, and put this day, and my thoughts, behind me.

I looked up to the door when the bell rang and I smiled when Enda Peterson strolled in. She was somewhat of an adopted auntie to me, she had been best friends with my mother since before I was born. I loved Enda . . . most of the time. The woman was as loyal as they come, but Lord, she was also a nosy old goat.

"Frankie, honey," she smiled, her brown eyes gleaming. "Can I get a cheeseburger to go? I've just come from bingo. Before that I was visiting your mummy and I'm starved."

"Coming right up, Auntie," I chirped. "How is she? I haven't spoken to Michael since this morning. It's been a hectic day here."

"She was in fine spirits. After she was bathed, she rested a lot."

I was happy to hear that.

I turned to tell Joe what would likely be the last order of the night when the door opened once more and in ran an out-of-breath, red-faced, teenage girl. Once she spotted the young couple, she darted to their booth.

"I have tickets to see Blood Oath at Wembley this coming Monday!" she screamed with excitement. "My dad got them for us, isn't he the best? But wait, it gets better! The band is coming to visit *tomorrow,* they're rumoured to be attending the retirement ceremony for Mr Jones. He was the one who gifted them their first instruments, you know? May, Hayes and Risk are coming home! I bet Angel will be with them too!"

My heart stopped at her declaration and I knew good and well it had nothing to do with excitement. I felt Joe's eyes on me from the kitchen, as well as Enda's. The kids paid for their meal, then left the diner amidst laughter and excited squeals all the while tapping away on the screens of their phones. When the door closed, silence filled the space. I stared at the booth the kids just vacated and my heart began to pound.

"Frankie." Enda tentatively inched her way closer to me. "Sweetie, are you okay?"

"No," I answered honestly. "I'm not."

I wasn't okay. Nothing was okay and both Joe and Enda knew it. It'd been nine years since I saw him in person and not on the cover of a magazine, or on the evening news in passing. Nine whole years and I still wasn't ready to face him. It didn't matter what I wanted because one thing was certain and it was one thing that I couldn't change.

Risk was coming home.

CHAPTER TWO
RISK

Fourteen years ago . . .

"Risk! Get out here, ye no good wee bastard!"

I waited for Owen Day, my foster father, to stop banging on my bedroom door before I opened it. I didn't brace myself quick enough because as soon as there was space Owen's hairy, fat arm jerked through the door and his hand clamped onto my hair. I shouted with surprise as both of my hands shot up to his, where I automatically tried to break his hold, but couldn't because he was a strong man. Tall, heavy set and as mean as they come. I was starting to take a stretch, but I was skinny and no match for Owen's brute strength and he knew it.

"I didn't do anything!"

It was a phrase I had come to squawk almost every single time my name was bellowed.

"Yer were *warned* not to answer my wife back, boy."

"I didn't!" I panicked. "She told me to get my bag and get to school and I said okay!"

"Ye said it with an attitude, ya wee prick. I heard ye. Ye think because ya turned thirteen yesterday that ye can act up?"

"No! I don't. I didn't mean it. I'm sorry."

He twisted his hand and it made me scream. I could feel strands of hair being ripped by the root from my scalp and it burned like hell. I smacked on Owen's wrist twice before he forcefully pushed me back by the head and let go of my hair. I stumbled, tripped over my feet and landed flat on my arse. I groaned in pain as I lifted my hand to my head and rubbed, trying to lessen the stinging pain.

I saw Owen's feet move closer to me and when I looked up I was knocked flat onto my back when his massive, meaty fist swung down and cracked me square in the jaw. For a second, I heard ringing in my ears and black dots skewed my vision. I shook my head and moaned in pain as fierce throbbing spread like wildfire over my jaw. I lifted my hands to my face and willed myself not to cry. I made a point to never cry in front of Owen or Freda, his wife, just so they would have no clue how much they broke me down.

"Get yer miserable hide to school."

I swallowed down the metallic tang of blood.

"Yes, sir."

My bedroom door was slammed shut and all of two seconds passed by before the tears started. Angrily, I wiped my face with the sleeve of my uniform jumper. I hated crying, I hated that Owen and Freda could hurt me enough to reduce me to tears. I pushed myself to my feet, grabbed my school bag and hooked the straps over my shoulders. I left my bedroom and went into the bathroom so I could gargle some water in my mouth. It tasted like I swallowed a litre of blood, but only a trickle came out when I spit into the sink.

I stuck my finger into my mouth and felt along the inside of my aching cheek. I hissed as the tip of my finger ran over a tiny, torn piece of flesh. When Owen punched me, the contact caused a tooth to slightly cut my cheek. It stung but it didn't hurt anywhere close to how much my jaw pained me. I removed my finger then turned on the tap, bent down and filled my mouth up with water. I swished it around then spat it out.

I wiped my hands down on a hand towel, folded it neatly back in place and made sure all of the blood was gone from the sink before I turned the tap off. If I left a mess, the Days would tear my arse up. Those two were so full of anger and misery I always did what I could to avoid being a target but there were days, like today, that I couldn't avoid their wrath. I didn't get them. I mean, I knew *why* they fostered kids, for the money. I just didn't *get* why they even bothered because it was as obvious as the day was long that they hated it. They hated me and they always had. I had known since I came to the Day household that I was never going to be part of their family. I had to refer to Owen and Freda by their names and never Mum and Dad. The first time I tried this, when I was five, I got my arse walloped until I could barely walk from the pain.

I made sure to never make that mistake ever again.

I was the first placement Owen and Freda ever had and I was the only foster kid to come into their household who was never adopted by a family. I was a long-term placement, not short-term like the kids who passed through. I had visits with families who seemed like they were too good to be true, happy and loving but not willing to take in a boy who couldn't express joy like that. I always figured part of me was broken and wasn't good enough to be with a real family, so I accepted the only one I would ever know would be with the Days.

I left the Day household on Trinity Street without a sound and made my way towards Cumberland Road, where May Acton, my best friend, lived. My other mate, Hayes Hurley, lived on Stradbroke Road and we always met up with one another at Cumberland Road to wait at the school bus stop. I made it to the stop five minutes earlier than usual. I adjusted my uniform so it didn't look creased or out of place. I was listening to my headphones, like always. Music was my solace, my haven, my idea of what heaven was like because when I listened to it, I felt the lyrics, the riffs, the kick and snares of the drums. I felt them all.

I loved music.

I sighed and switched off my MP3 player, wrapped my headphones around it and put it into my bag so I could think. I quickly devised a story in my head about how I was getting a pan from the top cupboard in the kitchen and it fell and hit me in the face. It sucked not telling my friends the truth, but I knew if I did they would tell their parents who would call the police who would contact my caseworker. I hated the Days, I didn't want to be within a hundred metres of them, but leaving their house meant leaving Southwold to be placed with another family and I didn't want that. The thought of moving away from the only place I've ever known on top of leaving my only friends made me feel sick.

I just had to stick it out for four years, three-hundred and sixty-four days more.

"Then I'll be eighteen and free," I mumbled to myself.

"Risk! Orrite, boy?"

I snorted as May jogged up the road and bumped his fist against mine when he reached my side. May was the happiest lad I had ever known, he always had a smile on his chubby face. He paused next to me and tried to catch his breath. He was breathing pretty heavily. May was overweight by a few stone and he wasn't all that fit so the littlest of exertions left him breathless. I waited, as I always did, for him to be comfortable before we started talking.

"Mate," he said, shaking his head and placing his hands on his wide hips. "I need to shift a few stone. My mum joined Slimming World last week and some of the dishes she made are super healthy and tasty as fuck. She said I can follow along with her plan too. I don't even care if you or Hayes rip me a new one."

This made me happy and not because I wanted to take the piss out of him.

"Good for you, mate. Soon you'll be able to come running with me."

"Ha!" May barked. "You run in the morning *and* at night like a fitness junkie, no thanks."

I wasn't a fitness junkie, not by a long stretch. I couldn't afford to lose any weight, but I still went running twice a day just so I could get out of the Days' house. They didn't starve me, but they only fed me three meals a day because that was all the human body needed, Owen said. Most of the time, I didn't even jog when I went out. I just wandered around until it was close to my curfew so I could go back to the house I lived in and go straight to sleep.

"We can walk too," I pointed out to May. "That's still good exercise."

"Yeah, I suppose you're ri— *boy*! What the *fuck* happened to your ugly mug?"

I lifted my hand to my sore face, forced a laugh and told him the story I had rehearsed in my head and by the time I finished, May was cracking up. Hayes showed up at that moment and May rehashed everything I just told him and soon, they were both laughing at me. I laughed too and pretended that the story I made up was real because it beat the alternative.

"Lad," Hayes winced. "It's all swollen and black and blue, you'd take less damage from a punch."

"Yeah," I snorted. "I probably would."

We talked about football, comic books and music as we boarded our bus to school and pulled up at Sir John Leman High School. I made it through the entire day without too many questions about my face until the last period of the day – History. Our teacher took ill over the lunch break and there was no substitute to look after us so we had a free period. We had to keep quiet;

the teacher in the classroom next door left the door open and she would frequently pop in to make sure we weren't acting up.

One of my classmates asked me what happened and the whole bloody room stopped what they were doing and listened as I repeated my story. By the time I had finished, I was grinning because of how much everyone was laughing but I couldn't help but feel like a complete and total fraud. I looked around the room at the smiling faces and stopped at one who wasn't so much as grinning my way, she looked proper pissed off if I was being honest with myself.

Frankie Fulton was a classmate and most definitely the best-looking girl in my year, or at least I thought she was. She had auburn hair, big green eyes and skin so fair she looked like she glowed. I had fancied her for as long as I could remember, but did nothing about it because I didn't know *what* to do about it. I tried to give her a smile, but she was looking at me so intently that I couldn't hold the contact and looked down at my workbook. I felt her gaze on me throughout the whole period and when class was over, she stopped by my desk before I could escape the room.

"Risk."

I looked up at her and froze because she was looking at me like she knew my deepest, darkest secret.

"Hey." My voice cracked so I quickly cleared my throat. "Hey, Frankie."

She blinked. "You get off the bus at Cumberland Road, right?"

May and Hayes stopped behind Frankie when they realised she was talking to me and they both widened their eyes and looked at me like I was some sort of bird magnet, but the reality was, I had no clue why Frankie was talking to me. She hardly ever spoke to anyone, let alone me. She listened to her headphones the majority of the time and liked to keep to herself. I was as stunned as my friends that she was interacting me with me at all.

"Uh." I blinked up at her. "Yeah. Yeah, I get off at that stop."

"Okay," she nodded. "I'll get off there today and you can walk me home."

She didn't ask permission, she was telling me what I was going to do and I wasn't about to disagree with her so I bobbed my head and said, "Okay."

She nodded then turned and left the classroom along with the rest of our classmates. May and Hayes both smacked me at different points on my body as I grabbed my stuff and shoved it into my bag at rapid speed.

"Mate!" May practically squeaked. "Why does she want *you* to walk her home?"

"Dumb arse," Hayes shoved May. "She's into him, why else would she ask?"

"Maybe to make sure he's not in danger of any flying pans on the way home?"

Hayes cracked up at May's teasing, but I barely heard them.

I grabbed my bag and bucked it out of the room after Frankie so I wouldn't miss the bus. I had no idea if Hayes was right and that Frankie liked me, but there was no way in hell that I was going to miss the chance to find out. My friends were trailing behind me as we left the school grounds. Frankie waited to board the bus until she saw me. She sat up at the front like she usually did and I had no clue whether or not I was supposed to sit next to her so I just sat a couple of rows behind her like I normally did.

It was a mild day not hot or cold, but I was sweating.

Quicker than I anticipated, the bus rolled to a stop at Cumberland Road. I stood up with my friends and some other students and we got off the bus. I glanced over my shoulder when I saw Frankie hop down from the steps onto the pavement and my heart thrummed in my chest. This was actually happening. She really wanted me to walk her home. Suddenly, I couldn't remember

how to walk and looked to my friends for help. Hayes's dark brown skin looked flushed on my behalf and May was smiling like normal, but his smile was a little *too* big.

I cleared my throat when Frankie came to a stop at my side. I wasn't massively tall, but I was taller than everyone else in my year and even taller than some of the older kids a few years ahead of me. I was five foot eight inches and, looking down at Frankie, I wondered if she topped off at four foot eleven. I had never realised how short she was until she stood next to me. She was seriously tiny.

"Uh." Hayes coughed. "Hey, Frankie. Me and May were just about to go to his house, which is this way," he pointed over his shoulder. "So we'll see you both later."

Hayes all but dragged May along as they walked away. I knew he thought he was doing me a favour by leaving me alone with Frankie, but he did the complete opposite. He threw me right into the deep end with no armbands because I had *no* bloody idea what I was supposed to do, or say, to a girl that I liked. I hardly knew what to say to a girl who I *didn't* like. My mind couldn't handle the stress of it.

"I live on Dulwich Road," she said, breaking the silence. "Where d'you live?"

I knew she lived on Dulwich Road, her stop was three stops before Cumberland Road.

"Uh, on Trinity Street."

Frankie nodded and turned and began walking away from Cumberland Road in a direction that would cut through a few streets and eventually lead to Dulwich Road. I snapped out of whatever the hell was wrong with me and hurried to catch up with her. When I reached her side, I had to take much smaller strides because hers were half what mine were. I glanced down at her and saw she was wearing a necklace with a pendant I had never seen before.

"I've never seen a necklace like that."

She lifted her hand to the pendant and brushed her thumb over it before dropping her arm back to her side. "It's a medical I.D.," she explained. "I have severe asthma so I have to wear one for medical purposes."

Right. Duh. I knew she had asthma. At the start of every school year for as long as I could remember we were reminded of her illness as well as a kid who had a peanut allergy. We knew what we had to do if either of them had one of their respective attacks. Get help immediately.

"So," I said, shoving my hands into my pocket. "Why'd you want me to walk you home?"

"So I could talk to you."

"Right."

Talk to me about bloody *what*? My head was about to explode with the confusion of what was happening. Frankie looked as cool as a cucumber while I was as jittery as a squirrel.

"I'm going to talk," Frankie began. "And you're going to listen, okay?"

I was going to shit myself is what I was going to do.

"Okay."

"Right," she said. "So, I know you're lying about how you got that bruise on your face."

Of all the things I expected her to say, that was *not* it.

"What d'you mean?" I looked down at her, feeling my body tense as I walked. "I'm not lying."

"Yeah, you are."

I stopped walking and so did Frankie, she turned to face me. She looked up at me with her big green eyes and she almost narrowed them as if to challenge me. I shifted, looking down at my feet.

"I'm not lying, Frankie."

"It's okay," she comforted. "You don't have to be scared."

I felt like I was suddenly in a tiny, dark, confined room.

"I . . . Look, I don't think I can walk you home." I blurted, taking a step back. "I forgot I have something to—"

"Risk, I'm going to tell Mr Jones what I think is happening to you."

I felt my jaw drop as surprise, and anger, filled me when she brought the school's counsellor into the conversation.

"What the hell are you talking about?" I said, dumbfounded. "*Nothing* is happening to me."

"Yes, it is," she pressed. "You come into school with more bruises and injuries than anyone I know. At first, I thought you were clumsy, but no one is *this* clumsy. Also, don't insult me. I'm not stupid, no poxy frying pan left your face *that* bruised and swollen."

I shifted my gaze and stared down at this girl who I had known since reception, but never really knew. I couldn't believe how she could see through the cloud of lies that not even my best mates questioned. I suddenly felt panicked. She said she was going to tell Mr Jones. He was probably the nicest man to walk the earth and he was the obvious choice for a student to go to when they needed help.

"Frankie." I wiped my forehead. "Listen to me—"

"Don't lie to me and I will."

I couldn't believe she was talking to me like this when we had *never* really talked before. Didn't she realise how out of order she was?

"You've got some neck, y'know?" I frowned. "You can't just go and say shit like this to people."

"Shit like what?"

"Like saying I'm being abused!"

"But I didn't say that." She raised a brow. "I said I was going to tell Mr Jones what I thought was happening to you. You said the word abuse, not me."

She was confusing me.

"Stop." I scowled. "I knew what you meant and you did too."

"Well, answer me this. *Are* you being abused?"

My heart hurt with how blunt her question was.

"I . . . I . . . No, I'm not!" I lied. "It's fucking creepy of you to think you know me when you fucking *don't.* I thought you were cool, but you're clearly a psycho bitch who—"

"You're not hurting my feelings." She interrupted as she folded her arms across her flat chest. "You're lashing out because you're scared and upset and I get it."

"What is your *problem*?" I snapped. "Why're you acting like you're an adult? You're no older than thirteen!"

"I'm actually twelve, thirteen next week, but just because I'm not older I'm supposed to not see what's right in front of me?" she demanded. "I can't just pretend I don't see that you're hurting, Risk."

"Why not?" I shouted at her. "Why the fuck *not*? Nobody else sees what they do to me, why do *you*? Why d'you even care?"

"Because I'm not heartless, wazzock. *That's* why!"

I couldn't believe she called me an idiot, I couldn't believe she was doing this to me at all. I was breathing heavily and I stumbled back when I realised I just confirmed her suspicions. I imagined her telling Mr Jones everything and then the police coming and taking me away. Everything flashed before my eyes and it prompted me to say what I'd been holding on to for so long.

"Please don't tell," I begged. "They'll take me away if you do. I won't get to go to school here anymore, or see May and Hayes every day or even you. Please, Frankie. Don't tell."

Her lips parted and sadness filled her lustrous green eyes, sadness for me.

"They're hurting you though, Risk. You're always so beat up coming to school and it kills me to see you like that. They're your foster parents, they're supposed to take care of you, not hurt you."

"They don't hurt me all of the time," I assured her. "Owen only does it when he's mad, Freda just shouts sometimes. She only smacks my head when she gets goin', she doesn't do anything worse."

"Risk." Frankie's eyes glazed over with tears. "One smack is enough for it to *be* worse."

"Please," I pleaded. "Don't tell. I don't want to leave Southwold. *Please*."

Frankie didn't reply.

"I'll be eighteen in a few years, then I'll be an adult and out of the system," I rambled on. "I just have to stick it out for a few more years, then I'll walk away and never look back."

"D'you promise?"

"Yes, Frankie. I promise."

"And promise you'll do everything not to make your foster dad mad."

"I promise."

"Okay." She rubbed her eyes. "I won't tell. I hate that you're asking me this. I shouldn't listen, but I don't want to hurt you so I won't tell."

I was so relieved, tears fell from my eyes. Frankie surprised me when she got up on her tiptoes and wrapped her short arms around my body. She squeezed me so tight it almost stole my breath. A wave of emotions I had never experienced before crashed into my heart. I had been a burden, an outcast, a misfit and unloved for as long as I could remember and this tiny, red-headed girl made me feel wanted with one conversation and one little hug.

"We're friends now and that means I'll take care of you, okay?" she mumbled against my chest. "You can come to my house any time you want to get away from them. I promise."

"O-Okay."

"Promise we'll do everything together, that we'll take care of each other."

"I promise, Frankie."

When I hugged her back, it felt right. Like I had found someone who liked me for me and accepted all that came with me. I knew we were going to be good friends because finding someone like Frankie, someone who saw through the façade I portrayed and still wanted to have my back was rare. *She* was rare. I think I started to love her that day because she made me feel like I wasn't the broken one, the stray kid who couldn't find a family.

When I was with her, I was wanted and I knew that she wouldn't ever send me away like everyone else did.

I just knew it.

CHAPTER THREE
RISK

Present day . . .

Home.

I had been back to the UK and travelled up and down it multiple times since I left to pursue my dreams in the States nine years ago, but this was the first time since I had left that I was returning to my home town. Southwold was a small town on the coast in the East Suffolk district of Suffolk, England. The town had a population of a thousand or so people and what kept the place afloat was the tourist economy. Tourists came for the pretty views and the beaches which Southwold offered, but the hotels, B&Bs, the golf course, cafés, restaurants and the market town atmosphere were the only reason people stuck around for their weekend getaways. Half of the homes in Southwold were second homes or let to holidaymakers so you rarely saw the same faces twice unless they were locals.

Growing up, I saw the appeal in Southwold that many of its residents were blind to.

I loved how calm, how quiet and picturesque it was. It was a place where someone could find themselves, or in my case, lose myself. When I left Southwold I was only eighteen years old, but

I was a broken person. I spent a long time forcing myself to never think of my past, to think of *her*, but being back home made that impossible. Everywhere I looked, I saw her. Frankie Fulton, my ex-girlfriend, *was* Southwold to me and I always figured that was why I loved the town, but never came back to it.

They say you don't know what you have until it's gone or that sometimes you have to lose someone to realise that you really love them. I never understood any of that because I always knew that I had the love of my life in Frankie and I knew I loved her long before I lost her. The shitty thing was, I knew all of those things and I *still* lost her. I had nine long years to think about why we ended and though I didn't think it was the right thing to have had happened, I accepted it. That didn't make it hurt any less. I knew I was a rock for Frankie, but what she didn't know was that she was an entire boulder for me.

She knew everything about my past. All of it.

May and Hayes had been my best friends for years, but even they didn't know the extent of the things that I had been through. Frankie was different. We started out as regular classmates at school, then when I was twelve I noticed that she was pretty and that was the beginning of how she became my entire world. She took care of me before I was hers to take care of. She gave me my first hug that I could ever remember. She had my back from the jump and didn't take no for an answer. A deep bond developed between us. She had always been there for me when I felt trapped and all alone in a home, and world, where I wasn't wanted. She kissed every bruise, allowed me to unload my troubles onto her and she kept my secret when I asked her to.

She gave me hell for it, but she still did it.

Once Frankie entered my life in a big capacity, I shared my coping mechanism with her. Music. I explained to her how I felt when I listened to music, how I could go into a new world and escape mine whenever I listened to a song. Whenever I listened to the riffs of a guitar, the ping of a piano, the beat of drums and the emotion in a vocalist's voice, I became part of a moment with them that took me away from all my anger, hurt and misery.

It was thanks to Frankie that I found out that I could sing.

She had severe asthma, I had known that for as long as I had known her, but I found out just how bad it was during the time that we became close friends because it was around the same time that her dad died. The day she ran towards me, screaming and crying. I knew I'd never forget how scared I was when she dropped to her knees before me and gasped for breath. Her lips had turned blue by the time I got her inhaler from her pocket and forced it into her mouth.

Hearing her inhale her medicine and listening as her wheezing faded to nothing gave me a relief I had never felt before in my life, but it also added a great worry to my mind too. Frankie was a girl who I quickly realised I needed in every way and the very thought of her dying because of her asthma terrified me whenever I allowed myself to think about it. It was the reason why I stole one of my foster mother's blue inhalers every few months. I made sure I had one of them with me at all times just in case Frankie was ever without one of hers.

Owen had caught me stealing one once and he sliced a line into my back as punishment. Out of all of the times that the man had beat me, that was the only time he had ever left a forever-lasting physical mark on me. Across my shoulders and down to the right of my back was a thick, jagged scar. Its pink colour was fading with time. It was always there to touch though, to feel, to remember.

That awful day, when Frankie's attack subsided, I sat on the side of the street with her and hugged her but it didn't seem like it was enough. I asked what I could do to help; she told me patting her lower back was what her parents did so I did that and then I began to sing to her to distract her from the pain she was feeling. I didn't know what it was like to have a real father. I never knew who mine was, and my foster father was never in the running for Dad of the Year, but just because I didn't have a father didn't mean I didn't understand the pain of losing one. I had never seen Frankie so broken before and I wanted to do something, anything, to take away some of that pain.

So I sang and to my great surprise, it helped her.

A long time later, when her sobs turned to sniffles, she turned her tear-streaked, blotchy red face to mine and stared at me through her swollen, bloodshot eyes and she offered me the sweetest smile I had ever been given. She leaned her face against mine and I could still remember feeling my heart stop when her lips brushed against mine. It was a simple, chaste kiss but it was my first, hers too, and I still couldn't imagine anything more perfect. It would be the only kiss we would share until just over two years later just after her fifteenth birthday when I bit the bullet and asked her on a date. During that date I asked her to be my girlfriend, and I kissed her, and that was that.

Her kissing me back had been enough to shake my world.

Ever since Frankie heard me sing, she almost demanded I sing to her all of the time. She encouraged me to start a band to put my passion for music into something I could create myself. It was like a switch had been flipped inside of me. I loved to sing, I just loved it. Singing felt like breathing to me. May and Hayes took to the idea of being in a band like fish to water. At our school, Mr Jones was musically inclined and he was delighted to finally have students to start an after-school music club with. He taught us how to play the guitar, piano, and the drums. We learned our other instruments on our own, but Mr Jones was the reason we could even do that.

He supported Blood Oath from the second we came up with our name and took our band seriously.

He didn't have much on a teacher's salary, but the man went out of his way and bought us our first instruments. They weren't new or even second hand, they were third hand and obviously not in the best of shape, but they were ours. Once we had instruments, May's parents sat up and took notice of us one day when we were jamming out in their back garden. Three weeks later, they allowed us to have their small garage converted into a makeshift soundproof studio for us to work out of. May's parents didn't know it then, but they gave me a place to escape to every single day and I always appreciated them for it.

The day I turned eighteen, I moved out of my foster parents' house with a bag full of my belongings before the sun had even risen, and I kept my promise to Frankie: I never looked back once I closed the door behind me. The day before that, Frankie and I had signed the lease to rent a cottage on Pier Street. She didn't turn eighteen until the twenty-first of January, a week after I did, but her mum allowed us both to move in together before that because she knew we were the real deal. Her boyfriend, Dr Michael O'Rourke, was our landlord. Frankie liked the man, she just never knew how to act around him because he had always been her family's GP, but he was a good guy.

Having a place of our own was better than anything I could have imagined.

Frankie and I had been dating almost three years to the day when we moved in together, but as far as our relationship went, we had never gone all the way physically. I wanted to, I had wanted to have sex with her since I was fifteen but she wasn't ready for that step in our relationship so we waited. We kissed and touched and she let me finger her once, but full sex had never happened until the night we moved in together.

It was a memory that I would never forget.

◆ ◆ ◆

"Frankie!" I hollered. "Babe, did you buy tea-bags when you went shopping with your mum?"

"Yeah," she shouted from the bathroom. "They're in the tea caddy."

I paused. "We have a tea caddy?"

"It's next to the sugar-pot."

"We have a sugar-pot?"

Frankie's musical laughter flowed down the hallway when she opened the bathroom door. I turned my head and watched as she walked into our kitchen looking good enough to eat. She had her long, curly auburn hair tied up in a high ponytail, she had a fitted green T-shirt on and a pair of black leggings. She was barefoot and wearing the most casual outfit a person could wear, but to me, she looked like a goddess. Knowing I was alone with her, and would sleep in a bed with her, was making my head – both of them – spin.

"I bought a set for coffee, tea and sugar when I was in Tesco." She pointed to the brown pots that were near the kettle. "I filled them up already."

I reached over and grabbed the pot that had 'Tea' written across it in bold, white letters. I took out two tea-bags, closed the pot and put it back before I grabbed two mugs and flipped the kettle on. I smiled when Frankie's arms slid around my bare waist and her head rested underneath my shoulder blades. I was being a little unfair to her and I knew it. I was starting to fill out a little, my shoulders were broader and my body was lean and I knew Frankie liked it best when I was shirtless and now that we lived together I planned on being shirtless a lot.

"If I get any taller," I commented, "you're gonna need a foot stool to hug me."

She reached up and pinched my nipple which made me yelp and her laugh. When I turned to face her, I looked down and snorted. I was eighteen and was already six foot four, she was a week shy of eighteen and topped the measuring stick at five foot even. She was an itty bit of a thing and I loved it. There was no woman more feminine to me than Frankie.

"You're not allowed get any taller." She stated. "I think my growth spurt is over."

Laughter bubbled up my throat.

"You grew two inches the year you turned sixteen and have capped off at five foot nothing. That isn't a growth spurt, Frodo, that's a growth *stall*."

I arched back when she jokingly pretended to bite me.

"Don't start with me, Groot," she warned. "Remember how much closer I am to your dick than your face and which one I can slap first."

I shuddered. "Messaged received."

She snorted then turned and helped me put away the rest of our shopping. After making and drinking our tea, we got to work. Once the perishable food was stored in the fridge and freezer, we took some time deciding on where everything else would go. I made the mistake of putting cups, bowls and plates into the top cupboards. I forgot my girlfriend was a hobbit so I had to take them all out and put them in a floor cupboard. When everything was put away Frankie beamed and hugged me for the hundredth time that day.

"I can't believe we live here. Together. We've leased this place, we both graduated school, have jobs and pay rent and bills. We're actual adults. It's terrifying. I love it."

I chuckled as I kissed the crown of her head.

"I'm not scared at all."

She looked up at me with wonder in her clear green eyes.

"You're not?"

"Nope," I chirped. "Because being here in this cottage with you is the first time I feel like I'm actually living. I wouldn't trade this for anything in the world, Cherry."

Her eyes suddenly glazed over with tears so I moved her over to the counter and helped her sit on top of it so I didn't have to keep looking down at her. She was still shorter than me, but the height difference wasn't as drastic now. I leaned in and kissed her pale pink lips, which were quivering.

"Don't cry."

She sniffled. "I just love you so much."

"I love you too," I smoothed some unruly tendrils of hair back from her face. "Only you."

When Frankie kissed me, I wasn't sure how I knew, but I was confident that this would end with us experiencing the other's body for the first time and the anticipation of it made me shake. I lifted my hands to her face and stepped between her parted thighs. I almost couldn't keep up with how desperately she kissed me until she surrendered herself to me and followed my lead.

I was a virgin like her; I had waited for her to be ready and according to her kiss and touch on my body, I felt that she had reached that point. This thought was confirmed when her hand slid down my bare stomach and shockingly dipped under the band of my trousers and boxer briefs. The second her soft, supple hand touched my hardened cock, I broke our kiss.

"Are you sure?" I asked, staring down into her lust-filled eyes. "We can just kiss and touch; we don't have to have sex."

When Frankie smiled up at me, I knew then just how dangerous she was because for that smile, for that overwhelming look of want for me in her big, round eyes, I knew that I would do just about anything. I'd give her the world if I had it in my hands.

"I'm ready. I want to be with you in every way," she said, her hand stroking me twice. "I hurt for you. Please."

Christ. She was testing me with her words and a couple of strokes. I had to regain control, so I picked her up and attached my lips to her neck as I moved. She gasped and pulled her hand from my underwear so she could grip my shoulders with both of her hands. Within seconds, I was in our bedroom and laid her back on our already-made bed. I moved my lips up to hers and kissed her until she wrapped her legs around my body and squeezed me tightly with her thighs.

"Please," she moaned against my lips. "Risk, please. Love me."

I could have dropped dead there and then from excitement alone.

My heart was at risk of exploding in my chest when Frankie removed her T-shirt as she lay under me. She had no bra on and while I had seen her small, perky breasts before, the sight of them still made my breath catch just like it did the first time. Without a word, I leaned down and sucked her right, hardened nipple into my mouth. She shifted, pushing her breast roughly against my lips. I flicked my eyes upwards and watched as Frankie's eyes squeezed shut and her mouth hung open in a silent moan as I swirled my tongue around her areola and then suckled.

"Yes," she hissed. "Fuck, *yes*!"

Blood surged to my already hard cock, it throbbed to the point of pain.

As I switched breasts, I multitasked by hooking my thumbs under the hem of Frankie's leggings and underwear and I began to push them down. She helped me by lifting her hips and kicking the fabric off her legs when I couldn't push them down any further without stopping what I was doing. I sat back on my heels and got my first look at my naked, red-headed beauty and I was already embarrassed because I knew I was going to come before I was supposed to.

My girl was a goddess who would have Aphrodite herself leering her way with jealousy.

Her skin was flawless, smooth to the touch and she was so fair she looked immaculate. Her cheeks were flushed with colour and her green eyes were hooded with desire. Her hair had come out of its tie and was spilled over the white bedsheets, the fiery colour popping out against the backdrop. That same auburn colour was between the apex of her thighs. My heart was a pounding mess and staring at her pussy didn't help matters. I didn't wait for an invite, I lay flat on my stomach, spread her lips apart and licked up her wet slit until my tongue slid over the swollen, pulsing bud of her clit.

Frankie's hips bucked against my face.

"Risk!" she screamed. "Oh my god. *Oh my god*!"

Except for hearing her cry my name, her words became inaudible as they jumbled together. I had never done this before; I took my cue from the pornos I had watched. I explored her pussy, devouring her taste and smell as I paid attention to her body's responses whenever my tongue made it twitch or jolt. She liked when I tongued the hole of her pussy's entrance, but she *loved* when I swirled around her clit before clamping it between my lips and sucking. I wasn't sure how long I had been eating her pussy, it could have been five minutes, or five hours, but time was lost on me because what I was doing was pleasurable for me too.

I loved eating pussy, or more importantly, Frankie's pussy.

It didn't take long for me to realise that her thighs were shaking as I flattened my palms against them to keep them wide open. There was no warning for me that she was about to come, but I knew when she did. She sucked in a strangled breath and her body went rigid as she held it. I was about to stop and ask if she was okay when her clit suddenly throbbed under my tongue, the second time it pulsed, Frankie released the breath she was holding and screamed.

It scared the shit out of me.

I faltered for a moment and she cried, "No, no! *Don't stop*."

I quickly sucked her clit back into my mouth and worshipped it as the pulses slowed down. The entire time, Frankie's moaning was ripping into my restraint. It was so sexy, so full of need that I was battling with myself to keep from stripping and sinking right into her.

"Risk," she whimpered. "Now. Please. Fuck me *now*!"

I nearly broke my neck as I jumped from the bed to my feet and rid myself of my trousers and boxers. I was as naked as the day I was born and back between Frankie's thick, creamy white thighs in one tenth of a second, a time that would have made any Formula One driver proud. I crawled up her trembling body and brought my mouth to hers when she reached for me. I forgot that she would taste herself on my lips and tongue, but it wasn't a problem as she plunged her own tongue into my mouth and moaned. It was such a fucking turn on knowing she liked her own taste because I fucking *loved* it.

"Please," she begged. "Fuck me. Make me come again, rock star."

"Condoms."

"We don't need them," she panted. "I'm on the pill, been on it since I turned seventeen. Remember?"

If I was excited before, knowing I was going to fuck Frankie raw was enough to make me cry. I reached down, fisted my cock, pumped my hand up and down twice, coating myself in pre-cum. I pressed the head against Frankie's soaking wet folds and ran it up and down against her. She twitched, I grinned.

"You like that, Cherry?" I moved my face back to hers. "You like when I play with this pussy?"

Her eyes rolled back as she bobbed her head, too focused on what I was making her feel to pay attention to my words.

I swallowed as I looked down. I bit my lip as I lined my cock up, but instead of watching myself sink into her hot, wet pussy, I looked at Frankie's face instead. Our eyes were locked as I moved my hips forward and slowly slid inside of her. Her face was flushed, her chest was rising and falling rapidly, but my fear of hurting her went out of the window when her legs wrapped around my waist and she used them to pull my hips forward, forcing me to sink all the way into her.

"Risk."

My eyes rolled back and my teeth sunk into my lower lip as euphoria consumed me. I had imagined every which way of having sex with Frankie and I knew it would feel incredible, but I never thought of just *how* incredible it would be. I felt like I couldn't move. I was so aware of every sensation that if a breeze blew over my balls, I'd likely come. I opened my eyes and focused on Frankie. She was in the tight clutch of desire, looking at me like I'd just hung the moon for her.

"Are you okay?" My voice sounded pained to my own ears. "Tell me the truth."

"I feel no pain," she hummed, her hands sliding up my arms to my neck then to my hair. "This is how I knew it would be. This is perfect."

I agreed with her wholeheartedly.

"Please don't hate me if I come too soon." I realised my body was shaking. All I wanted to do was thrust in and out of Frankie's body. "I don't think I can hold back, you feel . . . it's too much."

Frankie's grin was almost Cheshire Cat-like as she shifted her hips, drawing a groan from me.

"Cherry, *please*."

"Cherry," she mused. "You always called me that because of my hair colour, now you can add popping my cherry to the list of reasons why."

I leaned down and snagged her lower lip with my teeth; her eyes gleamed with a challenge and then, before I knew it, Frankie nudged me onto my side then she rolled on top of me. Somehow, I never slipped from her body.

"Babe," I hissed as she sunk down, taking the length of me. "Are you sure?"

"Is there a rule that for our first time you need to be on top?"

"What?" I shook my head. "No, but – *fuck*!"

Frankie rose up and down on my cock and I almost lost it then and there. I shifted my hips, almost bracing myself against what she was going to do to me as I placed one hand on her tiny waist and the other on her breast. She licked her lips, grabbed my forearms and kept eye contact with me as she slowly began to ride me. Instantly, my toes curled as I tried to force my body to remain absolutely still.

I understood in that moment why people became addicted to sex.

The raw pleasure that filled my body took over everything. My mind, my senses, my will to do anything other than come was insane. I lowered my eyes from Frankie's stunning, pleasure-filled face so I could watch my cock slide in and out of her pussy. I had gotten off to this visual of what that could look like over the past three years and, now that it was happening, I was happy to say that reality completely outdid everything my imagination conjured up, because *fuck*.

"Yes," I hissed. "Ride me, baby. Fuck me."

I bucked my hips up to meet hers as she slammed down on me and we both made sounds I couldn't describe. That was the flip of the switch on slow sex and almost instantly the pace changed and

Frankie was riding me, fucking me, like there was no tomorrow. I had no defence against her, she had me completely and utterly at her mercy and I loved every single second of it.

"Fr-Frankie." I panted. "I'm gonna come."

"Yes." She slammed down. "Come inside me. Fill me up."

Christ.

I moved both of my hands to her waist, squeezed tight and drilled my hips up into hers. She clenched around me and threw her head back. I was trying to look everywhere at once. Her face, her tits, her body, my cock slamming in her pussy. My senses were entirely overloaded with Frankie and when I locked eyes with her, I knew I was about to come. My lips parted as what felt like static electricity pinched my balls as they drew up tight. I groaned as the built-up pressure released and my cum shot out in spurts from my body to the inside of Frankie's. The sensation of bliss was so strong, I thought I might have blacked out for a second.

When I was spent, I was more satisfied and relaxed than I had ever been in my life. I closed my eyes and audibly thanked God for his method of reproduction. Frankie's laughter made my softening dick twitch inside her body. She lay her still-trembling body on my chest and brushed her soft lips against mine. I felt like I weighed a thousand pounds as I lifted my arms and wrapped them around her.

"Frankie," I opened my eyes and looked at her. "I love you."

She nuzzled her nose to mine.

"I love you too. Always have and I always will, rock star."

I kissed her before I let my head plonk back on the mattress. I was wiped. Or at least I thought I was, then Frankie sat back up and lifted her hands up to her head so she could finger comb her hair. I was still inside her body and as my eyes rolled over the porcelain white curves God gave her, I suddenly wasn't as tired as I thought I was. My slowly hardening cock agreed with me. Frankie's screeching laughter as I rolled her under me soon turned to moans and urgent demands as I loved her body with mine so thoroughly that I knew there was no way we would finish unpacking the rest of our things tonight.

Not a chance.

CHAPTER FOUR
RISK

"Risk, could you *look* any more miserable, boy?"

The sudden intrusion on my memory made my body tense. I turned my head in the direction of the voice that spoke and stared at May Acton, the first kid I had ever hung out with on the first day of reception at school. As I looked at him, I didn't think he'd changed all that much. He still had the same shoulder-length hair he'd always had, only it was blood red now instead of its natural dark brown. His face wasn't fat anymore since he'd lost over five stone of weight throughout the years, but he still looked like May and our success and fame definitely hadn't changed him. He was still the same idiot from Cumberland Road who thought farting was funny.

I wondered if I was still the same Risk to him, because I sure as hell didn't feel like I was. Instinctively, I lifted my hand to the coin on my necklace and thumbed it. Six months sober. The coin represented a lot to me, so did the others I had. I was hoping to switch it out for a new coin in a month's time. It was something I was looking forward to because it was entirely for me and me alone. Making the decision to never take drugs or drink alcohol again had been the first time I saw light in a very dark tunnel. My use had started gradually over the years. A line of coke here and there, a weekend bender every so often, to snorting and drinking daily. It was insane how a vice could take hold of a person so quickly.

I've never blamed her, but in the beginning of my career, taking drugs and drinking till I blacked out was the only way I could forget about Frankie and how much it hurt to be without her. The first time I fucked a woman after we broke up was about eight months after I left Southwold, and the only way I could force myself to do it was to be high. The method continued because using was the only time I didn't see Frankie's face every time I looked at another woman. I had become addicted to the high that alcohol and drugs gave me. The only time I never had to take anything was when I was on stage because the high of performing live was unlike any other. I tried to replicate that feeling when I had downtime because otherwise I felt like I was sinking into a black hole of darkness that was just waiting to consume me.

An intervention seven months ago by my friends and management saved my life. I shot heroin for the first time because the coke and drink weren't enough anymore and I almost accidentally killed myself. I overdosed, but I was one of the lucky few who lived to tell the tale. When I left hospital, I went straight into a ninety-day stint in rehab. I spoke with a therapist often and I wrote two dozen songs during my detox. I had clarity for the first time in years. I didn't want to live the way I had been living anymore and it was a huge step because I wanted to live for me instead of someone else.

"I'm not miserable." I shifted. "I was just thinking about something."

"What?"

"None of your business, cocknose. *That's* what."

May snorted. "Do you think it's weird being back here?"

"It *is* weird being back here."

Hayes, who was seated behind me in the van, said, "Good weird?"

"Just weird," I shrugged. "I've never had a reason to come back here."

"My parents haven't been back since they moved to France five years ago. Hayes's parents moved to London not long after we moved to LA," May pointed out. "They don't need to be here for us to visit. This is where we grew up, this is where Blood Oath was born. We wrote and released our EP here. We wrote some of our first album here. This place is part of us."

He was right, of course, but he still didn't get it.

"I know all of that," I began. "Being here is just weird—"

"Because your ex who dumped your sorry ass is still here."

May and Hayes both cursed at the same time.

"What?" Angel questioned, unbothered by their outbursts. "Someone needed to say it since both of *you* tools are dancing around the subject. He isn't a piece of glass, stop treating him like he's going to shatter. He's sober by his own choice; mentioning an ex isn't going to have him rushing for a needle."

Angel Reyes was not an original member of Blood Oath. Nine months after we moved to LA he joined the band after we had heard him play during a weekend gig in some bar. He was Mexican, he moved to the States when he was seven and bounced around from state to state before settling in LA with his mum and little sister when he was ten. Like the rest of us, he wasn't tied down to one talent. He was solid on drums, viola, and keyboards. Drums, however, was where he performed his masterclasses.

He was hardwired to say things no matter how blunt they were, which was the cause of more than a few arguments, but he was one hell of a drummer and he knew it. He was a good man too and just as much of a brother to me as May and Hayes; he was just too honest for his own good sometimes. When his topic of discussion hinted at Frankie, I wouldn't entertain him.

"Mind your business, Ringo."

"Please. I'm better than him."

"Whatever." I rolled my eyes. "Keep your bitchy comments to yourself or I'll break your sticks off in your arse."

Angel snorted, not threatened in the slightest.

"*Is* it a problem though?" May questioned. "About possibly running into Frankie while we're here? If you're worried, maybe this is too soon. You got out a rehab three months ago, you're sober six. You shouldn't be in a triggering situation. Maybe we shouldn't have come home."

I hated, fucking *hated*, how my addiction had messed with May's head. He and Hayes never touched drugs. Angel liked to smoke weed. They drank alcohol, but it wasn't a problem for them like it had been for me. They drank for fun, I drank to black out. My use was to mask the hurt I felt, then it almost became like something I needed in order to survive. I wasn't sure when my use became an addiction . . . it happened too fast for me to grab it.

"I *told* you what my therapist said." I nudged May's leg with my foot. "The space I'm in can take people recovering years to reach. I'm sober for me, I want to be healthy and have a clear mind. Frankie . . . she won't trigger me."

"How d'you know though?" May pressed. "You started taking everything to cover up everything about her, what if seeing her wrecks everything?"

"I can't run from her, May. I'll be running forever if that's the case."

"I think it'll be worse for her than him because she knows what she did to him," Hayes commented. "He's known her all of his life, dated her for a few years, then as soon as we get our big break, she dumps him when his life was already going through a massive change. I've always had a soft spot for her, but what she did to him was cruel. If anyone should be weirded out, it's her, not Risk."

"That's not fair, boy. She found out her mum was sick the week we got offered our record deal," May fired back, coming to Frankie's defence like he always did. "She did what she thought was best for both her and main man. She isn't a cruel person and you fucking know it, Hayes."

I lifted my hands to my face and groaned.

"Stop," I said, dropping them to my lap. "Look, it's been nine years. Nearly a whole decade since I've seen her or spoken to her. We're long past being weird in the other's company *if* we happen to cross paths. She has her life and I have mine. It's *cool.* I can handle being back here."

No one said anything, which pissed me off a little. I wanted someone to agree with me, but no one did. I leaned my head back against the headrest and told myself that the conversation was stupid. It'd been years since Frankie and I were anything to each other. If I was being honest with myself, it messed my head up to think of her because of how much she meant to me at one point. Being back in Southwold did turn out to be somewhat of a trigger because as we drove into town, she was all I could think about.

I even went down memory-fucking-lane while thinking of her.

Jesus. I cracked my neck. *That shit needs to stop.*

"I forgot Southwold was so small." May suddenly asked as he looked out of the window of the van, "How can everything be the exact same? Nothing has changed."

"Because it's Southwold," I answered. "The only thing that changes is the faces."

May and Hayes were staring around the place we grew up with intrigued eyes. I didn't have that same enthusiasm. Angel, who was on my right, was on his phone probably texting the woman who has been leading him around by the dick for the past month.

I closed my eyes until the van came to a complete stop and May suddenly burst into laughter before he jumped out of the vehicle. Hayes followed him and so did Angel. I looked at the driver who had picked us up from the airport as he lifted the privacy screen.

"Thanks, man."

He nodded then got out of the van and helped us unload our belongings from the back. I gave him a fifty-pound tip, which he didn't bat an eyelid at as he took it, nodded once more then got back into his tinted-window van and drove off. I turned and stared at the two-storey house that the other three were looking at.

"This," Angel said. "*This* dump is where you grew up?"

"I bought it when my parents were selling it so they could move to France." May laughed. "Isn't it beautiful?"

"Fucking gorgeous, bro."

I snorted, Hayes laughed and May beamed like he didn't have a care in the world.

"It may not look like much, but mate, this little house has nothing but happy memories for me. This is where Blood Oath was born . . . y'know?"

Angel reached over and gave May's shoulder a squeeze.

"I know, bro, I'm just yanking your chain."

"My chain does not need yanking from the likes of you," May paused, smirking. "Your missus on the other hand . . . I'm joking!"

May practically leapt away from Angel and the coward hid behind me, which made Hayes double over with laughter while I watched Angel with a knowing grin.

"He always ruffles your feathers when he mentions your new girl. Why is that?"

Angel's black-as-night eyes moved to mine and they narrowed slightly.

"Do I need a reason *other* than she is my girl?"

I shrugged. "No, but you've had dozens of girlfriends and never got bent outta shape over May making jokes. Mate, I'm pretty sure the last blond you dated fucked May after you kicked her from the tour bus in Vegas."

Angel rolled his eyes. "She wanted him from the jump. I'm just a good-enough friend to take a pass on pussy that wants to sit on my friend's dick rather than mine."

May popped his head out from behind me. "I fucked a blond in Vegas? I don't remember?"

"Big tits Brittany," Angel and I said in unison.

"Oh." May's eyes gleamed. "I remember *her*."

Angel shook his head. "Zoey is off limits for jokes of any kind, especially innuendos, May."

"Why're you singling me out?" May protested. "I'm not the only member of this band."

"No," I agreed. "But you're the biggest slut in the band, and sex and women are never far from your mind."

May paused for a moment then he stepped out from behind me with his hands up at his chest, palms out. "That's fair," he said. "I won't talk about your missus anymore."

"If you do, I'm breaking your fingers."

Angel turned and walked towards our luggage with May hot on his heels.

"My fingers?" he spluttered. "Of all things to break, why my fingers? I need them to play! You'd ruin the entire band and our Sinners would hate you and—"

May's rant was cut short when Angel grabbed one of our carry-on suitcases and shoved it into May's gut, winding him. I looked from the pair of them to Hayes and we both chuckled in amusement.

"I think he's serious about that new girl of his," Hayes mentioned. "He hasn't so much as looked at another woman since he started dating her last month. He smiles more too. You've noticed it too, right?"

"Yeah," I nodded. "I have. Our boy's all grown up. He's in a serious relationship now just like you are."

Hayes grinned. "I'm married, he's not."

"With Angel, I wouldn't be surprised if he married that girl next week and had her knocked up by the year's end."

"Don't jinx us," Hayes shuddered. "After the new album drops next month, we have one year before our next tour. This time tour is gonna be different, mate. Two hundred shows in thirty-seven countries. Can you fucking *believe* we make albums and go on tours? That shit still blows my head."

I slung my arm around Hayes's shoulder and said, "Lad, I hope it never gets old for us."

"Amen, brother."

We looked back at May and Angel, who were now scuffling and demanding the other apologise for something they said. I shook my head, not surprised because they pulled the same shit no matter what country we were in. I looked at Hayes and grinned.

"Home sweet motherfucking home."

CHAPTER FIVE

FRANKIE

For nine years, my day-to-day life could be depicted like clockwork.

I went to work, visited my mum and Michael, stocked my cupboards with food, paid my bills, refilled my inhaler prescription at the pharmacy. I read between four and five books a week and sometimes I went to the cinema by myself if I was having a really wild night. I didn't have any girlfriends; my co-workers were lovely, but our social circles did not cross outside of work. This worked well for me because I had a routine that I liked to follow. I knew what to expect, or at least I normally did.

Risk Keller being back in Southwold threw a wrench into not only my day-to-day plans, but right into my entire life.

"It's okay," I told myself as I walked towards the entrance of Sir John Leman High School. "This is *not* a big deal."

Trying to reassure myself had been a complete and utter disaster.

I didn't have social media accounts, so I couldn't check in and see if it was actually true about the band attending Mr Jones's retirement ceremony. I deactivated my Facebook account years ago because everyone would constantly post things about Blood Oath as they got more successful and even more famous. I understood it: three of the band's members were from Southwold and everyone was super proud of them. I was too, I just couldn't see or read about Risk because it hurt me too much.

I refused to ditch the ceremony out of fear of him showing up because Mr Jones didn't deserve that. He was a fantastic man who deserved to be celebrated for all of the work he had done for the school and the time he gave to his students over the years. For me, he was an angel after my father passed away. I spoke to him a few times a week and after each talk I felt immensely better. Nothing took away the pain of losing my dad, but Mr Jones helped me focus my pain and deal with it rather than let it consume me. I knew Risk, May and Hayes, if they were actually attending the ceremony, were going because they loved Mr Jones. He was their after-school music teacher and second biggest fan after me. He bought them their first instruments with his own money.

He had encouraged them to reach for the stars and now they were stars.

I wasn't going to let the possibility of seeing Risk mess with showing my respect to Mr Jones. I was a grown woman and even though I was worried about possibly seeing him again I wasn't letting that keep me from doing something that I wanted. It was likely that I was working myself up over nothing. Maybe I would get a little sad, but sure, who wouldn't? I loved him desperately at one point in my life but that was the past. Risk probably didn't even remember me, I was only his childhood girlfriend. He was a rock star now, and thanks to Anna and Hannah Porter, I knew he had been with a lot of women, some really famous ones, over the years.

The chance of him remembering me in his living-in-the-fast-lane life were slim to none.

I entered the school, the familiarity of it made me smile. I headed towards the school's PE hall where the decorated signs and pictures of Mr Jones all pointed. When I entered the hall, I wasn't surprised to see it full of people. How packed the place was made me smile. Understandably, not all of the student body could be present, there was just a couple of hundred kids taking up the first four rows of seats. Likely children who had a strong relationship with Mr Jones.

I made my way to an empty seat in the middle of the second back row of chairs. Ideally, I would have just stood at the back of the room, but there were people ushering everyone to sit down on any seat that was available so that was what I did. I ended up being wedged between two stocky men. I was thankful when the ceremony began a couple of minutes later. The lights in the hall were suddenly dimmed and a hush spread across the room. A projector switched on and on the back wall of the room, a film began to play.

"Hi, everyone!" A blond-haired girl wearing black-framed glasses appeared waving happily. "Thank you for coming along today to celebrate the wonderful career our dear Mr Jones has had during his forty-two years at Sir John Leman High School. My name is Sarah Marks. I'm a sixth former and I'm also the student who has been lucky enough to be selected to record and edit this short film for our lovely Mr Jones. I want to quickly thank every student, past and present, and each staff member who appears in the film because without you guys, we wouldn't get to show just how special Mr Jones is and how happy we are for him to start the next chapter of his life. I think everyone will agree that no man deserves to put his feet up more than him. This is for you, Mr Jones."

Instant applause filled the hall then it died down as *Dr Jones* by Aqua began to lowly play in the background of the film, making everyone chuckle. A roll of clips of Mr Jones throughout the years began to play and one thing that stood out was just how happy he was and how big the smiles were on the kids' faces around him. It wasn't all games and laughter though; there was a clip of a boy who looked down in one of the school's hallways and Mr Jones kneeled in front of him, talking to him before giving the student a hug and pulling a smile from him as he wiped his eyes. It showed the ups and downs that the counsellor of a school had but in the end, everything always ended in a smile.

I was smiling happily until my teenage face popped up onto the projected image on the wall, followed by Risk, May and Hayes as they played on their instruments in Mr Jones's office sometime during our last year at school. Students, and some parents, whooped and cheered before being shushed. There was audio with this clip and normally I would look away or run away, but I was trapped where I was and found that once I saw Risk, I couldn't tear my eyes away from him. My heart jumped when teenage Risk leaned over and kissed my cheek, my younger self smiled and looked at him like he was the only boy in the whole world as he sang his rendition of 'The Way You Look Tonight'. I could hear the teenage girls up front sigh dreamingly from my spot at the back of the hall.

I hadn't thought of that day since before Risk and I broke up, but watching it on film made it all come rushing back to me and I could remember it like it was yesterday. It was after school had ended, the guys and Mr Jones were waiting for the room that doubled as the music room to be cleaned by the caretakers and while they waited they sat in Mr Jones's office. I popped in to say hello, and goodbye, because I had to go straight to work since I just landed my first job at Mary Well's diner as a part-time waitress. Risk had asked me to wait a minute and he sang his version of the song to me. It was the best part of my day.

As Risk finished the song, I gave him a big kiss then got up just as a younger Mr Jones said, "Ew, can you both, like, not do that in front of me? Thanks."

The hall burst into laughter, but I couldn't move.

"Is that you?"

I jolted when the man on my right whispered his question.

"Me?" I shook my head. "No way."

"Huh." The man looked back at the projected screen. "Looks like you."

I said nothing further and neither did the man.

The film switched back to Sarah Marks approaching several children and as she asked them to answer the same question. Each answer was different from the last and it made me choke up a little because each word used was exactly the word to describe Mr Jones. It made my heart happy to know that he was beloved by students now just as much as he was when I was in school.

"Describe Mr Jones in one word . . . go!"

"Funny."

"Cool."

"Kind."

"Compassionate."

"Happy."

"Amazing."

"Nice."

"Patient."

"Understanding."

"*Legend*!"

The room erupted with laughter thanks to that last description from an energetic boy. The video then turned into a montage of pictures through the years with students and staff members. A bunch of staff members appeared on screen and said a few words about their colleague. Five minutes later, Sarah Marks popped back up.

"Mr Jones, you are one of a kind, sir. We're all so happy for you to get the break you deserve after helping so many people throughout your career, but we'd be lying if we said were weren't sad too. You mean so much to us and we're going to miss you every day."

The video zoomed out revealing hundreds and hundreds of children who all shouted. "We love you, Mr Jones!"

The video ended and everyone clapped, the projector was turned off and the lights to the room were turned up. Mr Jones stood up from his seat on the small, makeshift stage that was put together every year for graduation. He shook hands with the principal, who was on the stage with him, then Mr Jones moved to the microphone stand.

"Thank you for your hard work on the film, Sarah. I'll cherish it forever." Mr Jones smiled. "And thank you to the students and my colleagues for your lovely words. I'll be honest, I'm trying my very best not cry right now but it's very difficult because, from the bottom of my heart, I have loved my time at this school. I remember all of my students, past and present, and I appreciate every single one of you."

Everyone clapped again when he wiped under his eyes; I was right there with him wiping my own tears away. The man was an absolute gentleman and I wished nothing but the best for him. He deserved everything that was good in the world. He deserved to go on a six-month-long cruise with his wife; he had always talked about that when I was in school.

"Now that I've got the tears and the thank yous out of the way, I get to the very exciting part of my day. I've had permission from the top gun of this school to dish out this warning." Mr Jones rubbed his hands together, grinning. "If I see a single student rush towards this stage, or get up out of their seat, it's an instant suspension. That goes for any parents too, if you run up on this stage, your child will take the fall for you and will live in a bubble of shame for the rest of the term."

Everyone laughed apart from me because I knew what was coming. There was no way Mr Jones would put out a warning, even jokingly, if anyone other than who I thought it was was going to be coming on stage.

"Please, join me in welcoming past students and global superstars, Risk Keller, May Acton and Hayes Hurley. They've taken a break out of their busy schedule to come home to Southwold and attend this ceremony for my last year at Sir John Leman High School. They've brought along Angel Reyes too!" Mr Jones beamed. "Our very own Southwold boys are home! Give it up for Blood Oath!"

The noise. Christ. The volume was deafening, but when the side door to the hall opened, I had to put my hands over my ears because the sheer volume actually hurt. I didn't get to see a thing because everyone jumped to their feet while I remained seated. I seemed to be the only person who wasn't overjoyed to see Blood Oath, but they didn't have history with the lead singer and guitarist like I did. I remained seated, and for a solid two minutes, all that took place was screaming, cheering and clapping.

My bum was glued to my seat the entire time.

When the crowd finally retook their seats, I felt like I was having an out-of-body experience and that was because I saw him for the first time since I made him walk away from me nine years ago. The sight of him took my breath away and as an asthmatic, that was dangerous. I took deep breaths, but never took my eyes off him. Risk had changed, and he hadn't at the same time. His hair was still the same white-blond it always had been, but the style was different. He was rocking that typical Viking look. His hair was shaved on the sides and braided on the top of his head right back down his neck.

He was still gloriously tall but he wasn't skinny anymore. He had put on weight, but from what I could see, it only seemed to be muscle. His shoulders had always been broad, but now they were muscular and looked very strong, so did his biceps . . . he had actual biceps. Even his bloody thighs looked bigger. I swallowed as I continued my visual assessment of him. It wasn't hard to see why women, and a lot of men, lusted after him. Not only did he have a voice that sounded like a wet dream, he looked like one too.

He was more gorgeous than ever, he looked so healthy. I had heard he had gone to rehab after an incident of some kind with drugs and it obviously had done him the world of good. He truly looked incredible.

Risk, May and Hayes gave Mr Jones a big hug while Angel, the only non-original member of the band, shook his hand and smiled at something Mr Jones had said. I looked to May and Hayes and noted there were changes in their appearances too. May's transformation was incredible, even down to his blood-red hair. He was no longer overweight; his body looked just as fit as Risk's did. Hayes wasn't as muscular as the other two, but lord, he was a handsome man. A handsome man who had married his girlfriend of two years in a shotgun wedding last year so Anna had told me.

The three guys I once knew so well might as well have been strangers to me. The realisation of this smacked into me with the full force of a train. Yes, I had incredible difficulty getting over Risk, I was still struggling with it but seeing them made it clear to me just how stuck in the past I was. It'd been nine years since we were in each other's lives. Nine. They were famous rock stars now while I still worked in the same old diner and still lived in the same one-bedroom cottage near the pier. My best memories were in the past with Risk and the others, while they made new ones every day . . . this made something inside me shatter.

I couldn't do this. I thought I could, but I couldn't.

I stood up and quietly made my way across the row so I could leave. I apologised to every single person I had to step over and just as I reached the edge of the row, a kid who had walked from the front of the hall to speak to who I assumed was their parent at the back, stopped walking when she saw me. Everyone had quietened down as Mr Jones moved back to the microphone stand. The girl's eyes locked on my face and almost instantly they widened.

"Hey!" she gasped dramatically. "Aren't you the girl in the video who was kissing Risk?"

She may as well have used a megaphone because her voice carried throughout the whole hall. Everyone looked in my direction. I could have died there and then from embarrassment. I looked from the kid to the stage and my legs threatened to give out. Standing there, staring right at me, was Risk Keller. I nearly choked on air. Instead of smiling, nodding, or doing something, I turned and all but ran out of the hall.

I made it out to the car park. After I hurriedly got into my car, I grabbed my inhaler from my bag and took a few puffs. My heart was beating so fast I thought it would explode. He saw me. Risk looked right bloody at me. I was wrong. I thought I was grown up enough to take whatever happened in that hall on the chin, but I was a chicken shit. There was no way around it, I was a complete and utter chicken shit. The man probably thought I was some crazy ex-girlfriend who came by the ceremony just to see him.

"Jesus," I groaned as I drove out of the car park. "God in Heaven, what'd I do to deserve that?"

I drove all the way to work in silence as my mind kept replaying what had happened back at the school.

He looked great.

Better than great: he looked incredible. I'd seen glimpses of him over the years, obviously I couldn't avoid him everywhere I went with how famous he was, but I never ever stopped and truly looked at him like I did today. All the memories I had with him were when he was a boy. He was a grown man now. Who he was as an adult, I did not know. This was unsettling for me because it was a wake-up call to just how much time had really passed since we were together.

It'd been nearly a whole decade and I was *still* hung up on him.

When I reached work and entered the diner, I was actually happy to find that we were busy because it gave me something else to think about other than Risk, other than how pathetic I really was for not being over my childhood boyfriend. I threw myself into work, I barely spoke to Joe, or the other waitresses unless it was to do with orders. I didn't want to talk to anyone if I could help it and I think my co-workers could sense that. I knew they knew why too. They were aware that I would arrive late to work because I was attending Mr Jones's retirement ceremony. They obviously knew that Risk was there too.

It didn't take a genius to figure out that I was feeling sensitive because of him.

The day passed by quickly thanks to the steady flow of customers. My feet were aching. I worked myself to exhaustion and I couldn't wait to go home so I could shower and fall into bed where I would hopefully have a dreamless sleep. I was standing up, leaning against the hostess counter, checking over the inventory of our stock and making a note of what deliveries needed to be made the next day. Mary Well's was a themed diner so the only music that Joe wanted played was from the forties to the eighties by the original artists. I loved that. It made sure that I would never hear Risk's voice while I worked.

I was humming away to 'Greased Lightnin'' as the song filled the diner. I grabbed the tray next to me, intending to put it back in its spot, when the bell over the entrance door rang. I automatically straightened and turned with a smile on my face to greet the potential customer, but the face peering down at me was one that had been on my mind all day long.

"Hello, Frankie."

CHAPTER SIX
RISK

"Lads, I'm nervous." May paced back and forth in the hallway outside of the emergency exit of the hall of Sir John Leman High School. "*Why* am I fucking nervous?"

"Because you're not going out to a crowd of Sinners like you're used to. You're going out to people who taught you as a child and knew you before you were a rocker and you're worried you can't be cool because deep down you know that they know that you aren't really cool. Am I right?"

"Angel's right!" May's eyes turned wild. "I'm an imposter. Everyone knows it!"

"Leave him alone." I shoved away a snickering Angel and stood before May, placing my hands on his shoulder. "Relax, you're good."

"I'm good." He nodded frantically. "I'm fine, this is fine."

"Totally fine." Hayes said from my right. "Mate, breathe. This is home. We're *good*."

"Home." May nodded. "We're home. I shouldn't be freaking out."

"Exactly." I squeezed his shoulders. "Here, we're just a couple of regular lads."

"Regular lads that are global rock stars and carry the weight of the world on their shoulders."

May looked like he was going to collapse but he snapped out of his breakdown when Hayes got Angel in a headlock, shutting him up. He laughed and so did I as Angel spluttered curses and promises to kill Hayes, who smirked and shoved our drummer to the floor.

"Leave him be, dickwipe." Hayes grinned as he held his hand out to Angel. "Get your laughs by tearing into someone *other* than our brother."

"You three are no fun."

Hayes pulled Angel to his feet and clapped a hand on his back. Angel was chuckling again as he reached over and shoved May. His eyes gleamed with amusement telling me he wasn't being cruel with May, just a regular dick who thought stressing him out was funny.

"You're too easy to play with, Mayo."

"How can you be called Angel when 'demon' is so much more fitting?"

We all snickered, then leaned against the wall of the hallway, waiting for our cue. We had met with the principal of the school when we arrived and we were hustled to a staff-only hallway to avoid any kids seeing us and a riot ensuing. There was going to be a brief video some of the students had made for Mr Jones, then he'd make a speech and welcome us on stage. It was one of the more basic and least stressful appearances we had ever done, but the fact that it was for Mr Jones made it a big deal. That was probably what May was so worried about it in the first place. Like Hayes and I, he thought highly of Mr Jones. He probably thought he would mess up his retirement ceremony.

"Mr Jones is gonna be buzzing to see us," I commented. "When was the last time we saw him? Five years ago?"

"Four," May corrected. "He came to a gig we had in Manchester, we got him backstage passes. Angel was sick that night so he didn't get a chance to meet him. Remember?"

"Not really." I shifted. "I remember seeing him but nothing after that. I was likely out of it."

That made me feel like a piece of dog shit. Angel bumped my shoulder with his, gaining my attention.

"You'll remember this encounter with him and every other from now on," he said. "Focus on that."

Angel was a hard arse, but he cared about me and the rest of the guys like brothers. I appreciated him and Hayes and May. The three of them saved my life when they threw my arse into rehab. I was still alive because of them. I always reminded myself of that when I thought they intruded on my life a little too much. They, more than anyone, had the right to.

"Hey," May said and he moved closer to the door. "Look, they're playing that video the kids made for Mr Jones."

The glass of the doors was covered with sheer coloured paper on the other side of the panel, but parts of it were ripped, enabling us to peek into the hall without drawing attention to ourselves. We were bunched together like a group of schoolgirls as we watched the video projected onto the back wall of the hall. I smiled as I watched the video but then I saw my younger self along with a younger Frankie. A memory I had long forgotten was playing in front of me and it stole my breath.

I sang to her and her smile, her eyes, everything about her was for me in that moment. I had forgotten how she looked at me like I was her entire world. I'd forgot how much I loved that about her, I'd forgot how much I loved it when she looked at me like that.

"I take it that's the infamous Frankie?"

"Yeah, man," I answered Angel. "That's Frankie."

"She's cute."

Gorgeous. She was gorgeous.

The video came to an end and silently we all straightened away from the door and adjusted our clothing. I expected the lads to rip into me over what we had just seen on the video, but none of them said a word. I couldn't even look at them; I didn't want them to notice that seeing the memories I had forgotten about made my chest ache. Since we returned to Southwold, I thought of Frankie more than I had in five years, but seeing her face as I remembered it on screen, smiling my way with love shining in her green eyes? That was almost more than I could cope with.

It worried me. When I couldn't cope with something, I drank or used and now that I was sober I couldn't do either of them. It meant I had to deal with how seeing Frankie's face made me feel instead of simply blocking those emotions out. I tried to run through things my therapist told me to do when I found myself in a situation like this but, for the life of me, I couldn't remember a single thing he had ever told me.

One thing was on my mind, one person . . . Frankie.

"You good?"

Hayes put the question to me and I nodded instinctively to cover up my lie.

"I'm good, man."

Before any of the guys could say a word in response, Mr Jones's voice boomed as he introduced us.

"Please, join me in welcoming past students and global superstars, Risk Keller, May Acton and Hayes Hurley. They've taken a break out of their busy schedule to come home to Southwold and attend this ceremony for my last year at Sir John Leman High School. They've brought along Angel Reyes, too! Our very own Southwold boys are home! Give it up for Blood Oath!"

"Let's get it."

The door to the hall opened and, holy shit, it was only a small crowd but they made themselves heard. Everyone was on their feet, waving their hands and screaming our names. One by one we filed our way up onto the stage. I had a huge smile on my face as I clasped hands with Mr Jones and gave him a hearty hug.

"Great to see you, sir."

"And you, kid." He clapped his hand on my shoulder. "You're looking great, Risk."

I reached up and touched my sobriety coin.

"I feel great, sir."

I moved aside and snorted as Mr Jones ribbed Angel, offering to give him drumming lessons for free which made Angel beam happily as he shook the man's hand. When I turned to the crowd and waved, the screaming became deafening. I made eye contact with as many of the schoolgirls as possible because they ate that shit up. I didn't get it, but looking at them seemed to make their day and seeing how happy they were made mine so it worked out well for everyone. After a couple of minutes, the screaming died down and everyone retook their seats.

We remained standing side by side next to Mr Jones.

"Hey!" a girl suddenly shouted. "Aren't you the girl in the video who was kissing Risk?"

My eyes sought out the girl who shouted and my eyes zeroed in on the woman everyone else was staring at. Frankie Fulton. I felt like I had been kicked in the chest at the very sight of her. I felt like the ground fell away from under my feet.

There she was. My Frankie.

She was staring directly at me with big wide eyes. A burst of warmth filled my body at the familiar sight of her. Happiness filled me to the brim. Just as I was about to jump down from the stage and walk right up to her to say hello, to hug her, to do *something*, I quickly found that I couldn't do a fucking thing because Frankie suddenly turned and all but sprinted from the hall, leaving me to stare after her like a fucking idiot.

Hurt replaced the happiness that seeing her brought me and I wanted to crush that feeling and bury it away forever but I couldn't. I was aware that everyone had looked from the exit to me and I plastered a smile onto my face just so no one could see how much Frankie's reaction to me had hurt me. Mr Jones took everyone's attention as he asked us questions about being home and retold some old stories of our times together. I laughed at the correct moments and answered questions when they were put to me, but mentally I was no longer present in the hall.

I couldn't stop replaying Frankie's rapid departure upon seeing me.

I didn't even get a second to fully take in her appearance before she ran. I could see the bottom of the baby pink Mary Well's uniform under the coat she wore, and her mess of unruly red hair was tied up into a pretty high ponytail, but that was as much as I could see. Her coat had been puffy, so I couldn't tell if her body still looked the same or if it had changed over the years. I hated that I wanted to find out because I shouldn't have given a fuck about Frankie just like she clearly didn't give a fuck about me.

She wouldn't have run like a bat out of hell at the first sight of me if she did.

On the outside, I was still smiling and laughing, but on the inside I was seething as the hurt I felt turned into anger and all I could think about when Frankie's face popped into my head was, fuck her. If she wanted to act like she didn't know me then fine, I didn't give a shit. Fuck her. If she didn't want to sit in the same room as me, what-fucking-ever. Fuck her. If she couldn't spare me one fucking minute to say hello after nine poxy years then fine. Fuck *her*.

Bitterness filled me.

I held on to that emotion throughout the entire day, I couldn't even shake it when me and the guys jammed with Mr Jones in our old music room, nor when we returned to May's house later in the day. Frankie had taken over my mind. I couldn't stop thinking about how she saw me then ran like I was some sort of virus that she couldn't wait to be away from. It felt like a kick in the gut each time the scene rolled through my mind. I should have blocked her out, I should have forced her from my mind but I couldn't. I had an incredible urge to see her up close. She was wearing her Mary Well's uniform at the school so I knew where she would be.

Before I could think better of it, I asked the guys if they were hungry and only Angel said yes, so I drove us to Mary Well's in a flashy car that our manager had rented for us. I hated it. It didn't fit in with Southwold, it made us stand out. Angel was silent the entire drive, but when I parked the car and we both hopped out, he sighed out loud.

"Mary Well's diner. She works here, doesn't she?"

"Who?

"Don't play stupid, it doesn't suit you."

Angel knew what I was doing just as much as I did.

"I want food. I've been craving one of Mary Well's burgers for years. You can wait in the car if you want."

I started for the entrance. Angel cursed then fell into step beside me.

"You're gonna regret this, man," he said as I reached for the door's handle. "Don't say some shit you can't take back."

I ignored his wise words because I wasn't thinking. I didn't want to listen to reason. I didn't want to be the bigger man. For once, I just wanted to be an arsehole to make myself feel better. I wanted to see Frankie's face and I wanted to hurt her just like she had hurt me earlier that day.

After all, she broke me first.

CHAPTER SEVEN
FRANKIE

I dropped my empty tray in surprise and flinched when it clattered against the floor. I was in a state of disbelief. He was standing right in front of me. Risk. *My* Risk. His ice-blue eyes were locked on mine and I almost felt paralysed under their watchful gaze.

"Risk," I blurted. "Hi. Hey. Hi. How are you?"

His focus remained on me and his lips didn't so much as twitch. I bent down and quickly snagged the tray from the floor before I straightened up. The small action left me out of breath . . . seeing Risk left me out of breath.

"What're you doing here?"

"This is a diner." He raised an eyebrow. "I'm hungry."

"Right," I said, stupidly. "Right. This *is* a diner. Right."

"You said 'right' three times, Frankie."

"Right," I cringed and glanced at the man who was just behind Risk. "Uh, just the two of you?"

Risk nodded, still keeping his eyes on mine which made me feel all sorts of under pressure.

"Okay," I turned, put my tray down on the counter and grabbed two menus. "Follow me, please."

I hurried over to booth one but paused when the visual of Risk leaning over the table on our first date when we were fifteen, asking me to be his girlfriend, then kissing me, popped into my head.

"Problem?"

He was right behind me. The hair on the back of my neck stood up because I could almost feel his body brush against mine. Almost.

"N-No," I spluttered. "Uh, maybe booth two will be—"

"This one is fine," Risk interrupted. "It's just a booth, nothing special about it."

Somehow, I managed not to flinch. I shouldn't have been surprised that the booth held no memories for him. It's not like he remembered kissing a girl when he was fifteen and I was stupid to even consider that he would.

"Of course." Risk and his friend slid into the booth. "Here are your menus."

The man with Risk was Angel Reyes, the Mexican member of Blood Oath who they recruited when they were in America their first year. He was the drummer of the band and he was insanely talented, I had heard him play. I had heard all of the band play . . . I just didn't hear Risk sing. I bought all of Blood Oath's albums: the instrumental versions. I wanted to support their music and that was the only way that I could without risking my sanity.

I focused on the pair before me and forced myself to be calm and collected. I reached down, grabbed my order notepad from my apron and my pen from the top of my head and said, "Can I start you gentlemen off with some drinks?"

"A Coke," Risk said without missing a beat. "Cherry . . . Coke."

My eyes locked on his, but I said nothing. I wasn't sure if he was referencing the nickname he once called me, but he didn't look like he was teasing me in any way so I shook it off. I looked back to my notepad and jotted the order down then looked to his friend.

"Just a regular Coke is fine."

I nodded and placed my notepad back in the pocket of my apron. My eyes glanced to Risk's hands momentarily and my heart skipped a beat when I saw there were scribbles of black ink on the backs of his hands that disappeared up his wrist and forearm under his sleeves. He used to always write random lyrics and songs notes on the backs of his hands and on his arms. It was nice to see that hadn't changed.

"I'll be right back with your drinks." I plastered on a warm smile. "Please take your time to scan the menu."

When I turned and walked over to the opened hatch that led behind the counter, I flicked my eyes to the mirror on the wall and I saw that Risk's eyes were following as I moved. It made me conscious of every step I took until I rounded the corner and was out of his view. I leaned against the wall and placed my hand on my chest, willing my heartbeat to slow because I was at risk of either an asthma or a panic attack, or bloody both if I didn't calm my arse down.

I hurriedly made both of the men their drinks, then made my way back to their booth. I was very focused on my steps to make sure I didn't trip or do anything to attract notice to myself. The diner only had four booths filled, but it was only one booth I was concerned about messing up in front of. I reached booth one and smiled once again.

"Cherry Coke." I placed the cup in front of Risk then placed the other in front of Angel. "And a regular Coke."

"Thank you," Angel said.

"You're very welcome," I replied. "Are you guys ready to order or do you need another couple of minutes?"

"We're ready."

Risk's voice was so much deeper than when he was eighteen and I quickly found that I almost couldn't cope with it. It gave me goosebumps. It was ridiculous how much his voice made my body react like a sex-deprived animal . . . which I basically was, but still.

"Okay." I grabbed my notepad and pen once more. "Fire away."

I jotted down both of the men's orders as they spoke, ripped the page off my notepad and said. "That shouldn't be too long of a wait."

"No problem," Angel said.

Risk said nothing, he just stared up at me like I was a zoo animal. I cleared my throat, smiled again then turned and hurried over to the hatch and hung the order up on the rack. Joe spun the order rack around until the order sheet was on his side of the hatch in the kitchen. He looked over at the booth, then looked at me and raised his eyebrows. I shrugged my shoulders in response. I had no idea what was happening any more than Joe did.

The door bell sounded and I jumped when there was a sudden squeal.

I turned and watched as Hannah Porter walked into the diner ready to start her evening shift, from five until closing time at eleven. She spotted Angel and Risk and just about lost her bloody mind. I stared as she literally rushed over to the booth and started telling the guys how much she loved them and what a huge Sinner she was. Risk said something to her that nearly made her die then and there.

"You remember me!" she all but screeched. "I was the year below you and you remember me. Oh my god."

"Jesus Christ," Joe huffed from the kitchen. "Hannah. Work. Now."

She waved her hand at Joe without looking away from Risk or Angel. I didn't want to stand there and watch her gush over the men so I saw to the other three booths that had customers. They were all middle-aged couples and didn't appear to see what the big fuss was over two ridiculously attractive men.

"We're lost on who they could be," one man said. "Are they famous?"

"Yeah," I nodded. "They're in a rock band."

"Ooohh." The man's wife grinned. "They're lookers, too."

I chuckled. "That they are . . . can I get you both anything else?"

"The bill, please," the man answered. "We're finished."

"No problem."

I went to the till, checked the couple's booth out, grabbed their receipt and brought it to them.

"When you're ready, just come to the till and pay your bill. No rush."

I kept my eyes averted from booth one where Hannah was still talking with Risk and Angel. I knew what Hannah sounded like when she was flirting and she was *hardcore* flirting with both guys. More Risk than Angel and that hit me in the gut. She knew he and I once dated, but maybe because it had been so long ago she just didn't care. I mean, we were co-workers, not really friends, so I guess she didn't have a girl code to uphold with me.

I turned my attention to my inventory list and reread it nine times before Joe called booth one's order. Hannah didn't move away from Risk's booth to get the order so, with a sigh, I did it since it was my booth to wait on. I grabbed the plates and sides and put them on a tray then crossed the room to stand behind Hannah-bloody-Porter.

"Excuse me, Hannah."

She jumped, obviously startled by me.

"Oh! Hi, Frankie."

She stepped aside as I placed the correct plates in front of each man.

"Enjoy. If you guys need anything, give me a shout. Or just ask Hannah since she's already here."

Hannah's eyes narrowed slightly and I knew it was because she heard the slight sneer in my tone. Before I could turn and walk away, she touched my forearm and said, "Wait, Frankie. Have you caught up with Risk? You two used to date when you were kids, right?"

"Date?" Risk blinked. "Weren't we *just* friends in school, Frankie?"

I felt my cheeks burn with humiliation.

"We *did* date. That was a very long time ago though," I said to Hannah, lifting my chin. "It doesn't matter anymore."

I turned and walked back over to the counter to my inventory list and tried to focus even though I felt sick to my stomach. Risk didn't agree that I was once his girlfriend, he referred to me as a school friend. He didn't even look at Hannah when she mentioned we dated, he only stared at me as if daring me to say someone as good as him had dated someone as basic as me. I didn't know what was happening but this kind of interaction with him wasn't something I expected.

I stayed across the room, doing inventory and checking booths out when people paid their bills. I noticed Hannah eventually leaving the table when Joe came out and got her so the men could eat in peace. They ate quickly, in less than twenty minutes. When Risk raised his hand and beckoned me over with his finger, my gut twisted. Part of me wanted to stick my finger up at him for addressing me in such a way, but I didn't.

I walked over to the table calmly.

"Anything else I can get you guys?"

"No, thank you. I'm full. It was delicious."

I smiled at Angel. "Happy to hear it."

"Frankie."

My body was weak for him whenever he said my name. Whenever he uttered the word, it was like I was the only woman in existence. It was distracting and embarrassing and if he ever found out, I'd likely drop dead.

"Yes?"

"Hannah reminded me about us dating, I remember now. It got me thinking. I was just telling Angel here about our first date right here in this booth . . . how long ago was that? Nine years? Ten?"

I hated that it hurt my feelings because he couldn't remember when we went on our first date, or that Hannah had to remind him about our relationship in the first place.

"We were fifteen," I shifted my stance. "So twelve years ago."

"Twelve years." Risk whistled. "A hell of a lot has changed since then." He glanced at my uniform, grimaced, then looked up to my face. "Well, for *me* it has."

I felt my face drop when he finished speaking. Judgment for working in the same job all my life was not something I ever, in a million years, expected from Risk. He looked at me like I was . . . nothing.

"Good seeing you again, Frankie," he stood up from the booth, making me take a couple of steps back. "Great service, you've got this waitress thing on lock. Have a good one."

He didn't look at me as he stuck his hand in his pocket, pulled out a wad of notes, and dropped them on my notepad like he was handing a homeless person money. My mouth dropped open, not because the notes he gave me were fifty-pound notes, but because I had never felt so disrespected by a person in my entire life. I never expected that disrespect to come from Risk.

It hurt me deeply.

"Thank you, Frankie," Angel said after Risk walked on out of the diner. "Uh, it was lovely to meet you."

He turned and nearly jogged to catch up with Risk, who was already outside. For a moment, I couldn't move. I couldn't believe the person who had treated me so horribly was Risk. *My* Risk. I was flabbergasted but only for a moment because hurt quickly dissolved into anger and before I knew it I had his tip clenched in my hand and was out of the diner, rushing after the two men quicker than a hiccup.

"Risk!"

He paused mid-stride as he and Angel neared a flashy sports car.

"No autographs, Frankie," he said. "Sorry."

I nearly tripped over my feet with shock.

"Autographs?" I sputtered. "Are you *joking* me? I don't want your bloody autograph, Risk Keller."

He looked at Angel, who was looking at the ground, then looked back at me.

"No pictures either."

"Jesus, man. Stop it."

I ignored Angel and so did Risk.

"What is *wrong* with you?" I demanded. "Why did you treat me like that in there?"

"Treat you like what?" He blinked. "I barely know you, Frankie."

Don't you dare cry.

"You knew me once," I said, standing tall. "And I knew you too. Treating me like I'm beneath you just because I'm a waitress is downright disgusting, Risk."

"I can't remember a time when you were beneath me, Frankie. Only when you were on top."

I couldn't help but stumble back a couple of steps with the force of his hurtful words. It would have hurt less if he'd slapped me.

"I can't believe you just said that." My voice cracked. "Who *are* you right now?"

"Risk Keller." He winked. "You don't know me anymore, Frankie. People change."

"You're right!" I snapped. "People *do* change because you aren't the Risk I once knew. He wasn't cruel like the person you've become."

"Maybe you didn't know me as well as you think you did, Cherry."

Hearing my nickname come out of his hateful mouth was like a punch in the gut.

"I knew you inside and out, you fucking arsehole!" I bellowed. "How *dare* you tarnish the relationship we had by treating me like this!"

"I think that relationship was tarnished the second you dumped me, soft lips." He tilted his head, clearly remembering more about us than he let on. "What? Is my money not good enough for you? It's easy cash, you can put your feet up for a couple of weeks with that tip."

Risk's friend Angel shifted as he looked from his friend to me and back again. A surge of fury shot through my veins and I felt my face burn with heat. I bunched up the wad of notes he'd tipped me and threw them in his face like they were nothing more than scrap paper. Risk didn't flinch, but his gaze did harden and his posture went rigid.

"I have worked in this diner since I was sixteen years old." I lifted my chin and looked him dead in the eye even though I knew that mine were filled with tears. "I'm not a millionaire like you. I don't have the luxury of money and I never will, but every penny I have ever earned is worked hard for and you have the fucking audacity to treat me like less than you because you're rich and famous and can tip someone over a thousand pound like it's nothing. Are you better than me now, Risk? You forget where you come from, you forget you were one treated lesser and *I* was the person whose shoulder you cried on because of that." I looked him up and down, thoroughly disgusted. "There's no need for the likes of you in Southwold. We might not be the most glamorous people, but we are honest and hard-working. I'm heartbroken that someone as fake as *you* came from here."

"Is that all?"

His voice was so raspy it sounded like music all on its own.

"No," I stepped forward, tilted my head back to glare up at him. "Fuck you, Risk Keller, you piece of shit. *That* is all, arsehole."

Now I was done.

I turned and walked away from Risk and returned back into the diner, where I went straight into the staff bathroom and locked the door behind me. I fisted my hands and pressed them against my eyes to keep from crying. I tried to take deep breaths in and out, but the urge to sob was overwhelming me. I slid down the door until my bum touched the floor. I drew my knees up to my chest and tried to battle away the horrendous pain that ached within my chest. It had nothing to do with an asthma attack and everything to do with my heart breaking.

Risk somehow managed to break me all over again.

CHAPTER EIGHT
RISK

I was a no good, rotten piece of dog shit.

No one needed to tell me so, I knew it without anyone else's input. Angel, however, felt like I needed to hear how much of a prick I was the entire drive back to May's house last night. He didn't stop there either, when I woke up the following morning and went down to the kitchen to make some food, he was already seated at the kitchen table. He glared at me as he drank from his cup of what I guessed to be tea. I felt my jaw click from clamping my teeth together to keep from saying a word. I left the kitchen hungry, but it was worth it to get away from Angel's judgemental eyes. It freaked me out how he could glare at you and make you feel like he knew exactly what you were thinking when you were thinking it.

I felt bad enough without him making me feel worse.

We agreed that we would sleep in May's house until the first of our three concerts at Wembley Stadium took place in London next week. We wanted the nostalgia of the best part of our childhoods which was this house and the studio attached to it. Angel wanted to experience where we grew up too, so he was on board to bunk in the house with us, but I think he was regretting it after how much of an arsehole I was to Frankie the night before. I got it. What I did . . . that wasn't me. That was a prick who wanted revenge on a woman because she hurt his feelings in front of a group of kids.

I was massive fucking fanny.

Angel had told me not to do something that I would regret and I went and did exactly that. I treated Frankie exactly how she made me feel, worthless. It didn't feel good in the slightest. I didn't get that moment of 'screw you for hurting me', all I got was a wave of regret that Angel said I would have.

I fucked up.

I fucked up the first chance I got to see the very woman who didn't deserve a bad thing in the world. I knew I had to apologise, I knew I had to get on my knees if need be. I knew most people would just say sorry and go but Frankie . . . I had too much respect for her to do anything less than beg for her forgiveness.

◆ ◆ ◆

I spent the whole day in the old studio with the guys trying to straighten my head out. I began to write a song that I didn't have a title for yet. I was only a few words into it, but it didn't take a genius to wonder where I got my inspiration from. Just like the majority of my other songs, they all stemmed from a once-beloved muse whose life still remained in Southwold.

"I can't get enough of your green eyes, your soft skin, your sweet smile."

I looked up as Angel read out loud what I'd written so far over my shoulder.

"So, another song for Frankie is in the works, huh?"

I didn't answer him, I looked back down to my notepad and tapped my pencil against it.

"Don't you feel like a hypocrite, man?" Angel quizzed. "Writing so many songs about her then treating her like the scum of the earth when you first see her again after *nine years*? That's a coward's move as far as I'm concerned."

I wanted to punch Angel in the face but I couldn't. I was mad at what he said because it was the truth. I wasn't mad at him, I was furious with *me*.

"I fucked up," I acknowledged. "I know I did, she didn't deserve that. None of it."

"So what are you gonna do about it?"

I looked at Angel and frowned.

"Writing a song about her doesn't benefit *her*, it benefits *us* because your songs are hits. Even if a song doesn't work out for us, it does for another artist. That woman has some of the most beautiful songs in the world written about her and she probably doesn't even know it."

I had never considered that . . . surely she knew.

"Whenever I mention an eye colour it's green, or a hair colour it's some variant of red. A blind man would know she's my muse. I describe her in every way when I focus on her . . . her looks, her mind, her heart. I even have her personality in what I write. She has to know."

"Just because *you* know, doesn't mean *she* does. You aren't so forthcoming in your writing, bro. You don't straight out say you love a green-eyed, red-haired girl. You wrap what you say in layers so they could mean a bunch of different things. Why do you think our Sinners made a big deal last week when one of them realised you penned a song that went to number one for that Bieber dude? They were freaking out wondering who you were talking about. They love breaking that shit down to figure out what you're actually saying. They're convinced you're in love with Nora Maxwell."

"Good God." I rolled my eyes. "I took her out to dinner twice. Twice!"

"She has red hair and green eyes."

"She has brown hair that's dyed ginger and she has brown eyes, but wears green contacts."

Angel laughed. "To the world, she is the *chica* you sing about so much."

"Well, she's fucking not. Frankie is."

"Maybe Frankie thinks they're about Nora too. Maybe even more so after how you treated her last night."

I felt sucker punched.

"You're making me feel like shit, Angel."

"Enough to make you go and apologise to the woman?"

"Yes!" I snapped as I got to my feet and threw my notepad at him. "Don't lose that. Wazzock."

"I know you're calling me an idiot, but that word *still* sounds like a Harry Potter spell."

I clenched my jaw as I walked away.

"You're welcome, *puta*!" Angel shouted after me, laughing. "And good luck. With how mad that woman looked last night, you're gonna need it!"

I shrugged my coat on, grabbed the car keys and left the studio. It was a cold February evening, but the sky was clear and the stars were out so I decided to walk to Frankie's home to see if she was there. That was the plan until a flash went off on my right when I left the garden. I tried my best not to sigh because if the vultures got a picture of me looking sad, they would attach some ridiculous headline to it and piss me off.

"What's up, Risk? How are you?" a woman's voice hollered. "Enjoying being back home?"

I headed straight for the rented car that our manager had delivered this morning. None of us had wanted the flashy Audi, it made us stand out too much in Southwold, so we had a regular BMW SUV delivered to us instead. We were lucky so far that the residents didn't bother us, even though they knew we were staying in May's house. Throughout the day, teenagers and young adults would come to the gate of the front garden and take pictures and videos. May humoured a group of lads around lunch-time and went outside to talk to them, I joined him because they seemed like kids who were genuinely fans of music, just like we were. We took pictures and had a laugh with them.

I knew it was only a matter of time until the paps showed up, though.

"I'm having a great time, thanks."

I fisted the car key as more flashes went off. A glance to my left showed three more women with cameras jumping out of cars, and a man too. I shook my head.

"This road is for residents only, you know? You can't park in front of their houses."

"We move when they tell us to."

The man who replied to me had a camera, but wasn't flashing so I assumed he was likely recording his interaction with me.

"Nervous about playing in Wembley next week?"

"Nope." I answered the shortest woman as I approached the car. "We can't wait. Wembley filled to the brim with Sinners? You can't get a better atmosphere than that, love."

"Is Nora Maxwell going to be attending the concert?" another voice asked. "She's in London right now."

"I have no idea." I unlocked the car door. "If she has time in her busy schedule to come by and see a show, I'd love that."

"C'mon, Risk. We all know you're dating Nora."

I glanced at the woman. "That's news to me, darlin'."

She snorted, not buying what I was selling, but I didn't care. The media rarely believed the truth because most of the time it was boring and didn't earn them clicks or likes online. Attaching my name to Nora's was much more exciting because she was a beautiful, famous actress who, in the past two years, had blown onto the Hollywood scene. She was a Londoner, and although we went on two dates before I went to rehab, and had sex I could barely remember at the end of both of those dates, we weren't dating and never were.

The media thought otherwise though.

"Risk!" the man butted in. "What's all this talk about you and May having plenty of behind-closed-doors arguments? Are you kicking him from the band?"

For God's sake.

"Firstly, Blood Oath is *not* my band. It belongs to all four of us, just because I'm the main vocalist doesn't mean I run shit because I *don't*." I opened the car door and climbed into the driver's seat. "Secondly, I argued with May about how brown toast should be this morning so yeah, we argue a lot. Always have, always will, but he's my brother. They all are. No one is leaving Blood Oath so all that talk you mentioned is a load of squit. Just like everything else you've probably heard about us breaking up or going solo."

I closed the door before the vultures could ask another question. The flashes from their cameras continued to go off and I appreciated the tinted windows of the car. I started the engine and pulled away from the kerb, noting the paps rushing back to their cars in my rearview mirror.

"Fucking arseholes."

I knew they were going to follow me, so I couldn't drive directly to Frankie's house. Instead, I decided to take them on a wild goose chase. For two hours, I drove around Southwold, up to Reydon, then when I came back to Southwold, I drove down some of the one way lane roads. I cleared the lane before the paps behind me did and when a group of kids walked across the pedestrian crossing behind me, I grinned. One of the kids bent down to tie their shoelace and the paps blew their horn at them. The kids jumped, but instantly threw insults at the vultures for scaring them and didn't move an inch.

I laughed as I drove away and headed for Frankie's place.

All this would have been a waste of time if she wasn't home, or worse, if she didn't live there anymore. She could have moved into her mum's old house when I left Southwold. She could have moved in with a boyfriend. She could have moved into Dr O'Rourke's home. May's mum and dad attended their small wedding a few months after I moved away. I drove up Pier Avenue and it felt so familiar to me, a feeling of belonging filled me. I didn't have that feeling when I drove to my home in Beverly Hills or to my town-house in London. Southwold was my home even though I didn't live there.

I didn't even live in the cottage we rented from Dr O'Rourke for very long before I left, but I could remember driving along this street on my way home to Frankie most nights after a long session at the studio. It was a dream area to live in. The pier and beach were a stone's throw away from the cottage; waking up and looking out of the window in the morning and staring out at the ocean was a favourite pastime of mine. I loved it and I know Frankie did too.

When the cottage came into view, I saw a small, beat-up Ford Focus in the driveway. I stopped outside of the cottage and suddenly felt sick with nerves. I fucked up majorly with her the night before. I was cruel, just like she said I was. I turned into a massive prick just because she hurt my feelings. I should have been man enough to tell her that her reaction to me wasn't something I liked but, instead, I was a complete prick. Angel was right. I had to apologise and pray Frankie would forgive me because not only did she look incredibly hurt in the car park of Mary Well's, she looked spitting mad too.

I remembered that it took a lot to get Frankie angry but when she reached that point, she was a force to be reckoned with.

I exhaled a breath, shut off the engine and climbed out. I locked the car up behind me and walked up the pathway that led to the cottage. I hoped she lived here still, it would be really awkward if I knock on a stranger's door and they recognised me. Before I lost my nerve and chickened out like a little bitch, I lifted my hand and knocked on the door of the cottage where I once lived.

Relief flooded me when I heard a familiar voice after a few seconds say, "Who is it?"

"It's me, Frankie." I said. "Risk."

When silence stretched, I closed my eyes and sighed. I didn't think she would leave me outside in the cold, but I shouldn't have been surprised. I hurt her . . . I really fucking hurt her. I knew I did, I saw it on her face and in her eyes.

"Get lost, Keller."

I winced, she had only ever called me by my surname when she was *pissed.*

"Please, Frankie. I've come to apologise." I placed my hands on the frame of the door. "How I treated you last night was horrible. I was wrong and I'm so sorry. I'd take it back in a second if I could, Cherry."

The door was yanked open and I stumbled back a step in surprise.

"*Don't* call me Cherry," she snapped at me, pushing her curly auburn hair from her face. "You don't get to call me that when you hurt me like you did last night. What you did was horrible! Sorry isn't good enough, Risk!" She glared. "You hurt me and you did it on purpose so don't you dare act like—"

"Frankie, what the *fuck* happened to your face?"

CHAPTER NINE
FRANKIE

"Frankie?"

I looked up when Michael said my name. He was sitting right across from me on the other side of Mum's hospital bed, but when he spoke it sounded like he was a great distance away. I didn't think I had heard a word the man had said since I stopped by after my shift at work ended two hours ago.

"Huh?"

"Kid," he smiled. "You're miles away today."

He didn't know the half of it.

"Sorry," I said, shifting in my seat as I felt a little stiff. "I didn't get a whole lot of sleep last night."

As soon as I clocked out of work after my run-in with Risk, I drove home, had a shower then I cried for most of the night. I kept replaying over and over in my mind how Risk looked at me like I was nothing and spoke to me like I was a random person on the street. How dismissive and cruel he was hurt me more than I ever could have imagined. Of all the times I imagined meeting him again, him being a mean-hearted person was never ever a consider-ation. I had never known him to have a cruel side, because of who he was raised by, but I guess he had forgotten about his upbringing over the years.

"Are ye okay?" Michael asked. "Wanna talk about it?"

I exhaled a breath. "Well, it's just . . . Risk is home."

"Is he?" Michael's jaw dropped. "I had no clue."

"He and the lads came home to attend the retirement ceremony for Mr Jones." I explained, crossing my leg over my lap. "He stopped in at the diner for dinner last night and he was just . . . he said some things that just hurt my feelings. He's . . . he's different than the person I remember and I guess I'm just having a hard time with that."

Michael's frown deepened. "What'd he say to ye?"

"Nothing major," I lied. "Just spoke down to me a little."

I didn't want to tell Michael the truth because since the night Risk and I broke up, he had been there for me through thick and thin. He and I had formed a strong bond and he was very protective of me. If he knew how Risk had treated me, Michael would probably go looking for him. He wasn't a violent man, but I knew there was nothing Michael wouldn't do for my mum and I so I kept the details to myself.

"Well," Michael adjusted his glasses. "Maybe being in America for too long has swelled his ugly noggin'."

Everyone blessed with eyesight knew Risk wasn't ugly, far from it, but Michael's jab at his looks to show he was very much on my side amused me.

I tittered. "Maybe you're right."

"If he comes 'round again, tell him to feck off. We don't need the likes of that in Southwold."

"Already ticked that box." I bobbed my head. "I doubt he'd come back around, I told him exactly what I thought of him. I got the last word in too before I stormed off so I'm happy I didn't just take it lying down."

"I'm surprised that he would treat *you* of all people like that."

No one was more surprised than me.

"People change." I shrugged. "Nine years is a long time."

Michael nodded in agreement. We both looked to Mum as she began to stir from her evening nap. Both Michael and I helped her to sit upright. She began coughing violently so I grabbed her handkerchief and placed it in her hand so she could press it to her mouth. Her breathing sounded horrible even when she calmed down and stopped coughing. I knew from speaking to Michael that her lungs weren't improving and her pneumonia was worsening. Like me, mum suffered from asthma, hers just wasn't as bad as mine, but right now even her mild asthma was dangerous when paired with pneumonia.

"You're okay, Mum."

She rested her head back against her pillow and cleared her throat.

"Enda, when did . . . you get here?"

Stupidly, I looked over my shoulder to see if Enda was behind me, but I quickly realised that Mum was speaking to me. She was terribly confused more often than not and she always mistook me for someone else. It was a kick in the teeth each time she didn't know who I was.

"Not long ago," I answered. "How're you feeling?"

"I'm fine." She waved her hand, her voice sounded husky. "How is M-Molly?"

Molly was Enda's West Highland Terrier who died four years ago.

"She's great," I assured her. "She just got groomed so she's looking all pretty."

"Good, good," Mum sighed.

She looked exhausted, which was upsetting because all she seemed to do was rest. Michael reached over and gently took her hand in his. Mum glanced at him and her face lit up.

"Malcom," she beamed, squeezing his hand. "I didn't hear . . . you come in."

My face dropped, but Michael kept his composure when my mum called him by my father's name.

"I wanted to surprise you," Michael winked. "I missed ye today."

Mum chuckled to herself. "You say that a-all of the time."

"Because I always miss ye, gorgeous."

Even though she was wheezing and out of breath, she was giggling like a schoolgirl and it made my heart feel a little lighter. I knew Michael, like me, had his feelings hurt whenever Mum called us by someone else's name, but it had to be worse for Michael. Mum rarely recognised him and she often called him by my father's name. My stepfather took it in his stride and never showed he was upset, but I could see it in his eyes. He only found my mum a little over nine years ago and the time he had spent with her was when she was slowly losing herself. The man was a gentleman. Most men would have run for the hills, but not Michael, he stood by my mum and married her.

He loved her desperately and it broke my heart that when she was gone, his heart would be gone with her.

"The big black dog stole my b-best wool earlier," Mum rasped, looking back at me. "When I find the owner . . . I'm calling the police."

"I don't blame you one bit," I said, going along with her story. "That dog is causing too much trouble, he's been stealing everyone's best wool."

"Yeah," Mum nodded. "It's a disgrace how this c-country let's him get away . . . with it."

"I've a good mind to write a letter to the Prime Minister about it."

"I have his number," Mum informed me. "I'll set up a dinner date. We can talk about . . . him fixing the shower head. It's always dripping, I can't s-sleep over it."

Michael chuckled under his breath and even I had to hide a smile. When Mum was talking in circles like this and we went along with it, none of us ever really knew how the story would end. We were surprised, more often than not, at the outcome, just like now and myself and Michael always tried to find the humour in it. If we didn't, every evening with Mum would just be depressing and hard to get through.

There were no official visiting hours in the hospice, but the staff began to get the patients ready to settle in for the night from eight onwards. It was just after nine and my eyes began to feel heavy. I had worked a double shift at work. I opened with Joe and Deena at seven and didn't clock out until half six in the evening. I then came straight to the hospital to spend time with Mum and Michael. My body wanted nothing more than to sleep.

"Frankie," Michael said. "Get on home, honey. You're exhausted."

I didn't put up much of a fight. I hugged and kissed Michael goodbye, then did the same to Mum, careful not to wake her because she had just fallen asleep after having a pretty horrible episode with coughing. The nurse placed an oxygen mask on her face to help her breathe easier and it helped as she fell asleep.

"I'll see you tomorrow." I wiggled my fingers. "Love you."

"Love you too, kid."

I left the hospital with the strap of my bag on my shoulder and my hands shoved into the pockets of my coat. When I left the building, I yawned and headed in the direction of my car. I was practically dragging my feet along the ground when I heard a voice ahead of me. I looked up to the person who was shoving his phone into his pocket and cursing to himself. The voice was familiar and as I drew closer to the man, I practically felt bile rise up my throat like it always did whenever I was unlucky enough to cross paths with this vile human being. I hoped that he wouldn't notice me, but I didn't have such luck.

"Frankie Fulton." He sneered when he looked up. "What're you doing here?"

"Not that it's any of your business, Owen, but I was visiting my mum."

I moved right on by Owen Day without stopping and I could tell he had turned direction and followed me towards my car without having to look back and check. I could feel his presence, it made me very uncomfortable.

"I'll be havin' a word with ya, Frankie."

I rolled my eyes.

"I *told* you at Christmas that you're barred from the diner," I said to the man whose face I hated as much as his blackened heart. "I've nothing to say to you now any more than I did that day. I'm not lifting the ban after how you spoke to me."

"I don't care about the bastard diner," Owen griped. "I heard he's back."

I stopped as I reached the boot of the car and turned to face the tall, balding, overweight cruel menace behind me. He had his keys in his hand and on that set of keys was a black pocket knife that I knew had left the long, jagged scar on Risk's back. Owen had slashed him when he was fifteen for answering back, Risk had told me. I hated him for it.

"He is." I flexed my fingers. "You *know* he won't want to see you though."

"That wee bastard owes me," Owen sneered, his Scottish brogue thickening as his anger grew. "He lived under *my* roof for thirteen years."

I couldn't believe his audacity.

"He owes you *nothing*!" I snapped. "He was a cheap way to earn some extra money for you and Freda and you know it. You made his life miserable, you beat him and—"

"The last time ye accused me of beatin' that lad, I wasnae happy."

The memory of him grabbing my forearm hard enough to bruise me was never far from my mind. It was a few years ago and he had started an argument, similar to this one, in the car park of Tesco and it resulted in him hurting my arm.

I swallowed. "I'm not scared of you, Owen."

"Says the tremblin' wee lass."

Damn him, but I *was* shaking before him. I hated that.

"Owen, it's late." I adjusted the strap of my bag. "I've had a long day. Please move, I want to go home."

"Tell him to come and see me," he stepped forward. "He was always a sap for you. He'll listen to ye."

"He was *never* a sap for me," I bit back. "And even if he would listen to me, which he wouldn't, I would never tell him to go and see you because you're an abusive waste of space who made his life hell!"

I didn't register Owen moving his arm until his fist connected with my face and sent me sprawling back onto the ground. I couldn't even scream, I was too shocked to do anything other than lie back on the ground and put my hand over my throbbing face. Owen stood over me and I hated that I cowered beneath him, but I was worried that he was going to hit me again.

"Get . . . Get *away* from me!"

He took a step back then another.

"Tell that lad t'come and see me," Owen said, shaking out his hand. "I mean it, Frankie."

He turned and stormed towards the hospice's entrance. I had heard one of his friends was dying of cancer and was a patient at the hospice; that was likely to be who he was visiting. It didn't surprise me that he was heading inside as the staff were getting the patients settled in for the night; he did what he wanted. He always had. I got to my feet and before he changed his mind and decided to come back, I hurriedly got into my car, backed out of my space and drove out of the darkened car park. I didn't realise that I was crying until I was on the main road.

My face was on fire, it hurt so badly.

I kept touching my cheek and eye to make sure there was no blood to indicate that Owen had cut me. I found nothing, which was a relief, but only just. I could see perfectly okay out of my right eye, but my cheek bone under it felt massively swollen. The throbbing hurt so much worse than I ever thought being punched would. I found myself thinking of Risk, about how he had experienced this pain at Owen's hand when he was only a kid, and it made me cry harder. I made it home and into my cottage, where I grabbed a bag of frozen peas from the freezer, wrapped it in a tea-towel and placed it against my face.

I was too scared to even look in the mirror.

I looked down at my feet when a small body brushed against my shin, I reached down and picked up Oath, my eight-year-old ginger British Shorthair. I cuddled him then put him on the counter-top. I rubbed his head then put down my frozen peas so I could top up his food and water and clean out his litter tray. When I bagged up his dirt, I went outside and put it into the rubbish bin before returning inside and locking my front door. I went back into my kitchen and took two painkillers with some water before I filled my kettle up, put it on its stand and plugged it in.

I looked over my shoulder when a knock sounded at the door. I glanced at the clock and frowned, it was quarter to ten. I rarely had visitors, but none this late. I approached the front door cautiously and I said, "Who is it?"

"It's me, Frankie." I stared at my door in silence. "Risk."

For a moment, I didn't know what to do. Then I huffed with annoyance because Risk Keller was standing on the other side of my door after everything he had said to me the night before. I couldn't believe his nerve.

"Get lost, Keller."

"Please, Frankie. I've come to apologise." Risk pleaded his case. "How I treated you last night was horrible. I was wrong and I'm so sorry. I'd take it back in a second if I could, Cherry."

The second he called me Cherry, my blood boiled as I unlocked the door and pulled it open.

"*Don't* call me Cherry." I snapped, brushing my hair out of my face. "You don't get to call me that when you hurt me like you did last night. What you did was horrible! Sorry isn't good enough, Risk!" I glared. "You hurt me and you did it on purpose so don't you dare act like—"

"Frankie, what the *fuck* happened to your face?"

I felt my lips part and my eyes widen when I remembered how I must have looked. Wordlessly, I tried to close the door in Risk's face, but the stubborn idiot threw his body forward.

"Don't you dare," he warned, forcing the door open. "What happened to you?"

I stumbled back a few steps, staring up at Risk. I was gobsmacked. He was the last person I expected to be coming knocking on my door. My shock quickly melted away to anger when I remembered how he treated me the night before.

"None of your business, Keller." I stated as I pointed past him. "Get out of my house. Now."

"Fuck no," he closed the door firmly behind him with his foot. "Your eye is bruised and so is your cheek, it's red too and swollen as hell."

I scowled at him before I turned and went back into my kitchen to grab my frozen peas. I removed them from the tea-towel, wiped away the water droplets and placed the bag against my face. It was freezing and brought much relief to my burning, throbbing cheek.

"I'm not dropping this."

I grunted. "I walked into a door."

"The fuck you did," Risk stated. "Remember who you're talking to, Frankie. You don't get that big of a shiner from walking into a door."

I didn't answer him because I didn't know what to say. There wasn't an excuse that I could use that Risk wouldn't see through. He had used every one in the book to hide his abuse at the hands of Owen and Freda over the years.

"Look at me, Frankie."

"Risk," I exhaled. "Just leave. I am *none* of your business so please, just go away."

"Did someone hurt you?" he asked, ignoring what I said. "A boyfriend? Tell me. I'll kill him."

I looked at him and found him staring at me from the kitchen doorway, his hands were fisted and he looked as if any second steam would pour from his arms. I had no doubt that if I told him what happened then he would kill someone. Especially Owen. I couldn't let that happen.

"The only person who hurt me" – I looked him up and down – "is *you*."

He flinched.

"You're right," he swallowed. "I'm so sorry about the way I treated you, Frankie. I said horrible things to hurt you to get you back for hurting me."

My jaw dropped. "What did *I* do?"

"You treated me like a stranger, Frankie. At the school, you looked right at me then just walked away . . . or ran." He didn't look away from me. "That shit hurt me coming from you."

I dropped my gaze to my feet and stared at my tiled floor.

"I didn't mean to," I admitted. "I just . . . I just can't believe you're here, it's really surprised me. I would never purposely set out to hurt you, Risk. You know I wouldn't. I was just so shocked to see you."

He sighed, long and deep.

"I was an arsehole." I looked up as he lifted a hand to his head and ran it through his white-blond hair. "I was in my feelings about how you treated me at the school. I went to the diner and I treated you horribly to make myself feel better, but it didn't work. I only felt worse. I'm so fucking sorry about how I treated you, Frankie. I swear I am. That wasn't me . . . you know that wasn't me."

He was telling the truth.

That was one of the things I had always loved about Risk: when he told the truth, he didn't just tell it with his words, his eyes told the truth too. He was looking so intently at me that it made my heart skip a beat. I quickly realised then that Risk Keller was standing in the entryway of my kitchen . . . a kitchen that used to be his too.

"If I forgive you," I eyed him. "Will you promise to never treat me, or anyone, like that again? Acting all high and mighty doesn't suit you, rock star."

The second I called him his old nickname, his whole body practically deflated.

"I promise."

"Then I forgive you."

His shoulders sagged. "If I ever act like that again, I'll bend over to make it easier for you to shove your foot up my arse."

Surprise laughter left me, startling Oath, who was behind the kitchen door likely eating from his food dish. He darted around the door then out of the room between Risk's legs. Risk jumped with fright at the sight of him and banged the crown of his head on the top of the door-frame. He cursed, placed both hands on the top of his head and hopped from side to side in pain. I hurriedly grabbed my foot stool from its hook on the wall, opened it up then placed it next to Risk on the floor. I stood on the top step of the stool and ended up being the same height as Risk.

"Let me see," I said, trying to push his hands away. "Risk, drop your hands."

"It hurts!"

"I know, you big baby." I pushed his hands away. "Let me see."

He dropped his hands and once I saw he wasn't bleeding, I placed my bag of peas on his head. He hissed as he reached up and rotated the bag around, trying to kill the pain he felt. I hopped down from my stool, folded it back up and put it back on its hook on the wall.

"Just so you're aware," Risk grumbled. "That was possibly the cutest thing I have ever seen and I've seen a lot of cute shit."

My lips twitched.

"I'm five foot," I shrugged. "I can't reach the top cupboards so I need the foot stool."

"Like I said," Risk said. "Cutest shit ever."

I shook my head. "D'you want a cuppa tea?"

"Yes, please," Risk nodded. "Then we can sit down and you can tell me who hit you."

Tell him that Owen Day hit me? Absolutely *not.* I could foresee what would happen if I did that. Risk would take it personally because of his history with Owen, he'd probably show up at his house and beat him unconscious, getting his revenge for all the pain he put him through, and there was only one place that would land Risk. Jail. No, I wasn't telling him what happened to me. Not a chance.

"No one hit me," I stressed. "I literally walked into a door leaving the hospice by not watching where I was going. I'm so tired I can barely stand upright, Risk. I do clumsy shit like this all of the time, only I've never gone and actually hurt myself to this extent before."

"D'you promise?"

I felt a little sick when I said, "I promise."

Risk nodded once. "Okay then, I believe you."

It left a foul taste in my mouth lying to him, but it was for his own good.

"Thank you." I busied myself with getting two cups of tea ready. "Oath. Come to Mummy, baby boy."

Oath remained in my bedroom.

"Oath," Risk repeated. "You called your cat Oath?"

"He has red hair," I shrugged. "It seemed fitting to name him after Blood Oath."

Risk snorted as he sat down at the kitchen table. "When did you get him?"

"Eight years ago," I answered. "A neighbour couldn't find a home for him. He was the runt of the litter, I fell in love with him when I saw his big electric blue eyes so I took him home with me. He's been here ever since."

"You always were a sucker for blue eyes."

His more than anyone's.

"Yup," I played it cool. "He's my ginger pal. He's a scaredy cat though . . . kind of like you."

"I'm *not* scared of him," Risk protested mildly. "He just caught me off guard is all."

I grinned, keeping my back to him.

"Okay, tough guy."

I made our tea, turned and carried the cups over to the table, placing one on a coaster in front of me then the other in front of Risk. When I sat down and looked at Risk, I couldn't pretend this was normal.

"This is *so* bloody weird." I fidgeted with my hands. "I can't believe you're in my kitchen, drinking tea."

Risk leaned back in the chair, letting his long legs stretch out. He glanced around with fondness, if I wasn't mistaken.

"It feels smaller."

"You probably just got taller."

"Smart arse." Risk grinned. "I haven't grown an inch. I'm still six four."

"I haven't grown an inch either, I'm still five nothing."

"I've gathered that, Frodo."

"Don't start with me, Gandalf!"

Risk's amused smile made me laugh. The familiar teasing of one another's height helped break the ice that we walked on. While it eased the tension, it couldn't take away how bizarre it was to sit across from Risk while drinking a cup of tea. It was almost like not seeing each other for years wasn't a big deal, but it was.

"I thought you had changed," I said to him. "After last night, I thought you weren't the person I knew."

"I have changed. I'm just not cruel, you were right about that." He nodded. "I'm still the same person in a lot of ways, I've just grown up."

I guess I was in the same boat as him.

"Is it weird being back here?" I sipped my tea. "I bet it is, nothing has changed."

"It's *so* weird," Risk shook his head. "It's kind of scary how similar everything is, but it's also really nice."

"I bet." I nodded. "I always loved that the only thing to change about Southwold were the faces."

Risk glanced at my necklace then moved his eyes to the air box that was still on the wall. "Has your asthma improved any?"

I shook my head when he looked back at me.

He frowned. "I was hoping that was one thing that would change."

"Thanks." I smiled, touched he was somewhat concerned for my health. "My asthma is part of me, I honestly don't know what life would be like without it."

Risk ran his finger over the handle of his cup.

"How is your mum doing?"

"She's in St Elizabeth Hospice right now," I shifted. "She transferred from the hospital recently. She has pneumonia that is getting worse and worse. Her doctor said we're in the end stages now."

"Shit. I'm sorry, Frankie."

"Thank you," I smiled politely. "I always knew this time would come, but now that it's here, it feels like its crept up on me out of nowhere. Time really is no man's friend."

"Would be it okay for me to visit her?" Risk asked tentatively. "Your mum was always so great to me."

"Um, sure." I played with my fingers. "She won't remember you, though. She doesn't know who I am most days, Michael either."

"Fuck, Frankie. I'm *so* sorry."

He'd said that twice now.

"It is what is it." I scratched my neck. "I've known for a long time that this was going to happen."

We fell into a silence until Risk asked a question that seemed to bother him.

"Do you see them often?"

"Who?"

"Them." Risk cracked his neck. "The people I lived with."

I noted that he couldn't even say Owen and Freda's names and I didn't blame him one bit. It probably left a foul taste in his mouth.

I cleared my throat. "I see Owen every now and then."

"And her?"

"She died two years ago," I replied, looking up. "Lung cancer."

Risk looked shocked for a moment before he nodded once.

"Good." He clenched his teeth. "I'm glad she's dead."

I frowned at him. "You shouldn't be."

"I shouldn't be?" Risk repeated, gobsmacked. "Have you forgotten what *happened* to me in that house? By their hands?"

"No," I answered calmly. "I haven't, but I do know that you're better than them. You always have been and living your life to the fullest is how to get your revenge on them. I wouldn't be glad of anything for either of them, not the good or the bad. I wouldn't give them a second of my time if I was you."

Risk said nothing as he digested my words.

"They got three new kids not long after you left, but I made sure it didn't last long." I drank my tea. "I tipped off the police and the kids' primary school, a dozen times. The kids were removed from the Days' care a week after they arrived. An investigation was done soon after and, while neither of them went to prison, they did lose their license. They've never had another child to take care of since then."

Risk's jaw dropped and his eyes, there was a mixture of sadness and relief in his blue orbs.

"You wouldn't let me do it for you," I said, not waiting for him to ask why I did what I did. "I hated how you continued to live with them, I hated them both for the pain they put you through so when you left and they got new kids, there was no way I was sitting by anymore."

"I didn't think of them getting any more kids. Freda always said I'd be the last one."

"They must have needed the money," I guessed with a shrug. "We both know it's the only reason they fostered in the first place."

"What happened?" Risk asked, leaning forward to rest his elbows on the tabletop. "After the kids were removed from their care?"

"Nothing . . . well, except for Owen being furious with me."

"You *told* him what you did?"

Risk's eyes were as wide as saucers.

"No, but he knows it was me," I mused. "He asked enough times who gave filed complaints against him. I think he expected it to be you. But someone let it slip that a woman gave the information and he just guessed it was me. He can't prove it though."

Risk said nothing, he drank his tea in gulps and allowed my words to marinate.

"That man hates you because you're successful, rich and famous. He can't stand that you have the life you do while he is still here in Southwold with nothing to show for *his* life. I'd live an even better life if I was you; just knowing your happiness kills him slowly is all the revenge in the world that you'd ever need."

Risk swallowed and, suddenly, he didn't look like the big tough, rock star that he was. He looked exactly like he did the day after his thirteenth birthday when I told him I knew what he was going through. Without a thought, I leaned across the table and took his hand in mine.

"He's never going to hurt you again, you know?" I strummed my thumb over his skin. "He is a pathetic waste of space, and you . . . you're a superstar who chased his dreams when the odds were stacked against him, just like I knew you would."

Risk threaded his fingers through mine and held my hand.

"I've missed you, Frankie." He looked at me. "I've thought about you throughout the years. I should have reached out to contact you to see how you were doing, to see how your mum was doing but, after I left, looking back just wasn't an option. Not until now, at least."

I understood exactly what he meant. I couldn't think of our times together, I couldn't even hear him sing, or see his face, if I could help it. Doing those things were the only way I could function so I got it.

"I get it," I said. "Sometimes looking forward is the only way we can keep going."

"D'you think we can be friends?" Risk suddenly asked. "I know after I eventually leave here I probably won't be back for a while, but I'd like to be able to call you now and then to see how you are, you know? I miss talking to you."

Tell him no, Frankie.

I wanted to tell him that we belonged in each other's pasts. I wanted to tell him to leave and never come back . . . but I wanted to tell him to stay with me too. It terrified me just how happy sitting, drinking tea and talking to him made me feel. It gave me a sense of peace I hadn't felt in a very long time and I didn't want that feeling to go away. I didn't want *Risk* to go away. The very thought of going back to how I lived before he came home scared me, hiding behind my earphones and following the same schedule day after day made me feel trapped.

I didn't realise how much until that moment.

"Is that a good idea?" I wondered. "Us being in each other's lives after so long?"

"I think so," Risk squeezed my hand. "I miss you, Cherry."

Those four words melted me.

"I think we can be friends. We . . . we were friends before we got together, right?"

"Right." Risk laughed a little. "We were. What're you doing tomorrow?"

"Same thing I do every day. Work." I snorted. "My shift tomorrow is from ten until five then I'm going to visit my mum."

"Can I tag along?" Risk quizzed. "To see your mum?"

"Sure," I nodded. "That'd be lovely."

"Brilliant." Risk suddenly got to his feet. "Get to bed. I'll pick you up from work tomorrow . . . and Frankie?"

"Yeah?"

"Happy birthday."

I blinked. "My birthday was last month . . . so was yours."

"I know but since I missed it, I wanted to say it."

My lips twitched. "Risk?"

"Yeah."

"Happy birthday."

His smile nearly knocked me off my feet.

I expected him to just leave, but he didn't, he hugged me before he went and he kissed the crown of my head, just like he used to do. It lasted five seconds, maybe less, but the security and comfort I found in his embrace nearly stole my breath. I locked the front door when he was gone, then I wandered aimlessly into my bedroom. I sat on the bottom of my bed and felt my body shake as Oath brushed against my legs. I pinched myself and hissed. The pain was a vivid reminder that this was real, Risk had really been in my home and we somehow agreed to move forward and be friends.

I was both excited and scared beyond belief.

"*Please*," I pleaded with God. "Don't let this end badly again. I'm begging you."

I looked down at my hands and realised I was holding my phone. I must have grabbed it when I left the kitchen to see Risk out without realising. My hands were a little unsteady as I tapped on the screen, clicked into my messages and tapped onto Risk's name. It was his old phone number and nobody but Oath knew of a secret I had been keeping.

A few years ago, my therapist, before I stopped seeing her, suggested keeping a journal to express my feelings. I found a better coping mechanism to help me breathe through the pain of missing Risk . . . I sent text messages to his old number every so often, pretending that he got them. I talked to him and while I knew it was kind of crazy, it helped me focus my emotions.

I scrolled through the hundreds of messages I had sent Risk over the years. They varied in length from paragraphs to mere a handful of words. I almost couldn't believe that he was back in my life. It was so strange. He penned songs to project how he felt, I wrote message entries.

Texting Risk saved me . . . I wondered if writing songs saved him.

CHAPTER TEN
FRANKIE

Text message #1

Frankie: I'm texting your old number because I know you'll never see this message, but typing it out and getting it off my chest and sending it to 'you' will hopefully make me feel better. My therapist recommended it. My fucking therapist, Risk. I still can't believe I pay someone to listen to me talk about the things that keep me awake at night. My mum made my first appointment and though I didn't want to go, I'm so glad I did.

Maybe talking to 'you' will be my new thing instead of talking to the therapist and I'll save myself a few quid in the long run. This will be like my venting vice until someone gets this number and tells me to piss off. I'm supposed to message 'you' and tell you what is on my mind whenever things get hard for me.

Funny? Nah. Pathetic? Hell yeah.

I haven't seen you in exactly ten months and nothing has changed here, but I know everything has changed for you. Blood Oath being signed to an actual record label is all anyone can talk about in Southwold. You guys are already legends here as far as we're concerned. I heard you guys dropped a new single for the upcoming album you are working on. Mum told me she read that it went to number one on the Billboard Hot 100. That is huge, Risk. Huge. I'm so happy for you and the guys, I mean that with my whole heart. I wear my earphones everywhere I go just so I don't hear your voice by accident. I don't listen to the radio anymore. I'm afraid that if I hear your voice, something inside of me will shatter.

Keep chasin', rock star.

Text message #39

Frankie: I woke up today and I forgot that everything was different. For a few seconds, I thought you were still my boyfriend and that when I rolled over, I would see your handsome face on the pillow next to me. When I remembered that we broke up and you moved away, it felt like a kick in the teeth.

I did a silly thing after you left, you know?

You left one of your hoodies here by mistake when you collected your things and I put it inside one of those airtight bags to keep your smell safe. I've opened it twice, just for a few seconds, so I could inhale your scent. I have it sealed up tight because I'm so scared the smell will disappear one day. I miss it so much. I miss you so much. The reality that you're gone from my life is breaking me, but I know it's all for the best. You couldn't stay in Southwold and I can't leave. It's what's meant to be, but it still fucking hurts.

Keep chasin', rock star.

Text message #73

Frankie: I didn't think talking to 'you' would be worth my while, but it's actually helping me. It's been fifteen months since I last saw or spoke to you. Today I'm missing you really badly and I have to send this message to get this off my chest. It's crazy but I've started to notice that I don't feel as sad as I did when you first left and that's really good, Risk.

There were weeks where I wouldn't get out of bed after you left. Missing you hurts like hell. Loving you hurts like fucking hell. I have hope though, like there is light at the end of this dark tunnel I'm walking through. One day I'll be able to listen to your songs and see you on TV and I'll think, 'Get 'em, Risk.' Until that day, I'm just going to keep doing this for my sanity's sake.

Keep chasin', rock star.

Text message #142

Frankie: I was walking down Parade Road earlier today and I couldn't believe what I saw. On the ground was a magazine, and on the cover was you with that Kigi model, or whatever her name is. This is the first time in two years that I had seen evidence of you being with another girl. Anna and Hannah tell me what, and who, you're up to whenever they get the chance but for the most part, I tune everything about you out.

I've cried all day. You're moving on from me. I'm angry with you and I have no right to be, I know that, but I'm still angry with you. I'm so hurt, so fucking hurt, because I still love you more than all of the stars in the night sky.

Half-naked and drunk off your arse leaving a club – you're not even legal there yet! – with a bunch of people you likely don't even know is your new norm now, is it? It's considered cool in Hollywood, huh? FYI, it just means you're a dumb arse here. Please don't contract an STD, May's mum will kill you. Happy 20th birthday.

Keep chasin', rock star.

Text message #189

Frankie: I redecorated the cottage today. I've modernised it with a couple of coats of pure white paint and I got new furniture. I got rid of everything with Michael's permission. I love you, but I need to clear out my living space. Right now, I look at a piece of furniture and I remember how you did something on it, or near it, and it's slowly driving me up the wall. The hardest thing to get rid of was the bed and mattress because we made love for the first time on them both but it's time for a new start.

I need to try something, anything, to help me not feel so broken inside.

Keep chasin', rock star.

Text message #248

Frankie: Three years. We broke up three years ago today. I haven't seen your handsome, freckled face in person in 1,095 days. Yeah, I've been counting. On one hand, I can't believe it's been three years, and, on the other, I can't believe it's not more. Some days feel like minutes and others like decades. God. I miss you, Risk.

Keep chasin', rock star.

Text message #303

Frankie: I got a promotion today and a pretty sweet raise. You're the former boyfriend of . . . wait for it . . . the head waitress of Mary Well's diner. Eat your heart out, Keller.

Keep chasin', rock star.

Text message #346

Frankie: Guess who got caught in a bloody downpour? Yours truly. I'm literally soaked to the bone and I'm as cold as ice as I type this message, but I can't help but laugh. It reminded me of the time we got caught in the downpour not long after we started dating and when we got to my house and you realised my mum was at work, you convinced me to undress and share your body heat so I wouldn't get sick. Do you remember? You copped more than a feel you smooth-talking fucker. LOL.

I've noticed that I'm starting to laugh again and I don't even have to force it anymore. It only took three and half years for me to get here . . . that's steady progress, right? FYI, my mum said she saw you and the guys on The Ellen Show and that you were very funny. I didn't believe her because we both know you don't have a sense of humour.

Keep chasin', rock star.

Text message #391

Frankie: Blood Oath is a MULTI GRAMMY AWARD WINNING ROCK BAND. Did I or did I not tell you that you guys were gonna take the world by storm? I did. I totally did!

What the absolute fuck, Risk? I am SO proud of you guys. I can't even put it into words just how happy I am right now. I was working the morning shift when Hannah told me you guys took home five awards the night before. Five of those little babies are for the band and one for you as a songwriter. BABE! Best Rock Album, Best Rock Song, Song of the Year, Record of the Year and Album of the Year. You guys nicked three of the ceremony's most prestigious awards. WHAT?? This is actually real life. I'M SO PROUD OF YOU!

Keep chasin', rock star.

Text message #416

Frankie: Happy New Year, stupid head. I can't believe it's been four years since I last saw or spoke to you. I don't find the need to text you as often anymore. My mini breakdowns when I grab my phone to 'talk' to you are few and far between. I think that means even though I'm still struggling with you being gone, I'm starting to cope in this new, strange way. I don't know, it's probably mad, but I can breathe a little easier when I think about you now.

Keep chasin', rock star.

Text message #437

Frankie: I've been awake for hours. I had a dream about you, you touched and loved me. It felt real . . . I wish it was real. I hate you for leaving me, Risk. I told you to go, but I can't believe you really listened to me. I hope you're happy. Even though I'm hurting right now I know that when I wake up tomorrow, I'll still love you just as much, but I'll miss you a little less. Even though I don't have you anymore, there are times when I feel happy. Time really has helped heal the wound that you leaving ripped open. These periods of sadness when they come . . . Christ, they really do hurt, though.

Keep chasin' rock star.

Text message #471

Frankie: I had an asthma attack today. It was scary, it hurt, but eventually the pain went away. I wish the pain of missing you would go away. I hate it, Risk. I fucking hate it.

Keep chasin', rock star.

Text message #499

Frankie: Anna told me that you were making eyes at a Kardashian at an award show. You're such a PIG!

Keep chasin', rock star.

Text message #511

Frankie: A tourist in town asked me out on a date today. I turned him down, but it wasn't a flat out no, which tells me I might be ready for a new relationship soon. Maybe not, I'm not exactly sure. Being emotionally fucked up is so fun. Can you feel my sarcasm? I feel like you can feel it.

Keep chasin', rock star.

Text message #533

Frankie: I miss you. I love you.

Keep chasin', rock star.

Text message #567

Frankie: Hannah told me that you were all over Twitter. Again. Stop taking drugs and drinking alcohol, wazzock. I fucking hate that you're taking that squit! WHAT THE HELL IS WRONG WITH YOU? Please, please, please, stop. I can't lose you again. I can't. Please. Stop.

Keep chasin', rock star.

Text message #589

Frankie: I heard you're sober. Do you have any idea how happy this makes me? Do you, Risk? I've been so worried about you. So worried. I was terrified whenever Hannah or Anna mentioned you in case they would tell me that you'd died. I've been sick just thinking about it, but you're sober now. I'm so proud of you. Please, please, don't take that stuff again. It's not worth the risk. Don't take it.

Keep chasin', rock star.

My eyes rolled over my sent messages to Risk's old phone number. I skimmed past the similar-sounding ones and focused on the ones I remembered sending and how I felt when I sent them. I was still waiting to receive a message one day telling me I had the wrong number and to stop bothering the new number's owner, but until that day came, I was going to keep sending messages to 'Risk' whenever the mood struck me because it helped me. It really did. It was a form of expression and even though it was only me who knew about it, it helped me straighten out how I felt. Most of the time, anyway. I tapped on the message box and began thumbing out a new message and when I hit send, for once, I wished Risk would text me back.

Text message #600

Frankie: You're home.

Our first encounters were not good . . . not good at all, but you came to find me and you apologised for the things you said to hurt me. I think I gave in easier than I should have, but I couldn't help it. You were in my fucking kitchen, drinking tea and holding my hand. I could have died. We decided we're going to be friends, but what I want to know is how are we going to make that work? How can we be friends . . . ? How can we be when I'm still so deeply in love with you? I thought our love was past tense, I thought I was holding on to you because I was hurt and messed up inside but I'm holding on to you because I NEVER stopped loving you. We're going to be friends and I love you, how messed up is that?

Risk, I love you. Do you love me too?

Keep chasin', rock star.

CHAPTER ELEVEN
RISK

I hummed to a tune that was stuck in my head and before I forgot it, I rolled up my sleeve, revealing one of my many tattoos. From my inner left forearm down to my wrist, I had blank sheet music paper on my arm. I often thought of music and had to write it down before I forgot it. I had been writing lyrics and music notes on my skin for years, a tattoo of sheet music just made it easier for me to keep track of it until I transferred it to actual paper. I jotted down the music notes on the tattooed staff on my skin, then I scribbled a couple of lyrics in small print on the back of my hand with my fine-tipped, permanent Sharpie.

I knew I could have easily used the notes app on my phone to write the words down, but writing them on my hands and forearms had sort of been a rite of passage. I never wrote full songs on my body, just words here and there, maybe a sentence or two, but every song that I eventually penned had stemmed from a word or phrase I had jotted down onto my skin. I couldn't break that habit now.

It was sort of like a good luck charm, in its own way.

"Never enough," May leaned over and read the words I had just written on my hand. "New song?"

I bobbed my head. "Beginning stages, I'm just brainstorming a little."

May grabbed my arm and turned it slightly so he could see my inner forearm. He squinted his eyes and focused on the notes drawn on my arm. He mumbled the tune under his breath until he had it in his head. I ducked *my* head when he reached back into the boot and grabbed his guitar case. Hayes gave him a tongue lashing for taking off his seat belt while we were driving but May ignored him.

When he turned forward, he opened his case and removed his Fender Jazzmaster that he brought along with him for the car ride to London. We had an interview at *Rock Stop*, a huge podcast show that *every* rock band wanted to be on. We had interviewed with them half a dozen times and each time, good press followed.

Instead of taking the train, we opted to drive. It was less of a hassle because it wasn't public transport. I was glad we had decided on driving because unprompted writing sessions were what I lived for.

May grabbed a signed pick from his pocket, he kept a dozen on his person at all times. One for playing and spares for any fans we bumped into. He strummed the guitar, adjusted his hold, checked the tuning, then he played the notes I had written. In my head, I liked how they had sounded, but when May played them on the Fender, he brought them to life with a few simple flicks of his wrist. Hayes was driving the car, Angel was in the front seat but as soon as May began to play, he reached back into his bag that was at my feet, and grabbed his favourite pair of drum sticks.

He began doing his own improv based on what May was playing.

"Of course I'd have to be driving. I wanna play, too."

I snorted at Hayes, but I understood how he felt. I was our lead vocalist and guitarist, May was our rhythmic guitarist, and Hayes was our bass, but May took up most of the slack on certain songs because I spent a shit load of time interacting with the audience and running around like a headless chicken when we performed. The only person who never switched instruments on stage was Angel, he could play guitar well, and was wicked on the keyboard, but drumming was his thing and he stuck to it. I reached into Angel's bag and pulled out the different kinds of blank sheet music paper he always carried for times like this.

I uncapped my pen and wrote down what May was playing.

He started off with my notes, then improvised his own and one chord in the middle of the small set gave me chills. It changed everything about the set-up. I said nothing, I just let him go as he repeated the same chord layout a few times until he felt like adding something new.

I focused on Angel, switched a blank drum sheet and placed the notes I heard along the staff on the sheet. Because he wasn't playing on actual drums, I couldn't hear the music the way he could. I'd know which key he was hitting when he drummed his instrument, but because drumming wasn't a talent of mine, I strained a little to hear it the way he did.

"Angel," I said. "Fifth note, floor tom or mid?"

"Neither, high."

This was exactly what I was talking about, had he been playing on his drums, I'd have heard the difference. Angel turned around in his seat and peered down at the sheet I was writing on and said, "Bro, no. Rest for four beats on the whole, and that," – he pointed to the tenth note – "is supposed to be a snare, not a hi-hat."

I scowled down at my sheet. He plucked it from my hand, grabbed his own Sharpie from his bag, turned around in his seat, and fixed the drum key.

"Sorry, man."

"Don't be," Angel said. "You're much better at hearing the right notes now compared to a few years ago, you use to *suck*."

That was a backhanded compliment if I had ever heard one.

I focused back on May, he restarted his piece and I made the additions on to the staff that I missed before. I smiled as I wrote, Hayes got involved and told May which chord to add in and where. I made the additions, then used a separate sheet for the bass that I could hear even though it wasn't playing. In my head, I could hear it like it was behind May's guitar. When I wrote it down, I showed May and he nodded, "That'd be sick."

I showed it to Angel who held the sheet out for Hayes to glance at.

"I hate that we can't just lay this right now," he grunted. "I can hear this already, bro. Shit's gonna be fire."

"Right?" I beamed. "As soon as we get can get back to Southwold this evening, we'll lay what we've got and see what we think."

"I thought you had a date with Frankie tonight."

I capped my pen and put the sheets of paper back in Angel's bag while May put his guitar back in its case and then over his shoulder and into the boot. The fucker nearly took my head off again with the movement.

"I'm going to see her *very ill mum*," I reminded him. "Not a date. I told you, we agreed on being friends."

"How in the *hell* are you going to be 'just friends' with the person you write about like she is the only woman in this world who ever made you feel worth a damn?"

I didn't reply to Angel because I had no fucking clue how I was going to be 'just friends' with Frankie. No clue at all. I had asked her to be my friend because I couldn't leave her cottage without having reassurance that she would be in my life in some sort of capacity. I went there to apologise, and for the short time we spent together I knew I couldn't continue to live a life that didn't involve her.

I missed her too much.

"Leave him be," Hayes glanced at our friend. "Let him figure this out *himself*."

I was glad of the interruption when my phone rang, but when I saw who it was I groaned.

"It's Chris."

Chris Harrison was our manager and talking to him was sometimes draining. By sometimes, I mean all of the time.

"I'm not talking to him," Angel blurted. "He stresses me out when we're close to a performance. The guy is a wurryburt."

"A *wurrygut*," the three of us corrected.

Angel had picked up on some of our slang over the years because he thought the words sounded funny, but he still needed a little nudge here and there whenever he messed a word up.

"What*ever*." Angel grunted. "His anxiety gives *me* anxiety."

"I'm putting him on speaker."

Before anyone could argue, I answered the call.

"Hey Chris," I chirped. "You're on speaker."

"Where the fuck *are* you guys?" he shouted, the volume of his voice startling me. "You were supposed to be live on *Rock Stop twenty-five minutes ago*."

I cringed. "We're on the way, man."

"We're literally only ten minutes away," Hayes said. "Stuck in traffic."

London was known for many things: rubbish traffic was one of them.

"You all should've left for the interview *earlier*!"

"Chris." May exhaled a deep breath. "Remember your breathing, in and out."

"Bite me, May," Chris griped. "There's only so many excuses I can make for you guys. I know people love bad-boy rockers who scream 'fuck you' to the world, but your fans have this shit trending. They're waiting for you guys to go live. You know the media will run with this."

"Mate, *relax*," I urged. "I can fix this with one little tweet."

I grabbed May's phone from his hand, logged out of his Twitter account and signed into mine and tapped on the screen a few times and *voilà*. Crisis averted.

"What tweet?" Chris's voice rose an octave. "Risk, don't you fucking tweet anything—"

"Too late."

"*Motherfucker*!" Chris snapped. "You're the reason I have high blood pressure, asshole."

I snickered. "I've fixed the issue."

Chris continued to curse, then he read out the tweet I just tweeted.

"London, we love you, but *fuucckkk*. This traffic sucks. *Rock Stop*, we're on the way. Adult lady Sinners, stay wet for us. Every other Sinner, keep refreshing the page. Hang tight, we're coming!"

Angel snorted. "I've just retweeted it."

I laughed and so did the other two.

"Risk," Chris grunted. "When you get there and they ask if you're dating Nora, make sure you make a joke about it, but also make it clear you're single. The Sinners *loved* how you shut down the paps who cornered you last night. Shit was trending on Twitter for five hours straight."

"Got it," I stretched. "Don't worry so much, man. We've done a million interviews."

"Until it's over, *let me stress*."

I snorted.

"If rehab is mentioned, be as honest as you want to be. The support for your recovery is huge."

That was nice to hear.

"Will do. Is everything in order for the gigs next week?"

"A sold-out concert, one of three, in Wembley Stadium is *more* than a gig, you dopey Brit."

We laughed, not offended in the least.

"But, yes," Chris continued. "Everything is in order; the crew is already in London. Set-up started this morning since your stage is awkward as fuck and needed time to be set up and tested for safety. What date is it today . . . it's Thursday the eleventh. Show one is on Monday the fifteenth, you four are due in the stadium at noon on the fourteenth for soundcheck, costume check, full rehearsal and so forth."

"We'll be in London on the fourteenth," May offered. "We're staying at Risk's house, right?"

"What do you mean, right? You don't know?"

"Of course I know . . . I think."

"This is why I stress!" Chris exploded. "You dumb asses are slowly killing me."

I bit my lip so I didn't laugh.

"They're all staying in my townhouse rather than a hotel," I cracked my neck. "You know we hate hotels."

"Yes, I know, trust me." Chris sighed. "I know you all know the dates, but for my own peace of mind, I'll have Nolan email it to the four of you. He takes care of your itinerary. You know he's having a worse breakdown than I am because you four forbid him from accompanying you to Southwold. He gets chest pains because you refused Jacob, and the rest of your security team, tagging along too."

"Southwold is ours." I repeated what I told Chris before we even came home. "That town is just for us. We're safe there."

"Until crazy Sinners travel to Southwold and kidnap you all."

May shrunk low in his seat because that was an actual fear of his, which amused me greatly.

"He's joking, May."

My friend nodded, but didn't look like he really believed me.

"We're about to pull into the building's underground car park," Hayes said to Chris. "We'll call you after the interview."

"Just announce the new album and tour, making it exciting . . . and don't say shit you can't take back."

With that, Chris hung up. I pocketed my phone, cracked my neck again and cleared my throat.

"Why do I feel like he was directing that last part at me?"

"He was," my friends said in unison, then chuckled.

I looked at May, held my fist out. He bumped his against mine.

"We have to be cute," I told him. "You know our Ray shippers eat our bromance up. And you, Angel," I said. "The Rangel shippers *die* when we interact with each other. Be nice to me, princess."

"Suck my cock, asshole."

"Hell, if you did that," May clapped me on the shoulder. "You might kill the Rangel shippers altogether."

We all burst into laughter as Hayes parked the car and we climbed out. I straightened out my clothes, so did the others, then we headed to the entrance. There was a brown-haired woman waiting for us who looked like she was relieved to see us walk towards her. She put her phone to her ear and into it she said, "They just arrived, be up in five."

She ushered us into the building, into an elevator then up to one of the top floors in the building. As soon as we got out of the elevator, there was a guy pointing a camera at us. Podcasts were pre-recorded but they went live sometimes too; this interview was live. They put them on platforms like YouTube where a broader viewership could hear, and see, interviews. I winked at the camera when he turned to me.

"Fannies quiver everywhere with a single wink from Risk Keller," May mumbled behind me, but I heard him and laughed. We followed Katie, the woman who greeted us in the car park, down a few hallways then into a room full of people who cheered when the four of us walked inside.

"Blood Oath is in the building!"

Rock Stop was a huge podcast with twenty million monthly listeners around the world, this meant they had a big operation with different staff members. There were normally two hosts per episode and that was the case today. I had never met the man, Brian, who stood up to greet us, but the last interview we had done with them over a year ago had the same woman, Toni Marlow. I fucked her in an empty room not long after that podcast ended, she was cool and she knew her shit when it came to rock. It was sweeter that nothing came of us having sex, no nasty episode on *Rock Stop* where she dragged me through the mud like Chris thought she would.

She stood up to hug each member, but I was the only who got a kiss on the cheek when I bent down.

"How are you, gorgeous?"

"I'm good." She smiled and returned to her seat.

The four of us got in position in front of a microphone and put headphones on.

"Morning, everyone," I said into the mic. "Sorry we're late. London traffic, ay?"

"Tell me about it, Risk," Toni said. "How are you all? It's great to see you guys again."

We exchanged pleasantries then the interview started naturally.

"Back in the motherland, lads," Brian grinned. "How does it feel to be home?"

"Amazing," May answered. "We love the States, but home is where the heart is and that's in England. Isn't that right, lads?"

"Yeah," Hayes and I echoed.

"No," Angel answered, his tone flat. "Not for me. Stop excluding me, May. Our band is so fragile, this could be the tipping point if you don't make me feel loved like these two. I'll have a mental breakdown unless I'm treated exactly the same on camera just so everyone can see you three actually love me."

Angel, unblinkingly, stared into the camera as he spoke then rolled his eyes up to the heavens and said, "I'm being extremely sarcastic before any of you dumb fuckers think I'm serious."

Hayes and I snorted, May laughed and so did the hosts.

"I take it you read some of the more . . . interesting headlines about the band as of late, Angel?"

"Pretty hard not to when they're linked everywhere on social media," Angel answered Toni. "But it's all garbage. We read some of these headlines and we honestly just laugh. We rip into each other constantly but trust me when I say these guys are my brothers. Just because I'm Mexican doesn't mean they treat me differently, it's all love between us even when we're mad at each other. These articles are made just for clicks and likes for companies to gain revenue, that's it."

"Like most articles," Brian nodded. "Hard to tell what's real and fake these days."

"What's real," I said, "is our three *sold-out* gigs at Wembley Stadium on the fifteenth, sixteenth, and seventeenth."

The crew around us cheered, making me grin.

"Wembley packed with over one hundred thousand Sinners per night?" May shuddered. "I can't fucking wait."

"You've had a mini tour over the last year," Toni said. "A dozen dates in the States and now the three dates in Wembley . . . how come you guys didn't decide to visit other cities while in the U.K.? Was it all down to your stint in rehab, Risk?"

The woman was smooth the way she slid a heavy topic into a casual conversation.

"Yes," I answered. "The tour was always going to be small, but Wembley being the only dates we scheduled was down to my stint in rehab."

"I can see your coin hanging around your neck from here," Brian said. "What's the number say? Five?"

"Six," I corrected. "I'm six months sober."

I received congratulations and smiles from everyone.

"We know that Risk's sobriety has the full support of our Sinners but we understand many were left disappointed not to have a gig in a city near them," Hayes took over. "But this mini tour was just a practice run for our new stage with our new crew. It's all part of our preparation for our *next* tour."

There was a moment of silence.

"Next tour?" Toni repeated. "*What* next tour?"

I looked at the guys. "Did we not tell them we have a world tour coming up for our new album?"

"What?" Brian blinked. "New album, world tour . . . what the fuck, lads?"

"I *knew* we forgot to do something," May facepalmed. "We were supposed to announce our new album, *Lost in the Darkness*, and the accompanying world tour for it."

"Right," Angel snapped his fingers. "The album drops next month, right? On the sixteenth?"

"Yup," I nodded. "You've got it in one, bud."

"Look at the comments," Brian pointed to a monitor on the wall. "One hundred per second, I think you broke the live stream."

The comments on the stream were coming in so fast it was impossible to read them. I flicked my eyes to the number in the left hand corner. Just over eight million people were watching the stream . . . and the number was rising.

"I think our Sinners are excited we have a new album and tour on the way."

"Not just any tour," Toni said. "A *world* tour. Your first, right?"

"Yup," Hayes answered, beaming. "North and South America, Europe, Asia, Africa, Oceania. We're hitting six of the seven continents. Two hundred shows broken up into twelve legs. We're going global this time, baby."

"*Two hundred* shows," Brian said and took a sheet from one his crew members. "We have an official email from your management. Holy hell, guys, you're going everywhere and most of these venue are stadiums and arenas. This tour . . . this might be one of the highest grossing tours of all time."

Our team had calculated that the upcoming tour could earn anywhere between seven hundred and nine hundred million. So yeah, it's definitely going to be one of the highest of all time if that proved to be correct.

"We hope so," Angel chuckled. "That'd be pretty sweet."

"So your new album, *Lost in the Darkness*, releases on the sixteenth of March, next month, and the tour kicks off exactly a year later on the sixteenth of March 2021 in Paris, France. Leg one is for Europe."

"Yup," I nodded. "The exact press release you're reading is being uploaded on our website right now, so, Sinners," I looked at the camera. "Go and check out when we'll be in a city near you."

"I can already hear the screams and roaring of your Sinners." Toni chuckled. "But speaking of tours. We heard a rumour that you guys worked out a *really* sweet deal for upcoming tours . . . is it true?"

"What's the rumour?" Hayes asked. "There's a shit tonne of them."

"This rumour is about money . . . apparently you guys own all the earnings from merchandise sales on top of your sixty per cent earnings on ticket revenue per show."

That was public knowledge, but since Toni wanted an answer, I gave her one.

"Yeah, that's true. We're very anal about our contracts, we go through them with our solicitors with a fine-tooth comb. Singers, and bands, have been ripped off because they didn't read their contracts thoroughly and know their worth. We know how much money we make people, we just make sure we earn more on our careers than anyone can earn off us and by that I mean the big companies that are likely to take advantage of artists like us."

Tony laughed. "And that's the way it should be."

We spoke in depth about the tone of the new album, the writing and recording process for a solid thirty minutes before Southwold was brought back into the conversation.

"It all over Twitter that you guys returned home to Southwold to attend an old teacher's retirement ceremony, is there truth to that? I mean, we've all seen picture evidence and there's video footage of the paps questioning you, Risk, but that could have been in any location. Like in London, where Nora Maxwell happens to be."

I snorted. "Nora is shooting a new film. I haven't seen or spoken to her in months. I've said it a million times but we really are just friends. That's *it*."

"And *that's* how you to stamp out a rumour."

I smiled at Toni.

"It's true about why we were in Southwold though," Hayes chimed in. "Mr Jones, we've spoken about him a lot in interviews, was our school's counsellor, PE teacher and our after-school music teacher. He bought us our first instruments with his own money, the man is a gent. We honestly love him."

Toni pouted. "That's so fucking cute."

We chuckled.

"Angel," Brian prompted. "You didn't grow up with Mr Jones, how was meeting him?"

"He's a great man," Angel answered. "He was really welcoming to me, we jammed with him a little in the guys' old music room. I had fun. I've heard so much about Mr Jones and the school rock days, experiencing a little of it made me understand how much of a connection the three of them have to Mr Jones, and Southwold overall."

Brian was reading our fans' comments on the live stream chat window.

"MayActonSitOnMyFace has a question for you guys."

Each of us erupted into laughter, Hayes nearly fell off his bloody chair.

"Fuck's sake." May covered his face. "What's the fucking question?"

"Is Mr Jones the original Sinner?"

"He's actually not," I said, rubbing my cheeks to stop smiling. "Mr Jones was the second Sinner, not the original."

This surprised Brian and also excited him.

"Who was the original Sinner?"

"A girl who supported us from the get go," I shifted. "She went to school with us."

"She liked your voice?"

This came from Toni.

"Yeah," I nodded. "She liked it, she liked our style too. She's the one who encouraged me to put my focus into music, she's sort of the reason for Blood Oath being Blood Oath."

"Well," Brian shook his head. "Millions of fans around the world definitely have a lot to thank this girl for."

I chuckled. "We're just like any other band. We love rock, we love the music we make. We're just us."

"Says the man who looks like a Greek god," Toni mused. "Each of you are shockingly handsome, you're all so talented too. You do understand most rock stars just have talent, not looks. You have both in spades."

We knew we had more females as fans because of how we looked. The majority of our fans were hardcore rock fans, but we weren't stupid enough to think the extra attention we got was solely down to our music. Each of us was good looking, it had helped our careers so I never looked at it as a hindrance. I was the face of Hugo Boss and Calvin Klein, surprisingly they didn't drop me after my fuck up. Apparently, my sobriety journey was great business for them. I was the underdog and everyone loved an underdog. The other three members had endorsements deals as well from skincare and hair products to aftershave.

Not being ugly . . . it helped us and that was just the way it was.

"If anyone is the Adonis of the group," May said. "It's me."

Myself, and the other two, agreed wholeheartedly which made Toni widen her eyes.

"*May* is the band's frontman when it comes to women?"

I grinned. "He calls me the main man but that title really belongs to him."

"No way," Toni shook her head. "I've seen how some women take to you, Risk Keller. You're . . . mouth-watering."

I kept eye contact with Toni as she spoke; I wondered how far she was willing to go with this conversation. She was eye fucking me. Thoroughly eye fucking me.

"Everyone expects me to be fucking every minute of every day," I shook my head. "It's not true . . . unfortunately."

Everyone snorted.

"But you've had your fair share of, eh hem, pus-say."

I rubbed my neck at Brian's pretty blunt question.

"Yeah, but what rocker hasn't? You know the saying. Sex, drugs and rock and roll. You can't have one without the others. Trust me, I know what I'm talking about."

Everyone laughed at the jab to my own past, the crew more than my bandmates.

"You guys have been at this a long time . . . probably having sex longer, right?"

Only on *Rock Stop* would a person be asked when they had their cherry popped.

"Fifteen for me," Hayes said, then May and Angel said, "Sixteen."

I sighed. "I was freshly eighteen."

"Liar," Toni smirked at me. "I've seen pictures of you when you were eighteen, *no way* were you a virgin."

"I'm telling the truth," I assured her. "I was in a relationship back then so I waited until my girl was ready. It's simple really."

"I heard you mention a mysterious girlfriend a time or two in an interview." Toni raised a brow. "Would *she* be the original Sinner?"

"Yup."

I felt May look at me and I wondered if I'd revealed too much. I had always been selective when I spoke about Frankie, always making sure she was kept private, but something about the way Toni asked her question rubbed me the wrong way. Her tone was a little condescending. Like Frankie making me wait to have sex until she was ready was a lame thing to do. That irritated me.

Angel jumped in and casually turned the conversation back to our upcoming album and world tour next year. We answered some fan questions, Hayes spoke a little about his wife, Summer, and how she was adjusting to being married to a famous rock star. I zoned out a little. I kept thinking of the song we had begun on the journey here and that made me think of Frankie.

I can't get enough of your green eyes, your soft skin, your sweet smile.

Those were the lyrics I had written on my notepad last night. It was obvious it was going to be another song about Frankie but this one felt like it was going to be different. In every other song another her was connected to the loss of love, or living without something. Even our upbeat belters had her in them. This song . . . I wanted this to be about how I felt over the past nine years, but also about how I felt now, having her back in my life.

I *really* wanted to write the bloody thing.

I was glad that half an hour later the interview ended and we said goodbye to everyone watching the live stream. We had just removed our headphones and stood to hug Toni and shake Brian's hand when Toni leaned up and into my ear she whispered, "How about I show you a lovely empty room down the hallway?"

I hadn't had sex since before I went to rehab; when I got off drugs and alcohol, I binned sex too. I didn't even consider Toni's offer, which told me I was still well and truly on the wagon, but also because Frankie's face popped into my head.

"Sorry, Toni," I politely kissed her cheek. "Rain check, yeah? I have to get back to Southwold, I have a song I need to write."

She pouted up at me but nodded. When we left the building and got back into the rental, the guys turned and looked at me. I froze under their watchful gazes. I lifted my hands to my face, paranoid I had dirt on my skin or something. Or that I'd done something wrong.

"What?" I questioned. "I didn't do anything."

I hated that that was my go-to response even after all of these years of being free of the Days. It was a defensive stance I always took and had yet to shake off.

"Toni wanted to fuck you," May blinked. "You shot her down."

"Why?" Angel quizzed. "Why not fuck her? You're in a dry spell."

A *self-imposed* dry spell.

"I know why," Hayes grinned. "It has to do with a little redhead in Southwold, am I right? The one who you're *just friends* with?"

I scowled at the three of them.

"Suck my dick, the three of you."

They laughed and turned forward in their seats. We left London and headed back to Southwold. I checked the time and cringed; I would cut it fine picking Frankie up from work. I'd have to table writing the song until later with the guys, which they were fine with. It took over three hours to get back home, the guys got out at May's house and settled on ordering takeaway, while I jumped in the driver's seat and bucked it to Mary Well's. I pulled into the car park just as Frankie was walking out of the diner. I pulled alongside her and lowered the passenger window.

"Where are you off to, good looking?" I asked with a teasing grin. "I hope you were coming to find me."

"You said you'd pick me up so I didn't drive." She tucked a tendril of hair behind her ear. "I . . . I thought that maybe you forgot about me."

"Forget about you?" I repeated. "Cherry, if I haven't been able to forget you over the past nine years, eighteen hours isn't gonna do the trick."

When she smiled, calmness filled me.

"Get in, Frodo," I grinned. "I have something I wanna do after we visit your mum."

CHAPTER TWELVE
FRANKIE

"You look like you're going to rob a bank."

Risk's eyes crinkled at the corners, telling me he was smiling.

"Covering up is essential when I go out. Sinners are everywhere, y'know? Even in Southwold."

I snorted. "At least with it being winter you get away with covering up so much without sticking out like a sore thumb."

He nodded as we walked down the hallway of the hospice towards my mother's room.

"Remember," I reminded gently. "Michael might be a little cold towards you."

"I know," Risk straightened his coat. "He has every right to be pissed at me for how I treated you."

"I didn't tell him anything other than that you talked down to me a little, he would probably square up to you if he knew how much of an arse you were."

Risk glanced down at me, his eyebrows raised. "He's that protective over you?"

"He's like my dad in many ways," I said with a nod. "He loves me. I love him."

Risk was silent as I brought us to a stop. I knocked on the door of Mum's room, then let myself in. Mum was asleep, as usual, and Michael was perched in the armchair reading a newspaper. He looked up when I entered, adjusted his glasses and smiled, but that smile faltered when Risk stepped into the room after me, ducking slightly to avoid hitting the top of the door-frame.

"It's okay," I told Michael. "He stopped by my place last night to apologise, we've hashed it out."

Michael didn't look convinced.

"Ye apologised to her good and true?" he asked Risk, not blinking as he stared him down. "Because disrespectin' her is disrespectin' me. I don't care who ye are, I won't have it."

Risk stepped around me, removing his scarf from around his face as he went.

"Yes, sir, I apologised. I said things that I shouldn't have and I treated Frankie poorly. She didn't deserve it, I know that. I was a massive prick."

"I'll say," Michael grunted.

"I don't want to cause any trouble, Dr O'Rourke." Risk held his hands up. "I just wanted to visit Mrs O'Rourke, that's all."

Michael looked at me. "You're happy with this, Frank?"

"Yeah," I nodded. "We spoke about it last night when he stopped by."

"Okay then," Michael said, then took a couple of steps forward and held out his hand. "Thank you for comin' by and welcome home."

"Thank you," Risk closed the space between them and shook my stepdad's hand. "Congratulations, too. On your marriage . . . I know I'm a bit late."

Nearly a whole decade, but who was counting?

Michael snorted. "Thanks."

I sat on my usual seat on the right of Mum's bed, Risk pulled up the spare chair from against the window and sat next to me. When he was settled, I watched as he took in my mum's frail body. His eyes widened a little, but he quickly masked his expression of shock, probably not to hurt my or Michael's feelings. I leaned over and nudged him until he looked my way.

"It's okay to be shocked," I said gently. "She's very ill, and we know she's changed a lot over the past nine years."

Risk cleared his throat. "I'm so sorry that she is going through this . . . such a lovely woman, I hate when bad things happen to good people like her."

"Me too," Michael agreed, looking at Mum. "But me wife's illness has made sure that meself and Frankie never leave an 'I love you' unspoken. We never walk away in anger or leave a conversation unresolved and we always, *always*, thank God for each day we have with my Amanda. Every second with her is a blessin' and we know it."

I bobbed my head in wholehearted agreement.

Risk was startled when Mum suddenly began coughing. Both Michael and I got up to help her sit up when she woke up and automatically tried to move her body upright. I grabbed her hanky and gave it to her, she pressed it against her mouth and coughed until the fit passed. Michael didn't call for a nurse, he checked Mum's vitals and decided she'd benefit from some oxygen so he turned it on and fixed the mask over her face. She needed the mask more often than not now.

When she settled back against the pillow I had just fluffed up, her eyes landed on Risk, who was still sitting in his chair and staring at her.

"Who're you?"

The question snapped him out of his trance.

"I'm Risk," he smiled. "Risk Keller. Lovely to meet you."

Michael snorted and shook his head when Mum began to tuck her hair behind her ears and adjusted her nightgown with her shaking hands. I put my hand over my mouth, sat back down and laughed. Risk took her trembling hand when she held it out to him. She rubbed her thumb over the back of his hand.

"Very handsome," Mum told him. "Do you h-have a wife? I'm a . . . widower."

"Oh my god," I dropped my hand, laughing louder. "Mum!"

Mum didn't pay me any mind, Risk was her only focus.

"Well," Risk said. "It's my lucky day, because I'm very much single."

Mum's giggle was so wonderful to hear, her openly flirting with Risk made both Michael and I smile her way. This type of interaction with her massively beat one of her coughing fits or when she got angry or upset. She relaxed against her bed, looked at Michael and said, "I changed the alarm code."

I hated her wheeze, I wanted nothing more than to take it away from her.

"Did ye?" he asked. "To what?"

"Yeah," she replied. "I know. I wanted the big vase . . . instead."

I glanced at Risk and he looked at me, blinking.

"She's very easily confused," I murmured. "Having a solid conversation with her is rare. We just go with it."

"Nurse," she said to me. "I don't need . . . help, you can . . . leave."

I bit back a laugh at the dismissal.

"Can I stay a few minutes longer? I'm enjoying your company."

Mum sighed. "Okay."

She looked back at Risk and her eyes widened.

"*Hello*."

I laughed again. "Oh my days."

Risk and Mum had another introduction, then there were conversations about nothing for a couple of hours before she got a bit cranky and let Michael talk her into resting. When she fell asleep, I kissed Michael, and Mum, goodbye. Risk shook my stepdad's hand and touched Mum's. When we left the hospital, Risk was really quiet. I knew he was processing his reunion with my mum and I wanted to give him time to straighten things out in his head before we spoke because it was a lot to deal with, especially when you were new to someone who has a disease such as Alzheimer's.

When we drove back to Southwold, I broke the silence as we drove through town.

"You wanna talk about the visit?"

"Yeah," he answered in a rushed breath. "I just don't know what to say other than I'm sorry."

"Sorry?" I repeated. "What for?"

"For your mum being so ill . . . Frank, you have to deal with that every day. Her not knowing who you are, watching her get sicker. I hate that for you and Michael, and I hate it worse of all for your lovely mum."

A lump formed in my throat.

"Like Michael said," I looked out of the window. "We're grateful for each day with her, the good, the bad and the ugly."

Risk remained silent.

"She's dying," I said, clenching my hands into fists. "Her health is declining rapidly. She's been in the hospice for two months now; the doctor gave her six months at most. I know her time to go is fast approaching, Michael does too. It's just, if we focus on that we'll miss moments like the ones you shared with her tonight. You know?"

"Yeah, Cherry," I felt Risk look at me. "I know."

I laughed then when he said, “How does it feel to know that your mum thinks I’m sexy?”

“Sexy?” I repeated. “I believe she called you handsome, not sexy.”

“Are you sure?” he teased. “The way she looked at me, she thought I was more than handsome.”

I tittered, shaking my head.

“Mum’s always been a Sinner,” I mused. “But it’ll break your heart to know that *her* heart has always been May’s.”

“Typical.” Risk mock growled. “May is everyone’s favourite.”

Before I thought better of it, I said, “Not mine.”

I kept my gaze locked on the passing town. Risk said nothing, which I was thankful for. The feeling of embarrassment passed when confusion took over. When we parked in the car park at Southwold Pier, I looked at Risk, who pulled the handbrake up and switched the car off.

“This is where you wanted to go after visiting my mum?” I quizzed. “The pier? You want to go walking?”

“Yep,” he chirped. “The last time I walked to the end of this pier and stared out at the ocean was with you . . . I don’t like being here without you.”

I had no idea what to say to that, so I followed his lead by getting out of the car. Risk pressed on the car fob and locked the vehicle. I fell in step next to him and we began walking towards the pier’s entrance. It was night-time, so the café, restaurant and gift shops along the pier were closed. It was freezing out too so we were the only idiots dumb enough to be outside walking, but I kind of liked it. I liked that we had the place all to ourselves. Even though it was very cold, the ocean was calm and there was only a slight breeze.

“I can’t wait for spring,” I said as we walked, slipping my ice-cold hands into my pockets. “I’m so fed up with the cold.”

"Really? I don't mind it."

I glanced up at him. "You live in LA; the winters there are pretty much our summers."

Risk smiled, then he fixed his scarf in place, hiding most of his face from me. I wished I had brought a scarf of my own because my nose was so cold that it stung. I was confident that I already had wind burn on my cheeks too.

"God, I've missed that smell." Risk inhaled deeply and exhaled with a satisfied sigh. "Cool, salty air and no humidity."

I chuckled. "I guess I don't notice the smell anymore since I've never left."

"I've been meaning to ask you about that," Risk said. "Have you never gone on holiday anywhere?"

"Nope," I answered. "For lots of reasons. The main one is my mum, I was never comfortable with leaving her even in the early days of her illness. Another is money, I had to save every penny so I could buy my cottage off Michael upfront without needing to apply for a mortgage."

Risk jerked his head in my direction.

"You *own* the cottage?"

"Yeah." I shivered as a breeze swirled around us. "I bought it two years ago. Michael wanted to just *give* it to me, can you believe that?"

"Well, yeah, I can," Risk replied. "You and him are very close now compared to what I remember of you both."

"We are," I agreed. "But I wasn't about to let him just give me a four-hundred-thousand-pound cottage. It's tiny but the location is what makes the property value so high. Michael wouldn't take a penny over fifty thousand, though. I tried to work out a deal to triple it, but he refused."

"Why did you fight him so hard on it?"

"It's just the way I am," I shrugged. "I've always had to work for what I had and even though it's not much, I earned it. I guess I felt like I was robbing Michael if I just accepted the cottage from him. Paying him, even though it was such a small fee compared to the house's value, made me feel better. Like it was well and truly mine."

"So that little place is all yours?"

"Yep," I smiled. "I love it more than ever."

"I think you should invest in getting taller door-frames," Risk commented, his eyes crinkling at the corners. "It'd be nice not to have to duck every time I came by your place."

Was he planning on coming by often? I was too chicken to ask.

I snickered. "I'll add it to my to-do list."

We walked down to the very end of the pier and we both leaned against the railing and stared out at the ocean of darkness. In the distance, the lights of a ship could be seen, as well the flashing red light of a buoy. A wisp of light coated the waterfront for a second or two before disappearing only to return. I glanced over my shoulder and smiled at the lighthouse before I returned my attention forward.

"You always smile when you look up at the lighthouse. Why?"

"Because it's operational," I glanced up at Risk. "When the light of the lighthouse is working every night, it makes me happy because if someone gets lost out on this side of the ocean, they can follow our light all the way to Southwold where they'd be safe. That light is a beacon to someone's darkness."

"If everyone thought like you did, Cherry," Risk nudged me with his elbow. "There would be fewer wars."

I smiled, then I closed my eyes and hummed with content. Listening to the gentle clash of the waves on the beach not far away, and the slosh of the water against the support legs of the pier gave me a sense of peace that filled me from my head all the way down to my toes.

"It's so easy to forget the world when you're out here," I opened my eyes. "It feels like I'm in another world when I'm here at night, kind of like being free . . . you know?"

When I looked up at Risk, his body was turned so his hip and arm rested against the railing but instead of gazing out at the blanket of black water, he was watching me. There was something in his eyes that made my heart skip a beat and caused my throat to run dry.

"Why are you looking at me like that?"

"Because I wanna kiss you."

I jolted as if I was electrocuted by the force of his words.

"What?"

My voice was a hair above a whisper and even to my own ears it was filled with disbelief. Risk didn't reply to me, he just continued to gaze at me as if he wanted to take me in his arms and kiss me until my knees threatened to buckle.

"Risk."

"Don't you wanna kiss me?" he asked. Christ, he looked and sounded so vulnerable when he asked me that question. "Because I *really* wanna kiss you, Cherry. So fucking much. I can't stop thinking about it."

I heard his words as if he screamed each one.

"Don't do this to me," I trembled. "Don't tease me like this."

"Tease you?" he repeated. "I'm a second away from begging you to let me taste you again."

He stepped closer to me, so close that I had to reach out and grab his forearms just so I would have something to hold on to.

"Risk," I swallowed. "I don't think this is a good idea. We're supposed to be *friends*—"

"Yes or no," he interrupted, his eyes searching mine. "Just say one of those words. That's all you have to do, Frankie."

My mind was screaming to tell him no. To holler that no good would come from us kissing, but my heart and body were demanding I say yes. For years I had dreamed of what it would be like to kiss him again, to taste his lips, to feel them against mine. To be wrapped in his strong embrace and have his touch and smell invade my senses once more. My heart beating against my chest was the only sound I could hear for a moment, until I replied to his question and surprised both of us with my answer.

"Yes."

Risk didn't need another word, he dipped his head and covered his mouth with mine the second I gave him the green light to do so. His arms went around my body as quick as a flash and suddenly I was hoisted up into the air then my behind rested against the railing around the pier. I didn't have time to gasp with surprise. My hands instinctively went to his hair and the second his tongue pushed inside of my mouth, I moaned so loudly that he squeezed my hips painfully in response. He was between my parted thighs and through his jeans I could feel his hardened length snugly pressed against my heat.

I was so overwhelmed with his touch, his very presence, that I felt tears slip from my eyes and slide down my cheeks. Risk moved his mouth from my lips and he kissed away my tears without a word spoken. He was frantic with his movements, but gentle at the same time. It was like he felt what I felt, disbelief that we were together in this capacity again, but overjoyed at the same time. It was a bundle of emotions to sort through, but I didn't want to focus on how I was feeling. I just wanted to kiss Risk, and focus on his touch, so that was what I did.

Time was lost.

I could have been kissing Risk for ten minutes or ten hours. It didn't matter. All I knew was by the time our kiss came to a gradual halt, I wanted it to start all over again and never end. My hands had dropped to Risk's shoulders, where I gripped his coat tightly in my clenched fists. I was breathing heavily, so heavily, my chest was tight too. When I opened my eyes and found Risk holding a blue inhaler close to my mouth I parted my swollen, tingling lips and breathed in the medicine he puffed. If I was thinking rationally, I would have been mortified that kissing Risk had me on the verge of an asthma attack. After a few minutes, and a couple more puffs of the inhaler, the tightness in my chest faded and my breathing evened out.

"Look at me, gorgeous."

When I lifted my lids and stared into Risk's icy-blue eyes, I swallowed.

"Kissing you almost gave me an attack."

He moved his face back to mine and slid his tongue over my lower lip.

"Yeah?" he rumbled. "Imagine what having sex with me will do to you."

I shuddered and couldn't help but imagine our naked bodies moving together as one.

"Have mercy," I swatted his chest. "You'll bloody kill me."

Risk's smile made my pulse spike.

"You good?" he asked. "I don't hear the wheezing anymore."

I nodded. "I'm good . . . I didn't even realise an attack was incoming."

"I'm a good distraction from bad things," he winked. "Trust me."

I looked down as he capped the inhaler and tucked it into his pocket.

"Is that not mine?"

I figured he took it from my pocket when my eyes were closed.

"No," he answered. "I got this one before I went to London this morning . . . I always carried one when we were together. I feel safer having it."

I stared at him, and how I felt for him couldn't be described as anything other than raw love. I loved him. I loved him so desperately and I couldn't even tell him.

"Thank you."

"For what?" He nudged my head with his.

"For thinking of me," I said, lowering my eyes to the buttons of his coat. I began to play with them. "You don't have to carry an inhaler for me, Risk, but you still do . . . after all of this time."

"Hey. Look at me."

I lifted my eyes to his.

"Nine years have passed by, but right here with you, it feels like we've lost no time at all."

Butterflies fluttered around my tummy.

"What are we doing?" I asked. "Are we going crazy? Kissing each other like we just did?"

"If kissing you is crazy, Cherry, I don't ever wanna be sane."

I smiled. "Me either."

He lifted his hand and brushed his knuckle over my cheek.

"We're complicated," he murmured. "God knows we are, but can't we just kiss when we wanna kiss? Being denied your touch, your taste . . . I'd have to go to rehab for the rest of my life to cope, Frankie. I can't stay sober when it comes to you. I always want you."

"I feel the same way about you."

He leaned down and brushed his lips over mine.

"You wanna come back to May's house with me?"

I felt my eyes widen and Risk instantly chuckled.

"Not to do anything like *that*," he assured me. "The guys have been hassling me to bring you by, and by 'the guys' I mean May, and by 'hassling', I mean he has been nagging me half to death so he can see you. Please, put me out of my misery."

I covered my mouth with my hand as I tittered.

"Okay, rock star." I grinned as I lowered my arm. "Take me to see Blood Oath."

CHAPTER THIRTEEN

FRANKIE

"As I live and breathe, Frankie Fulton is in my front garden. O.M.Fucking.G!"

The teasing words had barely left May's mouth before I set out in a run towards him which caused Risk to say, "Oh, for fuck's sake," from behind me.

May caught me when I jumped at him and he just about squeezed the life out of me. He even gave me three kisses on the cheek that made me laugh like a little schoolgirl. A throat was cleared behind us, making May snicker and give me another peck on the cheek. A big one.

"Great to see you, gorgeous."

"May, give it a rest."

I ignored Risk and so did May.

"It's good to see you too, May." I smiled up at him. "I think you've gotten even *more* handsome since I last saw you."

He bobbed his head in wholehearted agreement.

"I've gotten one hundred per cent more handsome, sexy and everything in-between these past nine years. In case you didn't know, I'm a sex symbol now."

"*I* was voted *People*'s Sexiest Man Alive last year *and* three years ago," Risk interrupted. "Not you."

"I can't have anything with you," May hissed at Risk. "Bastard."

Their bickering amused me greatly.

"Still modest as ever, I see, Mr May."

He winked, looked over my head and devilishly grinned as he leaned down to kiss my face again, but he suddenly jumped backwards, laughing. The two men walking up behind him shoved May when he bumped into them. One man was someone I once knew well.

"Hayes!"

Without a word, he advanced on me and wrapped me up in a bear hug. He kissed the crown of my head which just about melted me. Hayes was always a fantastic hugger and it seemed that that hadn't changed a bit over the years.

"Congratulations, Mr Married Man." I squeezed him. "I'm so happy for you, honey."

He gave me another kiss on the head.

"Thanks, short stuff." He chuckled as we separated. "I thought my wife was small, but I forgot that you're a walking hobbit."

I playfully thumped him in the stomach as the others stopped chuckling and took a step back.

"I'm small," I eyed him. "But always dangerous, you'd best remember that."

"Wouldn't dream of forgetting it, Frank."

When I turned my attention to the person chuckling on the right of Hayes, I straightened.

"Angel," I held out my hand. "Lovely to officially meet you. If you don't mind, I'm not counting that night in the diner."

"I don't blame you." He grinned, taking my hand and surprising me by raising it to his face and gently kissing the back of it. "It's nice to meet you too, muse."

I frowned. "Muse? I don't understand—"

"He's takin' the piss," Risk interrupted. "Angel here is still a little jet-lagged. Aren't you . . . *mate*?"

"Oh, yeah," Angel smiled at me. "Just tired, is all."

"Well, that's nothing a cuppa and good night's sleep won't fix."

Angel winked. "Noted."

We never got a chance to go inside May's house to have any tea because he announced that he was hungry and the obvious choice, to me, for good food, was Mary Well's but Risk disagreed.

"You were working there all day, you aren't going back there for dinner."

I understood his logic, no one wanted to go to their place of work when they didn't have a shift to work, but I loved Mary Well's. It was a hard job and on most days it was exhausting, but I loved it. I loved the atmosphere, and for the most part there was no drama between co-workers and working for Joe was honestly a pleasure. In many ways, we were kind of like a family.

"It's after nine, Mary Well's is the only place open that does a good burger. Those fancy restaurants in the hotels aren't all they're cracked up to be."

Risk hesitated. "You're sure?"

"Of course."

With that said, we all piled into the SUV and Risk drove us five minutes away to Mary Well's. The guys were talking amongst themselves about how the paparazzi that had been staking out May's house had gotten into trouble with the police. They had been parking on a residential street and loitering, which was uncomfortable and disruptive for the residents so the police were called. They were talking about how it wouldn't keep them away, but for the time being, they had a little peace.

Once that conversation ended, May turned to me and told me a bunch of funny encounters he'd had over the years with some of the crazier Sinners. I was cracked up in the back seat the entire time and I was so happy when he asked me to get in a selfie with him because I didn't have any pictures of us together as adults.

He put his arm around my shoulder, mashed our faces together, and we beamed like two fools.

"*Don't* post that."

We both looked at Risk who was glancing at us through the rearview mirror.

"Why not?" May questioned, sounding a little annoyed. "We're just smiling, main man."

"It's not about the picture, it's about what the crazy Sinners will think of you posting a picture with a woman. That shit will spread online like wildfire and she's *not* getting a spotlight placed on her for it."

I didn't think of that.

May slumped next to me. "Yeah, you're right." He looked at me. "I'm keeping the picture though, I like it."

I chuckled. "Send it to me, I like it too."

"What's your number?"

Before I had a chance to say a word, Risk recited my number perfectly. I said nothing as May tapped on his screen and sent the picture my way. I checked my phone, opened the message May sent and smiled at the picture, then saved it to my phone.

"I'm going to get it printed and put it in a frame."

"You're cute," May chuckled. "Save my number, we're not losing touch now that you and main man are speaking again."

I happily did as he asked. When we pulled up to Mary Well's I hung back as the guys climbed out of the car. Risk came around to the open door and looked in at me.

"Everything okay?"

I tilted my head. "How did you know my number?"

"Frankie," he snorted. "I knew it by heart, it's just stuck in my head."

"How did you know I still used that number though?" I quizzed. "It's been nine years, I could have changed it."

Risk lost his smile. "Lucky guess."

I wasn't buying it and he knew it.

"Risk."

He shifted.

"I've called you a few times over the years," he lifted a hand to his hair and ruffled it. "When I wanted to hear your voice, I'd call you then when you answered . . . I could never make myself speak so I hung up. I didn't do it a lot, just a few times. I swear."

My heart just about stopped.

"You missed me?"

Risk's eyes found mine. "Of course I missed you, Frankie."

"I missed you too."

His shoulders lost some of their tension.

"Stop dawdling! You both coming or what?"

"Yeah," Risk said over his shoulder to Hayes. "We're coming."

I hopped out of the car, Risk locked it up and the five of us strolled into a pretty empty Mary Well's, which wasn't all that surprising seeing that it was half nine at night and a weekday. Kids usually came in for late-night dinners more on the weekends and during the summer. Three booths were filled and they were all older couples. Anna Porter, Hannah's twin sister, and Deena were on shift. Deena was busy cleaning tables but the second Anna saw the guys, she nearly dropped dead on the spot. I had to jump out of the way to avoid being shoved aside by her.

Wide-eyed, I looked from Anna to the guys and found that they were all smiling down at her. She was taller than me by a good five inches, but she was still shorter than all of the guys. Risk was the tallest at six four, next came May at around six two and Hayes and Angel were easily six foot. Anna beamed their way.

"Oh my god! I love you *so* much," she said in a matter-of-fact voice to May. "Like, so much. I'm the *biggest* Sinner!"

May smiled, but it wasn't a smile he gave me or his friends, this was his ladykiller smile and I'd be damned if it didn't make me stare a little longer than what was deemed polite. I jumped when fingers stuck into my waist. I turned to a stone-faced Risk, who was towering over me like the giant he was. I was so focused on May that I didn't even notice him move behind me.

"Hello." I bit my cheek to keep from smiling. "How's the weather up there, lanky?"

Risk's tempting pale pink lips twitched.

"Do I have to worry about May becoming your favourite month?"

"With a smile like his?" I wiggled my eyebrows. "Hell, maybe."

Risk moved so fast that I had no time to react when he backed me up against the nearest booth. I burst into a fit of giggles when he pressed his fingers into my waist until I was twisting and pleading through my laughter for him to show me mercy. I was the kind of person who was a danger to everyone around them when I was being tickled and Risk knew it. When he stopped, he was grinning down at me. I lightly thumped his stomach, making him snort.

I looked from Risk to the others, the guys were grinning at us and Anna was still looking at May like he was a mythical creature that she wanted to lick. He glanced back at her, saw he was still her focus and he switched his smile back to the one he reserved for women who wanted him. He lowered his head down and bumped his nose against hers. Her eyes momentarily widened and she bobbed her head like there was no tomorrow to something he said. Like the snap of my fingers, she hurried over to Deena and hurriedly said something to her. Risk tossed the car keys to May who caught them with one hand.

Bewildered as to what was happening, I watched as May, and Anna, left the diner.

"Where is he going?" I wondered out loud. "I thought he was hungry."

"He is," Risk answered. "His food preference has just changed though."

I looked up at him. "He's going to eat somewhere else?"

"Yeah," he laughed. "Something like that."

My eyebrows furrowed and then just like that, I realised what was happening.

"Oh." I said. "Oh. *Oh.* He's disgusting."

I felt my face burn, but it was more because I was embarrassed of being so naive as to what May and Anna were going out to the car to do. I held no judgements, I had had two one-night stands before too . . . but Jesus. I at least had a few hours of conversation with the men before we got physical. May *was* Anna's favourite Blood Oath member though; she had gushed over him enough throughout the years so hell, good for her.

"I'll go and get an order pad and be right back."

I walked away before Risk could say a word. I saw Deena walk towards the booth the guys were settling into, likely coming to take our order, but I hurried over to her just so I had a second for my face to return to its normal colour.

"Can you *believe* Anna?" She shook her head. "That girl is gonna catch something one of these days, either an STD or a baby."

Probably, but it was her business so I kept mute.

"I'll take my booth's order, you relax for a few minutes."

"Thanks," Deena rolled her head onto her shoulders. "I've been holding my wee in for the last ten minutes."

When she went to the bathroom, I grabbed an order pad and pen from the cup holder by the till then returned to the booth I would share with the guys. A glance at the mirror on the wall above the booth showed my face was only slightly flushed.

"Okay, what d'you guys want to eat?"

Thankfully, the guys didn't tease me, they ordered what they wanted to eat instead. When it came to Risk ordering his drink, I raised a brow and said, "Cherry Coke?"

"Strawberry milkshake," he grinned. "With two straws."

I stared at him as he reminded me of our first date when I told him we should share a strawberry milkshake or romance was basically dead for me. I couldn't help but smile as I scribbled the words. When I had everyone's order jotted down, including my own, I glanced out of the window to the darkened car park.

"Maybe one of you should order for May for when he's . . . finished."

"He'll be a while." Risk kept his eyes on me. "He always is."

"Yeah," Angel chuckled. "He'll order something to go, he'll have a bigger appetite."

I felt like I had suddenly swallowed a rock because I could *not* have this conversation. I was such a chicken shit when it came to talking about sex. I was twenty-seven years old, but I felt like a little thirteen-year-old whenever someone mentioned it to me. I wasn't a prude, I just was so easily embarrassed by the topic.

"I'll go and give Joe the order."

I heard the guys laugh at me as I walked away and I had to talk myself out of running out the diner during the entire walk away from the booth. Instead of just hanging the order up, I entered the kitchen. Joe looked up, then down, then back up when he realised it was me and not Anna or Deena.

"Frank," he blinked. "What're you doing here?"

"I'm with Blood Oath," I jabbed my thumb over my shoulder. "We're here for dinner."

I hung our order up then glanced around the kitchen. Joe was a perfectionist. He cleaned as he worked so his station was always tidy. I knew I had nothing to do and that I was just stalling so I didn't have to go back out front but I shook my head, mentally pulled up my big-girl knickers and returned to the floor. When I reached the booth, I slid in next to Risk, but he didn't move over by much even though he had the room.

Our thighs were plastered together and I was very aware of it.

"So," I cleared my throat. "What's it like being famous?"

The three superstars snickered at me.

"It has its pros and its cons," Hayes answered. "We do what we love on a global stage, we're successful, we earn great money and we get to perform to Sinners everywhere and see the world at the same time."

"I feel a big but coming on."

"But," Hayes grinned. "We no longer have privacy with the level of fame we've reached. Everything we do in public is documented. We can't fuck up because if we do, it makes headlines. We have to watch our Ps and our Qs. People, if we're not careful about who we keep in our circle, use us for money, fame or exposure for their own career."

I frowned. "I don't like the cons."

"Neither do we," Angel winked. "But the pros outweigh the cons so we cope."

I glanced at Risk. "Do *you* cope?"

"Now I do," he answered. "These guys are my brothers, if I didn't have a good bond with them, I don't know if I would have been able to climb out of the hole I dug myself into."

I didn't want to bring up any bad memories for him so I nodded. I was as still as a statue when Risk lifted his left arm and draped it over the back of the booth. I could feel the material of his jumper brush against me. I found myself imagining him lowering his arm so it rested around my neck and shoulder. I would snuggle into him and stay there forever. I cleared my throat and mentally shook those thoughts away. We kissed, and I knew Risk wanted to continue to kiss me when he wanted, but I was certain that was more to do with the sexual tension between us more than him just wanting to hold me.

We both knew nothing could happen between us, nothing long-term anyway. Nothing had changed in our situation: my life was in Southwold and Risk's wasn't. It was rubbish, but that was just the way it was. I hated it, but I accepted it a long time ago. I was sure he had too.

"Frankie baby!"

I jumped as a voice hollered across the diner, when I turned and saw the owner of said voice, I groaned.

"Jesus, not now."

Before Risk, Hayes or Angel could ask what was wrong, I got up and walked over to the entrance. Sky Ekeles, a sixteen-year-old local, and frequent customer of Mary Well's, sent a beaming smile my way as I approached him. Sky, dumbly, liked me and he made it his business to stop by as often as he could to hang out with me while I was on shift. I hadn't seen him in a few days so I knew he'd want a cuddle.

"I'm not working right now, little boy." I came to a stop in front of the kid. "I'm with friends so you can't be here unless you're ordering and eating."

"I know, I just stopped in to see if you were here and since you are," he smirked, "I'll have my usual."

The audacity of him made me laugh.

"Sky—"

"One hug, you know that's all I want."

I sighed, long and deep. Sky smiled in response. He was so bloody cute and he knew it.

"One hug then you'll stop bothering me and go home?"

"Promise, this is a flying visit."

I grunted as I leaned forward and gave the little terror a hug. I called him little but he wasn't, he was five ten or eleven which meant I had to get on my tiptoes to give him a good squeeze. His hands instantly when to my lower back but he knew better than to let them slip any lower. I wasn't opposed to knocking some sense, and manners, into him and he knew it.

"Now." I grinned when we separated. "Get on home."

Sky winked as he jokingly brushed his knuckles over my jaw then turned and walked out of the diner. I shook my head as I watched the kid go. When I turned, my eyes automatically moved to Risk's and I wasn't surprised to find him watching me. His gaze was so intense, I found I couldn't keep eye contact. I was glad that Joe called my booth's order. Deena was back on the floor and she helped me bring over the plates of food. When everyone had their food, I slid back beside Risk and instantly picked up my burger and took a big bite out of it. No one said a word until I swallowed my food.

"Who's the kid?"

"Sky?" I answered Angel. "He's just a lad who pops in every so often, he thinks he fancies me."

"You don't think he likes you?" Hayes quizzed as he popped a chip into his mouth. "He seemed to be liking you just fine with his hands that low on your back."

I laughed it off.

"He's just a little boy," I said. "No harm, no foul."

We chatted about mundane things for the rest of our meal, which took us more than an hour to eat because we'd stop and laugh at something someone said. We spoke about the guys' upcoming Wembley shows, the new album and world tour they just announced and we spoke about their interview that they had done earlier in the day in London.

Everyone was too full for any dessert, but when May strolled into the diner with Anna ahead of him, I tried not to make it obvious that I knew exactly what they had been doing. Deena said something as Anna passed her by which caused Anna's face to glow bright red. May came up to our booth and both Angel and Hayes slotted to the right when Risk made no attempt to move so May could sit next to me.

"I'm starving."

I wasn't sure why, but those words being the first ones he spoke after having a quickie – if an hour and ten minutes was considered quick – didn't surprise me in the slightest.

"I'll go and get an order pad—"

"Annie's got it covered."

"Anna." I corrected. "Her name is *Anna*."

"Is it?" he blinked. "Shit, I called her Annie the whole time."

The men laughed, I didn't because I thought it wasn't a very nice thing to do. Risk seemed to pick up on this because he changed the subject. It was winding down to closing time and I was exhausted. Normally, when I wasn't working until closing, I came home from visiting Mum around nine and then I went right to bed. It was going on quarter to eleven and I was ready to fall asleep sitting up.

Anna brought May his food in a bag. He stood up to thank her with a full-on kiss right in the middle of the diner. I didn't know where to look so I settled on looking at my empty plate. I jumped when I felt a hot breath next to my ear.

"You're so fucking cute," Risk said. "I hope you know that."

He thought I was cute? I felt terribly embarrassed, not bloody cute.

I said goodbye to Anna, Deena and Joe and left the diner with the guys. I screamed with fright when a flash went off to my right. It was so bright that it startled me. I tripped over my own two feet and fell back, but arms caught me. There were half a dozen people suddenly around us, cameras flashing and voices talking loudly over one another. I could barely see. I didn't know what was going on. I was scared.

"Risk, how's Nora?" a male voice hollered. "Does she know you're on a date with another woman?"

"Who's your lady friend, May?" a woman shouted. "We saw you had some car-rocking fun a while ago."

"Fuck's sake," I heard May grumble as we all walked forward. "Can you move? We're trying to leave?"

I latched onto the arm that hooked around my waist.

"Back the fuck up, bitch!" Risk snapped at a woman who was shoving her camera in my face. "Get the *fuck* away from her!"

I suddenly found myself in the middle of the guys as we moved forward as one, and it made me feel less panicky because I knew that they were protecting me. Soon, we were inside the car and my grip on Risk was vice-like because I couldn't breathe. My wheezing was loud in the car. I was in the middle of an attack and I didn't even know it.

"Fuck! Hold on, baby. I'll make it better . . . Here, open."

It was Risk who spoke, my vision had blurred so I couldn't see his movements. I could only focus on trying to draw in a breath. I felt his hand on the back of my head then he forcefully pushed the head of an inhaler into my mouth. The second he pressed on it, I sucked down the medicine with eagerness. The familiar taste of it, as always, brought me great relief. Even before it began to work on my lungs, knowing I had my medicine allowed my brain to begin to calm down so I could get control of the attack. It felt like it took longer for me to be able to draw in a deep breath than usual, but eventually the pain faded and all that remained was the fear of what could have happened.

I was shaking like a leaf.

"I'm sorry," Risk held me to him, moved his hand to my lower back and began patting. "I'm so sorry, Frank."

He remembered . . . he remembered that patting my lower back comforted and calmed me. I couldn't believe that he remembered.

I hugged him as I continued to breathe in and out. That was all that mattered. Big breath in and another one out. Over and over. We remained that way for a few minutes. I realised when I straightened in my seat that Hayes was driving the car. Angel was in the front seat, but he was turned around so he could see me. He looked worried as he stared at me with dark, unblinking eyes. I was between Risk and May, they were in the middle of working together to put my seat belt around me and click it in place.

"Are you okay, Frankie?"

"I'm okay," I answered May. "I'm sorry."

"You have asthma." Risk clicked his tongue. "Having an attack is *not* your fault . . . tonight it was mine. Those motherfuckers wouldn't have crowded you if you weren't with me."

"Bollocks," May spit. "Don't put the fault of those arseholes on your shoulders, they're vultures. What they do is on them, not you."

May was absolutely right. I leaned into Risk, finding immense comfort in his arms when they came around me.

"They're not following us . . . yet."

"Just drop me and Frankie off at her cottage," Risk replied to Hayes. "I'll walk back to May's in a bit. They'll just hang around her house if they spot the car there."

"How would they know it's yours? Two of my neighbours have the same model, the colour is just a little different."

"They likely made a note of the number plate," Risk explained. "They normally do that so they can tell if they're following the right car."

That shocked me.

"That's insane," I spluttered. "Like stalking."

"We know." Risk frowned. "We call them vultures for a reason."

I tried to think of what all of this suddenly meant for my quiet, predictable life.

"Will my face be all over the internet soon?"

Risk was hesitant in replying, but eventually he said, "Probably."

"Oh."

"Look, so the stories don't run wild," he continued. "May will post that picture of you and him to his Instagram. He'll put something in the caption about you being like a sister to him. People will still speculate, but once it's clear that you aren't a romantic interest, the frenzy will pass after a day or two. It always does."

I was in disbelief.

"I had no idea you couldn't be seen with a woman without this kind of hassle."

"Where have you been?" May lightly teased. "It's been this way for years."

I didn't let him know that I purposely didn't keep up with information regarding the band. Not long later, Hayes dropped me and Risk off outside my home. We hurried inside in case we were followed. I didn't feel safe until the door was shut behind us. I went straight into my kitchen and flipped on the light.

"Oath," I called. "I'm home, baby boy."

Risk laughed when Oath came strolling out of my bedroom, looking like he had just woken up from a long nap. I picked him up when he brushed against the back of my legs. I knew Risk was by the doorway watching me, but I said nothing. That whole situation was surreal. I thought I knew what celebrities went through with the paparazzi but my experience with it first-hand told me how little of a clue I really had.

"You wanna talk about it?"

Risk's question lingered as I filled my kettle up with water, plugged it in and flipped it on.

"It's just weird," I said as I prepared two cups with tea-bags. "I never knew something like that could be so scary. I felt stuck, trapped."

"It sucks. I know."

"I'm sorry you have to deal with that all of the time."

"*I'm* sorry you had to experience it tonight. I'll be more careful with you out in public in the future . . . being home kind of makes me forget who we are, you know?"

I nodded because I understood what he meant. Everyone in town loved the guys because we were all so proud of them, but Risk was just Risk to us and he'd let that familiarity catch him off guard.

"Next time we're back here, we'll have security with us. Everything is a mite easier with our team."

I quickly understood the importance of having a security team. It would have made fending off the strangers with cameras a whole lot easier, that was for sure. I shook off the incident and put it behind me because dwelling did no one any good. I looked down and softly smiled. Oath was super cuddly, like he could sense I had had a bad night, so I snuggled him and kissed his head.

"My best boy." I nuzzled him. "Aren't you my best boy?"

When he meowed in response, Risk laughed.

"Why am I jealous of a cat?"

I put Oath down and he pattered over to where his food and water station was set up next to the doorway of the kitchen. He barely even glanced at Risk. Risk, on the other hand, was keeping an eye on him, which amused me.

"I don't know," I turned and leaned against the counter-top. "Why were you jealous of a sixteen-year-old boy hugging me in the diner tonight?"

I had wanted to ask him that question since I saw the way he looked at me after Sky gave me a hug. Risk's smile vanished at the mention of it.

"Let's put it down to a bad case of 'mine'."

That surprised me.

"Really?"

"Yeah," he answered. "It pissed me off to see that kid hugging on you. Do I have any right to feel that way? Nope. Do I still feel pissed off? Yep."

I crossed the space between us.

"Risk," I placed my hands on his arms. "You hear how silly this sounds, right? He's a *child*."

"I'm aware." His eyes searched mine. "I just . . . I don't like anyone touching you, Frankie."

Like he said, he had no right to feel that way, but it was crazy of me to like that he didn't want anyone touching me, whether it was a kid or a grown man. At the same time, it just confused the hell out of me. I had no idea what we thought we were doing. We had kissed on the pier and now Risk was admitting he didn't like a boy, or anyone, touching me. It was weird ground to walk on because we weren't in any sort of relationship and I had to remind myself of that.

I loved Risk but I had to remind myself that we had no future.

"Let's just forget about it, okay?" I smiled up at him. "You're leaving soon for London, I just want us to have fun and spend time with each other while you're here. No drama, no complications, just us being friends again. Okay?"

Risk nodded. "Okay."

We were both in agreement, but a voice in the back of my head told me that both of us . . . we were lying.

CHAPTER FOURTEEN
RISK

It was Friday, two days before we had to leave Southwold and go to London.

It was interesting to me that just days ago I was dreading coming home to Southwold because of Frankie, and now I was dreading leaving because of her too. A handful of days, that was all it took for her to mess my head up a million different ways. She said we were friends, but when I kissed her, she kissed me back somethin' fierce. When I hugged her body to mine, she squeezed me to the point of pain. When she looked at me, I saw emotion for me in her eyes. Or at least I thought I did. I wasn't sure if I was imagining her reactions to me because I wanted them to be real and not just some figment of my own imagination.

It was fucked up, but that was just the way things were.

"When we leave on Sunday," May said, interrupting my thoughts. "Are you gonna come back?"

"Come back after the gigs?"

"No," my friend replied. "Are you gonna *ever* come back?"

I looked from the road, to May, and back again.

"Of course," I answered. "I'm not leaving Frankie again."

I realised that I had made that decision the second I saw her in the PE hall of Sir John Leman's High School. Now that I had her back in my life, there was no way I could just carry on without her in it. I couldn't do it; I didn't want to either.

"See, *this* is where I'm confused." May sighed. "You don't live in England, you stay in your house in London for maybe a total of six weeks throughout a year. You don't live in Southwold *at all* . . . Frankie does."

My hands tightened around the steering wheel.

"I'm fully aware of all of that, May."

"Are you really?" he pressed. "I don't think you are, main man, because ever since she forgave you for being the world's biggest dickhead in the diner a few days ago, you've wanted to spend every minute of the day with her. I don't give a fuck what you say, you are not *just* friends. Even back when you *were* friends you were never really friends. You both have always just been . . . more."

He was right. Frankie and I had always been more, we could never be 'just friends' with one another. I knew that and deep down she knew that too.

"I don't know what to tell you, mate." I sighed. "I thought seeing her again would go differently. I thought maybe I'd see her and feel nothing and that I'd be able to fully move on from her with a clear head but *fuck*, May. She's all I can think about, I want her so badly I can't think straight."

"Want her how? For sex? As your girl? What?"

"All of the above." I grunted. "I want her, but I can't fucking have her. Nothing about our lives has changed. She couldn't cope with the thought of long distance before we blew up and now with me being famous, and having no privacy, I think any chance of her wanting to have a relationship with me is out of the window."

"So what the *hell* are you both doing?" May demanded. "I've been watching the pair of you. You're both gonna get in trouble, man. I can see it happening."

"Just leave it," I quipped. "Please, May. We agreed to spend time together and just enjoy one another until we leave on Sunday. I don't want to think beyond that, I just want to stay in the now with her. I just want this tiny bit of time with her. That's all."

My friend sighed deeply.

"This is gonna be bad, you know that . . . right?"

"Probably," I swallowed. "But I'll deal with whatever comes my way once I can have these few days with her."

"But what about when things go back to normal but this time you guys keep in contact? What about when she gets a man?"

Instinctively, my hands clenched around the steering wheel.

"Main man, you can't even handle the thought of her with someone else . . . what will you do when it actually happens?"

I couldn't answer him because I didn't know what I would do. Die, probably.

"She's still into me," I said. "I kissed her on the pier the other night and she kissed me back. She was hungry for me, man. She wants me as much as I want her, I know she does."

"That's great," May said, dryly. "But fuck all has changed. She's still in Southwold and you're not."

I remained silent.

"Let's say both of you realise you're right for each other and you can both do long distance until Frankie's situation changes with her mum because the woman is, I hate to say it, dying. Let's say you get back together . . . d'you really think Frankie can handle being thrust into our lifestyle? The paps, the fans, the white-hot spotlight on her life. After last night and how she reacted, I don't know if she can hack it, man."

May was speaking nothing but the truth and the weight of his words was crushing me.

"I *know* she's not meant for this life," I hissed. "She's a small-town girl, she can't come on tours and live in America and have a camera in her face whenever she leaves the house. I'm stupid for even thinking she can. I know this, May. I know. I just . . . I just can't stay away from her."

"You've given up one addiction for another."

"Don't ask me to quit on her," I glanced at him. "I can't do that."

"I'm not asking you to, man, I just don't want to see you back in that pit you were in. You broke my heart when you crawled your way down that hole before. I won't let you do that to yourself again. I won't."

I stopped at a red light and looked at my best mate.

"I never meant to hurt you, or anyone, with the shit I've done but I know I did. I found a reason to start my life over and that reason isn't Frankie, it was me. I got sober for *me*. If I get hurt over her again, I'll cope. I won't go back to that place. I promise, May."

He bumped his fist with mine and I knew he believed me when he nodded. We drove to Mary Well's then, we were both hungry for some breakfast and, of course, I wanted to see Frankie. Knowing she was working the morning shift at the diner made Mary Well's the obvious spot for us to head to. When we pulled up, my eyes widened. Out at the front of the diner, there was a police car. Joe, the owner of the diner and Anna, the waitress that May screwed, were speaking to an officer. May and I got out of car after I parked.

Anna spotted me and she glanced over her shoulder.

"Is everything okay, Anna?"

She looked back at me and nodded. "Just a little incident, everything is fine though."

"Where's Frankie?"

Anna jabbed her thumb over her shoulder. "She's inside."

"Go ahead," May said to me. "I'm gonna stay here for a bit."

Anna's attention shifted to May and just like that, I was forgotten. Without another word, I walked into the diner. I saw Frankie leaning over the counter next to the till, she was looking at something. When the doorbell rang, she turned. I smiled her way but the look I received in response caused that smile to falter. I approached her and she turned her back to me and began wiping down the counter. She wasn't a rude person so there had to be a reason for her to give me the cold shoulder.

"Hey, Frank."

She mumbled a response that wasn't coherent to me.

"Is everything okay?" I questioned. "Joe is out front talking to—"

"I *said* I'm busy and I can't talk. Are you deaf?"

I didn't even have a second to ask what was wrong, but I knew *something* was wrong. Frankie turned and walked directly into the kitchen of the diner. The ice in her tone had caught me off guard. I watched her go for a moment before I snapped out of it and followed her. She was in the kitchen on her own and from what I could see when I entered the diner, the place was devoid of customers. It was just the pair of us.

"What's going on?"

"Staff only!" Frankie jumped with surprise, turned to face me and quickly put her hand behind her back. "You shouldn't be in here."

I frowned. "What's happened?"

"Nothing," Frankie blurted. "Nothing happened, so you" – she glared at me – "can leave."

I bristled at her tone.

"I'm going nowhere until you tell me what the fuck is going on."

"Don't you speak to me like that, Risk Keller," she snapped. "Get out."

Joe and Anna entered the kitchen just as Frankie shouted at me.

"Frankie," I said firmly. "What the fuck did I do?"

"Stop cursing!"

Christ.

"Tell me what I did to piss you off so much and I will. And while you're at it, tell me why the police are here."

Joe and Anna glanced at one another, then left the kitchen without a word spoken, leaving us alone once more. I was getting more and more pissed off by the second so I crossed the space between us.

"What. Happened?"

"Nothing." She shifted her stance. "I handled it."

"Handled it?" I repeated. "What the fuck is '*it*'?"

"Stop. Cursing."

I felt the muscles roll back and forth in my jaw as I stared down at Frankie.

"So help me, if you don't tell me—"

"You'll what?" she interrupted. "Write a horrible song about me? Too late, you've already bloody done that."

I felt as if I had been punched in the gut because I knew instantly what song she was referring to.

"Don't even deny it," she continued. "I know it's about me."

"You're talking about 'Cherry Bomb'?"

"Yes." Frankie sneered. "Real classy, Risk."

I lifted my arm and ran my hand through my hair.

"Why're you bringing it up now and not the night when I came by to apologise to you? We've been cool since then."

"Because I didn't listen to it until today. It was on the radio."

That surprised the hell out of me.

"That record was on our last album, it came out two years ago."

"Oh." Frankie held up her hands in mock defeat. "Am I supposed to *not* be pissed because I've only just heard it?"

"No." I held her gaze. "I'm sorry."

"That's bollocks and you know it," I snapped. "You wrote that to be hateful and cruel!"

She was upset. She was shouting at me and she looked meaner than a bee-stung dog, but I could see the hurt in her green eyes. She was sad . . . my song made her sad. If there was one record I regretted writing, cutting and releasing it was 'Cherry Bomb'. Christ, any time I thought about it, it left a bitter taste in my mouth.

"I didn't write it to be cruel and hateful," I said, trying to keep my voice calm and collected. "I didn't, Frankie."

"Bullshit," she practically growled. "I listened to every word, you evil bastard. Fuck you! We're not gonna be friends or anything of the sort. Get the fuck out of my life and stay the *fuck* away from me, you arsehole!"

In all the years that I had spent remembering Frankie, I forgot how mad she could get once she got going.

"Frankie, listen—"

"No!" she shouted. "No, Risk. D'you know what it feels like to have a song like that written about you? A song millions of people have listened to?"

She was right, millions of people had listened to it, I just didn't understand how *she* hadn't listened to it. Frankie was the original Sinner. Back in the day, she had been in the studio for each record we laid on our EP, and most of the records on our first album that were finished ahead of time, too. She heard our music over and over and she always did so with a smile on her gorgeous face. On one hand I was glad she hadn't heard 'Cherry Bomb' up until now, but on the other, it rattled my very soul to think there was a record of mine that she didn't hear.

I spoke to her through my records; if she didn't listen to them . . . how would she ever hear me?

"Why didn't you listen to it before today?"

Her eyes flashed with an emotion I couldn't decipher.

"Because I knew it was about me," she suddenly said. "'Cherry Bomb'. Even a dumb small-town girl like me could figure it out. We had broken up; I was scared to hear what you had to say about me."

Hearing her explanation made the weight that had settled on my chest lift instantly. She listened to my records, to my words . . . she just couldn't listen to 'Cherry Bomb' until now, and I couldn't blame her.

"I was right to feel that way. Wasn't I, rock star?"

"Yes," I answered. "You were, but if you let me explain—"

"No. Get out."

"Listen. To. Me." I raised my voice. "I wrote it when I felt angry and upset and was fucking *missing you*!"

"Missing me?" she repeated with harsh laughter. "I wonder which part of me you missed. Oh, I think I know. How do the lyrics go? 'My cherry bomb's hips keep me awake at night, she's got an ass that'd make a holy man cry. Big enough for me to take a bite,' and those are the nicest lyrics in the fucking song! You went on to objectify me to nothing more than a body that you missed fucking."

"Frankie—"

"I don't wanna hear it, you *prick*!" she bellowed. "All this time I've wished you nothing but the best and you've been objectifying the memories you have of me for the whole fucking world to hear. I can't believe you would do that to me, Risk. I just can't!"

I felt like the room was closing in around me.

"That's the only record where I've *ever* talked about you in that way and it was only because I was hurting. Fuck, Frank, I wrote that shit when I was out of it. I snorted coke and drank my weight in vodka that night. I can't even remember cutting the fuckin' thing."

She recoiled the second the words left my mouth.

"Stupid idiot," she spat. "You'll kill yourself ingesting all of that poison. Is that what you want? To die? You bloody dope. You think you're some big-time hot shot because you're famous? Well, you're still the stupid boy I've always known, but at least that boy didn't take drugs!"

I stared down at her and I surprised us both when a chuckle left my mouth.

"This isn't funny, wazzock!" She reached out and shoved me. "This is your life, you *don't* get to risk it like that. D'you understand me?"

"Yeah, Frank," I said. "I hear you."

"You don't look like you do. What's so funny?"

"You are." I shook my head. "All five foot nothing of you is ready to kick my arse because I said I took drugs."

It was dumb of me to be so happy that she still cared enough about to get angry over my drug use and alcohol consumption. She could have brushed over those facts or ignored them completely, but she called me out on my wrongdoing in true Frankie Fulton fashion.

"Only stupid people take that squit. I didn't think you were stupid. Or at least not *that* stupid."

"Frank, why are you going off on me only now about what I've done with drugs?"

"Because I'm mad at you and I might as well get everything that pisses me off about you off my chest!"

"Okay," I rubbed my hand over my mouth. "I get it. I'll be quiet while you rail on me."

Her eyes narrowed to slits. "I can't think of anything else."

When I laughed, she shoved me again, but this time there was no anger behind it.

"I'm sorry," I repeated and lifted my hand to my necklace. "I swear I am. That record . . . we don't play that shit on stage anymore and I cringe if I hear it on the radio. I pretend it doesn't exist."

"Really?"

"Really." I nodded. "I wish I never wrote it, never sang it . . . I never will again. I promise you."

Frankie exhaled. "And your drink and drug problem? I've never brought it up because I didn't want to upset you, but I'm so mad right now that I don't care. I won't have you in my life if you take that poison again. I swear, Risk."

"I've been sober from both for six months, remember? I've got my coin to prove it."

She stared at my coin then flicked her gaze to mine.

"*Stay* sober and I'll be impressed."

"I'm working on it every day, Frank."

She nodded, satisfied with my answer.

"You didn't mean what you said right?"

"What'd I say?"

"About me getting out of your life."

She sighed, long and deep. "No, I didn't, I'm just really mad at you."

"Then take it back," I prompted. "Tell me you want me in your life."

I needed to hear those words to feel like I could breathe.

"I take it back," she frowned. "I didn't mean it. Of course I want you in my life, you big dope."

I relaxed. She reached out with her right hand to lean on the counter-top, but instantly she hissed and brought her hand up to her face and thoroughly inspected her palm. Her *bloody* palm.

"What the *fuck* happened to you?"

"I cut myself."

She said it as casually as wishing me a good morning.

Frankie turned and walked over to the other side of the kitchen and retrieved the first aid kit from its spot on the wall. It was clearly difficult for her to unzip it with one hand but she didn't have to worry about it for much longer because I moved behind her, plucked the kit from her hands without a word, barely a second later. With a grumble, she turned to face me and sighed. She knew she wasn't going to win this battle with me so she didn't even bother to start arguing.

Out of the corner of my eye, I saw she cradled her injured hand against her chest while I removed the items I would need and placed them on the counter. Silently, I held out my hand and when she didn't give me hers, I rolled my eyes. I turned my head, looked at her and waited. Slowly, Frankie moved her trembling, injured hand towards mine and when my fingers skimmed over the back of her hand, she shuddered. I gripped her wrist and turned her hand over so I could see her palm.

"Just put a gauze and bandage on it. It's only a little cut, it'll stop bleeding soon."

I didn't look up at her as I said, "There's dirt in it."

It wasn't a deep cut but it was wide and just over an inch long. I knew it was hurting her and I wanted to do nothing more than quickly bandage it so it could begin to heal, but I had to clean it first.

"I could just run it under the tap," she hurriedly suggested. "That would clean any dirt away."

She was scared, which didn't surprise me; she never did have a high threshold for pain.

"Or you could be a big girl and let me clean your hand correctly so you don't get an infection and have to get your hand amputated down the line because you were too chicken to let me do what needs to be done."

She squeaked. "You're such a little prat, I hope you know that."

I made a point not to smile.

"Can I please clean your hand?"

"Oh, go on then! And be quick about it!"

I grabbed a small, sterile bottle of water. I twisted off the cap and poured it onto her hand. Frankie didn't make a sound. The water just washed away some surface dirt. It was the alcohol wipes that I knew she was worried about. I was worried about them too; I was sober and I hadn't been around alcohol of any kind since my stint in rehab. I was worried that the strong smell of the wipe would tempt me but I figured I needed to be tested because I couldn't go through my life hiding from drink. Like a hawk, Frankie watched as I ripped one of the packets open and removed the tiny, white antiseptic sheet. The smell was strong but I was relieved to find it didn't give me the urge to find the nearest bottle and down it. I focused on Frankie. I didn't give her a moment to prepare for the pain, I simply shook the sheet out and pressed it against her cut and rubbed away any visible embedded dirt.

Frankie's whole body jerked and I had to hold onto her tightly to keep her from going anywhere.

"Bastard!" she shouted. "Son of bloody whore!"

"My mum probably was a whore," I mused. "So you're not far off."

I angled my hips away because I wouldn't have put it past Frankie to whack me in the bollocks. She didn't move though. She remained still as a statue and because of her compliance, I hurried through cleaning away any remaining dirt in her cut. A couple of minutes later, and I was done. I raised Frankie's small hand to my face and gently blew on her cut which made her release a sound very similar to a sigh. I didn't look at her as I opened a package of gauzes and pressed one against her palm and sealed it in place by wrapping a small bandage around her hand before I grabbed a safety pin from the first aid kit and clipped the bandage in place.

"Thank you."

The sincerity in her tone told me her anger had cooled off dramatically in the last few minutes. I nodded, then gathered the empty plastic packets I'd used and put them into the bin next to me. I knew Frankie expected me to leave but there was no way in hell that that was happening. There was something going on at Mary Well's. Joe was speaking to the police, Deena too, the place was empty of customers and Frankie had somehow cut her hand. She said she 'handled it' and I wanted to know what the fuck 'it' was.

"You need to leave." She looked anywhere but at me. "Staff only."

"How'd you hurt your hand?"

"For God's sake." She huffed. "You're a persistent little shit."

"That's twice you've called me little."

"Does that hurt your *little* boy feelings?"

She was trying to be mean and engage me in an argument to distract me from what I wanted to know and it wasn't working.

"*You're* the one with the nickname 'little', Pippin. Not me."

"Don't come for my height today, Groot," she warned. "I'm not in the mood."

I moved closer to her, enjoying the widening of her eyes and the seductive little O that her rose-red lips made.

"Then tell me what happened to your hand," I pressed. "You said you 'handled it'. Tell me what 'it' was. Does it have something to do with the police being here?"

Frankie's sigh told me she was going to answer me, she always had little tells I copped before she actually did, or said, something.

She was the easiest person in the world for me to read, she always had been.

"Joe wants you and the rest of the band to be able to come in and enjoy your food without fans asking for pictures or autographs or anything like that. He put it up on Mary Well's social media that while you guys are at his diner, you are not to be hassled. There's a sign on the front door too."

I must have missed that. "He did?" I tilted my head and smiled. "That's kind of him. I appreciate that and I know the lads will too."

"Yeah, well, not everyone is so inclined to listen to Joe," she grumbled. "A man walked in through the back about forty minutes ago. He offered me one hundred pounds to let him get close enough to sneak some pictures of you eating in here without you and the others knowing. I said no and told him to get out. He tried to offer me more money so I grabbed the mop and warned him to leave. He got super annoyed at me, grabbed the mop and pulled on it. I lost my balance and fell. I banged my knee and cut my hand when I fell."

I wasn't a temperamental person; despite what a lot of people thought about me, I wasn't one who was quick to anger. However, listening to what Frankie had just told me made me question myself because rage was quick to flow through my veins at the thought of someone harming my girl. A voice in the back of my head reminded me that she wasn't my girl and I wanted to scream at it to shut up, but I put all of my focus on Frankie instead.

She must have seen the anger in my eyes because she put her hands on my forearms.

"It's fine. I'm fine," she assured me. "Joe came in and threw the man out by the scruff of his neck and Anna called the police. I doubt he'll try anything like that in here again."

How naive she was irritated me.

"Are you serious right now?" I demanded. "You doubt he'll try anything like that again . . . ? You don't know the man or what he will and won't do, Frankie."

Frankie frowned. "The police were called."

"That doesn't mean shit to paps," I stated. "D'you know how many warnings they get for doing shit like this to people connected to celebrities. Some of them even get arrested but they don't care once they get a good picture or piece of footage."

She didn't respond.

"Listen to me." My voice was firm. "*Never* get in the way of these people over me ever again. D'you understand me? The paps are vultures, just one good picture of me, or the guys, doing something they think is wrong is enough for them keep the lights on in their houses for a couple of months. People will do anything for money and me and the guys bring them money."

She scoffed with frustration.

"So I'm supposed to *let* strangers who want to exploit you for money just waltz in here like they own the place?"

"Just turn a blind eye to them; everyone else does."

"I'm not everyone else, Risk! I won't let someone do that shit to you if I can help it."

I couldn't believe it when her voice cracked, and neither could she, telling by the wide-eyed expression that washed over her beautiful face. She hurriedly turned her back to me and headed straight for the back door of the kitchen, but she barely made it two steps before my hands touched her shoulders and turned her back around. My gut clenched when a tear fell from her eye and trickled down her cheek.

"Why're you crying?"

She reached up and swiped away the lone tear immediately.

"I'm not."

I stared down at her, blankly.

"Fine, I am," she looked down at her feet. "I just hate that you can't even eat a meal in peace without someone bothering you. All those strangers want something from you, you giving them songs should be enough. I don't like it. If I can stop one of them from exploiting you then I will and I don't want to hear a word about it from you either!"

She tried to move past me, but I blocked her from doing so.

"What?" she hissed. "If you're gonna shout at me, just do it. I'm not gonna change my mind and there's nothing you can—"

I had enough of her running her mouth so I shut her up with a kiss.

A kiss that to anyone else would have looked chaste and innocent, but to me made my body weak and my head spin. My heart was just about to burst when Frankie parted her soft lips and her warm, wet tongue tangled with mine. I never knew someone could taste so familiar, but Frankie did. She reached up and wrapped her arms around my neck and pulled my body flush against hers. Like when we kissed on the pier, Frankie's mouth devoured mine in a heated frenzy. I wanted to kiss her all over, to touch her, to strip her naked and feel the heat of her tight cunt wrapped around my cock as I sunk inside her. A little taste of her wasn't enough. I had been craving her taste, her touch, her very presence for far too long.

It was a fine line I walked, nothing about our situation had changed, but I wanted her more than my next breath.

"Shit, sorry!"

Frankie jumped away from me like I was an open flame.

We both looked towards the door of the kitchen that was flapping shut. The voice of the person belonged to May so I wasn't bothered, but Frankie was red-faced at being caught kissing me. I got back in her space, lifted my hands to her cheeks and ran my fingertips over her hot, flushed skin. I noticed the bruising around her eye was starting to change colour. The darkness was fading to a yellow, green colour. It was healing.

"You're so beautiful." I smiled. "I love when you're embarrassed, your face glows like Rudolph's nose. You really are my little cherry."

Frankie sucked in a strangled breath as she pressed forward and hid her face against my chest, making me laugh.

"Only you could go from spitting mad to embarrassed in space of a few minutes." I chuckled. "God, I've missed you."

Her arms came around my waist and she held me tightly.

"You came by for breakfast, right?"

"Yeah." I said. "I wanted to see you too."

Frankie stepped back, cheeks still glowing as she said, "Come on, let's go get you settled and I'll take your order."

"May'll be happy." I grinned. "He's starving."

I followed her out of the kitchen. Joe, Anna and May were leaning against the service counter and when they saw us both, each of them relaxed.

"Thank God," Joe said, placing a hand on his chest. "I'd thought you were gonna kill him."

"Me too," Anna bobbed her head. "I've never heard you curse or shout so much, Frankie. You're pretty scary when you get going."

"Like I said, gorgeous," May said to Anna. "The littlest dogs always have the biggest fight in them."

Frankie rolled her eyes, I chuckled.

"Let's just put what happened behind us," she said. "What did the police say?"

"They took our statements after you gave yours when they first arrived and I filed a report. I've given them access to our security cameras so they can extract the footage of the man attacking you."

"He didn't *attack* me," Frankie stressed, glancing at me. "He just . . . pulled the mop and I fell."

"That fucker was trying to intimidate you," Joe stated. "He trespassed, and if they catch him I'm pressing charges."

I was in full agreement with Joe but I knew from experience that the paps could get away with a whole lot worse than trespassing and intimidating someone. I didn't tell that to Frankie though, she wanted to forget about it.

"Let's just get on with our day. Look," – she pointed at the doorway – "we have customers coming."

It turned out the customers were a group of teenage Sinners who were wearing our band's merchandise. Straight away, Joe told them not to hassle me or May and they listened. Since it was only a small group of five, May and I decided to get in some pictures with them and sign their T-shirts.

"Can you take our picture?" a kid asked Frankie. "Please."

"Sure." She took the phone happily, stepped back and said, "Say cheese."

"*Cheese*." Everyone echoed and smiled.

My smile was the biggest because as Frankie took the picture, I realised that she was smiling wide as well, like she was in the picture rather than taking it. It was so fucking cute.

"Risk." She gave me a pointed look. "Look at the *camera*."

"Sorry." I grinned. "I'm looking now."

She took a couple more pictures, then May and I sat in booth one and Frankie took our order while Anna took care of the kids. I felt them staring at us, but a couple of glances showed they didn't have their phones pointed our way which was a nice change. Frankie took down our orders; we each wanted a full English. She came back about ten minutes later with large plates of food. May put his phone down and I noticed he was scowling as Frankie placed our food in front of us.

"What is it?"

"I was on Twitter."

Uh-oh.

"And some cocksucker said our music is basic. He actually said playing our songs are easy." May grunted. "The fucking clown."

Frankie snorted. "They *are* easy-peasy to play."

I nearly broke my neck jerking my head so I could stare at Frankie, who flushed under my and May's wide-eyed stares.

"*You* can play our songs on guitar?" I asked, feeling my balls tingle. "Think very carefully before you answer because I'm going to get a hard-on in public if you say yes."

Frankie's eyes darted down, but the table blocked her view of my groin, so she flicked her gaze back up to mine and shrugged her shoulders.

"I can play them on Guitar . . . God."

When May and I shared a look we promptly burst into laughter, Frankie's lips twitched as she folded her arms across her chest.

"Oh. So you two think that doesn't count, huh?"

"Frankie girl," May tittered, shaking his head. "Guitar God is a *game*."

"I bet I could beat you on expert on *any* Blood Oath song on Guitar God," she challenged. "I could play circles around you even *with* an injured hand, March."

"Oh, mate," I baited May. "I *know* you aren't gonna let Samwise Gamgee call you out like this."

The hobbit reference didn't bother Frankie. I had called her Bilbo, Frodo, Samwise, Merry and Pippin for as long as I could remember. I was sure I had dubbed her with the names of the entire population of The Shire at some point in her life.

"You're on, dwarf." May narrowed his hooded eyes. "You're gonna regret challenging me, Fulton. It's on like fuckin' Donkey Kong!"

CHAPTER FIFTEEN
FRANKIE

I should have known better than to challenge May Acton.

After a pretty outrageous morning at work, I shouldn't have been surprised to find myself in May's sitting room at half nine in the evening. After Risk and May had had their breakfast, May demanded I accept his challenge to a Guitar God duel. My threat of playing circles around him really riled him up. It didn't help that Risk was whispering in his ear, baiting him every chance he got. I accepted the challenge with a smile. Risk and May left not long after and I put the duel out of my mind as I worked. I finished my shift at three, went to the hospice and spent time with my mum until half seven, then I hit McDonald's drive-thru on the way to May's house. I got there at eight sharp and I shouldn't have been surprised to find that May had been out and purchased a Guitar God console and accessories, but I was.

I walked into the sitting room and stared at the massive plasma screen on the wall. The room wasn't very big, and the TV took up most of the space on the wall above the fireplace. The game's home screen was opened, and every single one of the instrumentals for every Blood Oath song available on the game's online store was on the screen.

I know to the guys, and everyone else, Guitar God was a silly game people played to pass the time. To me, it was so much more. I was a Sinner before Sinners had a name. I loved Blood Oath's music, I loved rock and roll, but when Risk and I broke up, I had to cut Blood Oath out of my life to keep my sanity . . . then Guitar God was released.

I couldn't hear Risk sing or listen to the lyrics he wrote, that was entirely too much to ask of myself. Blood Oath's music, however, was a different thing altogether. I knew they all had a hand in writing the music to their songs, so knowing I could hear their music on Guitar God was like getting the chance to peek into a window of Blood Oath's life to see how they were doing.

Blood Oath didn't release instrumentals of their albums until recently so Guitar God gave me the chance to hear them . . . without hearing Risk. It connected me to the band, to Risk, in a safe capacity. I loved the game for that reason alone.

There was only one song I wasn't very good at on the game. It just so happened to be 'Cherry Bomb', the song Risk wrote about me when he was in a bad mental space. Ever since I had heard it, I tried desperately to forget the lyrics that made my heart clench. I know it was about me and that I should have never listened to it. It was like my subconscious knew I'd hate it.

I really hoped that song wasn't picked because I was supposed to show May up, not let him show me out.

"Have you been practicing, December?"

May snorted at my question and jabbed his thumb in the direction of the guys. "*They've* been playing most of the day, I've been biding my time until you showed up. I don't need practice to beat you, little girl."

I snorted. "We'll see about that, big boy."

Risk grinned happily from the sofa, when my eyes slide to his, he crooked his finger, beckoning me his way. I was in front of his parted thighs before I realised I had moved. I leaned down so I could give him a hug, but Risk surprised me by kissing my lips.

"Missed you."

His words were murmured, but I heard them. Felt them.

"Missed you too."

I straightened, hugged the others in greeting then I put my game face on as I removed my coat, draping it over the arm of the chair.

"I should get to choose the song." I looked at May as I picked up one of the toy guitars and hooked its strap over my head. "Ladies first and all that jazz."

May rolled his eyes, his guitar already in his hands and positioned.

"Like that's gonna help you, midget."

"I'm gonna take pleasure in this, August." I narrowed my eyes. "Risk, record this for proof."

"On it, Cherry."

May glanced over his shoulder. "Proof of *what*?"

"Of me," I said when his eyes returned to mine, "spanking you like the little bitch you are."

All of the guys burst into loud, gleeful laughter at my threat, even May was giggling like a little girl with his hand over his mouth. Their laughter was fuel to the fire May ignited within me. Their lack of faith in me was all I needed to want to whoop May from here all the way to London and back again. I turned my focus to the flat screen on the wall and gave it my complete focus. I was good at Guitar God, I had racked up hundreds of hours playing Blood Oath songs and I was about to prove just how good I really was.

"'Black Space'." I selected the song I wanted to play. "*That* is my song choice. You ready, little dick?"

May sucked in a dramatic breath.

"That was *hurtful,* you little piece of bum fluff, and for the record," he growled. "My dick is *huge*, thunder thighs!"

I tried not to laugh but it was hard because May's clapbacks were always so quick and personal but so funny at the same time. He bloody well knew it, too.

"My thunder thighs keep me warm at night so with your next insult, make sure it cuts deep, Nutty Professor."

The guys were a mess of laughter behind us, we didn't pay them a lick of attention. May's eyes narrowed at me, but his lips twitched repeatedly, which told me he was trying to keep a straight face as much as I was. That was the thing about me and May, we insulted one another brutally, but we never meant it and we both knew it. Nothing had changed between us since we were kids, it seemed.

"We talking, or jamming?"

"Jamming."

"Loosen your arms then," he ordered. "They're too stiff, don't grip the guitar like it's a weapon. Hold it against you warmly. Love it, caress it."

I looked down at the plastic toy.

"This is too big for me to caress."

"I've heard those words often," May winked. "Just start with the tip, everything else comes easy after that."

"May!" My face burned. "I'll hurl this guitar at your head. Don't embarrass me!"

Laughter filled the room once more and I considered using the guitar as an object to bludgeon May to death with. He was getting entirely too much joy from my red face.

"How's this?" I followed his instruction and mirrored the way he held his guitar. "Do I look like a rock chick now?"

"There's not a scrap of black eyeliner on your face or a stitch of black clothing on that curvy body of yours so *nope*."

I rolled my eyes.

"Not *every* girl Sinner looks like a princess of darkness," I told him. "Some of us are Plain Janes, thank you very much."

"There isn't a plain thing about you, gorgeous."

I looked over my shoulder to Risk. He was sitting on the sofa with Hayes and Angel. He held his phone up, pointing it in mine and May's direction but his eyes were lowered to my behind and when they lifted to mine, he grinned when he saw he had been caught checking me out. I had known for a long time that Risk was an arse man, it was lucky for me, really. I had a fat bum, but my breasts were non-existent. The curse of a pear-shaped body meant I was a head member of the itty bitty titty committee.

"Behave."

"Hell no, Cherry."

I looked at May and cocked my eyebrow.

"Ready to play, May boy?"

"Always, Frankie girl."

We positioned ourselves and just before I hit start I said, "Your arse is *mine*, Acton."

The song began and because it was on expert level, every single chord appeared on screen in time to the original song. No mistakes were allowed. You had to strum at the right time, hit the right chord and hold it for the correct amount of seconds before moving on. Expert level was all about precision, May obviously didn't bank on that. I hit fifteen perfect notes in a row, he only hit nine. I got a lot of greats and so did he, but he got a couple of misses as well which reflected in our scores that were in the top left and right corners of the screen.

I glanced at May and grinned, he was struggling. His tongue was sticking out of the corner of his mouth, his eyebrows were furrowed and his eyes were unblinking as he gave the game his complete and utter focus.

"Stop looking at me!" he shouted. "You're distracting me on purpose."

"I'm just adoring May Acton in action . . . sort of. You kind of suck if I'm being honest."

The guys behind us barked with laughter. May told them all to suck his dick.

"Boy, she's *whooping* you," Hayes chortled. "This is the best fucking thing I've ever seen."

"Try the sexiest," Risk's voice rasped. "Christ, this is so fucking hot."

"Shut up, Risk!" I barked at the same time May said, "Mate, shut *up*!"

When the song wound to an end a couple of minutes later, it was obvious that I was the clear victor. When the results showed on screen, May glared at them like they were all that was evil in the world. I got an A and he got a C. For a beginner on expert, that was a bloody *insane* score . . . but for a famous musician who lived and breathed his guitar, this was like pouring salt on an open wound. I knew it and so did everyone else. I tried not to gloat . . . too much.

"Guitar God isn't for the faint of heart." I reached up and patted him on the shoulder. "Anyone could lose. Don't take it so hard, honey."

May cast a look of unchecked fury in my direction. "I helped *write* the fucking song, Frankie."

"Well, in that case . . . you're rubbish."

May gripped his guitar so hard the plastic creaked under the sudden strain of pressure. He looked me up and down. Slowly. His eyes were calculating and I found myself willing to pay a lot of money just to know what the hell was going on inside of his head.

"I've killed men for less than that, Fulton."

I grinned. "You have?"

"In my head I have!" he hissed as he righted his plastic guitar. "Rematch. Now, hobbit."

I shrugged and turned my head back towards the screen with a grin.

"It's your funeral, June bug."

CHAPTER SIXTEEN
FRANKIE

"For as long as I live, I'm *never* gonna let him forget that." Risk was still laughing when we entered my cottage two hours later. "You whooped him *four times in a row*. He was so mad he smashed the plastic fucking guitar on the ground. Hayes had to stop him from picking you up and throwing you out of the fucking house. I couldn't even move I was laughing so much. Angel was *crying*!"

Risk had to rub away the tears that gathered in his eyes.

"May's so funny, but my *god*," I chuckled. "He is the worst kind of sore loser, I never knew he was so competitive."

"You've got that right." Risk sighed happily. "Can I use your bathroom?"

"Of course." I entered my kitchen and flipped on the light. "Would you like me to give you directions? My house is gigantic; getting lost is a serious problem."

Risk snorted. "I'll manage."

He walked down the short hallway and walked into the open bathroom. I forgot to tell him that sometimes Oath liked to sleep in the bathtub, but he realised that as soon as he flipped the light on and yelped with fright. I heard a hiss then a whole load of movement. Oath scampered into the kitchen and jumped directly onto my stomach. Since I was standing up, he hooked his nails into my clothing to hang on tight. I felt every single one of those nails scrape against my skin. I winced as I took Oath in my arms and gently pulled on him until his claws released the fabric of my uniform.

"It's okay, baby boy." I kissed and snuggled his head. "Did the big bad man scare you?"

"Scare *him*?" Risk asked from the doorway, his tone incredulous. "*I* nearly pissed myself."

I laughed. "Are *you* okay, baby boy?"

"Maybe you should kiss and snuggle me and I will be."

I laughed. "Go to the bathroom."

He grinned then left the room once more. Without even thinking about it, I filled the kettle with water and prepared two cups with tea-bags. I put Oath down on the floor and he pattered over to his food and water station. While Risk was in the bathroom, I cleaned out his litter tray and put the bag of dirt in the bin outside. When I returned, Risk was in the kitchen. He was leaning his bum against the counter, staring at Oath.

"Look at him eyeing me while he eats his food," Risk said. "He isn't blinking."

Oath was doing exactly that.

"He's not used to anyone. Especially not someone like you."

"Like me?"

"I'm small and soft spoken, you're definitely *not*. You're not a skinny, lanky kid anymore." I titled my head. "You're different."

"Different how?"

"Well." I raked my eyes over his body. "You're a man now."

When I moved my gaze back to Risk's, I swallowed. He was staring at me so intently it caused a soft pulse to thrum between my thighs. I was very aware of how alone I was with him and it was a nightmare trying to keep my head out of the gutter. I couldn't stop my mind from conjuring dirty, explicit visuals that played on repeat. I wanted to touch him so much it actually hurt. I need to cool down dramatically so I turned around and busied myself with making us tea just to give me something to do with my hands.

"I'm still the same person inside," Risk said. "I don't think I look that different either."

He *had* to be joking.

"*Puh-lease*," I snorted. "Your entire body is different. You've got muscles in places you didn't before and I know you said you're the same height, but I swear you're taller."

"I'm not, I'm just broader."

"Well, you make me feel even tinier than you used to."

"Because you're a little slip of a woman," Risk murmured. "I could fit you in my pocket."

"I'm thirteen pounds heavier than when I was in school," I teased. "I doubt you could still lift me—"

I sucked in a sharp breath as I was suddenly picked up from behind. A lone arm was around my waist and I clung onto it for dear life. Risk laughed when I slapped said arm as he lowered me back to the ground.

"I did that with one arm," his breathy voice drifted into my ear. "You were saying?"

His body brushed against my back before he stepped away and I could have sworn my legs turned to jelly because I had to grip onto the counter to keep upright. I pretended that the surprise of him lifting me up was the reason and not that him touching me was almost my undoing.

"I nearly shat myself, Risk Keller." I turned and glared at him as he leaned his arse against my kitchen counter and folded his arms across his chest, grinning my way. "I almost got air sick!"

Risk tipped his head back and laughed, and the visual, as well as the sound, made me smile too. His tone was so musical that even his laughter sounded like a beautiful melody. I loved his laugh. I remembered how I used to crave hearing it when I was younger. It would make my heart happy . . . it still did.

"You were barely off the ground."

"I was a whole foot higher off the ground than what I'm used to . . . you *know* I'm scared of heights."

Risk was so amused that he snorted.

"Remember," I pointed dangerously. "I'm closer to a certain part of you that I could punch before you could blink."

Risk's demeanour changed completely and I quickly realised I just spoke about his dick.

"Punching my cock isn't very nice."

I practically jolted the second the word passed his lips.

"*Don't* say that word," I scolded. "It's so . . . dirty."

Risk's eyebrows rose and a mischievous glint filled his ice-blue eyes.

"Is it now?"

I turned back to the cups and fidgeted with them as the kettle continued to boil.

"I love a good cuppa," I chirped. "Don't you?"

"Don't be such a killjoy, Frankie. I'm only teasing you."

I bristled. "I'm not a killjoy, I just don't wanna talk about sex."

"Sex?" Risk repeated. "I wasn't talking about sex."

"Good," I shifted. "Because we don't need to talk about something like that. You get enough of it from your harems."

I couldn't believe those words had left my mouth. I had no idea what possessed me to say them. I heard my tone when I spoke, I sounded pissed off. It was sudden, unexpected and I knew it.

"My harems?" Risk repeated, and if I wasn't mistaken, he sounded a little taken back. "Sounding a little jealous there, Cherry."

I was so jealous of any woman who touched him before. It killed me inside.

"Hardly." I tried to act unbothered. "I have a pretty lively sex life myself. Not harem standards, but I do okay."

The biggest lie in the entire world left my mouth.

"Really?" Risk practically hissed. "You wanna tell me about how you've had sex with other men, Frankie?"

Twice. I had sex with two different guys in separate years. They both came to town for the weekend before returning to their home countries. It had been five years since the second, and last, one-night stand. Both times I didn't enjoy myself, I was too busy comparing the men to Risk and by the time it was over I faked both orgasms. I never attempted to have another one-night stand again. I had nothing against them, they just weren't for me. I realised after the second time that I was the kind of person who had to have feelings for the person I was making love to. I wasn't a wham, bam, thank you ma'am kind of woman. I was the kind of woman someone kept.

"Hardly."

"No, no," Risk pressed. "Since we're on the subject, tell me how many guys you've fucked. Go on."

Forget sounding jealous, he sounded bloody furious.

"Am I supposed to remain celibate?" I quizzed, turning to face him. "You certainly haven't been from what I've heard."

He scowled. "The press twists everything and you know it."

"Does that mean you haven't fucked dozens, if not hundreds, of groupies who've thrown themselves at you over the years, or maybe even a supermodel or fifty? I hear you've been collecting actresses, models and singers and adding them to the endless notches on your bed-post."

What the *fuck* was wrong with me? I didn't know why I was throwing this in his face. I had absolutely no right to say any of this to him. I knew that, but the words just burst free of their own accord.

"*You* dumped *me*, Frankie." His jaw clenched. "That means you don't get to control who sits on my cock."

I flinched at his wording.

"You're right," I snapped. "I don't have any control or say. Just like you shouldn't have a problem with another man fucking *me*."

I sucked in a breath when Risk darted forward and got in my space. He placed his hands on either side of the counter-top I was backed against. He leaned his head right down to mine, I felt his hot, mint-scented breath on my face. I licked my lips as my heart beat overtime. He nudged my forehead roughly with his.

"I have no say in who you let fuck you," he practically growled. "But I'll always have a fucking problem with it. *Always*."

"Wh-Why?"

I tried to be tough, but holy hell, I felt like a cornered kitten with a hungry wolf looking to eat it up . . . and when I should have been scared, I wasn't. I was so incredibly turned on it was almost frightening. No one had ever invoked such a reaction from me, only Risk. My body was like a live wire. I wanted him to touch me so much.

"Because," he hissed, "I should be the only man to fuck this body and make you come. Only *me*."

I moved my hands to his forearms just so I had something to hold on to. My fingers skimmed over the veins that bulged against his skin. He was so tense as he glared down at me.

"You want to be the only man to fuck me?" I swallowed nervously. "You're the only man I see right here in this room with me."

"*Don't* fucking play with me, Cherry," he snapped, moulding his hard body against mine. "This isn't a game."

"I never said it was. I'm asking you a question."

"Ask it then."

I was too drunk on his presence to abandon the courage that filled me.

"D'you want to fuck me?"

I gasped when one of Risk's hands moved to my hip and squeezed my flesh painfully.

"Do I wanna fuck you?" he repeated. "That's like asking me if I want to breathe. I want to fuck this body six ways to Sunday and hear those sounds you make at the back of your throat more than I want my next breath."

Excitement surged through my veins.

"In that case," I placed my hands on his chest and pushed him back a couple of steps. "I have another question."

"Is that so?" Risk's eyes rolled over my body. "I'm listening."

"Will you sing to me, rock star?"

His eyes darkened. "Any requests?"

He knew where this was going just as well as I did, he was just letting me think I was in control when we both knew the ball was, and always had been, in his court. This was always how we played. He decided he was going to fuck me, but he liked to let me take the lead before I willingly surrendered all control to him.

"Oh, I don't know." I turned and began to unbutton my uniform top. "How about something out of your comfort zone? I always liked when you'd sing slowly when you touched me."

I heard Risk's slight hiss and it made me grin. The only times I knew he could remember singing slowly to me had been when we had slow, intense sex. Risk bled rock and roll, but I didn't. I liked a bit of everything.

"I've always liked the twist you put on songs. Your gritty voice and that low, sexy tone makes me so wet."

Risk moved behind me, I felt the heat of his body brushed against me.

"*The second I saw you,*" he began, his lips against my ear as he sang a song I had never heard before. "*I knew that this time, my head and heart fell for you . . . both at the same damn time.*"

His hands slid down my waist to the hem of my shirt.

"*One look your way, girl, you're a hell of a view.*" He gripped the fabric in his hand and pulled it over my shoulders. "*You're pure beauty and wonder and I hope that one day, you will be all of mine too.*"

Risk removed my shirt and dropped it over his shoulder without another thought. I heard the material hitting the floor and it excited me. I hummed when his lips touched my bare neck and his teeth gently grazed over my skin.

"*Girl, I told you,*" he softly sang. "*I'm going to love you forever.*"

My lips parted when he gripped my hips and rolled his pelvis against my behind, I could feel how hard he was through his jeans. I could feel how much he wanted me. He wanted me just as much as I wanted him. I revelled in that fact.

"*I'll always be here, right when you need me. Hoping and praying, you'll never leave me. One day soon, I'll get down on my knee . . . make you all mine, like I knew you would be and softly I'm gon say that I . . .*"

He turned my body to face his, slid his hand up to the back of my neck then up to my hair where he fisted it in his hold. He pulled on it, making me gasp as he forced me to look up at him. He lowered his head, then with his eyes locked on mine, he slid his tongue over my lower lip before sucking it into his mouth. My hips bucked forward and my clit angrily throbbed, jealous of the attention my lip was receiving.

"Told you," he said, cutting the song short as he plunged his tongue into my mouth.

Instantly, I wrapped my arms around his neck and pressed my body against his as I kissed him with fierceness. Risk's hands moved from my head, down my back and to my behind, where he palmed my flesh to the point of pain. I moaned into his mouth, he responded by roughly slapping my arse. He moved his hand up to my bra and undid it with one flick of his wrist. The straps fell down my shoulders so the fabric fell to the tiled floor beneath us. I gasped when Risk's hand covered my breasts and I gasped when he pinched my nipple.

I jerked my head back in surprise.

"Risk!"

His smirk was anything but playful.

"I love hearing you say my name, Cherry," he hummed. "But don't say it again unless I'm fucking you."

Christ. My legs just about buckled from wanting him so bad.

"What'll you do if I don't listen, big man?"

His smile was predatory.

"Say it and find out."

His challenge was clear and I didn't know if I had the guts to accept it and meet him head on. Part of me wasn't sure if I could handle what he would do to me, the other part wanted everything he threw my way. Without another thought, I leaned up on my tiptoes, brushed my nose against his, flicked my tongue over his lips and whispered, "Risk."

I screamed with laughter when he bent down, gripped the back of my thighs and not so gently threw me over his shoulders like a sack of potatoes. I smacked his bum and he returned the favour by smacking mine twice, and twice as hard too. I hissed a breath when he turned his head and sunk his teeth into the flesh of my exposed waist. He slapped my behind again. I sucked in a breath when we entered my bedroom and I was suddenly falling through the air before my back bounced against my mattress.

"You couldn't have given me a warning?"

I laughed again when Risk hopped on top of me, nuzzled his clothed hips between my parted, bare thighs. I still wore my work skirt but with one swipe of Risk's hand, it was zipped down and pulled from my body, thrown somewhere in the room. Risk's lips went to my neck, but they didn't stay there for long. When he trailed his way to my mouth, I was already in a pool of bliss. Just being here like this with him was enough to make me happy.

My body, however, wanted, *needed*, more from him.

"That laugh," Risk breathed against my mouth. "It's still the same."

I lifted my hands to his head. Where my fingers once tangled in hair they now brushed against the shaved sides of his head. I moved my hands to the strip of braided hair that moved from the top of his head all the way to the base of his neck.

"This hair-style," I flicked my tongue against his lips. "Is *very* different."

Risk snorted. "Not a fan?"

I hummed. "I prefer having something to hold onto."

"Oh, really?" he growled. "Naughty girl."

It was unfair that he could make sounds like that with his throat. Those raspy, sexy sounds were enough to undo a woman. His voice . . . it made me weak for him.

"*Your* naughty girl," I told him. "Every naughty thing I think of has you at its centre."

Risk brought his mouth to mine and his teeth nipped my lips.

"Tell me what you imagine me doing to this body." It wasn't a request, but an order. "Tell me every dirty thought you've had of me, Cherry. I want to hear it all."

Christ, I was already shaking and he had barely touched me yet.

"I dream of you licking and sucking on my clit," I told him, feeling bold, brave and everything in-between. "Your hands palming my tits while you feast on me."

"That sounds delicious," Risk hummed. "You want me to eat your pussy?"

Frantically, I bobbed my head. His grin was dangerous.

"Beg me."

"Risk."

"Nuh-uh. Beg me, Cherry."

"Please," I pleaded. "Suck my cunt. Make me come."

He hissed at my choice of words. He began to undress and I helped him. I was desperate to feel his hard, naked body flush against mine. When there was nothing but air between our heated bodies. *God*, I ached in the best way possible.

"Baby." I licked my lips. "You're *so* sexy."

"That's funny." His eyes rolled over my form. "I was just about to say the same thing to you."

"Risk." My body trembled. "Please, I'm aching for you."

He lowered down and brought his mouth below my belly button.

"You want a little kiss?"

"*Yes*."

"I better make it a good one."

I expected him to trail kisses down my pubic bone, then for him to tease me some, but he did none of that. He spread my legs wide, my pussy lips parted on their own with the movement and without a word, Risk zeroed in on my throbbing clit. I made a sound between a scream and a gasp for breath. Risk was the last person to go down on me. It had been over nine long years since I felt the flick of a hot, wet tongue on my flesh and *Christ* did I miss it.

So g-good.

"Oh my god," I shouted. "Yes, *yes*. I'm already gonna come, don't stop. *Don't stop*!"

"Say my name."

"Risk!"

"Come all over my mouth." His fingers bit into the flesh of my thighs. "Let me hear you scream, Cherry."

I became sensation. Risk alternated between licking and sucking my clit and I had to remind myself to breathe. I couldn't keep my body in one place on the mattress; Risk had to pin my hips down with his arms as he tongued me into a never-ending pool of bliss.

"Yes," I whimpered. "Oh, yes. I'm g-gonna . . . *come*."

The words barely left my mouth when the first pulse hit. I tipped my head back and screamed. I sucked in a staggered breath and held it as the next pulse rippled from my clit and spread outward. I whimpered when the third pulse slammed home, the pleasure and satisfaction was enough to undo me. When my orgasm ended and my body was nothing more than a tender piece of meat, Risk moved his lips from my clit and kissed his way up my body.

"That sounded like a good one to me."

I kissed his swollen lips. Risk's fingers palmed my breasts until I whimpered. I knew how much it turned him on when I did this. We lived together for only a short time and the handful of times we had sex together, I remembered how much he liked when I tasted myself on his mouth after he made me come.

"Should I be embarrassed I came so quickly?"

"*Fuck no*," Risk snarled against my mouth. "Trust me, love. You being so hot for me that you come undone the second I get my mouth on you is *not* a problem. It never will be."

My hands slid up his muscled arms.

"I want you inside of me so bad. Baby, *please*."

"Condom." He licked his lips. "Shit. Where are my jeans?"

"I'm clean and I'm still on the pill." I said, my hands kneading his deltoids. "I want to feel you in me. Raw."

"I want that too." Risk's eyes darkened. "I'm clean. Got tested when I was in rehab, haven't been with anyone since."

"Then we're good. Please, fuck me."

"*Fuck*. I've dreamed of this, Cherry," Risk rumbled. "Having you spread out beneath me just like this. With you trembling and begging me to fuck you. The sounds you once made when I was inside you have been stuck on repeat in my head all of these years."

"Please," I pleaded. "Risk, *please*."

"Tell me," he growled as he reached down and fisted his cock before rubbing the head up and down my slit. "Tell me to fuck you."

"Fuck me, Risk. Now."

"My—" He thrust forward and buried his cock to the hilt. "Pleasure."

I sucked in breath. "Mine too."

Risk lowered his body down and pressed his chest to mine as he slowly bucked his hips back and forth. He kissed me deeply as he slid in and out of my aching body at a pace so slow that it almost felt like he was teasing me. I clenched my vaginal muscles around him. He shuddered. He broke our kiss, snagged my lower lip between his teeth and sucked. I knew he was challenging me to do it again . . . so I did.

He groaned deep in his throat and released my lip with a pop.

"F-Frankie, fuck." He panted. "I *love* when you squeeze me, baby. I've missed this pussy."

Words evaded me as he sunk back into my body, as deep as he had ever been. I couldn't believe this was happening. I had dreamt of this kind of coupling over and over, but nothing my imagination conjured up held a candle to reality.

"You f-feel so g-good." I was a shaking mess. "It's been so long."

"Good." Risk lifted one hand to my hair. "Only remember me, understand? *Only me*."

When I didn't reply, he thrust roughly into my body and stole my breath.

"Yes," I moaned. "Only you. Risk. *Please.*"

He worshipped and worked my body in ways that I had forgotten he could. No patch of skin was left unkissed, his hands touched every inch of me and he made sure to love my body until I couldn't keep my eyes open. My legs were around his hips, pulling him in deep every time he thrust forward. I wanted all of him, every single inch.

"How hard do you want it, Cherry?" he growled. "How hard do you want me pounding this pussy?"

"H-Hard as you can," I choked out the words. "So c-close. *Risk!*"

When I opened my eyes, something in Risk's expression changed. His stare was intense and solely on me as he moved inside me untamed. There was a fire blazing within his blue eyes, he was burning hot for *me*.

"Look at me when you come all over my cock."

I could barely breathe let alone keep my eyes open.

"*Look at me*, Frankie!" His fingers fit into the flesh of my thighs. "I want those sexy eyes on me as I fuck this cunt right. If you close them, I'll flip you over and sink into your fat arse. I'll make you scream, Cherry."

Holy Christ in heaven.

I had never, *never*, known Risk to be so domineering during sex. He had always been so gentle, even when he was rough, but this Risk . . . this Risk was new to me. This Risk was the sex god everyone worshipped and wanted. I wanted him to give every bit of himself, even if it wasn't a part of him I ever knew.

"Please," I whimpered. "I'm sorry, I can't . . . *oh god.*"

I sucked in a breath when he slammed his hips so hard against mine that my body jolted.

"Look. At. Me."

I forced my eyes open and when tears fell from my eyes, Risk's expression slowly softened and his eyes widened. He remained fully buried inside of me, but he looked down to my trembling body and jerked his hands away from my skin like I was on fire.

"Babe," he looked at his hands then to me. "I'm sorry . . . I hurt you."

I shook my head. I wasn't hurting, I just felt everything tenfold.

"I feel everything." I swallowed. "I've never . . . this is *so* intense."

He leaned forward, brought his hands to my face.

"I'm sorry. I'm so sorry. I didn't mean to be so rough with you."

I moved my hips, my body desperately needing the friction. Risk's eyes fluttered shut with the movement, but only for a moment then . . . then he began to fuck me slowly, thoroughly, just like he used to all those years ago. I lifted my arms and pulled him into my embrace until his bare chest was pressed against mine.

"I want your gentle loving," I licked his lips. "But I want to be fucked hard and fast too."

He pressed his forehead to mine, watching my face carefully as I moaned under him.

"Your eyes," he whispered. "I just . . . I need to see them."

"Why, honey?" I asked, moving my hand to his hair. "Why?"

"I need to see them looking into mine when I love you," he said as he slid deep inside me once more. "For years, I pretended the eyes looking back at me were yours, but none of them were ever green, none of them ever looked at me with emotion filling them . . . None of them were yours. I need your eyes on me, I need this to be real. I'm so scared it's not real."

I whimpered as more tears fell.

"I'm here." I held him as he slid in and out of me. "You're loving me, Risk. We're real."

"We're real," he repeated, shaking. "I've missed you so much. I dreamt of you all the time, you're in everything I do. Your voice is my music. I hear it everywhere . . . your voice, Cherry. It's the echo in my every melody. I hear it in my head on repeat. I hurt for you, Frankie. Please, I need you."

I held him tightly.

"You have me." I kissed him. "You've always had me. Please . . . please, love me."

He returned my kiss and increased his pace. Minutes passed by until my body was twisting and bucking beneath him like a wild animal. He was speaking to me, telling me how good I felt, how he had dreamed of having my body under his for years as he fucked me into submission. Every word was like fuel being poured on an already raging fire.

"Yes, don't stop . . . *Risk*!"

My scream was tangled up with his groan as my cunt squeezed him as my orgasm unexpectedly slammed into my body. My lungs burned for air and my body was rigid as the spasms of bliss sucked me deeper and deeper into their electric embrace. I sucked in air greedily as the spasms of bliss rocked me.

"Christ, baby," Risk groaned. "You're so fucking beautiful. I love watching you come."

I couldn't respond, my energy was spent. Completely and utterly.

"Look at me." Risk moved his hand up to my hair and gripped it tightly. "Look at my face. Look what fucking this cunt does to me. Look what *you* do to me, Cherry."

I was a quivering mess, I could barely hold my head up, but my overly sensitive body was so in tune with Risk's erratic thrusts that staring at him was all I was able to do. I slid my hands over his hardened pectorals and I hummed. He was so sexy, so masculine, so primal. So fucking mine. I loved him. I never stopped. I loved him so much it scared me to death.

"Risk."

His lips parted, his hold on me tightened then, just like that, his eyes rolled back and he hissed as his hips jerked, stilled, then jerked again. The low, guttural groan of pleasure that left him was so primal it made my body twitch in response. Watching Risk's face when he fucked me was a pleasure, but watching his face contort with ecstasy when he came? That was a fucking dream.

"Frankie."

He collapsed on my chest, almost knocking the wind out of me. We lay like that until Risk rolled onto his side, sliding out of my body as he moved. I was breathing heavily but my chest wasn't tightening. Yet. Risk leaned up on his elbow and placed a hand on my stomach.

"D'you need your inhaler?"

"Both of them." I nodded. "Please."

I lay unmoving as he got up and walked over to the air box on the wall facing us. He returned to the spot next to me and held out my inhalers. I took the blue one first. I uncapped it and took a few puffs to open up my airways, just in case. I waited a few minutes them I took a few puffs of my brown inhaler to combat any symptoms that were lurking.

"You're dangerous," I told Risk. "Between your kisses and sex, I don't know which one is gonna off me first."

Risk smiled as he took my inhalers and put them back inside their box.

We both got under the covers of my bed then and instantly drew one another in close. I plastered myself against Risk's hard body and deeply inhaled. His scent was a mixture of his cologne and sweat, but it was so primal, so male, so him. I loved it. I closed my eyes and couldn't even remember falling asleep.

When I opened my eyes, I was alone in my bed and the room was dark. I sat up, catching my duvet against my naked chest. I touched the empty space next to me and it was still warm. My heart jumped.

"Risk?"

I heard a door open and close then my bedroom door opened.

"Hey." The door clicked shut. "Did I wake you? I was in the bathroom."

"I thought you'd left."

I couldn't see him; the room was too dark.

"What?" He climbed back into bed, tangling his body with mine and lying us back down under the duvet. "Why'd you think that?"

"Because you're gonna leave," I said. "You aren't staying here forever. I . . . I already miss you."

"Hey," he nuzzled my neck with his mouth. "Don't do this, Frank. Let's just enjoy each other and we'll figure out how to move forward when we have to, okay?"

"Okay."

The only reason I agreed was because I didn't want to think about a situation where we couldn't figure something out and we'd go our separate ways again. I couldn't be without him. I'd lived that way and it wasn't even living, it was existing. I wanted, needed, him in my life. Even if it was only for a little while, even if it was only through phone calls or the occasional visits. I would take it all.

I'd take Risk any way that I could get him.

CHAPTER SEVENTEEN
FRANKIE

I missed work.

For the first time in my entire time of working at Mary Well's diner, I overslept and missed work. I woke up to a phone call from Joe, he was very worried about me because I had never missed work before. If I knew I was going to be late, I'd call ahead to let him know. When I told him I overslept, he laughed. When I began to freak out, he told me to just take the day off and he'd have one of the other girls cover my shift. That was how I found myself home on a Saturday morning, lying on my bed staring at the ceiling. After the phone call to Joe ended, I realised that Risk wasn't anywhere to be seen.

He'd left a handwritten scribbled note on the pillow he slept on.

> *Had to go to May's, our manager needed us for a video conference call about us heading to London tomorrow. I didn't want to wake you. You're so beautiful, Cherry. Not an ugly sleeper at all. Risk x*

I laughed when I read it then I rolled over and quickly winced. I looked down, shifted my thighs and winced again. Oh, I was *tender*. I didn't know why I was surprised. I went from having a five-year-long dry spell to a five-times-in-one-night sexathon with Risk Keller. I lifted my hands to my face and giggled into them. I had sex all night with *Risk Keller*. Me! I bet there were millions of women, and a hell of a lot of men too, who would leer at me with jealously right now. I knew people who loved him would give a kidney to be in my position.

I felt like a sex kitten.

I grabbed my phone and stared at the screen. I really, *really*, wanted to google Risk. I wanted to watch videos of him, hear him speak in interviews and I really, fucking *really*, wanted to hear him sing but I was still scared. I knew I was in a little bubble of happiness right now because I had Risk for another twenty-four hours before he had to leave, I was worried I'd upset myself if went against what has kept me sane for the last nine years. I had heard 'Cherry Bomb' by accident when I turned the radio on the day before on my way to work. The second I heard Risk's voice I was compelled to listen to it. That song though . . . God, it hurt my feelings. I knew it was about me, he described my body to a T.

Risk swore that was the only song of its kind that he had ever written, recorded and released and I believed him.

"Be strong," I told myself. "Come on, just watch some of his interviews. Hearing his songs can happen later."

Before I chickened out, I opened up my YouTube app and typed 'blood oath interviews' into the search bar and exhaled a breath when thousands of results popped up. I swallowed as I scrolled down through the videos, glancing at the year the video was uploaded as I went. Someone of them were fan-made compilations. I clicked into one video that had a thumbnail of all the guys laughing.

'Blood Oath Being Cute Little Nuggets For 7 Minutes Straight XD'

The video opened with the guys doing an interview in a studio but before anyone could ask a question, the chair May was sat on broke and he fell. The way he fell was comical. His hands and legs flailed around and his face was a picture. His eyes were wide and his lips parted as the chair gave way, like he knew what was about to happen to him before it happened. Risk, Hayes and Angel laughed so much that they cried. Risk ended up on the floor with May, he tried to help him up but was so weak with laughter that he fell right on top of him.

I was laughing so much at their antics that I made myself breathless.

I got up, grabbed my inhalers from their box and took a few puffs of my brown inhaler then brought them both over to my bed so I could watch the rest of the video. It was a compilation video so it was a bunch of random video edited into one. After the interview where May fell, it switched to the guys walking through a shopping centre with their security team and a whole horde of teenage girls, grown women and men following them. One girl was screaming so loud for Hayes that she actually fainted and May nearly died from shock as he bent down to fan her with both of his hands only for her to spring to life and launch up and wrap her arms around May as he screamed with fright. In the background of the video, Risk had his hand on his hips and was shaking his head while he watched the scene unfold. To his left were Angel and Hayes, who were laughing so much they began smacking each other.

I was laughing so much that I had to pause the video. Again.

When I watched the rest of it, eventually, I was laughing and wiping my eyes by the time it came to an end. The guys were hilarious and poor May seemed to be the cause of their laughter most of the time. He always either falling or someone fell into him, the silly sod. One thing that couldn't be denied was that the guys genuinely loved being in the others' company, a blind man could see that. They weren't just bandmates or regular friends, they were brothers.

I scrolled down through the related videos and froze.

RISK KELLER TALKS ABOUT HIS LOVE LIFE! (NOT CLICKBAIT!!!!)

The title, in all caps, was intimating. I was scared to click on it but I had to. I knew he had other relationships with women, we weren't together for nine long years, of course he moved on. I moved on with those tourists, it just was a train wreck for me and made me steer clear of men altogether . . . until Risk stormed back into my life.

With a deep breath, I tapped on the video's thumbnail.

His face appeared on screen instantly. He didn't look real. He looked like he was generated from a computer, that was how good he looked. His white-blond hair was still shaved on either side but instead of it being braided back and styled like a Viking, it was lose and messy and looked like he had just crawled out of bed but God, it was sexy. His face was clean shaven and his freckles were darker and covered his fair face. Freckles were supposed to be cute and adorable, but somehow Risk made them look incredibly rugged. He wore a black long-sleeved T-shirt that was a little fitted and outlined his broad shoulders, hard chest and muscled arms. The only thing that was out of place were his eyes. They were bloodshot and his pupils were huge. He was high on something during this interview and that hurt my heart.

The interviewer had been introducing herself to Risk, and he had greeted her, while I appreciated the sight of him. They spoke a little about music, the band as a whole and their past and upcoming shows before my ears picked up that the conversation had switched to interest in Risk's love life.

"Have you ever been in a committed relationship, Risk?" the lady asked. "We know you're the wild, bad-boy rocker, but have you ever had a steady girl?"

"Yep."

"Who?"

"Her identity is private, she's not in the spotlight and I don't want her life put in it because of me."

My heart thrummed against my chest. He was talking about me. I knew it.

"Was she special?"

"Very," Risk answered. "I never had another girlfriend after her so make of that what you will."

"Wow," the interviewer said. "Do you see her often?"

"I don't see her at all," Risk said. "She broke up with me just before I moved stateside so it's been a long time since I've seen or spoken to her."

The interviewer's eyes widened.

"I bet she regrets breaking up with you now that you're *the* Risk Keller."

I could tell that Risk was tired of this interviewer just by the way he looked at her. He was bored and maybe even a little irritated.

"She was fine before me so I'm pretty sure she's fine without me too."

I paused the video and noticed that my hands were shaking.

I had heard enough of this kind of conversation, because it involved me directly. I was sure Risk had received questions like this dozens of times before and hearing him respect my privacy touched me but was made my heart pound because when he spoke of me, I could hear fondness in his tone. This interview was before we reconciled. I checked the upload date. Three years ago. Wow. It made butterflies fill my stomach to know he was thinking of me during a time period when we hadn't seen or spoken to one another in many years.

I knew he was asked a question but it was comforting to know that I was on his mind, because he was always on mine. I felt good about that, but that emotion was snatched away when I accidentally scrolled down to the comments and read what some of the more hardcore Sinners had to say. Apparently, they didn't have a filter, or manners, when it came to posting comments on the internet.

BabyMama4Risk: *No hoe is good enough for our Risk. NO DUSTY BITCH THAT WALKS THIS EARTH! That's on periodt!*

Like It Is: *I don't no who Risk's ex gf is but I STILL dgaf about Nora, she is SO plain. Not hot at all. Risk is a GOD. A FUCKIN GOD!*

DaddyRisk: *I wnt him 2 marry me!!!! Risk pls!*

HayesIsBae: *What psycho bitch would dump RISK KELLER? Is she gay? Fuckin' has to be because WHAT A DUMB FUCKIN BITCH!*

Angel's Angel: *My guy is SO stoned, he can barely keep his focus on the woman interviewing him. 420 bitches! Roll up!*

HayesChoice: *I bet that stupid cunt who dumped him is SICK with herself now that he's blown up. Stupid ass ho!*

I clicked the home button to get out of the video and the nasty comments. I felt a little sick after reading them. These people were insulting me and calling me horrible names without knowing a single thing about me or about my and Risk's relationship. They had no fucking clue that if I *didn't* break up with him they wouldn't have their superstar Risk Keller. I felt myself get frustrated with the commenters but I took comfort in the fact that they didn't know I was the woman Risk spoke about. I was just a faceless and nameless person to them. That relaxed me . . . for all of two seconds.

I accidentally hit the trending option on my screen and when I saw what the number one trending video was on YouTube, I nearly had a heart attack. I jumped with fright and gripped my phone when I read the title of the video.

RISK KELLER AND MYSTERIOUS WOMAN KISS ON SOUTHWOLD PIER!!

I screamed when I clicked into the video and both Risk and I came into view. We were at the end of the pier, leaning against the rail as we gazed out at the ocean. The lighting on the pier showcased our faces easily. We laughed and it was obvious we were speaking to one another but then Risk turned this body to face mine. I had my eyes closed but when I opened them and realised he was looking at me, my entire facial expression changed. I looked up at Risk, and, Christ, I could see on my own face just how much I wanted him to kiss me.

We spoke for a couple of minutes then just like that, Risk's mouth was on mine.

I swallowed as I watched us hungrily kiss one another like it was the only chance in this life that we would ever get to taste the other. I gasped in real time when Risk picked me up and settled me on the railing and continued to kiss me something fierce. My hands were all over him, my legs were wrapped around his body and I could tell I was squeezing the hell out of him. I was shaking as I checked the upload time. Seven hours ago. We had kissed a couple of days ago but the video was just released.

With trembling hands, I scrolled down to read the comments.

Risk4Eva: Damn! GET IT GIRL!

Blood Oath's Biggest Sinner: Nooo! Why does he kiss ugly bitches like this when he has NORA? Does he feel sorry for them? UGH!

May Gal: OMG. I'M SO FUCKIN' JEALOUS BUT GET IT, BABY BOY!

Facts4Dayz: Another gold-digging ho who wants into Risk's pockets and how does she do that? By getting into his pants! I fucking hates these ho ass bitches. THOT!

PrettySophiaBabbyyyyy: Ew! Ewww! She's so ugly though!

Jameson Oz: My guyyyyyyyyyy, I thought he was gonna fuck her there and then. LMFAO!

MaySinner5426: I swear I've never seen him kiss a natural redhead before, this is INSANE!

Lazy A-Hole: I'm mortified for her. She looks so desperate for him, she's like a dog in heat.

I clicked out of the video, my face was burning and I quickly realised that I was crying. I grabbed my blue inhaler, took a few puffs and tried to calm down but, my God, I was freaking the hell out. My face was in the number one trending video on YouTube. Hurriedly, I googled Risk's name and the first articles to pop who were ones about the video of us kissing on the pier. I whimpered when I saw another video had been uploaded; one that was filmed through the windows of the diner when I was having dinner with the guys. There were videos of May and Anna getting into a car and obviously having sex by the way the car rocked and the sounds coming from inside the vehicle. I scrolled and it just got worse and worse. I was labelled a 'mysterious beauty' but it was as obvious as the day I was born that I was scared shitless as the paparazzi crowded me.

The pictures, and video, they got of me leaving the diner with the guys left no room for doubt. It seemed to excite everyone that Risk was so protective of me. There were articles about his fans praising him for telling the paparazzi to fuck off. I dropped my phone onto my bed and tried to think clearly. I didn't know what to do. Someone in Southwold was bound to say 'Hey, isn't that Frankie Fulton? The waitress at Mary Well's?'

"It's fine, it's fine," I spoke out loud. "Just relax."

I couldn't relax, I needed to try and fix this.

I needed to speak to Risk.

CHAPTER EIGHTEEN
RISK

I should've told you that when you trusted me,
When you looked at me, and saw the real me.

I wrote down the lyrics that floated around my head. I had been working on it over the last couple of days and it was starting to take shape. As I wrote, I hummed the melody that myself and the guys eventually wrote and lay just a couple of hours ago. I had put the MP3 of the instrumental on my phone, popped my AirPods in my ears and put it on repeat. That was how I wrote. The melody came first then the lyrics followed. None of the other guys took part in the lyrical aspect of our records, they were all about the music.

Luckily, I had a knack for both.

"Oh, fuck," I heard May say from downstairs. "*Shit.*"

I was upstairs, lying on the bed in the room I was crashing in. I sat upright when footsteps pounded against the stairs and May nearly fell into the bedroom. I jumped with fright and pulled my AirPods out.

"Mate, what the *fuck*?" I shouted, jumping to my feet. "What's wrong?"

He shoved his phone in my face.

"You have the number one trending video on YouTube and your name is the number one trending topic on Twitter."

"What the fuck did I do?" I thought out loud. "You fucked a woman in a car park just the other day and only trended at number five for a few hours. How the hell am I number one?"

"Your video is fresher and you can actually *see* what you're doing."

"*What* am I doing?" I grabbed the phone. "What fucking video?"

May reached over and tapped on the screen of his phone. I watched, in silence, as my on-screen self, along with Frankie, kissed the senses out of one another at the end of Southwold Pier. I sat down on my bed and watched the video from start to finish. Twice.

"Mate," May grunted. "If you get a hard-on, I'm smacking you."

I shifted because I *did* have a hard-on.

"She's gonna lose her fucking mind." I swallowed. "Frankie, *fuck*."

"Is she at work?"

"At home," I answered. "When I woke up, it was close to eight. She had her morning shift at seven so I just left her in bed. She was exhausted."

May grinned. "Dirty dog."

I snorted. "Don't tease her when you see her, you know how shy she is about sex. Having you poke fun at her for fucking me five times might just leave her face permanently red."

May blinked. "Five times . . . in one night?"

"I haven't had sex since before rehab and I can't even remember it." I shrugged. "Sex with Frankie, there was no way in hell once or twice was gonna be enough. Five times barely scratched the surface. I was sober for the first time since I last had sex with her, there was no chance that I was missing out on a second of touching her."

"Like I said," May chuckled. "Dirty dog."

"Woof woof."

We both froze when there was a pounding on the front door.

"Hayes and Angel are out."

"Go see who it is then."

"May? Risk?"

I tensed. "It's Frankie. Go open the door."

"Why me?" May demanded. "She's *your* girl."

"This is your house."

The pounding intensified.

"But I'm scared!" May lifted his hands to his face. "She scares me when she's angry!"

"Just let her in before she kills us *both*."

"I can't stand you!"

With that said, May left the room and jogged down the stairs. I heard the door open.

"Hi, Frankie."

"*Where* is he?"

"Upstairs," May answered faster than a sinner in a confessional. "First door on the right."

The door closed.

"Did something happen?"

Motherfucker knew good and well what had happened.

"Oh, just a video of me and Risk kissing on the pier the other night has gone viral and my face is plastered all over the internet. You know, the usual stuff I deal with on a Saturday morning?"

I cringed. Oh, she was *pissed*.

I looked down at myself and thought it would be safer if I wasn't clothed, she never could focus very well when I was naked. Like the fucking Flash, I stripped out of my jeans, T-shirt and socks. I dove under the covers of my bed and shoved May's phone under my pillow. Stupidly, I pretended I was asleep. I heard her enter the room and the second I heard her little gasp, blood surged to my cock. My mind flashed back to the multiple times I was one with her body just hours before. Those sounds she made, the look on her face and in her eyes. I knew I would think of them always.

I made sure not to tense when she approached me.

I swallowed when the bed dipped and her cool, soft hand slid over my back. She hadn't done much but I was ready to fuck a hole into my mattress to find some relief. I shuddered when I felt her lips touch my skin as well as her soft hair as it feathered over me. I groaned when her teeth nipped my flesh. I rolled over onto my back, opened my eyes and reached for Frankie in the same movement. Her eyes widened when I grabbed hold of her arms and pulled her body down on top of mine before she had a chance to blink.

"Risk!"

I grabbed her hand and moved it down to my rock-hard length.

"I want you," I told her. "Fuck, I need you."

"You can't be human." Frankie pressed her mouth to mine. "You can't be."

"I'll always want to fuck you, baby. Always."

She groaned. "I came to see you because there is a *problem*."

"Yeah," I hummed. "The fucking problem is I'm not sinking into your tight, wet cunt."

"Risk."

Jesus.

One little syllable and she just about had me ready drop to my knees before her. Her breathy tone of surprise sent a shiver up my spine and caused my aching cock to throb. I had never in my life wanted someone as much as I wanted Frankie. I couldn't get enough of her. She was wearing a lot of layers so as I pressed my lips to hers, I began to remove them. Her coat was the first to go, then her jumper. When her leggings hit the floor I reached to palm her pussy through her lace knickers but I paused because she winced.

I opened my eyes and stared at her.

"What's wrong?"

Her face was flushed.

"Risk," she licked her lips. "Last night was the first time in a long time for me. We did it so many times . . . I'm sore."

I felt my eyebrows rise.

"But in your kitchen . . . you said you had a lively sex life."

"I only said that because I knew *you* had had sex with so many women," she mumbled. "I had sex with two guys to see if I could have a physical relationship with another man. I couldn't. The last time was five years ago."

"Two blokes?"

"Two."

That was still two too many for my liking but the sheer level of jubilance I felt was un-fucking-real.

"No need to look so happy about it."

"I am happy, I know our time apart meant we could do what we wanted but holy *hell* am I happy, baby."

She frowned. "Wish I could say the same about you."

That was a low blow, but I deserved it.

"Do you know you're the only woman I've had sex with when I'm sober? The only woman I remember being with?"

Frankie blinked. "What?"

"I've taken drugs or drank a shit load in order to be with others. Their faces were always blurred, their hair was never red and their eyes were never green. I always saw you staring back at me. Last night, that was the first time I was naked with a woman while being completely sober and do you know why?"

"Because you're sober now?"

"I've been sober for six months and still didn't have sex when I'd gotten the offers. The reason is *you*, Frankie. Having sex with other women is a blur of nothingness . . . I only remember you. I only want to remember you."

She pressed her face to mine, I put my arms around her body and held on tight.

"Now *I* wish I wasn't so sore."

Surprise laughter bubbled up my throat.

"We can always play a little." I slid my hand down her behind. "I'm wicked with my tongue, as you know."

"Hold your horses, big man." She schooled her features. "I'm here for a reason."

I sighed. "I know."

"You *know*?"

"I just found out before you got here about the video . . . I pretended to be asleep because you sounded mad downstairs with May."

Frankie tried to appear angry, but her lips were twitching too much for her to be really mad.

"You're so cute," she said.

I tried to kiss her but she moved back as she sat up. She ended up straddling me, which I was more than fine with. I got comfortable under her, put one hand behind my head and the other up her T-shirt so I could hold onto her bare waist. She had the tiniest waist. She had wide hips, thick thighs and a big arse but everything else was tiny. Except for her mouth.

"Are you gonna shout at me?" I asked, rubbing her skin with my thumb. "Because if you are, I vote you must always sit on me when you do it."

Frankie rolled her eyes.

"I'm not gonna shout, this isn't your fault, but I *am* freaking out."

"I know." I nodded. "I get it, this is the first time any sort of spotlight has been on you. I know you're scared but it is honestly okay."

"I just don't get how us kissing on the pier is *more* newsworthy than May and Anna having sex in the diner's car park."

Risk laughed. "Because all that video of May shows is the car rocking for ages . . . in the video of us, it's clear to everyone what we're doing. It's obvious to anyone with eyes that I'm weak for you."

I wanted to make this all better for her because she genuinely looked stressed out over it, but there was nothing that could be done. Once something was made public, there was no taking it back.

"This is a big deal, Risk." Frankie stated. "You should see the awful comments about me under that video on YouTube. So many people think I'm fat and ugly and—"

"Stop it." I interrupted. "Look, trolls are all over the internet. People like that are miserable and haven't got a good word to say about anyone because they're sick inside. You could be the most flawless, kind-hearted woman to walk this earth and you will still be dragged through hell and back because I kissed you."

Frankie frowned down at me.

"I just . . . why be mean?" Her shoulders slumped. "The world has enough hate, why not be kind?"

"Darlin'." I smiled up at her. "You're a sweetheart, other people are mean-hearted. That's just the way it is. The best thing for you to do is never read the comment section on anything you're posted on. Ever. Your mental health will thank you."

She nodded. "So I've just to ignore it?"

"That's what I do."

She nodded. "Can I ask you a question? As I read those comments, a woman's name popped up a lot. I just want to be certain you're not in a relationship of any sorts with her because if you are whatever is happening between us is over."

"I've no clue what you're talking about."

"Nora."

One word. That's all she needed to say for me to sigh.

"No, Nora and I aren't in any sort of relationship and we never have been. I haven't seen her in months, babe. I swear. The media . . . they twist everything."

"I believe you."

Her trust in me made my heart soar. Frankie exhaled a breath then she glanced down at her positioning on my body and she froze.

"Are you . . . naked?"

I grinned. "No, I've got underwear on."

She scooted back and looked down to make sure that I was telling the truth which made me snort. She stared down at my stomach, reached out and ran her fingers over my abdominal muscles, then followed the trail of dark hair that ran from my lower abdomen to beneath my boxer briefs. Her eyes scanned their way up my body. Slowly, and good god . . . She looked like she wanted to eat me up and I was *so* here for it.

"You look like you're sculpted from stone."

I shifted my hips so my erection brushed against her pussy; she hissed a little.

"I've something else that's a lot like stone too."

"I'm sore," she reminded me.

"And I'm good with my tongue." I reminded her.

Her lips twitched.

"You're looking at me like you wanna see me naked, Cherry."

Her hands flexed.

"No, I'm not."

"Liar."

"How d'you know I'm lying?"

"I can see it in your eyes." I moved the hand under her T-shirt up to her breast and brushed my thumb over her nipple through the lace of her bra. "I know what you look like when you wanna fuck me, Frankie."

Her eyes fluttered shut, she shifted her hips, rubbing herself against me. I wanted nothing more than to reach down, free my cock, then push her knickers aside so she could sink down on my length but her comfort was my first priority. I came second. Always.

"You're full of yourself." She licked her lips. "I don't wanna have sex with you. I think I've had my fill of you, rock star."

"Oh yeah?" I sat up and came a hair away from my lips touching hers. "You don't wanna fuck me?"

Her little "No" was fucking adorable.

"How about a kiss?" I pressed. "You wanna give me one of those?"

I lowered my voice an octave and added a little rasp to my tone, just how I knew she liked it.

"Don't seduce me with your voice." She glared at me. "I won't fall for it."

"You're too clever for me, Cherry. You always were."

Her hands slid to my head when I grinned, then she suddenly tangled her fingers in my hair and said, "Maybe just one little kiss."

I didn't have time to respond before she pressed her lips to mine, forced her tongue into my mouth and kissed me fucking senseless. I always let her control our kisses when they first began, she was always so desperate to claim my mouth with a ferociousness but when she surrendered that control to me and let me control the pressure and the pace, I knew she was like putty in my hands to do whatever I wanted with.

Our kiss broke when a voice came from her bag. My voice. Frankie sucked in a breath, jumped off me and dove for her bag on the floor. I stared at her, her arse really, but I was aware of how frantic she was to silence her phone. When she stood up and turned to face me, I stared at her.

"I heard my voice."

"No, you didn't."

"I did," I said. "I hear it enough to know what I sound like."

"No, you don't."

I smiled. Slowly.

"Frankie, were you watching a video of me before you came here?"

"No!" she replied, horrified. "I was watching the video of us on YouTube earlier and I must have turned the auto play feature on and this video of you just happened to be up next and it played all by itself."

I felt smug. She was watching videos of me.

"I see."

My little redhead's face glowed. I beckoned her to come back over to me, which she did. I took her phone, settled her between my legs with her back against my chest.

"Pick a video," I said. "I'll watch it with you."

"O-Okay."

She scrolled through a bunch of videos then settled on one of the band playing a festival that I had no memory of. The audio was so shit you couldn't even hear me sing over the instruments, but the visuals were quality.

"How d'you do that?"

"Do what?"

"That!" She pointed to me on stage in front of thousands of people on the screen. "That makes my asthma flare up just thinking about it."

I kissed her head. "I honestly don't know, when I'm on stage with the guys, it just feels like I'm home. You know?"

"No."

I laughed. "Being on stage gives me the same feeling you get when you wake up in the morning and look out the window at the ocean or when you walk to the end of the pier and watch a sunset."

She turned her head and looked at me. "You feel at peace?"

"I feel at peace and so alive at the same time. It's another world kind of experience."

She turned her attention back to the video and I leaned forward so I could see her face, and my heart thudded against my chest when I saw that she was mesmerised. She slid her tongue over her lower lip without realising she did the action, and when she glanced at me and found me watching her, she clamped her lips together and cleared her throat.

So. Fucking. Cute.

"D'you think you could come on stage one time and look at me just like you are right now?"

Frankie's lips parted. "Like what?"

"Like I'm the only man in existence for you."

She leaned her face against mine, my eyes closed at the sweet gesture.

"I kind of can't believe you're leaving tomorrow." My eyes opened at her words. "You just came back into my life and now you're leaving again."

"Hey," I moved my hand to her face when she looked at me. "I'm coming back this time."

"Promise?"

"I promise." I kissed the tip of her nose.

Frankie smiled. "I know we don't really know what we're doing with each other but I'm just happy to be able to be with you like this."

"Me too, Cherry. Me too."

She pecked my lips then looked down at her phone when it vibrated. She tapped at the screen and her eyes widened almost instantly.

"What's wrong?"

"It's Anna and Hannah texting me," she said. "They're at work. Anna said a group of girls came in and asked for me. Saying they're all mad at me for kissing you on the pier." Before I could say a word she continued. "Hannah said they were really rude and called me . . . oh my god! *Look* at what your fans are saying about me. I've never been called fat and ugly this many times in my life."

"You're not fat or ugly, these people are *not* Sinners." I took the phone and scanned over the twins' messages. "They're just obsessed with me or the guys and think they get to decide who we date. It's kind of our own fault though . . . we're rock stars, we're aren't perfect. We've all had sex with groupies, we talk shit during interviews, we talk a certain way to our Sinners on social media because they like it. Sex is always a topic. Women are always a topic. Especially sex with women . . . fuck, we've actually been heartless bastards when it comes to women. I didn't realise we objectify them so much because they always come to us so willingly."

Frankie remained quiet.

"Maybe if we didn't link women and sex together so often, our Sinners wouldn't do the same when it came to the women in our life. *Fuck*. Looks like I've a shit load more to work on than just being sober."

Frankie brushed her hand over my chest.

"You're a good man," she said. "No, you aren't perfect, but realising flaws like you just spotted and knowing you have to make a change makes you perfect to me."

My heart felt lighter.

"I'll work on that and I'll talk to the guys about it but even if we change our ways you just have to realise that some people are just hateful. Summer, Hayes's wife, has her comments turned off on Instagram because she gets so much abuse over being married to him. She's Chinese so a *lot* of people have a problem with that. He's black, she Asian. Interracial couples have it insanely hard still."

"Well, the comments I've seen are mainly about my appearance, and a few about me being a gold-digger, so it's not nearly as bad as what Summer goes through."

"Just because she gets abuse over something different doesn't matter, you both are receiving it because you're connected to members of Blood Oath. To some of the crazier people, we're off limits to every woman. Some of the teenage girls even write fan fiction where me and the guys are secretly in love with one another and fuck like rabbits behind closed doors."

Frankie's face was comical.

"You're *joking*!"

"Nope." I shook my head. "May reads one about me and him and he's such an avid reader and fan of it that he hopes we end up together at the end of the story."

Frankie burst into gleeful laughter.

"That's actually brilliant."

I chuckled. "Surely you've gotten one insult that you actually thought was a *little* funny."

"Well," she shifted. "I read one when I was walking into May's garden. One commenter said I looked like a long-lost Weasley sister from the Harry Potter series, that made smile."

She pinched my nipple when I snickered.

"See?" I smiled. "You have to find the fun in some of those comments because if you didn't, you'd reach a real low point.'

"I guess."

"Always remember these people are insecure and want to be dating me, or one of the other guys, when they tear women down who are connected to us. It's jealousy that fuels it. Even if some of them *did* find you unattractive and think I could do better than you, the main reason they comment hateful things is because they wish they were in your position."

She processed my words and nodded, accepting them.

"Besides," I looked down at her phone. "They now know that you're my muse, that's likely why some of the more hateful ones are being extra cruel when speaking about you."

Frankie titled her head.

"What do you mean?" she quizzed. "How am I your muse?"

She had to be yanking my chain.

"You're joking, right?"

"No."

"You've heard our songs, right?"

"I've heard all of your band's songs, I have the albums downloaded."

Definitely yanking my chain.

"Then you *know* that you're my muse," I stated. "You've heard the songs. You know."

Frankie played with my sobriety coin and didn't reply. I assumed she was embarrassed to have me confirm that she was the reason I wrote so many songs. She was too modest to take credit so I knew that was why she was quiet.

"I think you should post something about me," she then said. "You know, something about me being an old girlfriend so your fans can relax. I know May posted that picture of us and called me his sister from another mister but I think your fans need an update from *you*."

"You're not just an old girlfriend though," I said. "You're the only girlfriend I've ever had. That's why that video is making the rounds so much."

Frankie rolled her eyes and the action took me back.

"What the hell was that for?"

She tried to take her phone back from me, but I held it out of reach.

"Answer me and I'll give it back to you," I said. "What'd you roll your eyes for?"

"C'mon, Risk," she grumbled. "I've seen magazine covers over the years and I've heard Hannah and Anna talk about you. You have been with models, the real ones and the Instagram ones as well as actresses, singers and I think Anna even said you dated a famous zoologist before."

The fucking media twisted everything. I didn't date a zoologist, nearly all animals scared the shit out of me. I went to dinner with that woman to prove to May that I could sit near a woman who took handled snakes, lions, bears and a bunch of other animals that would make me piss myself on sight.

"God's sake." I pinched the bridge of my nose. "Frankie, I just have to be pictured with a woman to make headlines about being in a secret relationship."

"So you're telling me you've never dated any of the women you've been pictured with?"

"I've gone on dates with a lot of them," I admitted. "But I've *never* dated any of them. You're the only girlfriend I've had. Ever."

She looked me in the eye when I spoke.

"Okay," she said. "I believe you."

"Look," I smoothed her curly hair back. "I don't want to talk about the shit people post. Chris will call me any minute now asking what the hell I'm doing. It's not a big deal, this shit happens every other day and it always blows over. I just wanna be with you. All day, here in this bed. Just the two of us."

Frankie ran her fingertips over my jaw.

"Well, I've left Oath his food and water so I can stay with you all day, rock star."

"How about going one step further for me?"

Frankie blinked. "How?"

"You don't work on Mondays, right?"

"Right."

"Come to London to see us play at Wembley."

Frankie's jaw dropped. "Risk . . ."

"Please?" I nudged her head with mine. "You've never seen us play live."

Frankie looked down.

"C'mon, Frank." I tightened my hold on her. "I want to look side stage and see your face when I play my first show sober. It will mean a lot to me, Cherry."

It will mean everything.

Her eyes found mine and when she smiled, my heart skipped several beats. This woman. I was weak for her. She truly had no idea just how happy she made me. She didn't know that I would give up every little thing in my life for her to be mine again. She didn't know I was still in love with her. There was no point in denying it to myself any longer. I held on to Frankie for nine years. I found myself in a dark hole because I was broken without her.

I fucking loved her . . . and she had no idea.

Her arms came around my neck and her lips hovered just over mine. I looked into her emerald green eyes and I saw my whole life reflected within them. When she smiled, I mirrored it.

"You'll come to London? You'll watch me play live?"

"I wouldn't miss it for the world, rock star."

CHAPTER NINETEEN
FRANKIE

"Hello, pretty girl."

I opened my eyes when her gentle voice roused me. I sat upright. I lifted my hands to my tired eyes and rubbed them thoroughly. When I dropped them, I smiled. Warmth wrapped around me at the sight of her.

"Hi, Mum."

Mum stared at me and, as usual, I saw the gears in her mind turn as she tried to place who I was. She gave up after a few seconds and said, "I'm cold."

"We can't be having that now, can we?"

"Nope."

I chuckled as I stood up and tucked her blankets back around her body, giving her a kiss on the head as I went. I retook my seat and winced. God, I was sore. After all the protesting I did about how tender I was to Risk earlier in the day, I was the one who ended up begging him to love my body until I couldn't think straight. I spent the entire day in bed with him at May's house. When we weren't upstairs wrapped in one another's arms, we were playing Guitar God and making food in the kitchen with the guys. It was one of the most peaceful days I ever remembered having and because of that, I wanted to go and spend some time alone with my mum.

The day with Risk had given me a glimpse of a possible future where I smiled and laughed and felt at peace. I loved my mum, God knew I did, but I hadn't felt a semblance of peace with her since before we found out that she was so ill. I always worried for her. I always waited for more bad news about her condition. I always had this bone-chilling fear that because she had forgotten me . . . did it mean she didn't love me anymore? How could a person love someone they couldn't remember, right? That thought plagued me.

Having a carefree day reminded me that, eventually, I wouldn't get the honour of worrying about her because she'd no longer be here for me to fret over.

I knew she was dying and I knew that no matter when her time came I wouldn't be ready for it. I wanted my mum to be free of pain, to finally find her own peace but I selfishly wished that was a long way away. Helping Michael take care of my mum these past nine years had become my life and it terrified to me to think of what would become of me when she was no longer here for me to take care of.

Those thoughts entered my mind as I lay in bed with Risk. I had a strong urge to come and be with my mother, even if it was just to watch her sleep, so that was what I did.

"I missed you today," I told Mum. "Did you know that?"

"Yes," she answered.

I'd wager she didn't have a clue how much.

"You're my best friend," I told her. "In the whole wide world."

"That's nice."

I chuckled, amused by how unbothered she was with me.

"These last nine years have been hell on you, Mum. On me and Michael too because we've had to watch you lose yourself but we're still here for you and we're not going anywhere. Do you want to know why? Because you're our girl."

Mum smiled at me, then turned her head and looked out of the window of her room. I knew she likely didn't have a clue what I was talking about and that her mind was wandering elsewhere but telling her what was on my mind made me feel better.

"I want to go to the zoo."

"So do I," I replied. "I hear it's lovely this time of year."

"Me too. I want to see a . . . dinosaur. A big one."

I smiled when Mum looked at me and blinked.

"Who are you?"

"My name is Frankie."

"I love that name," she wheezed. "Beautiful."

"Thank you."

Mum wiggled around her bed until she found a comfortable spot and sighed. She rested her head back on her pillow as she looked up at the ceiling, blinking slowly. I gazed at her beautiful face and felt my heart clench.

I loved this woman so much, I couldn't fathom my life without her and I didn't want to. She was my whole world and she was being snatched away from me by an enemy I could not fight. My eyes misted with tears and when I swiped away the few that fell, Mum looked back at me.

"Now, honey bear," she said in a very matter-of-fact tone. "Don't you . . . be crying. There are too many things . . . to smile about. Even if everything goes wrong . . . it's all gonna be okay. You'll see."

I stared at my mother as she beamed my way. When she blinked and looked around, I knew her moment of clarity had passed but her words struck a chord deep within me. Those words could be applied to every little thing that scared me right now. My relationship with Risk, my fear of my life without my mother, a possible future without them both in it. I could fret and cry about the unknowns that were to come but what good would it do? I still didn't know what would happen. All the fear I felt was taking away from my time with two people I loved so desperately in the here and now, and I had to force that feeling to take a back seat.

I just had to trust that things would end up being the way they were meant to be and that I could somehow live with whatever that turned out to be. It was still scary, *so* bloody scary, but letting go of what I couldn't control made my heart beat a little easier.

My mum was right. Even if everything went wrong, it was all going to be okay.

CHAPTER TWENTY
FRANKIE

"Frankie, relax."

I looked at Angel when he spoke to me and I knew I had a deer-in-the-headlights expression on my face.

"I *am* relaxed. I've never been as relaxed as I am right now. I'm insanely relaxed."

I looked at Hayes when he simpered. "No, you're wound up tighter than a—"

"Hayes!"

He burst into laughter. "I was gonna say clock."

He bloody well wasn't.

"Stop it." Summer, Hayes's wife, elbowed him and winked at me. "Leave her alone."

I beamed her way. I had only met her a short while ago but we instantly hit it off.

"You're still not relaxed, muse."

I looked at Angel. "Stop bringing attention to it."

"Tell me why your back is as stiff as a board and I will."

I glanced from Angel to Hayes and Summer before I cleared my throat.

"I don't think I should have come along today," I glanced around the living room that was bigger than my entire cottage floor plan. "I feel very out of place here."

On Saturday, Risk asked me to come to the band's first concert of three at Wembley Stadium. I agreed. When he left on Sunday morning, I damn well felt like I was sending him off to war instead of London. Fast forward to Monday morning, I woke up extra early and went through the works for beautifying myself. I showered, shaved and exfoliated my entire body until I was smooth to the touch. I cleansed my face and lips with a scrub then applied a mask to help my oily skin.

I applied roughly one hundred different products to my hair to tame it because I was born with hair like Merida from the Disney movie *Brave*. If I wanted it to look cute, I had to put in a shocking amount of effort for it to be that way. Even then, I prayed to God until I diffused my hair and was happy with how it turned out. The make-up part stumped me because I didn't wear it. I had the kind of skin that oiled up fast so wearing make-up had never been worth it. I wanted to look nice for Risk's big night so I sat through a make-up tutorial to cover up my healing bruise. I didn't have half of the stuff the guy used in his videos, but I had the basics. Primer, foundation, concealer, setting powder, eyebrow stuff and blush.

I had no clue how to contour so I didn't even attempt it, and making my eyes look nice with my skill set wasn't an option.

When I was finished, I looked in the mirror and wanted to cry. I looked like a five-year-old got into her mother's make-up bag and had the time of her life. By the time I was finished, it was too late for me to start over so I did what any normal person would do, I rang Risk on the new number he gave me and I told him I wasn't going.

"You're coming," he told me. "If I have to go back to Southwold and get you, you're coming."

"I don't look cute!" I told him. "My make-up is a joke, you can still see my bruise. I have nothing to wear to a rock concert. I don't even have a Blood Oath T-shirt! People will think I'm lost!"

"Summer is here, she'll help you put some of the crap on your face if you're so inclined to have it. Put on a pair of jeans and I'll have a T-shirt here for you. How does that sound?"

It sounded like I was losing the argument.

I found myself in Risk's London townhouse four hours later. I sat in his living room with Angel, Hayes and Summer. Risk and May were busy speaking to the band's manager in another room. I had yet to meet Chris Harrison and from the random shouting that flowed in the from hall every so often, I knew meeting him could have been delayed a million years and I wouldn't have minded a bit. He seemed like a stressed-out person.

"Why do you think that?" Summer frowned. "You look great and, girl, your make-up is on point now that I've helped you contour and we smoked your eyes. Your bruise is completely hidden. Your eyes are huge and so green; you look gorgeous."

I looked down at the Blood Oath T-shirt Risk gave me to wear and I messed with the hem.

"You're talking about the house when you say you feel out of place," Angel interrupted. "Right?"

I glanced up at him, guiltily.

"It's a long way from Southwold being in here."

"Frankie."

I looked at Hayes.

"Risk has this big house, but he's still Risk. I'm still me and May is still May. We're still the three prats you knocked into line when we were kids. That hasn't changed, Bilbo."

I smiled as Hayes's words took root. I knew I shouldn't let Risk's wealth affect me but it was just such a contrast to the life I once shared with him. His home in London . . . it was breath-taking.

I looked to the doorway of the room when a lady walked in, she was wearing a navy uniform and she didn't even look at us as she crossed over to the coffee table and began to gather all the used and empty tea cups.

"Oh, let me help you."

I jumped up to pick up the cups and the lady looked as if I'd just offended her entire family. "No, madam," she bowed her head. "This is my pleasure."

Awkwardly, I stepped back and lowered myself back down to my seat. I refused to look at the guys because I could hear Hayes's stupid wheezing sound he made when he was trying to hold in his laughter. It sounded like whistling kettle.

"Mrs Clover," Angel snorted when she left the room. "She takes her job seriously."

"Does she only work here when Risk is home?"

"No, all year round," Hayes answered. "She has her own key. On the top floor, in his entertainment room, Risk has this huge aquarium that is made into the walls, it wraps around the room and has hundreds of saltwater fish. It's gorgeous. She comes by daily to feed and check on them and she does whatever cleaning she has to. She stocks up on food when she knows Risk is coming home."

Wow.

"I wonder if she'd come and work for me in Southwold."

Everyone chuckled at me but I wasn't joking.

I tried to relax as best as I could but I was glad when Risk came into the room not long after Mrs Clover left. He sat right next to me, slung his arm over my shoulder and stared at me. Instantly, I was embarrassed.

"What?"

"You look extra sexy." His eyes scanned my face. "I've never seen you wear eye make-up before."

"Thank Summer," I said. "She said I needed a smoky eye and winged eyeliner if I was attending a Blood Oath concert."

He stared at my eyes.

"She made it look like little drops of blood are dripping from your eyeliner."

"Nice, right?"

"Sexy," he corrected. "So fucking *sexy*."

I flushed. "Risk, everyone can hear you."

"She's so cute," Summer gushed to Hayes. "How can a caveman like him have a sweetie like *her*."

"Because she's not around him enough to know how boring he really is."

"Eat my dick, demon."

Angel laughed, not insulted by Risk in the slightest.

I leaned into him. "Are you nervous?"

"Nope," he answered. "I can't wait."

He looked ready to bounce off the walls with excitement.

"Is it different?" I murmured. "Being sober?"

"Yeah," he kissed my nose. "Like I'm gonna be fully present for it, you know? I never used or drank on stage, but I did before and after so my mind was always clouded when I performed. This is a reset for me, for the band."

I nodded. "I can't wait to see you in action."

"And what about me?" May asked, entering the room. "I'm the best performer in the band."

"Here we go," Summer rolled her dark brown eyes. "Modest May in the flesh."

I laughed. "Modest May."

May scowled between myself and Summer.

"There are two of them to try and tear me down now," May nudged Angel's leg. "Your missus better be nice to me."

"Not likely."

We laughed.

"Let's get moving, guys!" a voice hollered from the hall. "Curtain drops in three hours, wheels up in five."

Everyone got up, but Risk held me down onto the sofa.

"What is it?"

"I want to give you something."

I leaned in to kiss him, he smiled and pecked my lips.

"Thank you, but not a kiss."

I blinked. "What d'you wanna give me then?"

"A gift . . . Happy belated Valentine's Day. I wanted to give this to you yesterday but you were so upset that I was leaving so I saved it for today instead."

He pulled out a black box from behind his back and handed it to me. My face burned because I had completely forgotten the significance of the day because I hadn't celebrated it in nine years. I felt pressured because everyone in the room was watching us. With shaking hands, I lifted the lid of the box and I gasped when the most stunning white gold bracelet I had ever seen stared back at me. Hanging from the bracelet were two charms, a small microphone and a little guitar that appeared to be made completely out of diamonds.

"Risk." I whispered. "Oh my *god*."

"D'you like it?"

"Like it." I looked up at him with tears in my eyes. "I love it. I've never owned a bracelet before, this is absolutely beautiful. Thank you so much, but I didn't get you anything."

"Yeah, you did," he smiled. "You're coming to my first sober show . . . this is my biggest first and you're gonna be here for it."

"Oh, honey." My chin quivered.

"Oh, fuck! Eye make-up, eye make-up!"

Summer's shouting was a reminder that I had make-up on and I instantly used my free hand to fan my face to force my tears to go away. Summer grabbed some napkins that were sitting on the coffee table and thrust them into my face. I grabbed a bunch and placed them under my eyes until the threat of crying passed. When I lowered the tissue, I saw some black smudges on the white cloth.

"Did I wreck it?"

Risk eyed me. "Looks perfect to me."

I looked at Summer. "Same question."

Risk snorted about his answer not being good enough for me. Summer carefully inspected my face, my eyes mainly, and when she nodded, I relaxed.

"Thank God."

I returned my attention to the bracelet and I carefully removed it from the box. I ran my fingertips over it, not being able to believe it was mine.

"Thank you, Risk."

"You're welcome, Cherry."

He helped me put it on and I was pleased to find that the fit was perfect.

"This is the nicest thing I own." I stared at it, mesmerised. "I'll have to buy a safe to put it in when I'm not wearing it."

Risk snickered as he pulled me up to my feet. We were all about to leave the room when Hayes held up his hand and got everyone's attention. We all paused and looked his and Summer's way.

"Before we go." He put his arm around Summer's shoulder. "We have something to announce."

You could have heard a pin drop.

"We're having a baby!"

My scream frightened both Risk and May, which cracked Hayes, Angel and Summer up. I shot across the room and wrapped my arms around both Summer and Hayes. This was the first day I had ever met Summer and we became fast friends. I was over the moon for her and Hayes, but Hayes . . . I couldn't believe it.

"Congratulations! You're gonna be a daddy, Hayes!" I leaned back and lifted my hands up to his face. "*You*! A daddy! My God. I'm so excited!"

The guys hugged one another, each of them gave Summer a squeeze too.

"How far along are you?" I asked. "You aren't showing yet."

She was very petite, I think it would show even if she ate a large meal.

"Nine weeks." Summer beamed. "I'm due the twentieth of September. I would have kept it a secret longer but holy *shit*, morning sickness is killing me and pretty much all food smells make me puke."

I winced. "Poor mummy but a little *baby*!"

Summer hugged me again, laughing. When I returned to Risk's side, he nudged me.

"You like kids?"

"Are you joking?" I questioned. "I love children, I love when babies and toddlers come into the diner. They're so bloody cute I want to gobble them up."

Risk looked thoughtful as he draped his arm over my shoulder. We all left his house and piled into a bus that was waiting outside. Joining the band, myself and Summer were ten members of the band's personal security team. I only knew two of their names so far, Jacob and Tobias. Jacob because he was the head of the team and Tobias because Risk informed me that I was his responsibility while at the venue. I didn't mind that I had a babysitter, it made me feel better knowing I had someone looking out for me when Risk wasn't around.

Blood Oath's manager, Chris Harrison, and the band's personal assistant, Nolan Kennedy, were aboard the bus too. Nolan greeted me with a big smile but Chris didn't. He wasn't rude, just a little cold. Risk mentioned they had just flown in from LA the day before so I guessed he was a little jet-lagged and likely stressed out with the upcoming concerts. It didn't take long to reach the stadium from Risk's house, but when we pulled up, my hand in Risk's tightened as I stared out at the sea of people that were behind the barriers.

I knew that Blood Oath were famous, but until I arrived at Wembley Stadium with the band, I didn't understand the full extent of what that actually meant. I had never seen so many people bunched together before. They were all screaming and waving signs in the air or had their phones held up high to take pictures. Risk removed his hand from mine, slid his arm around my waist then plucked me onto his lap.

"Look at me," he said into my ear. "Not them."

"That's a *lot* of people."

"A bunch of them always chance coming to different entrances of venues we gig at to see us when we arrive and leave.

I lifted my hand to the coin on his chain and I played with it.

"It's gonna be okay," Risk kissed my cheek. "You're gonna love seeing us live."

I felt a little guilty about keeping it a secret that I had never seen them perform at all, nor had I heard their studio version of their songs, only the instrumentals. I didn't know how to say it without hurting Risk's feelings. His music was his life and I could only imagine how it would feel if he knew I had worn earphones everywhere I went just to avoid hearing him sing.

It'd break his heart.

"I'm excited," I told him. "It's gonna be so cool seeing you sing to thousands of people."

"Tonight, after the gig, when I take you back to my place, I'll sing only to you."

I smiled. "You singing to me all alone might bring me to my knees, rock star."

"Baby," Risk's eyes darkened. "You before me on your knees is a sight sweeter than anything else. Suck my cock into your mouth and I'll—"

"Risk!"

The men behind us laughed and so did Risk until I leaned in and clamped my teeth down on his neck. For as long as I had known Risk, I had never been the bolder person but I felt a little bit of courage on the bus with him. His fingers squeezed me tight. When I pulled back, his mouth caught my lips in a deep, desire-filled kiss. I shifted on Risk's growing erection and he growled, deep in his throat.

"You're doing this on purpose, Cherry."

A statement, not a question.

I pecked his lips. "Maybe."

He kissed me again, deeply, but we quickly separated when a voice called Risk's name. "Remember what we said?" Chris, the band's manager, called out. "Behind closed doors."

"*You* said that," Risk quipped. "I remember telling you to suck my dick."

Angel, who was in the same row as us on the opposite side of the bus, began to chuckle at Risk's response to their manager.

"Are we not allowed to kiss?"

I felt like we were kids again and couldn't be too handsy around my mum.

"Ignore him." Risk rubbed his nose against mine. "I do."

The bus came to a gradual stop and I jumped when pounding began from both sides of the vehicle. "It's okay." Risk's hold tightened. "Fans broke the barrier, security will get them under control. This happens a lot."

We had to wait ten minutes but eventually we were ushered off the bus. Risk was separated from me as he was led quickly into the venue. Him and the guys were jogging and waving at everyone until they disappeared into the building. The volume of the screaming was insane. There was a man on my left and Tobias had a tight hold of my hand on my right. When I made it inside the kitchen, Risk was right there waiting for me and I was relieved to see him.

"That," I said as the doors closed behind us, "was crazy."

"Cherry," he grinned. "You've seen *nothing* yet."

CHAPTER TWENTY-ONE

FRANKIE

"This is a *dressing room*?" I exclaimed as I entered the room that looked like the living area of a fancy apartment. "This is nice, boy."

There were racks and racks of clothes on each side of the room, a buffet table of food, a machine for cold refreshments, a huge plasma screen television, video games consoles, big comfy-looking sofas and even a make-up station. I was very impressed and that seemed to amuse the guys. Hayes dropped a surprise kiss on my head.

"So cute."

His wife chuckled as she crossed the room, making sure to give the table of food a wide berth; this amused Hayes, who followed her. I jumped when arms snagged me around my waist. I smiled when Risk's face nuzzled the side of my neck.

"Do my make-up."

I was positive I had heard him wrong.

I turned my head. "I beg your pardon?"

"You heard me." He grinned. "Do my make-up."

I heard him alright, but I couldn't believe what he said.

"Risk." I blinked. "I can't even do my *own* make-up."

"I wear stage make-up," he laughed. "I don't use what you use, just eyeliner and a little bit of lipstick. It doesn't have to be pretty."

I wanted to tell him that his die-hard Sinners would be upset if he didn't look appealing to them but I held my tongue. He wanted to do this for me and secretly, I wanted to as well. I bobbed my head, he smiled.

"Great, I'll get changed and you can have an abundance of time to finish my look."

There were a couple of hours before the band was due on stage. In an hour and fifteen minutes, the opening act would take the stage to warm the Sinners up for the guys, until then, the plan was to hang out in their dressing room. May and Angel were already getting comfortable on the sofa with PlayStation controllers in both of their hands. Hayes and Summer were eating, and me? I was looking around at the items in the room like I was in a museum while Risk changed.

"Miss Fulton?"

I turned and smiled at Tobias when he approached me.

"Please, call me Frankie."

"Frankie," he nodded. "I just want to remind you that during the show, you're to remain at my side, or in my line of sight, at *all* times."

I didn't think Tobias was much older than me but I felt like a little kid when he spoke to me.

"I will, sir," I said. "I promise."

He nodded then backed over to Jacob where they discussed something in hushed tones. I moved over to Angel and May and sat between them on the large sofa. May was no longer playing with Angel, he was watching Angel play a very scary-looking game that made me jump a couple of times.

"I don't like that music," I told them, feeling uneasy. "Why is it getting louder?"

"It's boss music."

What the hell is boss music?

I was about to voice my question to May when a terrifying-looking monster grabbed Angel's character. When I screamed, May jumped then laughed. Angel fell against me as he cracked up. I placed my hand on my chest and I was laughing too, but it was nervous laughter at best.

"She's fine," Hayes suddenly cackled. "Your fly is down."

I sat up and turned. Risk was staring directly at me from the doorway of the bathroom as he zipped up his jeans and buttoned them.

"You," he said, "scared the shit outta me."

I clamped my lips together to keep from smiling.

My humour fled when my eyes dropped to his body. He had on skintight, black distressed jeans that had a silver chain hanging from one belt hole at the front to one around the back. He had on a black fitted denim vest that was hanging open. His washboard abs, his treasure trail, his whole toned-as-hell torso was on display. His muscular, tattooed arms were such a visual delight that I stared at them. He had full sleeves from the back of his fingers all the way up his arms, which ended half-way up his neck. I had seen him naked. I spent the day in bed with him on Saturday, I got to see his tattoos but when he was dressed as Risk Keller, global rock star . . . my vagina took notice.

I got up from the sofa, rounded it and approached him. His eyes never left mine once.

"You're looking like you wanna fuck me, Cherry."

He had *no* idea.

"The others don't dress the same?"

"Nah, the emo look is my thing on stage and in music videos." He grinned. "You like?"

More than liked.

"I've never seen the whole emo look on a guy that isn't super skinny." I scanned him from head to toe. "You look healthy, buff . . . *so* sexy."

Risk bit his lower lip and grinned . . . a lower lip that had a silver ring in it.

"Is that real?"

"Clip on," he winked. "I'm too scared to get a real one. Don't tell anyone."

I laughed as I slipped my hands under his vest and slid my arms around his waist.

"Later," I told him. "You better leave that lip ring on when I'm loving you."

"Yeah?" His eyes darkened. "I've a whole bunch of them, I'll wear them all if you want me to."

I giggled up at him. I followed him when he took my arm and led me over to the make-up station. He sat down on the chair in front of the vanity and clapped his hands on both of his muscular thighs.

"Straddle me."

I hesitated. "I've never done make-up on someone before. I think I should stand so I can concentrate better."

"And *I* think you should sit your fat arse on my dick while you do my make-up."

My face burned and I reached out and pinched his nipple without a thought, making him hiss. "You don't have to be so bloody crude, Risk."

Risk's laughter set everyone off as he rubbed his nipple then patted his legs again. I eyed him, exhaled a breath, then straddled him. I rested my feet on the bars that went across the legs of the chair and I got myself comfortable. Risk's hands, surprise surprise, went to my behind.

"Eyes and lips?"

He nodded. "Google me, you'll see pictures of me on stage and what it normally looks like."

I leaned back and removed my phone from my pocket and did exactly that. He was right, he didn't wear a lot of make-up, his eyes were lined on the top and bottom and smudged on the outer corner. His lips were darkened, but only in the centre of his lips. They looked like May's hair; blood red.

"If I mess up," I said, "Summer will fix it, she's really good at that."

Risk watched me as I grabbed one of the black eyeliner pencils. I bit down on my lower lip, cleared my throat and got to work. He closed one eye so I could draw a line tight to his lash line then when he opened it, he looked up so I could apply liner to his lower lash line and water line. I held my breath until I was finished because I was very aware of the fact that I could possibly blind the man. I repeated my steps on the other eye then I grabbed a little pencil with a sponge on the end of it and I smudged the liner above and below his eyes. I leaned back when I was done and nodded.

"What d'you think?"

Risk looked in the mirror. "Looks good to me."

"Really?" I gnawed on my lip. "I won't be offended if it's rubbish, I'd rather Summer fix it."

"It's good," he chuckled. "Now lips."

I leaned in and pressed mine to his.

"You meant my lips on yours, right?"

He hummed. "Always."

I chuckled as I leaned back, reached over and grabbed the lone tube of lipstick. I uncapped it, rolled it up and puckered my lips. Risk mirrored my action so I dabbed the colour on the centre of his plump lips then used my baby finger to feather it out so it blended into his natural lip colour. I tilted my head. He looked sexy.

“I wanna kiss you but I’ll get the lipstick all over me.”

“Pity.” Risk grinned. “How much d’you wanna kiss me?”

I shifted, grinding my behind over Risk’s groin. He hissed, looked down and groaned when I rotated my hips slowly.

“So badly.”

“Vixen.” He snapped his teeth at me. “You’re being naughty.”

“I can’t help it. I want you. Can we have a quickie?”

I had seen fleeting images of him on stage, but never studied them. I had never seen him up close and personal with his stage clothes and make-up. It was really turning me on.

“No.” Risk shook his head. “Wait until after the show. I’ll be so full of adrenaline that I’ll fuck you hard and for so long that you’ll walk funny afterwards.”

I felt my eyebrows shoot up.

“Really?”

“Really,” he slid his hands up my back. “This is another first for me. A new kind of foreplay that I think I’m going to like. I’m going to tease myself with you while knowing I have to perform a whole set before I can have you. Hell. I’m so hard, baby.”

I felt his thick length under me.

“Does it make you harder to know I’m wet and swollen for you?”

“Yes,” he hissed. “How wet are you, baby?”

“Dripping.” I licked my lips. “I can already feel the fat head of your cock sink into my hot, tight cunt. You’ll fuck me slowly, pull my hair and bite me because you can. I want to feel pain when you fuck me.”

“Christ in heaven.”

“Jesus, Frankie . . . that was hot.”

“It’s always the quiet ones.”

“Leave her alone you three, she’s *so* cute.”

I forgot people were within hearing distance and I felt my face burn under my make-up. I locked eyes with Risk and when he laughed, so did I, but I swatted his shoulders.

"I'm gonna kill you," I warned him. "I never talk like that."

"I'm glad I bring the vixen out in you, Cherry."

"Just hush."

Risk chuckled as I got up. I was embarrassed, and to take myself out of the situation I had put myself in, I grabbed my phone and dialled Michael's number as I joined Risk on the sofa with May and Angel. Games weren't on the television anymore. An action movie was.

"Hi, Frankie."

"Hi Michael." I put my finger in my free ear. "How is Mum?"

"The same," he answered. "She's slept most of today. How is the concert? Are you having fun, kid?"

"I am." I smiled. "It's hasn't started yet, I'm backstage with Risk and the guys. It's so cool, I want to touch everything."

Michael laughed, Risk snorted next to me.

"I'm glad you're lettin' your legs stretch, girl. Ye need this break."

I didn't realise how right Michael was until that moment, but guilt quickly followed.

"Are you *sure* Mum is okay?" I pressed. "I feel guilty not being home in case she needs me."

Risk kissed the side of my neck, comforting me.

"Frankie," Michael sighed. "Your ma would be the first person to push ye into experiencin' the world. There is more to life than Southwold, y'know?"

I was beginning to grasp that.

"Yeah, I know."

"Have fun." Michael stressed. "No worryin', just have *fun*."

"I will." I smiled. "I promised."

"Good. Now, go and rock out, or whatever it is Risk and his bandmates do."

I laughed. "I will. I love you."

"I love ye too, kid."

When the call ended, the guys were being told they had to get ready. I remained seated while Angel, May and Hayes got to change clothes. Like Risk, they got dressed quickly. They didn't wear make-up like Risk so they had one step to skip. A short while later, the guys were getting their wireless in-ear packs clipped onto the backs of their jeans. I noticed that each pair of in-ear headphones were a different colour. Risk's were dark green, May's were red, Hayes's were blue and Angel's were black.

"I like your in-ear thingys," I said to Risk when I got up and crossed the room to him. He left his in-ears hanging around his neck for the time being. "The colour is pretty."

"Ask me why they're green."

I raised an eyebrow. "Okay, why're they green?"

"Because it's my favourite colour," he answered. "Ask me why green is my favourite colour."

"Uh, why is green your favourite colour?"

"Because your eyes are green, Cherry. Dark emerald green. They are my favourite colour."

My throat ran dry.

"Risk."

"I know," he grinned. "You think I'm cute."

"You are," I leaned up on my tiptoes to kiss him. He had to lean down to meet me half-way. "The absolute cutest."

We shared a chaste kiss then I stepped back and stared at the group and I had a 'what the fuck' moment.

"I've just had a moment of realisation that you guys are *actually* rock stars." I swallowed. "I mean, I know you're famous and successful and all of that jazz but holy shit, you guys are actual rock stars. You made it out of Southwold and took the world by storm. I knew you would."

May made a sound between a whimper and a cough. He balled his hand into a fist and pressed it to his mouth that was clamped shut. I beamed his way and when I moved towards him with my arms open, he pulled me against him and hugged me tightly. Laughter and clapping surrounded us.

"I can't *believe* I almost cried," he said into my ear. "Fuck you, Fulton."

I laughed, squeezed him then hugged the other guys. Things happened quickly then. People were buzzing around like bees, shouting different things and talking into walkie-talkies while I was just watching them with keen interest. Chris announced it was time to head to the stage.

"Your guitars!" I gasped. "Where *are* they?"

"Breathe," Risk chuckled. "They're on stage waiting for us on our marks. Everything is where it should be, beautiful."

I placed a hand on my chest.

"Ignore me, I'm freaking out."

"You have your inhalers, right?" Risk tilted my chin up so I was looking at him. "Both of them?"

I grabbed my bag and patted it. "I triple checked."

"Good." He flicked his eyes over my head. "Tob, you've got the inhalers I gave you, yeah?"

"Got them right here, man."

He gave Tobias back-up inhalers?

I smiled up at Risk. "You're so good to me."

"Returning the favour is all," he said. "You've taken care of me for long enough, it's time I took care of you."

"How about we take care of each other?"

He leaned his forehead down against mine.

"Sounds like a dream to me, Cherry."

He pecked my lips then was ushered over to the other members as the crew were doing checks on their in-ear monitors amongst other things. I hung back, not wanting to mess up anything that was important in the build-up to the band going on stage. I couldn't take my eyes off Risk. He looked so fucking good.

"Hello, Frankie."

I looked up to my right and smiled.

"Hi, Chris."

"Having fun?"

"Loads."

"That's great." He looked at Risk. "Listen, Risk needs to focus right now on his first sober show with the band. In order for him to do that, I need you to your take yourself *out* of the equation because you're taking that focus away from his music."

I felt my smile fall from my face.

"Oh . . . uh, yes, sir." I shifted my stance. "I'll just wait over—"

"Cherry? Let's go. I want you side stage, babe."

I didn't even look at Chris as I ducked away from him and hurried over to Risk's side.

"Everything okay?"

"What?" I blinked. "Oh, yeah. Fine."

Risk nodded, hooked his arm around my shoulder and led me from the room. We lagged a little behind the other three members and Summer. There were crew members all around but my eyes were on the Blood Oath members. May was something else. He had on black distressed jeans, very similar to Risk's. His boots tied all the way up to his knees though, unlike the others, whose combat boots stopped midway up their shins. Apart from this little black scarf thing around his neck, and black suspender straps over each shoulder, May's torso was completely naked. I didn't realise he was so heavily tattooed. He was inked up way more than Risk.

"He's such a heartbreaker."

"Don't tell him that," Risk leaned down and kissed the crown of my head as we walked. "He'll think you want him and rub it in my face."

I giggled happily.

I wanted to document this moment so I got my phone from my pocket, turned the face fronting camera on and held it out. Risk instantly leaned down, pressed his head on mine and smiled. I mirrored the actions and snapped a couple of photos. Risk took my phone got more pictures from better angles. He was taller and had longer arms, his pictures did us justice. He did the same with his phone then before he gave it to a crew member for safe-keeping.

"I'm so excited," I said as I took my phone back and tucked it back into my pocket. "But I'm so nervous too. This is so huge."

We reached the end of the hallway. This was where I would part from Risk. Him and the guys rose up onto the stage so they had to go a different route. I grabbed his face, leaned up and kissed him. I quickly made sure his lips were still a desirable red when we separated.

"I'm so proud of you," I told him. "You know that, right? So bloody proud."

"Really?"

"Really." I reached around and smacked his bum. "Go get 'em, rock star."

Risk's smile was bigger than I had ever seen before. He took my face in his hands, pressed his lips to mine once more before he backed away. "This is for you, Cherry. Every single song . . . for you."

Then he was gone.

CHAPTER TWENTY-TWO
RISK

"Let's go, baby!" May whooped. "First Blood Oath gig."

I looked at my friend as we ducked below the stage and huddled towards our stage lifts that would carry us up onto the stage when the gig began. The roar of the Sinners out in the stadium was already off the charts. It made the hair on the back of my neck stand up.

"First gig?" I repeated when he didn't finish his sentence. "This is our millionth gig."

"This is our *first* gig," May stressed. "When you and Frankie broke up, you didn't perform on stage or record in the studio unless you had drink or drugs in your system. This is the first Blood Oath gig because you'll be really present for it. This is first *real* one, main man."

My chest tightened and a fucking lump formed in my throat.

"Why'd you have to go and say nice shit like that?"

Angel poked his head over my shoulder.

"Are you crying? *Please*, tell me you're crying, *puta*."

I shoved him out of my space, clearing my throat as he and the others laughed happily. The four of us were hunkered down because we were way too tall to stand up under the stage without whacking our heads. We were sort of huddled together and it gave me the chance to look at each of my friends, each of my brothers, and smile.

"I wouldn't want to do this fast-lane life with any men other than you three arseholes," I grinned. "We're Blood Oath."

"We're Blood Oath," they echoed as we bumped our fists together.

"Can you believe we do this shit for a living?" Hayes quizzed, his voice filled with wonder. "We're about to go and perform in front of one hundred thousand Sinners in Wembley. Those are people who love our sound, love Risk's lyrics, love us, and want to see us live. I still can't believe it."

"Me either, bro," May agreed. "This crazy shit is what our dreams are made of."

I grinned. "Amen."

"This feels different to you three as well, right?" Angel questioned, glancing at each of us. "Like this isn't just a standard show because our lives have changed so much since the last one? Hayes is gonna be a daddy, Risk has his muse back, I've got me a steady girl back home and May . . . May is still STD free, so that's something."

We cracked up with laughter.

"It *is* different," I affirmed. "This is how every one of our gigs should feel. I love being on stage with you guys but having a clear mind makes me feel like I'm experiencing all of this for the first time. I'll see the faces of our Sinners as they sing our songs back to us. They won't just be a blur of nothingness anymore."

Hayes clamped his hand on my shoulder. "This is the first gig of many for us."

I nodded. "The first of many."

"Let's get it!" May whooped. "I'm *so* fucking ready."

My boy looked as excited as I felt.

"I'm buzzing, man." I couldn't hold still. "Frankie is here, she's gonna hear me sing her songs. I've wanted this for so many years, just to see her face as she hears me . . . hears what I have to say to her."

It was incredibly important to me that I see her when I'm singing the songs she inspired. I had never been able to sing them directly to her before, and I wanted to see her face, her eyes as she heard me. I knew she would hear my love for her when I sang . . . I knew she would. She'd hear me. She had always been the only person able to hear me when everyone else just listened.

"She's not going anywhere," May assured me. "Trust me."

May's words struck a chord within me and suddenly, I felt like I was about to burst.

"I'm telling her tonight."

"Telling her what?"

"That I love her," I answered. "That I can't be without her. That I hadn't felt alive until the moment she came back into my life."

"It's about fucking time." Angel punched my deltoid. "I was going to tell her for you if you didn't."

I laughed as a voice behind us shouted, "On your marks, guys. Good luck!"

I felt a surge of adrenaline rush through my body as me and the guys bumped fists once more and moved onto our marks on our separate lifts. We all settled our in-ears into our ears and shook our arms out.

"May's mic is live for introduction. Show time in ten, nine, eight . . ."

The voice of Edward, our sound engineer, filled my ears, and I knew that the others got the same message. When he reached one, May's voice filled the stadium.

"Looonnnddddooonnnnn, Blood Oath is calling."

The stage lit up as we were lifted into view. The screams, holy shit, they were loud. Right next to our marks were our guitars, Angel had to hustle to jump behind his drum set, but like a well-oiled machine, we were strapped with our instruments and ready to go in a matter of seconds.

Without warning, I strummed my guitar and grinned when the riff sounded. It sounded like a lover's slow caress to my ears. Once the first one echoed, another one from the rhythm guitar followed its cue, then the beat of drums, then then bass line . . . then my voice.

CHAPTER TWENTY-THREE

FRANKIE

The world could have ended around me and I wouldn't have noticed because my entire being was focused on Risk. On his alluring, soul-touching, clit-throbbing voice. The throaty growling sound he made when he screamed certain lyrics sent a shiver up my spine. I had no idea *what* lyrics he was singing, I was entirely too captivated with how he looked and sounded to really *listen* to the words that were coming out of his mouth.

When the first song of the night wound to an end, the lighting on stage changed and each band member could be seen clearly by me at the side of the stage. There was a flurry of activity with the crew behind me still but I blocked them out and focused on Risk.

"London!" Risk shouted into his microphone. "What's happening, you beautiful bastards?"

The screams, holy Christ, they were deafening.

"That," Angel said into his mic from the back of the stage behind his drum set, "is what I like to fucking hear, Sinners. Don't you agree, Hayes?"

"Oh, yeah. Nothing better than Sinners screaming."

More screams quaked the stadium. I knew Angel and Hayes didn't sing like Risk, who was the lead, and May, who provided some backing vocals, but Summer had mentioned earlier that they recently started having their own microphones so they could speak and interact between songs because the fans loved it so much. It was clearly a good decision.

"Ha!" May suddenly shouted. "Barely finished the first song and I've got my first thong thrown my way." He bowed in the direction of the woman who threw it. "Thank you, darlin'."

He hung it off one of the guitar's tuning keys and I burst out laughing because that was such a May thing to do. A bunch of underwear was suddenly launched onto the stage, making Risk and Hayes laugh. With their fingertips, the lads followed suit and decorated their guitars with knickers and bras. I knew I couldn't be the only one to wonder if they were worn or new.

"Lucky bastards," Angel grumbled. "Where's my panties at?"

More flimsy pieces of fabric were hurled onto the stage, all of the guys laughed when May grabbed a bunch of them and ran up the steps in the middle of the stage so he could reach Angel. He decorated his drum kit and when he was finished Angel high-fived him.

"I've always got my brother's back when it comes to knicker decor."

I giggled like a silly schoolgirl. They were so funny, so charismatic and *so* happy. They were all smiling, I loved to see it. Them being happy made me feel happy. It was infectious.

"Long time no see, London," Risk shouted. "You're looking . . . good."

He needed to *stop* if he wanted me to *stay* side stage. He was using that low sexy tone of voice that melted me in seconds . . . the man was seducing the audience with nothing more than words, and he bloody well knew it.

"Good enough to eat," May continued. "I hope you're extra excited because you heard about our new album dropping next month and the accompanying *world* tour kicking off next year?"

Screams on *top* of screams.

"Nah, I don't think they heard you right, man," Hayes mused. "They don't sound hyped enough."

"Not even a little bit," Angel agreed. "I thought we had *Sinners* filling this place to the brim?"

He twirled his drumsticks expertly in his fingers as the screaming managed to get louder and it drew a musical laugh from Risk.

"Oh, our Sinners *did* hear about our new album and tour. Isn't that . . . fun?"

I was going to dry hump his leg if he wasn't careful.

May strummed his guitar, Risk followed suit, then Hayes and Angel joined in. I knew which song it was right away. 'Black Space', the song I whooped May on when we were playing Guitar God. I laughed and jumped around, which earned me a smile and head shake from Tobias, who was hovering close by. I was dancing and having fun but I slowed down to bobbing my head so I could focus on the lyrics of the song. It was an upbeat song about living life in the fast lane but needing the promise of a lover to always hold a person's hand so they couldn't get lost along the way.

The lyrics . . . they were beautiful.

A lump formed in my throat when I realised it was a song about the promise Risk and I made when we were kids, to always do everything together and have each other's back. It could have been depicted a million different ways, the lyrics weren't straight forward, but that was my take and I just *knew* it was the right one. I could hear what he was saying . . . I could hear *him*.

A tap on my shoulder startled me as the song drew to a close. I turned to my right and found Chris right there.

"He's looking at you!"

I turned my head to where Chris was pointing and I realised Risk was speaking to the audience, but looking right at me. I missed what he said, but when he held his hand out, I fully understood what he meant. He wanted me to go out on stage to him. Me. On stage. I reached into my bag and fisted both of my inhalers.

"Go to him!" Chris bellowed in my ear. "Get fucking out there!"

He pushed me from behind and I stumbled onto the stage, just barely catching my balance to avoid falling flat on my face. I wasn't completely on the centre stage, but I wasn't hidden by the side stage any longer. I glanced up at one of the huge screens next to the stage and my wide-eyed face was plastered up there for the thousands of fans to see. Screaming erupted when I forced myself to walk towards Risk. I knew the hardcore Sinners who followed the band in the media knew who I was instantly.

I closed the distance between myself and Risk, his hand came up to cradle my face instantly. I latched onto him like a spider monkey would its mama.

"Breathe," Risk lowered his face to mine. "You're okay, everything is okay."

I nodded, inhaling and exhaling.

"That's my girl."

"You're amazing, Risk."

He squinted and I realised he was reading my lips, his in-ears made it impossible to hear my voice. I smiled, letting him know I was okay and he relaxed. He lifted the microphone to his mouth and said, "Sinners, I would like to introduce you all to the *original* Sinner, the very woman who discovered I could sing and pushed me into making music. Miss Frankie Fulton."

I lifted my hands to my ears and laughed when the crowd screamed and cheered for me. A pair of black, lace underwear was thrown my way and it landed on my shoe. I kicked it off with a yelp which Risk, and the others, laughed over.

"I wanna sing my Cherry a little song."

I put my inhalers back into my bag and placed my hands on my cheeks, feeling my face burn through my make-up. Music to another song began, I recognised it from the instrumental of 'Think Up Love'. I didn't look away from Risk as he began to sing, I tried to focus on what he was singing, but I was too overwhelmed with him to keep up. He came to a stop in front of me and held the microphone out to me. My heart dropped. I stared from the mic up to Risk and suddenly felt sick.

Risk's smile slowly faded and the urge to run away was climbing up my spine. He reached out and took hold of my wrist, I knew he could feel how fast my heart was beating when he touched me.

"Risk, please. I can't."

His hold on my wrist tightened, he lowered his mouth to my ear.

"What's wrong? Just say the words if you don't want to sing them."

I couldn't move. I could only shake my head. Confusion filled Risk's ice-blue eyes, he didn't understand what was going on.

"Please, Frankie," his voice filled the stadium. "Please. Sing your song."

I couldn't move.

"I don't . . . I don't know . . ."

"One word, Cherry." He suddenly glared down at me. "Just sing *one fucking word* of the song. Of *any* fucking song."

The mixture of anger and confusion in his eyes was overthrown by a wave of hurt that filled his gaze. He knew . . . he knew I didn't know his songs. In that moment, we weren't on a stage in front of thousands of people, it was just the two of us. I knew Risk forgot about his surroundings, I was his entire focus. He processed me not knowing any of his songs.

I saw his heart break.

A body came up behind Risk, it was May. I saw his blood red hair out of the corner of my eye, but I couldn't look away from Risk's eyes . . . they had glazed over with tears. I blinked and my own tears fell.

"You don't know any of the words . . . d'you?"

The crowd nearly lost their fucking minds when I shook my head. Their screaming and booing was almost unbearable, but the sounds blended together the longer they carried on. I knew exactly what they were thinking. Risk had announced me as the original Sinner and I just threw that special honour back in his face, and the lads' faces too.

"You don't know them . . . you don't hear me."

As long as I lived, I knew I'd never forget the raw pain in his voice. It was as if his very centre, his reason for being, was snatched away from him.

I couldn't take the way he was staring at me, like I had just upended his entire world. I looked from him and out to the sea of faces who looked angry as they stuck their fingers up at me, angrily shook their fists and shouted words that blended to nothing but rage-filled noise. I looked back at Risk, whimpered when I saw how broken he looked, then I turned and ran off the stage and right by a red-faced Chris and a wide-eyed Tobias.

I ran and ran until I burst into a random bathroom and slammed the door behind me, locking it.

I fumbled for my inhaler, grabbed my blue one and inhaled some medicine to open up my airways. My chest was tightening so I focused only on breathing until I could draw in a deep breath without struggling. I inhaled a few puffs of my brown inhaler, then I capped them both and put them back into my bag. The music from the band was still playing and I could hear Risk singing. I didn't realise I was crying until banging sounded on the door behind me.

"Frankie?"

"P-Please," I sobbed. "Just leave me a-alone."

Tobias's sigh was loud and clear.

"I'll be right outside," he told me. "Take as long as you need. Do you have your inhalers."

"Yes," I choked. "I have them, I'm fine."

I was *far* from fucking fine.

I couldn't believe what had just happened. Risk brought me on stage and I humiliated him and the band. The look in his beautiful eyes when he pleaded with me to sing one word of his song, any song, haunted me. I cut him like a blade. He wasn't simply disappointed in me, he was deeply hurt. I saw how his face dropped when I couldn't sing a single word. He looked defeated. I cried harder knowing I had hurt him in the one place where I knew he felt free . . . on stage.

I wasn't sure how much time had passed by, but eventually there was no music coming from the stage. Tobias had banged on the door to check on me several times, each time I told him to leave me alone. He didn't leave though. Risk made me his responsibility and he took that seriously. My hands were shaking and my tears had dried onto my cheeks. I stood up and looked in the mirror. I looked disgusting. My eye make-up was ruined, twin trails of mascara ran down my cheeks and down onto my neck. I reached into my bag, grabbed the face wipes I brought with me and wiped away the make-up until the face I was used to seeing stared back at me.

My eyes were swollen and red, my cheeks were blotchy and my yellowing, fading bruise was on display for all to see too. Overall I looked like a train wreck.

I threw the used wipes into the bin, walked over to the door, unlocked then stepped out into the hall. Tobias was leaning against the wall facing the bathroom. His straightened up the second I opened the door. He shoved his phone into his pocket. His brown eyes stared at me with concern.

"I'm okay."

"No, you're not."

I sniffled. "You're right, I'm not, but I need to see Risk."

I had to explain myself, I had to make him understand why I didn't know his songs. I had to. I didn't wait for Tobias to respond, I turned and began walking. He cursed and jogged to reach my side. He directed me where I needed to go when I didn't know which turn to take. I looked up when I heard a voice shouting.

"You!"

I braced myself against the venom I knew was coming my way.

"You're fucking *lucky* you didn't ruin the entire show."

I swallowed. "I didn't mean for any of that to happen, Chris."

"Bullshit," he snapped, making me flinch. "You humiliated Risk and the band. Original Sinner my ass. You've been fucking Risk this past week and you're telling me you don't know one Blood Oath song? *One*?"

"My relationship with Risk is none of your business." I lifted my chin. "It's no one's but mine and his."

"His life belongs to the public, you stupid fucking bitch," Chris snapped, his face getting redder by the second. "I've worked overtime this past week calming the fans because you wanted to dry hump Risk on some shitty pier and just when that's blown over, you fuck up his first sober show. Are you *shitting* me?"

Each shouted word made me flinch.

"Ease up, Chris," Tobias practically growled. "Risk is a big boy, he made his decision. You get paid to do your job, not dictate his life."

"And *you* get paid to babysit so shut the fuck up or you're fired."

I didn't have to look at Tobias to know he was glaring at Chris.

"You don't know me," I said to him. "You didn't like me from the second you met me—"

"Because I knew something like this would fucking happen, you dumb *bitch*! You're no different than any other slut who wants the bragging rights of saying she fucked Risk Keller."

I didn't care for this man. I wasn't giving him another minute of my time because he had no clue about mine and Risk's history. Not a single one. I brushed by him but gasped when his hand grabbed my arm and he shoved me into the wall. For a second, I had no idea what was happening but then Chris's hold on me disappeared. My arm throbbed. I turned and saw Chris on the ground, moaning as he held his face. His bloody face. Tobias stood over him, his hand fisted.

"Oh my god!"

Tobias had punched him to help me.

"You're fired!" Chris spat. "Motherfucker."

"I work for Blood Oath, not you," Tobias snapped. "If I'm sacked, *they* will tell me."

Tobias turned, gently took my arm and led me away.

"It's your fault, bitch!" Chris bellowed as he stumbled to his feet. "His relapse is *your* fucking fault!"

If Tobias hadn't been holding me, I think I would have fallen to my knees with shock. Chris's words hit me with the impact of a train.

"No!" I clung to Tobias. "No, *no*! Please, don't tell me he's using."

Tobias couldn't look me in the eye.

"They got off stage thirty minutes ago . . . he's been drinking since then. He won't leave the building because he knows you're here somewhere, he's in the dressing room."

No.

I whimpered. "Take me to him *now*!"

I needed to stop him. I needed to explain. I needed to fix this.

"*Dios me!*" Angel straightened up, away from the wall outside the dressing room, when he saw me run down the hallway with Tobias right by my side. "Frankie, this is *not* a good time."

He tried to stop me, but I pushed by him and kicked the door open. The first sight that greeted me was Risk snorting a white substance off a woman's naked breasts. My stomach lurched as I stepped into the room. May was in the middle, shouting at one of the women, while Hayes was grabbing the piles of alcohol bottles on the table in front of Risk and was in the process of dumping them into a sink.

"Frankie," May looked shocked to see me. "This is *not* what it looks like. These girls just got here two minutes ago, he hasn't kissed them or anything. I swear."

The fact that May had to reassure me of this hurt my chest. Four women were all but sitting on Risk, kissing on his neck, face and anywhere else they could. He was fully clothed still but it looked like things wouldn't stay that way for long. My stomach churned with the sight. The four women looked my way. Risk looked like he was barely aware of their presence next to him.

"Leave," I said to the four. "Now."

There must have been a fierce look in my eyes or it was the finality of my tone, but the women didn't argue with me or try to make me change my mind. They simply stood up and left the room even while Risk was lazily calling for them to come back.

"Spoiling m-my fun, Cherry."

Risk sniffed repeatedly and rubbed the leftover white powder on his fingers over his gums. May smacked his hands away while Hayes, who had finished emptying all of the bottles, grabbed the open bag of drugs, poured it into the same sink and ran water over it. As they did this, Angel barred the door from the women who were pleading for re-entry, they were promising all of the members a good time. It shocked me to see just how much of a system the guys seemed to have, like they had done this very routine a million times before. Risk shouted insults at his friends but they didn't pay him any mind as they cleared away every bit of substance he wanted to consume.

"Who got you this shit?" May snapped at Risk, getting right in his face. "*Who*?"

"The tooth fairy."

"Mother*fucker*!"

Risk laughed at May, the magnitude of what he was doing was not registering with him. *I* knew what he was doing though. He was trying to escape the pain he felt. He was hurting deeply, he was looking to numb himself with drink and drugs, he was looking for the blackness to take him away from what he was feeling.

"Look at the state of you." I stared at him, my body shaking. "You're a fucking wreck."

He pushed himself clumsily off the sofa and onto his feet. If it hadn't been for May and Hayes reaching out and catching him, Risk would have slammed, face first, into the glass coffee table in front of him. Summer was on the far side of the room, out of any possible harm's way, with her hand over her mouth as she watched the scene unfold before her.

"You fucking *liar*!" I suddenly shouted. "You promised you wouldn't take that stuff anymore. You *promised*!"

"I'm a liar?!" Risk screamed in anger as he ripped his sobriety coin from his neck and threw it at my feet. "Me?"

"Yes, you! You said you wouldn't use anymore."

"And *you* said you had heard my songs."

I wiped away falling tears.

"I have a reason for that!"

Risk humourlessly laughed as he struggled against his friends but couldn't break their hold on him.

"I thought you had changed," I whimpered. "But you haven't."

Risk twitched left, right and centre.

"I thought everything had changed for the better for us. I hoped and prayed and d'you want to know why? Because you're the only one who fills the empty space inside of me."

He said nothing as he tried to focus on me, sweat beading on his forehead.

"Why did you do that to me out there? Why would you hurt me like that, Risk?"

Risk couldn't stand up straight, the drugs he had taken mixed with the alcohol were working their way quickly into his system. May was on his left and Hayes on his right, all three of them were staring at me. Risk was the only one who looked furious.

"Did you bring me here just to humiliate me in front of your fans?" I demanded. "D'you hate me that much that you wanted to hurt me like this?"

"I never want to hurt you, but you always hurt me," Risk slurred. "You don't know your own so-songs. You d-don't know th-them."

I had no idea what he was saying.

"My songs?" I repeated. "*What* do you mean?"

"*Your songs*!" he snapped. "They're all y-your songs and you don't know any of th-them because you've erased me! You're su-supposed to hear me and you *don't.*"

I felt as if he'd slapped me.

"Those songs . . . they're about me?"

Risk laughed like a mad man.

"It's why I call you muse, Frankie," Angel said quietly from behind me. "You're *Risk's* muse."

"Every song I've ever wr-written is about you because I'm fucking stupid and c-couldn't let you go even after nine years, but guess what, you heartless fucking bitch? Tonight you made it cl-clear. We're over. *Forever*."

His insult stung more than it should have because he had never called me a name like that before.

"You've got it wrong, Risk."

"Oh, do I, te-temptress?" He tried, and failed, to break out of his friends' hold once again. "Stupid Risk is wrong a-again, am I?"

"Yeah," I nodded. "Stupid Risk, you are, because I'd have told you why I don't know Blood Oath's songs if you had *asked* me. I wasn't keeping it from you on purpose, I just didn't know how to tell you!"

"Then t-tell me." He stared me down. "Tell. Me. Frankie."

"I don't know any of your band's songs, because I've never listened to them out of choice." I trembled. "I don't listen to your songs because your voice breaks me. D'you understand that? It breaks me!"

Risk struggled to remain upright, but his eyes never left mine. Not once.

"What?"

"You heard me," I shouted. "I couldn't hear you sing because I couldn't cope with how much I missed and hurt for you. Not because I hated you. I *never* hated you. I've loved you since I was fifteen, you callous bastard! You're my night and day!"

Tears poured from my eyes and I tried my best to quickly wipe them away. I hated that I was crying in front of May, Hayes, Summer and Angel. Mine and Risk's drama shouldn't have to be put on their shoulders but everywhere he was, they weren't far away from him.

"I wear my earphones everywhere I go because, like a fool, I'm weak for you." I hiccupped. "It's pointless to try and block you because I hear you every night in my dreams. You're haunting me and you have the nerve to tell me I don't know your songs because I've erased you? Risk, erasing you would mean erasing myself."

He looked like he was struggling to breathe and I knew all too well how that felt.

"I shouldn't have come here. I shouldn't have left my mum. I shouldn't have agreed to being friends with you. I shouldn't have had sex with you. I shouldn't have let you walk back into my life." I exhaled a painful breath. "Nothing has changed, we're still worlds apart from each other and I think we always will be. You're not good for me and I'm *definitely* not good for you. We can't do this. We were stupid to think that we could try to be something. We can't be anything."

"Frankie, just . . . just wait. I can't think."

"Goodbye, Risk." I backed towards the door of the dressing room. "Keep chasin', rock star."

When I turned and fled the room, Risk screamed my name and the raw pain I heard in his voice hit me like a tonne of bricks but I didn't stop running. I needed to get away, I needed space, I needed to think . . . I needed to go home to Southwold and put Risk and this too-big-for-me world out of my mind. It was time I closed Risk's chapter in my life.

The problem was . . . I didn't know how to do that.

CHAPTER TWENTY-FOUR
FRANKIE

Nine years ago . . .

My entire life had changed in seven days.

My every waking hour was consumed by my mum. A week after her accident I had maybe seen Risk for a total of ten hours because whenever I got home, I usually went straight to bed. Most nights Risk would be in the studio until late so when he came home, I was already asleep. When I woke up for my morning shift at Mary Well's diner, he would already be gone to work.

I knew it wouldn't last forever, just until my mum was in a routine and could move around easier, but I missed my boyfriend and I knew he missed me too. I wanted to spend some time with him so I left Mum and Dr O'Rourke's home – she had just moved in with him so he could keep a constant eye on her – just after six in the evening, exactly one week after her illness was revealed to me, and I walked the twenty minutes to Cumberland Road, where May lived. It was pitch black outside, lightly raining and freezing.

I didn't tell Risk I was stopping by, I wanted to surprise him.

When I reached May's home, it suddenly began to pour from the sky. I hurried into the garden and up to the studio next to the house and silently let myself in since I knew the door's key code. The studio wasn't huge, but the lads made the space work by only using whatever instruments they needed at the current moment.

They hung nearly everything else on the walls to keep them out of the way. It would have been easy for them to find a studio in a big town not far away and rent some hours of studio time, but that was money the band didn't have. All of their money went on upgrading their third-hand instruments to decent second-hand ones. It was a struggle, but a band was only as good as their instruments and because Blood Oath were virtually unknown, they needed to work hard to get better equipment to improve their sound.

I heard Risk's voice as I closed the door behind me and, from the tone, he didn't sound too pleased.

"You're not listening to us," Hayes sighed. "We have to leave in *two days* and you still haven't told her. Telling her is the right thing to do."

"He's right, Risk," May grumbled. "Look, I know you think you're doing the right thing but the *last* thing Frankie needs right now is another massive surprise."

I remained behind the stack of amplifiers that were piled up near the door. I had no idea what conversation I had walked in on, but it had something to do with me. The familiar sensation of dread that settled in the pit of my stomach when Dr O'Rourke told me my mum was injured and sick reared its ugly head and smirked at me.

"Both of you have *no clue* what you're talking about," Risk snapped at his friends. "Her mum almost died in a car accident and she found out in the same hour that she has Alzheimer's too.

Telling her that the band got offered a record deal now is *not* the right time."

"But she'll be happier than anyone on this planet for us," May argued. "Frankie is our number one fan. She is the first Sinner, she loves us."

"Being signed isn't what my issue is, mate," Risk grunted. "That isn't the hard part."

"Then what is?"

"Moving country," Hayes answered May. "He doesn't know how to tell her that."

I tried to understand what I was hearing, but I couldn't. Blood Oath had been offered a record deal? When had this happened? And they had to move to another country? Which country? Why was I finding out about it by accident?

I felt trapped in the small space so I turned and opened the door to the studio to get fresh air. I heard a noise behind me and when I looked over my shoulder, I locked eyes with May and his face dropped. I turned and hurried outside into the rain and cold of the January evening.

"Frankie!" I heard May shout. "Fuck! Risk, Frankie heard us! She knows!"

I broke out into a jog as I rushed away from the studio, my mind running wild. I gasped when I heard footsteps behind me and then felt arms come around him, bringing me to an abrupt stop. I struggled until lips pressed against my ear and his voice said, "Please, let me explain. *Please*."

"You want to explain now?" I repeated. "You were bloody adamant in there that I wasn't supposed to know anything of what you said."

"Cherry, please," Risk pleaded, using the name only he called me. "Just listen to me."

He turned me to face him and brushed my wet hair back out of my face. I looked up at him, blinking as the rain fell heavier from the night sky. We were standing under a broken streetlight that flickered every few seconds. The wind howled around us and the cold air of the night burned my lungs as I inhaled.

"What's goin' on?" I demanded. "I don't understand any of what I heard."

"Come inside out of the rain—"

"I'm not going *anywhere* until you tell me what the fuck is goin' on!"

Risk leaned his head back and exhaled, his hot breath fogging the air around him. When he looked back down at me, water ran from his matted, sopping wet hair down his sculpted face.

"The day your mum had her accident, Hayes got a phone call from a representative from New Chord Records. It's a small American record label. They saw videos of us online and they listened to our EP. They love our sound, our lyrics and our look. They're flying us out to Los Angeles on Wednesday so we can meet the executives of the company. They're offerin' us a record deal and if we like what they have to say, we'll be signed to their label."

I stared up at Risk, my heart hammering inside my chest.

"What's the catch?" I asked. "I know there is one, you wouldn't have kept this from me otherwise."

"They let us know that if we sign with them, we have . . . we have to move to Los Angeles for a couple of years to work with them on improving our sound and searching for a fourth member. They know we've been looking for a drummer and they're giving us time to find someone who fits in with the band. They mentioned putting us up in an small apartment while we write and record an album. They're a small company so they need us to be committed to them as they haven't got extra money to waste.

We need to be in the same city to cancel out travel expenses. It'll be hardcore work for us until we release the album we've been writing—"

"Why didn't you tell me any of this?" I interrupted. "Why? This is huge."

I felt sick. Processing his words was incredibly difficult.

"Because of your mum," he stated. "How could I just spring the best news of my life onto you when your world was crashin' down around you?"

"Because this is somethin' I need to know, Risk. *That's why*!"

He reached for me and for the first time in our relationship, I recoiled from his touch. Hurt filled his blue eyes and his arm dropped limply to his side. He didn't take his eyes off me once as I reached into my bag and grabbed my inhaler the second I heard the wheeze in my throat. I closed my eyes and focused on taking my medicine.

"Slow breaths," Risk urged. "That's it, baby. Slow."

The attack never had a leg to stand on, so when I felt the threat of it pass by, I relaxed. I held my inhaler in my hand, opened my eyes and looked back up at my boyfriend.

"I can't go to America."

"Not on this trip," he said. "I know that. This is just a three-day thing to see if what they're offerin' is the real deal. We'll have to have a solicitor look over whatever contract they give us before we sign anythin', but—"

"Risk, no." I shook my head. "I can't go to America. Not now, not ever."

Risk's whole body seemed to tense.

"What?"

"My mum's disease is only startin' and it is progressive. That means she's goin' to get *really* sick over time and she'll need me. I can't go to America while that is happening."

Risk blinked repeatedly. "But . . . But she lives with Michael now and he's a doctor."

"So?" I said. "Just because she lives with her boyfriend doesn't mean she won't need me. D'you understand how seriously ill she is? People think this disease is just someone forgetting things here and there, but it's not. It's cruel and it's horrible and it's going to erase her, Risk. It robs someone of themselves piece by piece over time until basic functions are a challenge. I can't leave her when she needs me the most, Risk. I won't. She's my mum."

Over the past week I had educated myself in my mother's disease and the things I learned utterly devastated me. When I thought of the times my mum would misplace something, I would tease her over it. I would constantly joke and tell her that she would lose her head if it wasn't attached to her shoulders. All those jokes and the harmless teasing about how forgetful she was were no longer funny in any way, shape or form. Forgetfulness was one tiny part of something much bigger that my sweet mother was now dealing with. This illness would rob me of her over time and I would be able to do nothing but stand by and watch as it happened.

It had taken me just a couple days to accept it, and the only reason I did was because I knew time wasn't a luxury I had. If I denied my mum's sickness, I would only be hurting us both. I accepted her disease, but I was still struggling with knowing that slowly but surely, I was going to lose the woman I knew and loved right before my very eyes. She was going to change so drastically and I couldn't stop it from happening. All I could do was be there for her and make sure she was loved and cared for so that in her darkest hours she had someone there to keep the light on.

"Frankie," Risk stepped forward. "What do I do then?"

"What d'you mean?"

"If this works out and we sign our deal, I have to go to America."

"For two years," I said, my body beginning to shake. "And that's only to find a new member and write and record an album. What about when you actually release it and have to promote it and do a bunch of other stuff related to it? What about when you guys blow up into superstars and have to spend a lot more time in America and go on world tours for months out of the year?"

Risk blinked and shook his head, but said nothing because he and I both knew that I was right. This was Blood Oath's big break, this is what they had been working for, this is what they deserved. It had to be full steam ahead, there could be no setbacks or distractions and I realised in that moment that that was exactly what I had become. Risk realised it too.

"This mi-might not work out though," he stammered. "This could be a complete bust."

Tears filled my eyes as I smiled.

"Not a chance, rock star. This is Blood Oath's beginning. This is what you've been chasing . . . you're gonna get your dream."

He stared down at me. "But you're not gonna come with me, are you?"

"No," I rasped. "I can't take the risk of leaving my mum."

"Frankie."

"I think . . . I think we need to step back from each other."

Saying those words ripped a hole in my chest.

"You once told me I was the only risk you'd ever take, but you're risking everything we have right now and for what? Because you think we can't do long distance?"

"I love you," I said, my body trembling. "I love you with my whole heart, but I *cannot* go with you. Your career just got its big break, you know where this ends if we do long distance. You know and so do I. We won't see each other for months, video chats and calls and texts will dwindle because we're both busy with our lives, and I don't want us to end like that. I don't want us to just . . . fade."

"Who says we'll fade?" he demanded. "You're making excuses now, Frankie, and you know it."

"I'm not!" I argued. "I'm thinking realistically!"

Frustrated, Risk turned and lobbed his phone at the garden wall next to us. I didn't flinch when it cracked off the concrete and smashed onto the ground.

"Why'd you do that?" I demanded. "You need a phone now."

"I'll get a new one with a new number since it's obvious you won't be calling me anymore, right?"

He was hurting. He reacted with anger when he was hurting because it was the only defence tactic he had. Risk had been fostered for most of his life by a family who never treated him like anything other than a stranger and a punching bag. He didn't learn to love until we got together. His biological mother died of a drug overdose when he was four and he never knew who his father was. He didn't have a real family until me, May and Hayes formed a bond with him.

"Please," I begged. "Don't be angry with me."

"Don't be angry? We've been dating for three years, I've known you almost my whole life. I thought we were stronger than this, Frankie. I thought everything in life we were going to do, we would do together. Wasn't that what we promised?"

It was. When we started dating at fifteen we promised we'd always do everything together. That'd we never leave the other one alone.

"I'm sorry," my voice cracked. "I wish things were different, I'd leave with you in a minute if they were but they're not. My mum has Alzheimer's, Risk. She's not going to get better, only worse. I have to take care of her, I have to."

"I can take care of you both." He reached for me and gripped my arms. "Just come with me. When I make money, I'll pay the best doctors to help your mum."

"Baby, *listen* to yourself. My mum's sickness is very mild right now, but she's eventually going to forget everything that's new to her and only have old memories. How would she cope living in America where everything is strange to her?"

"I don't fucking know!" he snapped. "I'm trying to think of something to keep this from happening."

"This is the only way, Risk. I wish it wasn't but it is. You're going to live in America for the next couple of years while your band grows and finds success. I'm still going to be here in Southwold with my mum when you're a worldwide superstar. Don't you understand that? I'm always going to be here, Risk. My life doesn't leave this little town . . . but yours will."

"So what?" he snapped, his blue eyes aflame with hurt. "You're setting me free, is that it? Am I supposed to fucking thank you for doing this to me? You think breaking up with me is what's best for me?"

I was sobbing now.

"It *is* what's best for you! How can you chase your dreams if you're stuck in this town with me for the rest of your life?" I pushed against his chest, hating how he thought this was easy for me. Like breaking my own heart was something I wanted to do. "How can you live if you're trapped here with me? How will you be able to breathe when I feel like I'm suffocating?"

I was screaming now, tears were flowing and my hands were beating against Risk's chest.

He put his arms round me and held me as I sobbed. I clung on to him like my life depended on it. I pressed my face against his soaking wet chest for a moment longer, then I looked up. Risk was staring down at me, his eyes glazed over with unshed tears. I had never seen him look so angry, so hurt, so helpless. I was the cause of each of those emotions and it cut me like a blade knowing that.

"We're done, Risk," I said, lifting my hand to his face. "I'm b-breaking up with you."

The muscles in his sharp jaw rolled back and forth as his ice-blues stared down at me. I scanned my eyes over every inch of his face, memorising it all so on the nights I was alone and hurting for him, I would know exactly how he looked in this moment.

"Why are you doing this to me? You're my girl, why're you pushing me away?"

My chin quivered. "I have to."

"No, you don't. You *don't* have to. You're the first person I have ever loved, you're the first person I have said those words to in my entire life. You reached me before May and Hayes could, before music could. I thought you loved me, Cherry."

"I *do* love you! I'll love you my whole life," I whispered. "I promise."

"You couldn't keep your first promise . . . what makes this one so special?"

The tone in Risk's voice changed, it suddenly turned emotionless and when I looked up into his eyes, it was like I could see him building up a wall protect himself from further hurt . . . to protect him from me.

"I wish things were different."

He licked his lips. "So that's it?"

I couldn't move.

"I . . . I guess it is. You have to go."

"Everyone in my life has sent me away. My mum sent me away when she picked drugs over me, all those families I went on visits to sent me away when they didn't want to adopt me, Owen and Freda drove me away when I was no longer in the system and couldn't earn them money . . . I never ever thought you would send me away, too."

My heart shattered as Risk took one step back from me and then another, I sobbed a little more with each one.

"Risk, please."

His jaw clenched. "*What*?"

"Please," I whimpered. "Just . . . just . . . kiss me before you go."

I thought I would have to beg him, but I didn't.

The words were barely out of my mouth when he surged forward and wrapped me in his embrace. We were soaked to the bone, but it didn't seem to matter when he lowered his head and his lips met mine in a furious passion. I lifted my hands to his soaking hoodie and pulled him as hard against me as I could. Our kiss was filled with broken promises, unimaginable hurt, heartfelt love and the brutal reality that this was likely the last one we would ever share.

I didn't want the kiss to end, but, like all good things, it did.

"I'll keep your mum in my prayers," Risk said against my lips before he took a step back and lifted his hand to wipe away the rainwater on his face. "I'll come by tomorrow when you're at work and I'll get all of my stuff. The rent money for this month is in an envelope under the mattress on my side of the bed. Make sure you *always* have your inhaler . . . your prescription needs to be refilled next week. Don't forget."

I choked out the word, "Okay."

Risk bowed his head. "Take care of yourself, Cherry."

"Keep chasin', rock star."

I had always told him that. No matter what life threw at him, I always told him to keep chasing his dreams.

Without a word, Risk turned and walked away from me, I had to force my legs not to run after him. I lifted my hand that still clenched my inhaler and inhaled a couple of puffs of my medicine.

I wasn't sure if I was about to have an attack or not. I felt horrendous pain in my chest, but I didn't know if it was because I was struggling to breathe or because I had just forced the love of my life to walk away from me. All I knew was I was hurting, and watching Risk disappear from view was like someone stabbed a blade into my chest and twisted it.

Somehow, I turned around and began walking. I was replaying my conversation with Risk over and over in my mind and I couldn't see a way that it could end where he didn't have to give up everything he had ever dreamed of to stay with me in Southwold. I knew in my heart that that was the direction things would have headed for us. Risk loved me most in the entire world and there was nothing on God's green earth that he wouldn't give up to be with me. That included his dream of being a successful musician. I wasn't going to be the person who killed his dream.

I refused.

I ended up at my front door without realising I had been walking home. When I got inside and closed the door behind me, the silence in my home was deafening. I began to strip out of my clothes where I stood. The sound of the sopping wet fabric smacking against the floor was barely audible because a new sound filled the silence. My crying. I couldn't believe what had just taken place. I had broken up with Risk . . . with *my* Risk. Nothing in my life was the same as it had been a week ago.

Everything was different now.

My home, my town, my mum, my life, me.

All of it had been flipped on its head. I had to actively live without the relationship that my new adult life had been built around. It hurt. God, it hurt. I felt like I couldn't breathe past the pain, yet I continued to breathe. I was somehow surviving even though on the inside I crumbled to nothingness. When I woke up that morning, I had no idea that my world could be turned inside out again. Just like the snap of my fingers, the life I planned to have was snatched away from me and the worse thing about it all . . . everything that led to right now was my decision.

Naked and shivering, I turned on the lights inside my home then I walked into my bedroom. I sat at my vanity table and stared into the mirror, wondering how I could look exactly the same, but feel so changed inside. The life I had planned with Risk was nothing more than a pipe dream now. The path we had walked together for so long had now become divided and I was quickly finding out that the road I was on was a one-way street. I couldn't make a U-turn and go back to the start because that time had come and gone.

Risk was following his journey to stardom and it was a path I knew in my heart that he would succeed in reaching the end of. Risk, and his talent, were too big for our small town and much too big for me. Letting him go was my gift to him and though he didn't understand that now I knew someday that he would. I was freeing him from a life that bound and constricted someone like him, someone who was born to take the world by storm. Someone who gave so much to people with his voice that his very presence would bring them happiness. I knew that because he and his voice brought me happiness for a very long time.

He would be okay, I knew he would be . . . me on the other hand, I would have to remember to put one foot in front of the other and tell myself to breathe. I would go to my quiet place where nothing was wrong. Mum wouldn't be sick, Risk wouldn't be leaving and I would be calm, collected and happy. All I had to do was remember to breathe.

In and out and in and out.

Just keep breathing.

CHAPTER TWENTY-FIVE
FRANKIE

Present day . . .

Three in the morning.

I found myself walking along Southwold pier after just arriving from London. When I fled the dressing room, Tobias followed me. He took a taxi with me back to Risk's townhouse and saw me safely to my car, which was parked in Risk's driveway. Tobias tried to convince me to sleep on my decision to walk away from Risk, but he and I both knew the only thing that would help Risk was me being far away from him. What happened a few hours ago could have been avoided if only we both were completely honest with each other.

Risk . . . he wouldn't have relapsed and I wouldn't be so broken.

It was nearing midnight when I left London, and I reached Southwold just as it turned 3 a.m.. I couldn't go home, not yet. I needed to be out in the open so I could breathe. I was having trouble processing what had happened. I didn't understand how a wonderful night had turned into such a pitiful nightmare. I kept replaying the look on Risk's face when he realised I didn't know his songs . . . or my songs. He wrote songs for me . . . and I didn't know them.

That knowledge hurt me so I knew it killed him.

"He looked devastated," I murmured as I walked along the wooden boards of the pier. "I made him feel that way."

I believed what I had said right before I fled Wembley . . . I wasn't right for him.

We weren't good together. I really didn't know if we were meant to be because we had only been back in one another's lives for a week and the level of shit that had kicked off was unbelievable. It was a bad omen if I had ever seen one. I sniffled, used the sleeve of my coat to wipe my nose. The top of it was sore from blowing and rubbing it so much with tissue on the drive from London. I knew it was likely scorched red.

I wrapped my arms around my middle and walked. I could hear the crashing sound of the waves under the pier and I could hear laughter and singing from somewhere up the beach. The pubs would have recently closed for the night so people tended to wander around town a little before they headed home. I paid them no mind. I walked all the way to the end of the pier like I usually did and my heart jumped when I saw a large man leaning against the rail at its end.

He heard me approach and when he turned my gut twisted.

"Owen."

"Frankie," he said, sounding surprised to see me. "Bit late for ye to be wanderin' along the pier, isn't it? All alone too."

I looked around the empty pier and the space where I normally found solace suddenly felt like it was a bottomless pit. The small buildings along it were closed and, apart from myself and Owen, the place was devoid of people.

"I didn't think anyone would be down here." I shifted. "Like you said, it's late."

"And yet here ya are."

I exhaled a breath. "It's funny, because I was just about to leave."

"Hold your horses." He rolled his eyes. "No need to run off."

I had *every* need to run off. I knew better than to be left alone with such a cruel, weak man who solved his problems with his fists when it came to women and children.

"How's your mum?"

I didn't move a muscle.

"If you say a word against her, Owen . . ."

He looked out at the ocean as my threat hung in the air.

"I'm not that heartless," he said. "I know how it feels to watch someone you love die day by day until they're gone."

My throat nearly closed up.

"I have enough on my mind right now," I rasped. "I *don't* need you reminding me that my mum is dying."

I didn't need *anyone* reminding me of something that was always at the back of my mind.

Owen shrugged. "I heard somethin' happened with yerself and the boy tonight . . . some just barely legal kids were in the pub yappin' on about it. Some rubbish about a concert."

I tensed. I shouldn't have been surprised that what happened was public knowledge but I was. "What happened is no one's business." I glared at him. "Especially not *yours*."

Owen pushed away from the rail.

"You and the boy have had some huge fallin' out and ya *still* jump t'his defence?"

"Always." I straightened. "He could hang me out to dry, Owen, and I would *always* defend him from you. I didn't do it when I was child, I should have, but I didn't. I swear to God that I'll do it from now until the day I die. You'll *never* get to say so much as 'boo' to him if I have any say about it."

Owen tilted his head.

"Ye didn't tell him I wanted to see him, did ya?"

The gall of this man truly astounded me.

"I *told* you I wouldn't!" I snapped. "I told you."

"And I fuckin' told *you* t'give 'im that message."

"Well, I didn't give it and I won't." I lifted my chin. "I don't care that you hit me or if you do it again. He doesn't owe you a fucking thing, Owen. *You* owe *him*!"

The lighting on the pier wasn't brilliant, but it was enough for me to see Owen's meaty face turn a repulsive, angry purple. He took a step towards me but stumbled slightly. I frowned.

"Have you been drinking?"

"Yeah," Owen shrugged. "I just came from a lock-in at the pub, so what?"

He didn't sound drunk, he didn't slur his words but I saw in his eyes when he moved closer that he was intoxicated, the evidence was in his steps too.

"You could tip yourself over that rail right there and drown," I shook my head. "Go on home, Owen."

"Why?" he asked. "No one's waitin' for me there."

I stood aghast. Was this no-good, child-abusing utter waste of flesh feeling sorry for himself? After all of the hurt he had put Risk through during his life? Was he *actually* serious?

"And whose fault is that?" I tilted my head, fury shooting up and down my veins. "Whose fault is it that no one in your life wants to be close to you? It's *your* fault and you bloody well know it! You could have had a son in Risk, he would have come home to see you, to take care of you and Freda but you used and abused him because you're a waste of space who—"

I screamed when Owen lurched forward quicker than I ever thought was possible. He reached out and used his large hand to grab a handful of my hair as he yanked my body towards his. The force of my body banging against his bloated belly knocked the breath out of me. My bag went skidding to the edge of the pier. Instinctively, I reached up with both of my hands and tried to pry my hair from Owen's grip, but he was too strong so I switched tactics.

"No!" I banged my fists on his chest. "Let go! Get away from me!"

"Yer a smart-mouthed wee tramp." He twisted his hand. "Thinkin' ye can talk t'me whatever way ya like!"

He was roaring every word as if I was miles away instead of right in front of him.

"This is why I had those kids taken from you!" I screeched. "*This is why*! You cruel son of a *bitch*!"

The sound of his hand clattering against my face seemed to echo in the still of the night. I hit the decking of the pier floor with a sickening thud. I thought I heard shouting from up the pier, but I couldn't turn to see what was going on because Owen yanked me back to my feet by my hair, pulling another scream from my throat. I could have sworn I heard my name being shouted, but I couldn't focus on anything other than the pain that swam around my head and throbbing face.

"I knew it was you!" he slobbered. "I fuckin' *knew* it."

"You're fucking right it was me!" I reached up and dug my nails into his face. "I'd do it again and again and *again*!"

I yanked my hands down, my nails scratching crevices along Owen's sweating, flushed skin. He released his hold on my hair as he shouted and raised both of his hands to his bloodied face. My scalp was burning but I didn't dare lift my hand to inspect any possible damage, I kept my eyes trained on Owen as I pushed myself onto my knees.

"Frankie!"

I jerked my head to my left. I couldn't see anyone because the pier's small restaurant was in the way, but I'd know his voice from a million miles away. I had heard it in my dreams enough to recognise it at a whisper.

"Risk!"

I was in the middle of getting to my feet when Owen stepped forward and kicked me so hard in the stomach, I partially vomited. His hands were tangled in my hair again within seconds. He was speaking so fast that I couldn't understand him but I got the gist of what he was implying. He wanted to hurt me or worse. I sucked in a breath when Owen's body was speared from the side. He smacked into the railing of the pier and a creaking sound echoed. It took me a few seconds to realise what was happening, but when I did, I was beside myself. Risk was bent over Owen and he was beating him violently.

My screams could have been heard out on the ocean.

"Risk, please!" I pleaded. "He's not worth it, he's nothing. Risk, *stop*!"

He didn't listen, the only reason he stopped was because Tobias and Jacob suddenly ran onto the pier's end and both of them physically dragged Risk off a sobbing, and badly beaten, Owen Day. His face was covered in blood. It was a horrifying sight. Hayes, May and Angel rounded the corner of the restaurant; the three of them were breathing heavily.

"Frankie!"

May was in my space with his hands on my face in seconds.

"Your head."

My head?

I lifted my hand to my forehead, just above my eyebrow, and hissed when stinging, throbbing pain registered. The slickness of warm, wet liquid coated my fingers. I pulled my hand down and stared at the blood on it. Owen had cut me, but I had no idea when it occurred. The pain in my head was nothing compared to the hurt I felt in my stomach that had suddenly spread upwards to my chest. Owen's kick was crippling and I knew I was in the grasp of an asthma attack before I realised it. I wheezed and looked around for my bag, panicking when I couldn't find it.

I fell to my knees within seconds. My ears were ringing, my vision distorted and my feet were tingling. It felt like someone was sitting on my chest, preventing me from taking in a deep breath.

"'haler," I wheezed. "My . . . inhaler. Bag."

"Fuck!' May shouted. "She needs her inhaler, where's her bag?"

"There!" Angel answered.

Before Angel could even finish speaking the head of an inhaler was pushed into my mouth. Instinctively, I inhaled the medicine, feeling more panicked, more unable to breathe than ever before. I heard Risk's voice, but it was lost on me what he was saying as I closed my eyes and inhaled my medicine. The familiar taste of albuterol coated my tongue as I sucked it down my windpipe and held it for a few seconds within my expanded lungs. Four or five more puffs were delivered from my inhaler before the world around me slowly began to come back into focus.

I didn't know how much time had passed.

"Frankie, look at me. Baby, eyes on me," Risk's voice prompted. "Are you okay?"

"Yes," I answered, still breathing heavily. "I can breathe now."

"Thank Christ."

His arms came around me and I felt him kiss the side of my face. I didn't have the energy to hug him back, only to breathe. I was exhausted. I have never had an attack that scared me so deeply before, nor one that left me feeling so utterly drained.

"What are you doing out here, Frank?"

"I . . . I needed to think." I looked at Risk. "Why are *you* here?"

"For you," he answered. "You left London before I could blink."

I looked down. "Risk . . . what happened tonight . . . it's a sign that we're not meant to be together."

"I've never believed in fate so I'm not gonna start now."

My eyes found his. "A few hours ago you told me we were done forever."

"That was before you told me . . . told me why you don't know your songs." He licked his lips. "I jumped the gun, Frankie. I didn't stop to think about why you didn't know them, I just reacted to the fact that you *didn't* know them. The pain I felt consumed me. I thought . . . I really thought you blocked them out . . . blocked me out because . . . because . . ."

"Because you thought I was trying to erase you?" I finished. "Trying to forget you?"

At his nod, my heart clenched.

"Risk, I meant what I said. Erasing you would mean erasing myself. I could never do it."

"Why didn't you tell me?" he asked, looking simply defeated. "On Saturday I told you that you're my muse, I asked if you heard my songs and you said you downloaded every album."

"The instrumentals," I explained. "I was too scared to buy the studio albums."

"Cherry . . . we *really* need to talk about everything."

"Right now?" I asked. "Because I really just want to go home and go to sleep."

"I can't wait—"

"You broke ma nose, ye fuckin' bastard!"

I grabbed hold of Risk's arms when his entire body tensed the second Owen spoke.

"Don't! All he has is his strength, hitting us is his only weapon. Hitting you, hitting me . . . it's all he has."

Risk didn't move, he just kept his eyes on my face. On the fresh cut above my eyebrow to the fading bruise on my cheek.

"You didn't hurt your face accidentally last week, did you?"

I wasn't keeping any more secrets from him.

"No," I sniffled. "Owen hit me because I refused to tell you that he wanted to see you."

Risk's eyes closed and he was so tense that when he clamped his teeth together, his jaw popped. I felt him tremble with rage.

"I couldn't tell you," I whimpered. "I couldn't because I knew you'd do this and you're better than this, better than him."

"Maybe I'm not!" Risk shouted, reaching out and taking hold of my arms. "Maybe I'm *not*, Frankie. Did it ever occur to you that I'm nothing? That you put me on a pedestal? That maybe I'm just a fucking junkie who can sing?"

Each word he spat felt like a slap in the face.

"No, none of that has ever occurred to me because it's *not* fucking true!"

Risk looked weak, like life was suddenly too much for him.

"Believe me," I pleaded. "You are a million times the man he is. You're so much more than you give yourself credit for. So much more."

I leaned in and rested my head against his.

"You need to let him go, all he and Freda did to you . . . it all needs to be let go. He should suffer with the weight of what he did, not you. Never you."

Risk got to his feet and helped me to mine, I held tightly on to his arm and both Jacob and Tobias stepped forward, just in case Risk attacked Owen, but he didn't. He simply stood and stared his abuser down. Owen had managed to get himself to his feet and was using the rail to support his weight.

"You hit her because you wanted to see me . . . why?"

"I . . . I raised ya," he sputtered. "Ye have yer life because of me and my Freda!"

"I had a roof over my head because of you two, but I never had a life. You controlled me, beat me and tried to break me from the time I was five years old."

Owen tried to string a sentence together but couldn't; he likely didn't know what to say to the truth when he couldn't physically beat the person down like he had done to me, like he had once done to Risk.

"You're nothing!" Risk bellowed at him. "Nothing. I used to cower at your feet like a scared dog. I begged my girl to keep your twisted secret. *Your* secret, not mine. What you did to me was *your* shame but I've been carrying it as my own all these years but I'm fucking *done*. You no-good waste of flesh. I'm done with anything to do with you. You'll have no part of me, my mind and soul are free of you, you pathetic bastard."

Owen lifted a shaking hand to his severely broken, gushing-with-blood nose.

"Turn around and leave." Risk stepped forward. "Leave this town. Get the fuck out of Southwold. If you don't, I'll go public and tell everyone what an abusive, fat pussy you are. I'll wreck Freda's memory and expose her as a cruel, heartless cunt to those who hold her dear . . . I swear, Owen. I'll ruin you way worse than you thought you *ever* ruined me."

Owen was bobbing his head up and down, then just like that he turned and hurried away from Risk, from me, from Southwold, as fast as his legs could carry him down the pier. This was going to be the last time I ever saw Owen Day. The second I saw Risk put the fear of God into his eyes with his threat of exposing him to the residents of Southwold, I knew it was enough to send him running. Owen was a pathetic man who valued others' opinions of him, that's why Risk's threat hit home. He didn't care that he could be arrested for child abuse, neglect and other things . . . he was scared that his friends and neighbours would know that he wasn't a poor, sweet widower who once fostered children out of the goodness of his heart.

No, they would learn the truth and that terrified Owen Day more than a prison cell ever would.

"Risk." I stepped forward. "You did it . . . you beat him."

Risk whirled to face me and with a choked sob, he enveloped me in a bone-crushing hug that, after years of pain, held nothing but relief and justice in its embrace. He held me for a long time but when we separated and I took a step back so I could stare up at him, my heart ached painfully. I looked into the eyes I loved . . . and I didn't recognise them.

"You've taken more, haven't you?" I asked. "More drugs?"

He shook his head.

"Don't lie to me." I warned. "I can see it in your eyes."

His jaw jumped around and his eyes were wild.

"I had a couple more lines of coke . . . that's it."

Half a line of that poison was more than enough.

"Where is Chris?" I asked. "He is your manager! He should stop you from doing this."

"That arsehole is sacked, Frankie."

I turned and looked at May with wide eyes. "What?"

"Tob told us that he grabbed you and shoved you into a fucking wall, and about the things he said to you," Hayes said, his body rigid. "He's done."

I looked back at Risk. "You guys fired him?"

"He spoke down to you and put his hands on you," Risk practically growled. "Of course we sacked him, he's lucky I didn't kill him."

I couldn't say I felt any love lost for the man, something about him rubbed me the wrong way from the second I clapped eyes on him.

"You guys need a manager. You *have* to go back to rehab, Risk. Someone has to deal with all of that," I told him. "Your body isn't used to taking that stuff anymore, you'll kill yourself. You have to go back."

"Please. I'm fine." He pressed his body to mine. "Don't send me away again. We can fix what happened tonight at the gig. Okay? We can fix it, Frankie. We'll get a new manager and me and you will be okay again."

Denial. He was in denial.

"Risk, you *need* to go back to rehab." I lifted my hands to his face. "You need to get clean again."

"I can handle this," he swore. "It's only a couple of lines."

I couldn't believe he was trying to talk me round to being okay with him using.

"D'you want me in your life?"

"You *are* my life."

I lifted my chin. "Then go back to rehab and get clean."

Risk's eyes darkened. "Or what?"

"Or tonight will be the last time we ever see one another."

Risk's lips parted, he looked like I just told him the world was ending.

"Why d'you keep doing this to me?" he asked, the hurt in his tone weighed heavily on my shoulders. "Why do you keep doing what I never thought you would?"

"What am I doing? What have I done?"

"You're sending me away."

I froze.

"You weren't supposed to send me away!" He shook. "Never you!"

I couldn't speak. His arms dropped limp to his sides. Tobias, Jacob, May, Hayes and Angel were standing a few metres away watching us, listening to every word we spoke.

"May and Hayes became my friends because their mums told them to play with me when we were in reception. I know they love me, but I wasn't their choice for a friend. I wasn't Owen and Freda's choice for a foster kid, I wasn't a choice for any family who met with me to adopt me. I wasn't wanted, I was no one's choice . . . until you."

A sob left my mouth.

"You wanted me just for me." His eyes were glazed over with tears. "Before I was Risk Keller, I was *your* rock star. You showed me what it feels like to be loved so completely, you showed me what it's like to be in a family. You were everything to me, Frankie . . . and you sent me away. Just like everyone else. You sent me away."

I knew he was going to turn and walk away from me and I knew that if I left him, there would never be a chance for us to be anything to one another, not even friends. Before he had a chance to move, I rushed forward and wrapped my arms around his middle. I squeezed him so tight, I heard his breath catch.

"You would have resented me," I said, my throat hurting from the need to cry. "You would have given everything up for me, I knew you would have. I couldn't live with being the person who dimmed your light, Risk. I broke my own heart when I ended us."

I held on to him tightly when his hands touched my back and gripped tightly on to my T-shirt.

"You didn't believe in us, Frankie," he said. "Not like I did."

I looked up at him. "I believed in us more than anything in this world, but can you look me in the eye and tell me that you would have lived the life you have knowing I was here in Southwold? Would you have settled for seeing me a few times a year or would you have given everything up just to be with me?"

"So what if I would have given it up?" he demanded, his jaw clenched with anger. "Who fucking cares about Blood Oath?"

"You do. I do." I lifted my hands up to his face. "I couldn't make you choose, honey. No matter how much I wanted to tell you to forget it all and stay with me forever."

He froze. "You wanted to tell me that?"

"Risk," I whispered, rubbing my thumbs over his cheeks. "I talked myself out of it every day for six months after you left. I wanted to get on a plane and go to you. I cried myself to sleep countless nights because I hurt for you. I loved you so much, rock star . . . I still do. I love you, Risk."

The tears that had gathered in his blue eyes fell.

"I love you more than anyone has ever loved another person . . . but we don't work, honey. We don't. Look at you. Look at me. Look at the hurt we have put one another through."

Risk's eyes were wild, he couldn't make them focus.

"Why can't we work?" he rasped. "You're the only woman I want. Only you."

And I only wanted him . . . but I couldn't have him. I couldn't.

"Not like this." I shook my head. "We can't be together like this. I'm still needed here in Southwold; my mum still needs me."

"I need you too, Frankie."

"And I need you, honey . . . but not like this."

He said nothing.

"Look at me."

His eyes found mine.

"When you first left, it broke me. I mean that literally, I was devastated. I need you to know that . . . that I had a coping mechanism of my own to help me get through it. You had your music and I had diary entries, you could say . . . only they were text messages . . . that I sent to you."

"*What*?"

"I've sent messages, God, hundreds of them over the years to your old phone number. 'Talking' to you helped me, it was therapeutic for me. I'm going to do something I never thought I would do, I'm going to forward every single one of them to your new number just so you can see that I could never have erased you. You've always been with me even when you weren't, you were always on my mind, always in my heart."

I turned when Angel held out my bag.

"Thank you, sweetie."

I dug out my phone and with shaking hands, I went into my messages and group selected every single text then I forwarded them to Risk's new number.

"It might take a while for them all to come through, there are a lot of them. I want you to read through them all then sit down and think about what you want from your life."

Risk was stunned into silence.

"This is your choice." I lifted my free hand to his face. "Get clean again and we can try and figure out a way where we can be completely honest with one another so any relationship we have can stand a chance. That is the only way this will work, Risk. Get clean or this right here . . . it's goodbye. A *final* goodbye. Make your decision, rock star."

I turned and walked away. Risk didn't call my name or chase me. He remained at the pier's end with my words hanging in the air, and with every single step I took, I felt Risk Keller's eyes on me as I merged into the clouded fog that had descended upon Southwold.

CHAPTER TWENTY-SIX
RISK

Eight days later . . .

"You can't keep doing this, main man."

I exhaled and a white cloud of smoke filled the space between myself and May.

"Says who?"

"Me, dicknose. That's who."

I snorted. "You gonna kick me out?"

"I'll kick you out and kick the shit outta you along the way."

I took another drag of my joint then held it towards Angel who took it from me. May glared his way as he smoked.

"You're enabling him."

"I'm smoking weed with him." Angel rolled his eyes. "I've smoked for years. I'd rather him smoke this than take coke or shoot up."

My eyes fluttered shut at the thought of heroin. I had only taken it once and it was the time when I accidentally overdosed, but I remembered how it made me feel. I wanted that sensation of bliss then numbness to take over my body and mind so I could escape the torment I felt. I wanted to feel nothing ever again. I wanted to be numb to everything in my life, the good and the bad.

"It's been a week since shit hit the fan in Wembley," May said. "We got through the other two concerts, just about. Nolan and our team of publicists are *still* doing damage control. Everyone knows Risk has relapsed, it's all anyone wants to fucking talk about."

I opened my eyes and laughed. "No one gives a fuck about me, it's just—"

"*We* give a fuck about it, *puta!*" Angel snapped. "I'm supposed to be back in LA right now celebrating my baby sister's eighteenth birthday, but I'm here with your stupid ass because I know if you get past May and Hayes, you're going straight for the hard stuff."

I said nothing, I stared at a spot on the wall.

"You *need* to accept that you've relapsed," May leaned against the wall, folding his arms across his chest. "You've snorted coke, drank a fuck tonne and I know you got one of the guys to get you pills to help you sleep. When I find out which one, he's gone."

Again, I said nothing.

"We're going back to LA—"

"I'm not going fucking *anywhere*."

Angel snapped at me in Spanish. I didn't know what the words meant, but I assumed he was calling me an arsehole in a colourful way. I reached for the joint but he stubbed it out in an ashtray, glaring at me while he did it.

"Risk," May snagged my attention. "The facility in LA helped you before, it'll help you again."

At the mention of rehab, my fingers lifted to fiddle with my coin on my necklace, but they touched nothing but skin. I remembered I tore it off and threw it at Frankie, a wide-eyed, heartbroken, crying Frankie. The pain in my chest whenever I thought of her made me hurt enough to want to puke. I needed to block her out. I fucked up so bad that I knew I couldn't fix it so I had to find an escape. I needed to use.

"I can't leave Southwold."

"We shouldn't have fucking come back here," Angel stated. "We shouldn't have let you talk us into it. We should have stayed in London, not here. This place, that woman . . . she fucking rules you. *Look* at you because of her."

"*Don't* put his actions on Frankie," May warned Angel. "He's hurt her just as much as she's hurt him. The only difference," his eyes cut to mine, "is that she never went out of her way to break his heart like he has done to her."

I felt an inch big as May projected an expression of disgust and disappointment my way. He has looked at me many ways before but he had never looked at me with such indifference. He was my best friend, he always had my back even when I didn't deserve it, but it looked like he wasn't making excuses for me anymore.

"You guys should go back to LA," I shifted. "I'll sort myself out here."

Both men scoffed, not believing me.

"You're a selfish prick," Angel sneered. "The only thing you'll do if we leave is use. You don't give a fuck about us and I'm sick of it. Everything is about precious baby boy Risk, isn't it? If you suffer, we all suffer, right? It's all about fucking you."

I jumped up from the bed. "Shut the fuck up."

"Hell no, bitch," Angel shot to his feet too. "You think you're a tough guy, you think I won't beat the *shit* out of you just because I love you?"

My voice was tight with emotion.

"Fuck *you*," I bellowed. "Don't love me. Just hate me, everything will be fucking easier."

"It'll be easier for *who*?" Angel snapped. "You? If you think we hate you, it'll be easier to use because you think we won't hurt, is that it?"

That was exactly it.

"I don't need this," I shook my head, feeling like the room was closing in on me. "I'm not a fucking child, I won't be beaten into what I don't wanna do anymore. I don't live under his thumb, you can't break me like he did."

Angel looked at May and May stared at me with wide eyes.

"We're not Owen or Freda," Angel said roughly. "We heard everything you said to that fat fuck back on the pier . . . they abused you and broke you down but we are *not* them. We *love* you, idiot."

I felt my body shake.

"Why didn't you tell me, main man? I'm your best mate."

May looked hurt that I didn't confide in him.

"Because you would have told your mum and dad, Hayes would have too. They would have taken me away and you guys were the only good thing I had."

"You should have told someone, Risk. Fuck, man . . . I didn't know. I can remember you always being bruised or hurt but I thought you were just clumsy as hell. I'm so sorry."

"Don't be." I rubbed a hand over my face. "Frankie knew."

"*What*?" May and Angel said in unison.

"She knew when we were *kids*?" May demanded. "You didn't just share this with her recently?"

"No, she's known for years. When we were thirteen, I said a pan fell from a cupboard and hit me in the face which is why I was all bruised." I lifted my hands to my eyes. "She didn't believe me. She called me out on it, she was even shorter than she is now and she took none of my bullshit. I made her promise to keep it a secret and she hated it, but she did it for me. From then on, she took care of me, you know? She's always taken care of me and look what I've done to her, May? She's my girl and I wrecked her."

Fuck. I was going to fucking cry. I pressed my fists against my eyes.

"This is so fucked up," I croaked. "I thought she was lying to me. She said she heard our records, I didn't know she meant the instrumentals. I didn't know she couldn't hear me without hurting . . . I thought when she sent me away it was because she wanted to. I got everything so wrong."

The guys said nothing so I dropped my hands.

"I stood her on stage in front of one hundred thousand people and I humiliated her. I insulted her and belittled her . . . all because my feelings got fucking hurt. Again. I fucked up so bad, man. So fucking bad. She told me goodbye." I shook my head. "Even when we broke up she didn't tell me goodbye."

May came my side, Angel too. Both of them clapped their hands against my back. I knew they were going to give me a speech about how the first step in righting my wrong was to go back to rehab, but before either of them had a chance to say a word, Hayes walked into the room. His face was passive.

"Risk."

I stared at him.

"What?"

"Enda Peterson just called."

I blinked. Slowly.

"Who?"

"Mrs Peterson?" Hayes frowned. "A friend of the Fulton family."

I had no idea why he was telling me this.

"Well, what'd she want?"

"She thinks one of us should go and be with Frankie."

My body was like a live wire at the mention of her name.

"Why?" I demanded. "She doesn't want me. She walked away from me on the pier, why would she want any of you."

"Because we're her friends and she needs us."

"Why does she need you?" I snapped. "*Why*?"

"Because Mrs Peterson was delivering bad fucking news, you selfish fucking *prick*! That's why!"

It took a moment for his words to sink in.

"What bad news?"

Hayes looked down and my gut lurched.

"Hayes," I stepped forward. "*What* bad news?"

"It's Frankie's mum," he lifted a hand and rubbed it down his face. "Earlier today . . . she died, Risk. She died in front of Frankie and the girl is broken. Enda is worried sick about her."

I felt every emotion under the sun in the space of a few seconds. I heard my friends shout as I rushed out of the room and went barrelling down the stairs. I didn't stop, I didn't listen, I didn't. Getting to Frankie . . . it was the only thing that mattered.

CHAPTER TWENTY-SEVEN
FRANKIE

Just keep breathing.

Those three words had gotten me through what was possibly the worst week of my life. I thought the week that followed my Mum's diagnosis and my break-up with Risk nine years ago couldn't be topped, but it had been. At least back then, I grieved the loss of my relationship and the boy I loved in private. I had the peace of my own home and the comfort only a mother could provide. This time around, that hadn't happened. I had no privacy and my mother was no longer the woman she used to be, she didn't recognise me any more so seeking comfort from her was impossible.

One thing Risk had said was true: the first four days after the concert there were paparazzi lingering outside of my home but from the fifth, they seemed to simply disappear. I followed my normal schedule, I went to work then to the hospice and that was it. I think my routine wasn't exciting enough for the media so they sought out bigger fish to fry. If they asked me questions, I didn't answer them. I treated them as if they weren't there. A time or two when my work was disrupted by paparazzi having the balls to enter the premises, a couple of customers and Joe stood up for me. Three very expensive cameras were broken in a single altercation.

The police were called but everyone in the diner sided against the paparazzi who were saying they were attacked. They got the short end of the stick, they got in to trouble with the police and their expensive cameras were smashed to pieces. Joe also stole their memory cards and broke them so any images of me that were on there were lost. I appreciated the support; it was nice to know that I had people who had my back.

It was Wednesday and I had to leave work early so I could go to the hospice. Michael had an eye test he had to attend because he needed a new prescription for his glasses. He had been putting it off for months and finally decided to get it over and done with. Neither of us liked my mum being left alone in the hospice because of how her health was declining. Once he called and told me he was delayed, I got Joe's permission, left work early and headed straight to the hospice. I had just walked through the doors when I spotted Erica, one of the lovely nurses.

"Frankie." She smiled when she saw me. "How're you, hon?"

"I'm good," I lied.

I wasn't good, all of mine and Risk's issues were still up in the air. We hadn't spoken since the night of the concert on the pier. I gave him an ultimatum and I had no clue if he made a choice on it or not. He hadn't contacted me so for all I knew he made his choice and it probably wasn't going back to rehab. I hurt to think that was a possibility but I powered on because life didn't stop, it kept on going . . . no matter how much I wanted to hit pause.

After I spoke to Erica, I walked down the hallway towards my mum's room when my phone rang. When I saw it was Michael calling, I answered.

"I just got here," I told Michael. "Erica says she is a little off today."

"I'm on my way," he said. "Bloody machine acted up, but it's done. I collect my new glasses on Wednesday."

"Don't rush, take your time." I opened the door to my mum's room. "She's asleep."

"Okay, see you soon, kid."

I hung up and closed the door behind me. Mum's body jolted and her eyes suddenly opened. She managed to lift her hand to her chest and, for a moment, I worried she was in pain but when she dropped her hand and sighed, I relaxed.

"Hello there," I smiled fondly as I approached her and removed my bag and coat, draping them over the chair. "D'you know who I am, lovely lady?"

My mum stared at me, tilting her head slightly as she tried to place me in her mind.

"It's okay if you don't," I assured her. "I can tell you a nice story of how we know each other, if you'd like?"

"You don't have . . . to do that," Mum shook her head after a moment. "I know who you are."

Her words were mumbled, but I heard her.

"Oh, yeah?" Amused, I hung up my coat and asked, "Who am I?"

"You're my baby."

I felt my lips part for a moment as shock consumed me before I hurriedly moved to sit on the side of my mother's bed. I grabbed her hand and lifted it to my mouth. I kissed it gently and never wanted to let it go.

"D'you know my name, Mum?"

"Yep," she grinned, her voice was no more than a whisper. "My Frankie."

My heart jumped.

"Yes, Mum," I trembled. "Yes, it's me. It's Frankie. *I'm Frankie*!"

"I know who you are," she tittered to herself, wheezing as she went. "I'd never forget you . . . you're my girl."

I couldn't believe it. She recognised me. She knew me! I wanted to jump and scream and cry my eyes out. My mum knew who I was!

"I love you, Mum." Tears welled in my eyes. "I love you so much. You're the best mother to me, you gave me all the love in the world. I am the woman I am today because you raised me to be her. I love you. Always remember that, okay? Frankie loves you so much."

"I l-love you too, little."

Hearing her nickname for me, and her declaration of love, caused me to choke back a sob. Mum frowned at me. I could see confusion in her eyes but I didn't want this moment of her knowing who I was to end. I leaned over her, kissed her face and hugged her tightly. She returned my hug and when I cried she chuckled and patted my back. When I leaned back from her embrace, she stared at me and sighed.

"Did a boy hurt you, sw-sweetheart?" She clicked her tongue in frustration. "Tell me all . . . about it."

I wiped my tears away.

"I'm okay, Mum."

She nodded, yawned then wiggled a little in her bed. She busied herself with her covers and by the time she looked back at me, the familiar squint of confusion had her in its grip once more.

"Who are you, hon?"

When she asked the question this time, it didn't hurt as much because I knew that inside her beautiful mind, and warm heart, I was there. I was her little and even though she didn't always know who I was, I knew that deep inside, I was protected by her like I always was.

"My name is Frankie," I smiled and wiped my cheeks. "I thought I'd sit with you a while, if you wouldn't mind?"

"I'd love that," Mum beamed. "What's your name?"

"Frankie," I repeated.

"Oh, I *love* that . . . name for a girl . . . be-beautiful."

I smiled. "I like it too."

I picked up mum's roll of knitting and handed it to her. She took it from me instantly, unwound her patch and positioned the needles correctly in her hand and began knitting. As I watched her, I wondered how long it would be before she forgot how to knit or lost the mobility in her hands to be able to do it. How she gripped the needles right now was already clumsy, like she didn't know how to do it. I thought of things like this whenever I was with her. I wondered how long it would be before she could do anything for herself. Every single one of those thoughts scared me to death.

"That wool is a beautiful colour," I said to Mum as she knitted. "Do you like that colour."

"It's okay," Mum replied with a shrug. "It's my daughter's . . . favourite colour, you know? She's only a toddler. I'm knitting . . . her a cardigan."

She was struggling to speak and I had to strain to hear her and when I realised what she said my heart clenched. What my mum was knitting was nothing more than mess of a random stitches. She wasn't following a pattern, each time she began to knit, the end result would always be different to whatever she was working on. It didn't really matter though, she never remembered what she had previously knitted, she just enjoyed the activity of doing it. Her mobility was getting worse and worse and I knew that soon she wouldn't be able to hold her knitting needles. Simply holding them was a victory of sorts for her.

"It's going to look beautiful on her."

"I know."

I snorted as I moved to the chair next to Mum's bed, I took out the paperback I was reading and flipped to the page that I had bookmarked. Ten or fifteen minutes had passed by when Mum let out a big sigh. I bookmarked my page and returned my book to my bag.

"What's wrong, Mum?"

"Enda," Mum smiled at me. "When did . . . you get here?"

"Just now," I said. "What's wrong with you?"

"I'm tired. My chest . . . is heavy."

I stood up, got her oxygen mask, turned it to the level Michael always did and fitted it over her face. She didn't smack my hands away or fight me on it, which I was grateful for.

I tucked her blanket around her. "I'll go and make you a cuppa, okay? It'll help you relax."

She reached out and touched my hand. "Two sugars, sugar."

I laughed, lifted her hand and kissed it. "Coming right up."

I left the room, feeling like a weight had fallen off my shoulders. I leaned against the hallway wall for a moment and I processed what had just happened. She recognised me. My mum knew who I was. I held back tears of joy as I pushed away from the wall and walked towards the tea and coffee station. As I placed the tea-bag into a cardboard cup, and filled it with boiling water, I kept replaying over and over in my head my mum saying my name and calling me her little. A little thing like that brought me so much happiness, I knew I would never forget it as long as I lived.

With two cardboard cups of tea in hand, I turned and walked back down the hallway and into my mother's room. I was half-way across the space before I looked at her and I stopped dead in my tracks. For a second, I thought she was asleep but she didn't look right to me. I got a sick feeling in my stomach.

"Mum?" I stepped closer. "Mum, are you okay?"

When she didn't respond, I hurried over to her side and it took me all of two seconds to realise that she wasn't breathing. I dropped both cups of tea to the floor. I stood as still as a statue. Inside, I was crippled with pain, and fear welcomed me into its open arms, but on the outside I could barely breathe. I felt myself stumble over to the door of Mum's room, Erica was walking by when she caught sight of me.

"I think she's gone."

I heard myself say the words but instantly my heart firmly denied them. This wasn't real. This was too soon. Much too soon.

Erica shouted something then hurried by me into the room. Somehow, I walked over to the bed's end without collapsing. Two other nurses entered the room. Their focus entirely on my mum.

"This is too soon, Erica. The doctor said six months, she's only been here two."

I sounded so calm, so serene, it confused me because inside I was screaming.

"You have to help her, Erica." I felt my hands shake. "I'm not ready for her to leave me. Please. We were supposed to have more time."

Erica and the other nurses didn't help my mum at all and I knew why. She made the decision to not be resuscitated when she . . . when she died. She was at the end of her life; when she went, she wouldn't get any help from anyone.

"I'm so sorry, honey," Erica said. "Time of death, 2.06 p.m.."

"No." I moved to the bedside. "This is wrong, this isn't real." I took my Mum's warm hand in mine. "Don't leave me."

She didn't reply and I couldn't accept that she never would.

"God," I felt my heart pound against my chest. "Please, don't do this to me. Don't take my mum away from me."

I didn't realise I was having an asthma attack until drawing in a deep breath was suddenly impossible. I gasped as my hand went to my chest, which felt like a weight was sitting on it. My vision distorted and a loud ringing sounded in my head. I felt hands on me and I heard voices but none of them were clear. Everything was out of focus and inaudible. It was only when my mouth was opened and the familiar tip of my inhaler entered that I forced myself to inhale. The usual taste of chemicals coated my tongue. It was odd, but I always liked the taste because I associated it with being able to breathe. I thought of this as I inhaled a few more puffs.

Slowly, I blinked the room back into focus.

"There we go." Erica's face came into view. "Slow and steady breaths for me, Frankie. That's it, girlie."

I kept my eyes on Erica as I followed her instructions. I realised I was sitting on the floor after a minute or two, I just wasn't sure how long I had been down for. Nothing throbbed or ached, which told me I didn't fall. My brain told me that Erica and the carers likely eased me down to keep me from collapsing and hurting myself.

"My mum," I rasped. "My mum."

"Just breathe for me, sweetheart. Just breathe."

I could breathe now, I could inhale and exhale a breath without struggling, but on the inside I felt choked with pain. I ignored the women as I pushed myself to my feet. I turned and stumbled over to my mother's bedside. I reached out and put my hands on her face. The calmness and confusion that I previously felt fled, and wild panic overcame me when my mind began to comprehend what was happening. I screamed and cried until no sound came out.

I thought I felt pain before, but that was nothing compared to the hollow, aching darkness that claimed me once the light of my mother's life went out.

CHAPTER TWENTY-EIGHT
FRANKIE

People said the words 'I'm sorry' a lot when someone died.

Hours ago, when my mum passed away, I thought I would die too. The pain I felt consumed me and it grew stronger until I couldn't scream anymore, until it hurt so bad that silence enveloped me in its embrace. Everything became a blur. I remembered Michael running into the room, I remembered him crying and kissing my mum, I remembered him hugging me. I recalled the moment Enda arrived and her whimpers sent echoes around the room. Then her sons came by, then Joe and even Anna. The nurses popped in and out to check on us.

All of them told me they were sorry but what they didn't know was that I was more sorry than any of them could ever have been for my mum dying. I had silently pleaded with God, hoping if He knew just how sorry I was that He would take pity on me and give her back to me but I knew that now God had the wonder that was my mum there was no way He was ever going to let her go.

She was love, happiness and light. All of the things meant for heaven.

The whistle of the wind outside drew my attention. I realised I was once again alone with Mum. Michael and Enda had tried talking to me, but once I sat down on the chair next to my mum's bed, I couldn't hear anything. I could barely see. My mind wandered elsewhere . . . just like my mum's once did. I flicked my eyes to the closed door, I heard voices outside. I knew one of them belonged to Michael.

I turned my head and felt the ache of pain in my chest that had come to make itself comfortably at home. I couldn't stop looking at her beautiful, serene face. I kept willing her to open her eyes and start breathing again just so I could feel like I could breathe again. The logical side of my brain didn't even argue with me, it wanted her to wake up too.

"Cherry?"

Through my haze I turned, and through swollen, stinging eyes I saw him in the doorway. He was a presence and he had no idea how happy my heart was to see him even though part of it was broken because of him. Everything that happened between us at his concert seemed like a distant memory. The past few hours had been the longest of my life.

"My mum is dead, Risk."

He crossed the room, got on his knees before me and placed his hands on either side of my face. I stared into his bloodshot eyes and I didn't think it was possible for my heart to hurt any worse but it did. He had taken something before he'd come by to see me. The evidence was in his beautiful eyes.

"I know, baby. I know."

I leaned my face against his, too empty inside to even shed another tear.

"I'm dead without her too." I shook. "I have nothing."

"You have me, you have Michael, you have Joe and Enda. You have a whole load of people who love you more than you could ever imagine."

My chin quivered. "But my mum . . . Risk, how do I breathe without my mum?"

"By living for her," he leaned in and gently pressed his lips to mine. "By being her beautiful girl with the biggest heart God has ever given a person. By honouring her every single day and remembering her life and the wonderful lady that she was."

I lifted my hands to his broad shoulders and squeezed.

"I don't know how to do any of that without her," I admitted, my voice nothing more than a rasp. "I'm terrified to live a life without her in it. I need her to breathe. I'm all alone without her."

"Alone?" Risk repeated. "Who said you're going to be alone?"

I tried to look down, but he wouldn't let me.

"Who said that?"

"Risk, I don't want to do this." I felt my body just droop. "Letting you go once almost killed me, I can't do it again. Not now when I'm already broken. My life is in Southwold, yours isn't. Your world, and mine, are too different. We don't fit together. I meant what I said at Wembley and on the pier . . . we were stupid to think we could work. We can't. We have no future together. We were once pieces to a beautiful puzzle that fit together perfectly, but we've both changed, our edges are sharper now . . . I don't think we fit together anymore."

Risk said nothing, he only leaned in and rested his forehead against mine. This was what I needed from him. Just his touch, his very presence . . . not empty words or promises that we couldn't keep. We had never been very good at keeping our promises, no matter how hard we tried. Risk and I were like currents in the Southwold harbour, no matter how hard we tried to stop it from happening, we would always unexpectedly clash, then drift far apart.

CHAPTER TWENTY-NINE
RISK

Two weeks later . . .

"Risk. Let's go."

I looked over my shoulder. "Already?"

"You've been in here for over an hour. Time's up."

The finality of that statement made my gut clench.

"Tell Hayes and Angel to come in here, I want to talk to the three of you."

May furrowed his eyebrows but did as I asked. He left the studio we spent so much of our youth in then returned minutes later with the rest of the guys. Hayes closed the door behind him and sealed the four of us inside. I was sitting on one of the sofas and they joined me by sitting on the other seats in the room. They stared at me, I stared right back at them.

"This studio is home to me," I said. "This is where Blood Oath began and I think it's always going to be a place I remember and love."

May leaned forward. "Why're you talking like you're not gonna be back here again?"

I didn't answer.

"Hold the fuck on." May frowned. "Are you *quitting* the band?"

"What?" Hayes gasped. "No way, man!"

"Is that what's going on here?" Angel demanded. "You're taking a step back from Blood Oath, from us?"

"What?" I blinked. "No, dumb arses. Right now, the band, you three, are all I fucking have."

May was so dramatic that he put a hand on his chest and had to take a few deep breaths. I watched him, shaking my head.

"I know I'll come back here, I just don't know when . . . I know we're leaving for LA today and you guys were planning on hog tying me if needed to get me back to the facility that worked for me before but you guys don't have to do that. I'm willing to walk through those doors myself."

Angel visibly relaxed. "What changed your mind?"

"You guys. Frankie. Her mum dying. Me finally confronting Owen and ridding myself of the shame I didn't realise I was carrying around. This morning, I snorted a few lines. I didn't want to, but I still did it, so I *know* I need to go back to rehab. I'm not strong enough right now to get better. I need help."

"I'm so proud of you, man," May said. "So fucking proud."

"Thanks," I said. "I'm ready to be sober again. It's only been a few weeks but I'm ready to think clearly again and not crave the high of the numbness. I want to straighten my thoughts out without anything in my system."

"You'll get there," Hayes said. "We're with you every step of the way."

A lump formed in my throat.

"I'm so sorry," I cleared my throat. "I know me using for so many years has been hard on all three of you. I've ruined gigs, and parties, and interviews and even downtime because I was thinking of myself. I'm so fucking sorry . . . Hayes, I ruined the day you told us you're going to be a dad. I'll never forgive myself."

"Well, you better," Hayes said firmly. "Because Summer and I have and we're backing you one hundred per cent."

My chest tightened as I looked to Angel.

"I'm sorry you missed your sister's birthday because of me."

"I forgive you," he said, then grinned. "She'll just make me buy her a better present for the next one."

I looked at May.

"I'm sorry I lied to you," I said to my best mate. "I promised you weeks ago when we were driving around town that I wouldn't fall back into my old ways and scare you, but I did."

"I forgive you," May said. "You're not perfect, no matter how much our Sinners say you are," he teased. "I know you struggle, but you're my boy and I'm always going to be there to help you whenever you need it. Just like you'd be there for me. The four of us are brothers, looking out for one another is what we do . . . smacking some sense into each other is required now and then as well."

We all chuckled but they didn't know how hard I was trying to keep from crying. I apologised to each of them and they didn't brush it off and tell me it was no big deal. They accepted what I had done was a problem but they forgave me. I was lucky to have a group of men who loved me like they did. I really couldn't have asked for better friends in my life. I thanked God for them.

"I can't believe you guys recorded your EP and some of our first album in here." Angel glanced around. "I love it."

I felt myself smile. "It's cute, right?"

"Adorable."

Hayes leaned back. "Are you going to see her before we go?"

"Yeah," May nodded. "It's been a week since her mum's funeral, you haven't seen her since. I stopped by Mary Well's yesterday just to look in through the windows . . . she was working as usual."

"She has to stay busy," I said. "That's how she copes, she can't just sit at home. It'd drive her crazy."

May and Hayes nodded.

"Answer the question," Angel pressed. "Are you going to go and see her?"

"Yes," I answered. "We have to do one thing before I go and say goodbye to Frankie."

"What?" the three of them said in unison.

"We need to lay the song."

May sat up straight. "You finished writing it?"

"Yeah," I answered. "I wrote it then rewrote it five times, but it's done."

"Why cut it now though?" May asked. "Why not after rehab?"

"While I'm in this headspace of feeling broken and angry and so fucking sorry for what I've done to hurt her, I need to get it out. I need this song to be the last one I write and sing that harbours pain about Frankie. I need this to be the end of that part of my life."

"Okay," Angel nodded. "Let's cut the record."

"Hell yeah." May got to his feet. "What's the title?"

I stood up, swallowed and shoved my hands into the pockets of my jeans. I looked at my friends, my brothers, and I knew that there were no other men on this earth that I'd rather jam with and take the world by storm. I smiled, feeling my strength, both physical and mental, begin to return. I had a long road to walk, but I knew my friends would be at its end waiting for me . . . maybe even Frankie too.

"'Never Enough'," I said. "It's called 'Never Enough'."

CHAPTER THIRTY
RISK

Mary Well's diner.

If there was ever a place in Southwold that I'd be sure to find Frankie Fulton if she wasn't on the pier, it was Mary Well's. I sat in the car park in my new rental staring at Frankie through the windows of the diner. I didn't take my eyes off her. I memorised everything. The way she smiled at customers, the way she nibbled on the end of her pen, the way she treated strangers with the utmost kindness. I wanted to remember everything about her in case this was the last time I ever saw her.

How is she real?

I remembered thinking of that often when we were teenagers. I would stare at her and think, how does this girl actually exist? It was more than her physical beauty, her inner beauty knocked me on my arse more times than I could count. She was a woman who loved with her entire being and life fucked her over in more ways than one. She lost her mum and her dad and through her involvement with me I believed she lost a piece of herself too.

Women like her belonged in books, in films, in plays.

Imperfectly perfect.

Selfish people like me didn't deserve her. I knew that.

"I don't wanna say goodbye to you, Cherry."

It didn't matter what I wanted, what mattered was Frankie. She deserved the best and what was best for her was me leaving her life. I wasn't good for her, especially not now. I knew that, but having relapsed I found myself making excuses for my behaviour. Falling back into old patterns to get what I wanted. I told myself, during those selfish moments, that I would be fine if I could just have Frankie. I'd give up the drugs, the drink, I'd give up Blood Oath . . . if only it meant that I could have her. But I was lying.

Now that I had once again tasted the numbness using brought, I craved it just as much as I craved Frankie. All day every day. I wanted it. I wanted her. Life didn't always give us what we wanted though and, in my case, that was a good thing. If Frankie overlooked my using, I would continue to snort and shoot up. That would break her . . . I was done breaking her.

I had to say goodbye.

I glanced around the darkened car park and when I was sure there were no vultures lurking in the shadows, I climbed out into the crisp March evening. I locked the car, jammed my hands into the pockets of my jeans and approached the diner. My eyes were still on her, but when a voice called my name, I looked to my left. It was Anna. She was standing outside smoking a cigarette.

"Hey, Anna."

"Leave," she sneered. "She is hanging on by a thread . . . just leave her alone."

My gut twisted.

"I'm coming to say goodbye, not to cause any more trouble."

Anna's eyebrows rose. "You're leaving?"

"Yup." I shifted. "Going back to LA."

"Humph." Anna took a drag of her smoke. "Can't say I'm sad to see you go."

I smiled sadly. "No longer a Sinner?"

"I'll *always* be a Sinner," she said. "I'm just not a *Risk Keller* Sinner anymore. I know the rest of the fandom has made you out to be the saint in the Wembley situation and Frankie is the red-headed siren who broke Risk Keller's heart, but you and I know that she is the sweetest woman in all of Southwold and you trampled all over heart when it only beat for you."

This was the most I had ever spoken to Anna Porter and I'd be damned if she didn't know where to stick the knife in and just how much to twist it to rip me apart.

"I didn't know you and Frankie were such good friends."

"We're not." Anna looked me up and down. "I always thought she was an uptight prude, but I was ignorant to the tough life she has lived. I thought she was boring and lived to work but I was wrong. She devoted most of her life to her dying mother, she was always on hand to help Joe, me, my sister and Deena with shifts here at Mary Well's and when you came home, she gave up everything for you without blinking. In the past two weeks her mother has died, she buried her, she was humiliated in front of thousands of people, but you know what? She still gets up every day and comes to work with a smile on her face. She's been knocked down in life more than someone like her deserves, but she keeps getting back up. I think she is wonderful and I'm working now to befriend her because I *really* think she could use one . . . don't you?"

"Yes," I answered instantly. "I do."

"Good." She dropped her cigarette and stood on it. "Go around back, I'll send her out to see you."

"I can't go inside?"

"Your relationship has played out in public enough, don't y'think?"

My shoulders slumped. "You're right, it has."

Anna turned and walked towards Mary Well's entrance.

"Anna," I called. "Thank you . . . for sticking up for her. Take care of her while I'm gone. Please."

She didn't turn around, but I saw her head nod in acknowledgement. I exhaled a breath, removed my hands from my pockets and flexed my fingers. I felt nervous. I wished I had weed to relax because I was so fucking jittery but I didn't want to smoke in front of Frankie. I knew I shouldn't have snorted before I came here . . . I just couldn't help it. I walked around to the back of Mary Well's and glanced out at the ocean. Off to the left, up the beach, was the pier.

Mine and Frankie's pier.

I looked at the back door when it opened and the second I saw her I had to force my feet to remain rooted to the spot. Her eyes were a little wide as she closed the door without taking them off me. Instantly, I was worried for her. She had dark circles under her eyes and her cheek bones were a little more prominent that usual. Was she eating? Sleeping? Her bruising from Owen's attack was nearly healed, the cut above her eyebrow was just a thin line now.

"You're going back to LA?" she asked. "Anna said you were."

"Yes," I answered. "I am."

Her chin did that small, cute little quiver it always did before she began to cry. My instinct was to step forward, wrap my arms tightly around Frankie's body and pull her into my embrace but I couldn't do that. I came here to say goodbye to her and that was exactly what I was going to do.

"I have to go," I said. "Me being here has caused nothing but trouble."

She didn't disagree with me. I shoved my hands deep into my pockets because I was tempted to reach out and touch her stunning face, to curl my finger around her ginger hair. I could see that the last couple of weeks had taken a physical toll on her but she looked as beautiful as ever to me. Maybe because I knew this was probably the last time I would see her.

"Are you going back to rehab?" she quizzed. "I want you to leave right now if you aren't."

After everything I had done to hurt her, she still wanted me to get sober and healthy . . . I really didn't fucking deserve this woman. Her heart was too big, too pure to be wasted on someone like me.

"I am," I said. "I'm due to check in as soon as I land in LA."

"Which is when?"

"I leave in about four hours." I swallowed. "When I leave here, I'm going straight to Heathrow."

Frankie's hands flexed, then she shivered.

"Maybe you should go back inside," I suggested. "It's warmer in there."

"I'm not cold," she said. "I'm just shaking."

I didn't know what to say to that.

"You're gonna be okay," she said to me. "You're gonna get sober again."

"You think so?"

"I know so."

I smiled, she trembled.

"I'm sorry, Frankie. I'm sorry for all the hurt I've put you through."

She wrapped her arms around her waist.

"I know you are," she said. "I'm sorry I wasn't more forthcoming with you. Things wouldn't have been so crazy if I had just been honest with you. I hurt you too. I wish I had done things differently."

I shifted. "Hindsight is a great thing, huh?"

She lightly chuckled. "Tell me about it."

My eyes rolled from her face to her medical ID and I paused when I realised she had two rings on the chain.

"Are those . . . ?"

She looked down and touched them with fondness.

"My parents' wedding rings," she looked at me, smiling sadly. "Michael gave them to me after the funeral. We buried Mum with Dad, and Michael felt it was right that I hold on to their rings."

"I'm glad you have them and that you'll keep them close."

"Me too, Risk."

"I hate that I'm doing this," I said. "Jesus, Frankie, I hate it. I don't wanna say goodbye to you."

"You can say it without it being final, you know?" she said. "Neither of us know what the future holds. I know that now, it took me a long time to realise no matter how much I overthink or fear something, I can't control whether or not it will happen."

That sentence alone gave me hope that I didn't know if I deserved.

"I read all of them," I said. "I read every message you sent me maybe a dozen times over the past eight days."

"You have?"

"Yes."

"D'you believe me that I never erased you?"

"Yeah, baby, I do. You love me."

"I love you so much."

"That's why I'm going to LA. I want to get clean for me, to be sober for me . . . but I want to do it for you too. You're my shining star, you know?"

Tears fell from Frankie's eyes.

"Say you'll do something for me?"

Frankie sniffled and tentatively nodded.

"When you want to talk to me, like you did before, don't text my old number. Text my new one. I won't ever text you back, I won't even see the texts until I'm out of rehab but knowing I'll get a peek into seeing how you're doing will give me a lot of strength while I'm away."

"Okay," she nodded. "I'll text you a lot."

"Thank you, love."

She wiped her cheeks.

"I don't wanna cry," she smiled sadly. "I've cried enough for ten lifetimes."

"Sometimes crying helps." I reached up and thumbed away another tear. "Sometimes it gives the pain we feel a way to escape."

Frankie nodded.

"I wish I didn't have to leave you . . . not right now just after your mum's passing."

Frankie swallowed. "I have Michael, Joe, Enda and even Anna now. It hurts but I don't think that will ever stop, it hasn't for my dad. With time, I just learn how to live with it I guess."

The door to kitchen opened and Anna popped her head out.

"I'm sorry, Frank," she said. "I need a hand. Joe has three orders ready and I just seated two more booths."

"I'll be right in."

Anna nodded and disappeared again leaving the door slightly ajar.

"I better get back," Frankie exhaled a breath. "Duty calls."

I stepped into her space before she finished speaking and her little gasp was one I knew would haunt me late at night.

"Can I kiss you?" I murmured. "Just once?"

"I'm scared," she trembled. "I might not want you to stop."

I kissed her before she could deny me, deny herself, and instantly she went up on her tiptoes and wrapped her arms tight around my neck, pulling my face down to hers. Our kiss was hungry, but not brutally intense. We explored the other's mouth slowly, seductively, savouring every single moment. I tasted Frankie's tears as they fell once more and my heart broke. This was either going to be just another kiss of many for us or it was the last.

The thought terrified me.

"I love you," I said. "I love you, Cherry."

"I love you too."

I stepped away from her and before she could hug, or kiss me, again I turned and walked away because I knew if I touched her again, I'd never let go.

"Keep chasin', rock star."

Tears fell from my eyes as I jogged back to my car, hopped in and drove away from Mary Well's. I drove back to May's house, switched seats and sat in the back with May while Hayes drove all four of us to London. The guys didn't have to ask how it went, I was still crying when I jumped into the back seat of the car. May kept his hand on my shoulder the whole car ride to London. He sat next to me when we were settled into our business-class seating. I didn't speak the entire time, I was scared if I spoke, then I would sob.

My friends understood.

With my phone in my hand, I scrolled through the photos of myself and Frankie that were taken the first night we played at Wembley over a week ago. Frankie's smile was huge and so was mine. We looked insanely happy. This was before everything went to shit. I hated that a few hours after these pictures were taken everything was ruined. I couldn't delete them though, I needed to keep them. I needed to see her, to see those big, round, beautiful emerald-green eyes and wide smile to give me something to cling to in the dark hours that I knew would come when I began my detox.

Frankie was my shining light, I couldn't put her out.

My phone vibrated in my hand as the plane began to taxi towards the runway. I clicked into the message without thinking and my heart stopped when I realised who it was from. On my screen was a text message from Frankie. I clicked into it so fast

I almost broke the screen. I read through her text ten times with unblinking eyes and when the plane took off into the air and left England, Southwold and Frankie behind me . . . I had a smile on my face.

Text message #1

Frankie: I said goodbye to you again today. I miss you, I miss you and you have only been gone a handful of hours. You're probably in the air right now on your way back to LA, but I'm keeping my word and texting you, just like I always did, to get things I need to say off my chest. I wish things had turned out differently for us. I wish my mum hadn't died. I wish I wasn't so scared for my future. I wish for a lot of things. This fucking sucks but that's life, right? I'm going to pray for you every single night before I go to sleep. I'll pray for your health, both physical and mental, and I'm going to pray so hard that you find peace. I want that more than anything for you.

Please, don't worry about me, okay?

Like you said, I have Michael, I have Joe and Enda and I'm getting a friend in Anna now too. I'm hurting, but I know I'm going to be okay because my mum told me so. I didn't tell you this earlier but I don't think this is the end for us, Risk. I can't tell the future but when we parted earlier, it didn't feel like a forever goodbye. We always have a way of finding each other in the strangest of times. I just want you to know when your mental health is stable and you're sober and you find your happiness and peace for you, and you alone, then if you want me still . . . you'll know where I'll be.

Southwold isn't a big town.

Keep chasin', rock star.

CHAPTER THIRTY-ONE
FRANKIE

Four months later . . .

Clashing waves, the cool, crisp air, idle distant chatting and a blanket of cold, swaying water. This handful of things were my solace when my thoughts were so loud that they made me want to scream. The late July evening was paired with a stunning sunset, which granted me an abundance of peace not even my chaotic mind could spoil. Four months. It had been four long months since I last saw Risk in person outside the back entrance to the kitchen of Mary Well's. I leaned against the rail of the pier, where I had found myself recently spending more and more time. Weather permitting, I took a stroll along the pier most evenings to unwind from a long, hard working day.

I looked down and smiled when a knock in my tummy caught my attention.

2021 had been a whirlwind of a year for me and it was only the twenty-eighth of July, only half-way through it. Risk Keller, my ex-boyfriend and the love of my life, came barrelling back into my predictable, quiet life and his very presence turned it upside down. Even though our relationship was rekindled rapidly and went downhill just as fast, I'm glad it happened the way it did because everything that occurred during that handful of weeks Risk was in Southwold led me to now.

Pregnant with his baby.

I didn't find out until I was ten weeks along and Risk had already been in rehab by then so I kept it to myself. May had been giving me updates on him when he got them, which I greatly appreciated. I knew Risk's stint in rehab had ended just over three weeks ago and every time I thought of why he hadn't come to find me yet made me feel guilty. Just because Risk completed his ninety-day program didn't mean he was just able to up and come back to a place, and person, that made him relapse.

If he would come back.

I closed my eyes trying to force away the fear and doubt that crept into my mind whenever I wondered about him coming home. In my first text message to him the night he went back to LA, I told him point blank that if he wanted me, I would be here waiting for him. That offer was still on the table and I knew it would remain on the table for the entirety of my life. Risk was my one, my person, and I believed I was his. I could only pray he returned to Southwold because I wasn't the only person he would be coming home to, the baby in my belly wanted him home too.

I wanted to wait.

I wanted to wait until Risk decided when, or if, coming back to Southwold, to me, was the best decision for him. There was no way I was going to contact him and let him know I was pregnant because I knew he would be on the next plane to England. If he chose not to be my romantic partner, it would crush me but I would survive. I would only tell him about the baby once he had made his decision so it wouldn't sway his choice. It would be devastating if he wanted a life that didn't involve me, but that would be my issue to work through. I knew he would never turn his back on his child.

The not knowing what was going to happen was a head wrecker . . . and I wasn't exactly running on an unlimited supply of time when it came to our baby.

"C'mon God," I looked up. "Give me a sign . . . something, anything. Just give me a hint of what I need to do, please."

The waves slapping together below the pier were my response . . . until a voice answered me.

"What kind of sign are you looking for, Cherry? Maybe I can help you look for it."

Time itself stood still. I turned around slowly because I was terrified I was imagining hearing his voice, but when I saw him, standing a few metres away from me with his thumbs resting in the pockets of black jeans, black boots, a black Nirvana T-shirt with rips in it and with a head full of white-blond hair that slightly curled at its ends, I was gobsmacked.

He was stunning, he was healthy, he was smiling . . . he was my Risk.

"Risk." I placed my hand on my chest. "I was just thinking of you."

"I know."

I blinked. "You do?"

"Yes," he nodded. "The pier, the sea, and me, are your favourite things. You always think of me when you look out to the sea."

I couldn't remember ever telling him that, but it didn't matter because it was the truth.

"You're really here."

"I'm really here. I would've been here a couple of weeks ago," he said. "But I had some business to take care of."

"Oh, really?"

"Yeah," he answered. "I was buying some land near the beach, you know, so I could build a new house."

Pain stung at my chest.

"You're building a beach house?" I swallowed. "Lucky dog. Anywhere nice?"

"Somewhere very nice."

I figured he didn't want to tell me where the location was, so I didn't press the issue.

"How come you're here at the pier?"

"I saw you walk from your cottage all the way down here about half an hour ago . . . figured I'd come and say hello."

I stared at him and he stared right back at me.

"Did someone see you?"

"Nope. No one knows I'm here except Nolan and the guys. He's taken over Chris's job for the time being. They're down at the entrance of the pier, Jacob said he'll scare away anyone who wants to take a walk down here. Tobias too."

I blinked. "There are already people on the pier though, I passed by two men fishing and others watching the sunset closer to the gift shops."

"Fine," Risk grinned. "He'll stop anyone who looks like they get paid to take pictures for a living from following me onto the pier . . . happy?"

I snorted. "You should've just started with that."

"Maybe," he smiled. "How have you been holding up?"

My mum's beautiful face flashed across my mind.

"Some days are worse than others," I answered honestly. "Today, I feel calm. I can think of Mum and smile. Yesterday I couldn't breathe past the pain of missing her, it brought on an attack but Michael was with me so I was okay. Tomorrow? Who knows, I won't know how I'll feel until I wake up."

Concern washed over Risk's face.

"How are *you*?" I quizzed. "You look great, Risk."

He really did, he looked so much healthier than when I last saw him.

"Four months sober," he said, touching the coin that hung from his neck. "This is the second time I've gotten this coin, but I know this time it'll be my last."

"I'm so proud of you. I truly am, honey."

"Frankie," he shoved his hands in his pockets. "I'm sorry for everything I've ever done to hurt you. What I did to you at Wembley . . . I hate myself for it."

"Don't," I told him and walked towards him until I came to within a few inches of him. "You've already apologised. You can't change what happened any more than I can. I know you're sorry and I know you didn't want to hurt me. I know you didn't even realise we were on the stage during that moment, your mind just went blank except for what I had done. You just wanted to hear me sing one of your songs because it killed you to think I blocked myself away from hearing you. I know you speak through your songs . . . it's why I never listened to them before the concert, I was too afraid to hear what you had to say."

The sadness in Risk's eyes was haunting.

"Can I tell you something?"

He nodded.

"I swore I was going to forget you when I ran out of that stadium," I told him. "When I left London, I promised myself I was going to just remove you from my life so I could learn to breathe without you, but I couldn't."

He exhaled. God, he looked so scared.

"Because you love me though loving me hurts you?"

"Because loving you is a pleasure I want for my entire life."

"But why?" he asked. "Why, after all I've put you through?"

"Because you're my risk and I pray that I am yours."

He moved closer, reached his arms out and placed his hands on my shoulders.

"You are, Frankie. It's always been you, since I was thirteen. Only you."

"Have you decided then?" I asked, my stomach flipping. "Have you?"

"I'm standing in front of you, aren't I?"

"I need to hear you say it," I lifted my hands to his waist. "I need to hear you say you want me, please. I need to hear you say that you choose me."

"I want you. I choose you." His hands moved to my face. "God, woman, I want you for life."

Tears filled my eyes. "Good because I've a second reason that I really needed to know that."

"What d'you mean?"

I didn't want to drag the conversation out, so I just said the words plain.

"I'm pregnant," I said, looking up into his widening eyes. "I'm sorry, I know this is the last thing you need in your life right now, but I couldn't keep it from you. He's your baby too."

"A baby? A he?" Risk rasped. "He's a *he*? *You're* pregnant with *my* baby?"

I nodded, feeling a lump form in my throat.

"I went for my ultrasound last week and the lady told me his sex by mistake but I don't regret knowing. He's a he."

"How pregnant are you?" Risk looked down. "I mean, how far along?"

I gripped the sides of my sun dress and pulled it tight against my skin, revealing my small, but growing bump.

"Nineteen weeks and three days today," I answered. "I'm nearly five months. I'm due on the nineteenth of December."

Risk said nothing, he looked pale.

"I didn't find out until a few weeks after London and you were already in rehab. I didn't want to ruin any progress you had. I've been struggling with how to tell you. I knew I couldn't just text you something so huge . . . I'll admit I was thinking about telling May to tell you but then you just showed up here."

"Frankie." His voice was barely a whisper. "Fuck. I can't think."

"It's okay," I told him. "I know it's a shock. Close your eyes."

He did so in an instant.

"Slow breaths, in through your nose and out through your mouth," I instructed. "There you go, honey."

With his eyes still closed, he reached out with his hands and flattened them over my stomach. Even though there was a thin layer of fabric between us, the contact sent a zing of electricity throughout my body. I whimpered a little when Risk lowered himself to his knees and brought his face to my belly. I gasped when he pulled up my dress so he could see my stomach.

"Risk, someone could be taking pictures—"

"Everyone thinks I'm in LA," he said, tucking my dress under my bra to keep it from falling down. "Besides, no one from the beach can see us down this far, not with the building blocking us. It's just you, me, and the sea."

I placed my hand on his cheek.

"And our baby."

Risk leaned in and pressed his lips against the underside of my swollen stomach, just above my pubic bone. With his hands on either side of my tummy and his face pressed against me so intimately, my breath caught.

"You aren't angry, right?" I asked. "About the baby? I swear, I didn't plan for this to happen. I didn't miss my pill once, and Owen kicked me in the stomach that night. This just . . . happened. *He* just happened."

He looked up at me, rose to his full height, which made me tilt my head back just so I could keep eye contact with him. He took my face in his hands and said, "You've made me the happiest man on the face of this earth, only one thing would make me happier than you having my baby."

I froze. "What?"

"Being with you again. Waking up and seeing your face first thing in the morning, holding you when I fall asleep at night. I want you, Frankie. Now more than ever."

Risk lowered my dress back down, but he never took his eyes off me.

"Not just because I'm pregnant?" I pressed. "You want me for me, right?"

"Of course, just for you. I've wanted you back since the moment you sent me away when I was eighteen." He shook his head. "The only difference now is I'm fighting for you, for my family. I won't walk away, not even if you send me away. I'll fight for you, for us, until I've no breath left in my body."

It was like I had been sucked into a recurring dream where I had heard Risk say all of this to me before. I was so scared I was going to wake up and find myself all alone again.

"I love you." He pressed his forehead to mine. "D'you love me?"

"Yes," I answered without hesitation. "So much. I love you."

"Then be with me," he said. "It's as easy as that. Be mine again . . . we'll figure everything else out along the way. As long as we're together, we can figure everything out."

"Okay," I said, surprising us both with my quick acceptance.

"Yeah? Just like that?"

"Yeah," I squeezed him. "I've wanted to be yours, and only yours, since I was fifteen. Nothing's changed about that, rock star. I don't think there will be a perfect time for us to get together but I'm not wasting any more time. I want to be with you. My mum's passing has shown me I need to live my life to the fullest, I need to create my own happiness. I know that happiness is with you."

"Thank God," he took my face in his hands. "Because I was hoping you'd be living with me rather than being a neighbour when I have the new house built."

A veil of confusion washed over me.

"I don't understand."

"A piece of land a few hundred of metres that way," he pointed past the colourful beach huts, "has been for sale the last year," Risk smiled. "I closed on it today. The land is just behind the beach so while the beach won't be ours, the land will be. We can build on it whatever way we want, we can wake up every morning and see the ocean and the pier, two things we both love."

I was so surprised that I was momentarily speechless.

"You . . . here in Southwold . . . but LA?"

"Cherry," he chuckled. "I can live anywhere in the world. LA was easier because so much work took place there but also because it was far away from you. I needed to be far away from you if I couldn't have you. Me and the guys have been talking it over and we want to split our time. Angel wants to continue to live in LA, his girlfriend just moved in with him. His mum and sister both live there so that was the obvious choice for him. Hayes and May will keep their homes in the Hills, as will I, but they're both buying houses in London, too. May already owns his childhood home here in town which I'm sure he'll continue to happily use."

I felt as if I swallowed my tongue.

"Nolan is going to take care of our schedules, he's our acting manager now that Chris is gone. He's searching for a competent assistant in the meantime. When we want to record, we'll schedule it. When we have to promote our music, play festivals, tour, go to award shows and do other work shit, we'll know about everything in advance. That way you can decide whether you want to come along with me or stay here until I come back."

This was all too wild to believe.

"It can't be as simple as that . . . it can't be."

"It is now that we're successful and earn good money. At the start this was never a possibility but it is now, Cherry."

"Why does is sound like you knew that we'd get back together?" I quizzed. "This is all very well planned out, Risk."

He brushed loose strands of hair from my face.

"Because I wasn't going to walk away this time, Frankie. I was going to get on my knees and beg you if I had to. God, baby, you have no idea just how much I love you, d'you?"

If it was anywhere near as much as I loved him then yeah, I knew.

"I may have a vague idea."

"Only a vague one?" His lips twitched. "I guess I better get a jump on letting you know just how much I love you."

"I think you should."

He lowered his face to mine. "What d'you propose?"

"Well," I smiled. "I think a kiss would be a good place to start."

"I've a question first."

"Ask it."

I sucked in a breath and flung my hands over my mouth when he dropped to one knee, he reached into his back pocket and pulled out a drop-dead gorgeous diamond ring.

"I didn't think I'd be doing this right now," he said. "I bought this ring the day I got to LA and I kept in in my pocket my entire stint because I knew one day I would ask you to marry me with it. I went to see Michael this morning and I asked his permission to marry you when I earned your trust back. He gave me a bit of a hard time but he shook my hand and said yes. You're my light, Frankie Fulton. You have been since I was thirteen. You would made me the happiest, and luckiest, man in the world if you would do me the honour of becoming my wife. Will you marry me, Cherry?"

"Yes!" I screamed as I burst into tears. "Yes, Risk."

Risk put the ring on my band finger then shot to his feet and in the same moment, his lips were on mine, our forever was sealed the second his lips touched mine.

CHAPTER THIRTY-TWO
FRANKIE

"What're ye thinkin' so hard about, kid?"

I looked up at Michael and shrugged.

"Everything," I answered. "I can't focus on one thing, it's just a jumbled mess up there."

"I know the feelin'," he placed a cup of tea in front of me.

I was in the home Michael and my mum had shared. It looked the exact same as the last time it did when my mum was alive, but it didn't feel the same anymore. It was as if her presence had vanished even though all of her things were still here. I thought coming here would make me feel close to her, but it didn't.

"I want to ask how you're doin', but I know ye've gotten that question as much as I have."

Wasn't that the truth. The year-round residents of Southwold had gone above and beyond for my mum. They had sent flowers, cards, homemade dishes and offered to be on call for a chat 24/7 should either Michael or myself need it. I loved my town and I loved the people in it even more.

"Today is a good day," I admitted. "But God, I miss her, Michael. I miss her so much."

"So do I, kid. We always will."

"It's weird though," I toyed with the handle on my cup. "The woman we knew left us a long time ago, but now that she's gone completely, I feel like I'm grieving that part of her being gone all over again."

"That's the thing about grievin', Frankie. None of it makes any sense. We know there are stages to grief, but no two people actually grieve the same. We're human, we aren't made to just accept the people we love most can be gone forever. It's why we hurt for so long then eventually reach a place when we can smile when we think of them. Even smilin' when you think of a passed loved one is grievin'. Don't let anyone ever tell you different."

"You're right," I said. "I know you are. I'm just trying to find a way to cope with this feeling. It hurts."

Michael reached over and clasped my hand in his.

"I know it does, love."

I looked up at my stepdad and my heart broke.

"Michael, have I ever truly told you how much I love you?" I asked, squeezing his hand. "I know I call you by your name, but you're very much my dad. You know that, don't you?"

He smiled wide, tears glistening in his eyes.

"Of course I know you love me," he said. "And you're me baby girl. You're nothin' less than me daughter, Frankie."

I got up at the same time as he did and we hugged tightly and cried. We both felt the same level of pain because we both missed one hell of an incredible woman.

"I have to speak to you about something."

"Does it have anythin' to do with that rock on your finger?"

"Risk is back," I smiled. "But I guess you already know that, right?"

The way I peeked up at Michael made him laugh.

"Did he ask you down on one knee like he better have?"

"Yes," I smiled, flushing. "You're so sneaky."

He reached for my hand when I held it out to him and rubbed his fingertips over my engagement ring. I stared down at it, still not being able to believe it was mine because Risk had asked me to marry him and I said yes. This morning when I woke up, I was at war with myself, wondering how I was going to tell him I was pregnant after everything we had been through and now I was engaged to the man and planning a future together for our family. Our family. Me, Risk and our son. It was all too good to be true and I thanked God for every second of it.

"He's excited?" Michael asked. "About the baby?"

I had told Michael I was pregnant when I was twelve weeks and he was so excited to be a grandfather.

"Madly." I shook my head. "You were right, I was scared over nothing."

"Told you so."

I snorted. "That you did."

I looked at the man who was once nothing more than a GP to me but was now the only parent I had left on this earth and my spirit felt a little crushed.

"What's wrong?"

I exhaled a breath. "Risk can't permanently stay in Southwold year round. He has to travel a lot for work. He said we're going to make it work so we're here in Southwold the majority of every year but there will be times he is touring, or has to go back to the States and I want to be with him when he goes."

"I'd expect nothin' less than a wife wantin' to be with her husband." Michael smiled. "So what's the issue?"

I looked down. "I . . . I don't want to leave you and Mum."

I felt horrible when I thought about it.

"Look at me, little."

I lifted my eyes to Michael's and the love he had for me shone bright within them.

"Your mam will be with you everywhere ye go." He squeezed my hand. "She knew, more than anyone, how much ye loved Risk. I know she would want you to spend your life with him in happiness."

I whimpered. "But how can I just leave her here . . . how can I leave *you* here all alone?"

"Oh, sweetheart," Michael smiled. "I'm not alone. I have me friends nearby, and, just like you, I still have your mammy with me."

"I just . . . I'm so scared. Southwold has been my life for so long."

"Are you scared everything will change again if you leave?"

Wordlessly, I bobbed my head.

"I understand." Michael's thumb brushed over my knuckles. "Ye've been here for so long because of your mam. Ye've dedicated the last nine years of your life to her, but now, kid, it's time for ye to live your life for *you*."

I processed his words.

"And don't be scared about not comin' back," he said. "Like ye said, ye'll be here the majority of each year, other times will be like a holiday for you. Ye couldn't stay away from Southwold even if ye tried and ye know it."

Surprised laughter bubbled up my throat as tears slipped from my eyes. Michael smiled, then pulled me into his embrace. I wrapped my arms around him as tight as I could and he returned it tenfold.

"I love you," I told him. "You know that, don't you?"

"I do." He kissed my head. "And ye know I love *you*, right?"

"Right."

I left Michael's home feeling lighter and happier than I had in a very long time. I walked back in the direction of the pier and texted Risk where I was going. He went to Mary Well's for food with the guys while I went to speak with Michael. I wasn't hungry. I just wanted to walk and breathe . . . I hadn't been able to breathe this easily for as long as I could remember. When I once again reached my favourite point on the pier, it was dark out. The lights of the pier and shine of the lighthouse burning bright.

My phone pinged.

Risk: When I first came back to Southwold, I began writing a song that was, surprise, about you. I wrote different parts of it when I felt different things. When I was dreading seeing you again, when I was elated to have you as mine for a little while then when I was broken after things ended between us at Wembley and on the pier. I want this song to be the last one I ever write about you that had doubt in it, that has 'should haves, would haves' buried in it. I need to close the chapter on my life that had longing and indecisiveness about you. I only want to look to the future knowing that I'll always see myself by your side and you by mine.

I wrote this for you.

You are the echoes of the heart for me.

You are my Never Enough.

I love you, Cherry.

I clicked into the MP3 link that was attached to the message and with shaking hands, I grabbed my earphones and plugged the pods into my ears. I clicked play, closed my eyes, and the guitar riffs and the beat of the drums surrounded me before Risk's voice did.

I can't get enough of your green eyes,
Your soft skin, your sweet smile.

You make my life so much better,
Just by being there, you're my healer.
My protector, my lover, you know me like no other.

Then a storm rolls in, and you switch it up,
Just to suit when you really give a fuck.
I love you, I show it, you use it against me, and you know it.
I hate you, I don't need you,
Those are white lies, I can't breathe without you.

I walk in and you walk out,
You left me, what's that about?
I begged you, I pleaded,
I laid it all on the line, you wouldn't believe me.
Would've given my life for yours, no thinking necessary,
Would you have done the same for me, my pretty cherry?

But no matter what's been said or done,
You'll always be my never enough.
My never enough.
My never enough.
You'll always be my never enough.

I should've told you that, when you trusted me,
When you looked at me, and saw the real me.
I wish everything turned out different,
I wish you had my last name, my children.
You ripped me apart, I came undone,
But if you called me now, you know I'd run.

This happened for a reason, that's what you told me,
But I can't justify this, it burns a hole in me.

I miss your red hair, your gentle laugh,
Your hell cat ways, the way you've got my back.
I know I fucked it up, but baby you did too,
We're a match made in hell, I'm meant for you.

Maybe it's too late, you've probably moved on,
But this is one song, I want your view on.
'Cause no matter what's been said or done,
You'll always be my never enough.
My never enough.
My never enough.
You'll always be my never enough.

You'll always be my never enough.
My never enough.
My never enough.
You'll always be my never enough.

You'll always be my never enough.
My never enough.
My never enough.
You'll always be my never enough.

Tears fell from my eyes. I listened to the song from start to finish eight more times. I sobbed through each replaying. We had been through so much, so much necessary hurt, so much unnecessary hurt but it all brought us to right now. We had done what I always prayed for. We worked through our problems, we didn't give up and we finally made it to the other side and we were stronger because of it. I lifted my hands, wiped my cheeks then took out my phone.

Frankie: You're my never enough, too, rock star. You're my always and forever.

I looked from my phone to the ocean and when I inhaled a breath, I felt like I could do anything. It felt good, really good. I looked down at my phone when it vibrated in my hand.

Risk: You like it?

Frankie: I love it. I'm honestly speechless. I don't know what to say.

Risk: That'd be a first, I've a phone full of messages from you. You type essays.

Frankie: Smartarse.

Risk: A smartarse you're marrying.

Frankie: Too bloody right I am. I can't believe you're going to be my husband, I want to kiss you so bad. Where are you?

Risk: About ten or so metres away from you.

Frankie: It's going to be so creepy if I turn around and you're there.

Risk: I was going for romantic.

Frankie: I can't move.

Risk: I can.

I had just put my phone back into my dress pocket when arms came around my waist, settled on my stomach and a hard body pressed against my back, moulding itself to me.

"I should let you know, sir." I leaned my head back. "My fiancée is pretty protective of me, he'd kick your arse for touching me. Maybe you should leave me alone."

"Or maybe he'll let me show his lady a good time at the end of the pier?"

I laughed and whacked Risk's hip, making him chuckle as he kissed my head.

"'Never Enough' is beautiful," I said. "It had everything in it. Our hurt, our anger, our confusion but most of all our love. I heard you. I love it, Risk. I love it. I love *you*, honey."

He turned me to face him. His hands moved to my face.

"I'm marrying you," he said, not able to hide his smile. "We're having a baby. This is the life I've always wanted, Frankie. Making music with Blood Oath and having you by my side with our little family in tow. I know you always thought Blood Oath was my sole dream, but it's not. This is my dream. You, me, our family, music, the guys, the band. All of it. I have my dream now."

I cried. Again.

"These hormones make me cry at the drop of a hat so you need to stop being so bloody sweet."

Risk smiled as he thumbed away my tears, then he leaned down and brushed his lips over mine.

"You're my dream, Frankie."

"You're my never enough, Risk."

I lifted my hands to his waist and gazed up at the man I loved so completely. He wasn't just my dream, he was my everything. My risk in this life. My whole world and he was all *mine*.

ACKNOWLEDGMENTS

This is the nineteenth novel that I have written and thankfully, I still get that '*oh my god*' feeling when I reach this point of production because it means I've written another book. Writing one book was such a huge feat for me, now having nineteen of them tucked under my belt is simply mind-blowing.

To my daughter, thank you for being you. You're the best you in the whole entire world. I love you more than you'll ever know, sweetheart.

To my sister, who is not only the best sibling, but the best sounding-board. Thanks for not thinking my book ideas are crazy.

To Mark Gottlieb, my agent, I'm truly happy to have an agent as brilliant as you. You always have my back and I truly appreciate it.

To my editor, Lindsey Faber, thank you for your hours of endless work helping me get my story to where it deserves to be. Developmental edits are a stage in book production that I dread, but you really do turn it from a daunting task to something I know I can get done with confidence. Working with you truly is a delight.

To my copy-editor, Laura Gerrard, thank you for going through my book with a fine comb from start to finish.

To my proofreaders, Eleanor Leese and Sarah Rouse, thank you for taking the time to scan every single word to catch any lingering errors.

To Sammia, and the team at Montlake Romance, thank you for always keeping my book's best interest at heart. I appreciate all your hard work.

To my readers, writing *Echoes of the Heart* during 2020's lockdown was an escape for me during a time when the world was going through great hardship. I hope reading Risk and Frankie's story gives you an escape into a world where things are a bit lighter.

ABOUT THE AUTHOR

L.A. Casey is a *New York Times* and *USA Today* bestselling author who juggles her time between her mini-me and writing. She was born, raised and currently resides in Dublin, Ireland. She enjoys chatting with her readers, who love her humour and Irish accent as much as her books.

Casey's first book, *Dominic*, was independently published in 2014 and became an instant success on Amazon. She is both traditionally and independently published and is represented by Mark Gottlieb from Trident Media Group.

To read more about this author, visit her website at www.lacaseyauthor.com.

Did you enjoy this book and would like to get informed when L.A. Casey publishes her next work? Just follow the author on Amazon!

1) Search for the book you were just reading on Amazon or in the Amazon App.
2) Go to the Author Page by clicking on the Author's name.
3) Click the "Follow" button.

If you enjoyed this book on a Kindle eReader or in the Kindle App, you will be automatically offered to follow the author when arriving at the last page.